Avril Flower was a teacher for 40 years of her married life. In her early married life, she spent the first seven years in Assam, north-west India, as the wife of her late tea planter husband Oliver. Since retirement, she has written a bevy of books in fiction and fantasy, some of which are based in Assam.

It was when she began thinking about this story and had commenced writing that her daughter saw a documentary about a 'horse lady' whose withered skin was tattooed. She had been discovered surrounded by buried horses in a grave in the steppes. She felt she had to finish the story after that. Flower lives in Auckland, New Zealand with her youngest son and his wife, and three bossy cats.

Dedication

To Oliver, my friend, husband, and lover. You are still alive in
my heart and soul.

All my writing is thanks to Rod and Shelley, Leonie and John –
adamant stalwarts – and to good friends Claire and Nina who keep
me to the grind. Latterly, I have had strong help from Marion and
Miles. Technology is not my forte, so thanks to Mark, Haydn and
mainly Rod for their support in this area. Also, gratitude to Dirk
and Gari for their moral support.

My thanks also go out to Vinh Tran and his team who were always
there with their constant support and help.

Avril Flower

THE TOTEM

AUSTIN MACAULEY
PUBLISHERS LTD.

A CIP catalogue record for this title is available from the British Library.

ISBN 978 1 78455 308 1 (Paperback)
ISBN 978 1 78455 310 4 (Hardback)

www.austinmacauley.com

First Published (2015)
Austin Macauley Publishers Ltd.
25 Canada Square
Canary Wharf
London
E14 5LB

Printed and bound in Great Britain

ERM

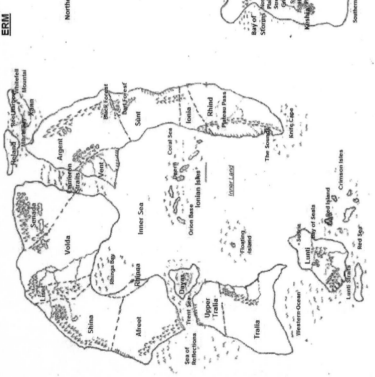

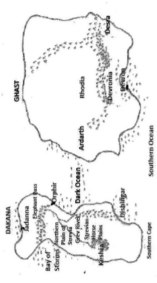

PROLOGUE

In the twenty-first century of recorded history on Earth, space ships left the planet to seed other galaxies.

One such was founded on the planet Erm in the solar system known as Mut. The continent of Dakana was where the settlers landed.

As time passed and the old world technology could not be sustained, the inhabitants were inclined to revert to their racial types, using the skills inherent by generations on Earth, for their farming and animal husbandry.

To provide a feeling of home the spacers brought wild animals with them, as well as herds for food. This meant that all the folk stories could be continued, as well as mystical myth and legend.

Eventually, like called to like, and the climatic conditions had influence on where groups decided to dwell.

As the hottest conditions existed in the north, this land was taken over by people of Middle-Eastern descent, and so Jaddanna came into being.

To the west the land was settled by people of the Far-Eastern races. Their fishing skills were paramount and the bays to the west were to their liking. The oriental city of Keshia was thus established.

The centre of the land was occupied by the mystical Celts, who herded horses there. They lived lives influenced by magic. Their chieftains were ritually tattooed, and were always female. A matriarchal society developed with the 'Horse Lady' as chief.

Other groups left Dakana and made their way to the land over the sea to the east called Ghast.

There was plenty here – an idyllic climate with fishing in abundance. The people who settled there, lived a life which would have suited medieval royalty. They were of European descent from Viking extraction.

All people spoke a version of English, rarely reverting to native speech apart from the Kordovans, who were of Welsh extraction. Kordova was an island kingdom to the south of Ghast.

Chapter One

Sunlight splintered through gloomy grey clouds, massing on the mountain peaks. Fingers of brightness stretched through Strevia, shooting across the far-reaching lands, the domain of the 'Horse Lords'. Fragile blooms, scattered through the grasses, uncurled, raising their faces to greet the light. The land became covered with a blanket of mauve, interspersed with indigo and dusky pink.

At the first signs of light, small creatures ventured out of nests and burrows, whiskers twitching, ready to find the pleasures or dismays held in the new day. A morning breeze, carrying sweet smells of wild mint and clover, set the grasses in motion, shifting them into green waves, tossing and rolling across the undulating land.

Westward, the deep green forest, could not be seen from the Horse Lord's camp, as such a vast expanse of hip high grasses stretched away from the main ytwurt, then disappeared in the mist between land and sky.

Inside the main yurt, Merthaylis woke to the usual sounds and smells of morning. Her sleeping quarters were partitioned from the others by a heavy blanket, which separated herself and her sisters from prying eyes.

She heard the fire being readied for the morning meal, and listened to friends and family getting ready to meet the day. The leather sides of the yurt had not yet been raised. The living quarters felt safe and secure. Motes of dust danced in the sunlight, entering the interior through the smoke hole.

She watched the smoke from the newly-made fire drift in erratic wisps towards freedom. Snuggling down in her coverings of wool, her fingers followed the raised whorls of embroidery on the blanket's outer leather covering. The design echoed the patterns the smoke was making.

Her mind wandered to the events of the previous day. Instantly, her instinct was to jump and flee. As she pushed herself out of the enclosing blankets, the sudden cold in the air made her light skin frisson with bumps.

Merthaylis was a young, rounded girl. Her almost knee-length brown hair had been plaited in small thin plaits, and decorated with various beads and feathers.

These plaits swung around her face as she reached for her clothes. Impatiently, she pushed her hair out of the way. Gazing out at the world from under chiselled straight brows, her slightly-slanted brown eyes could be vivacious, but now they held the expression of a frightened child.

Thickly-lashed, her eyes were magnetic, and conveyed authority, though she was unaware yet of their ability to instill her leadership. As quickly as she could, she crawled out of her sleeping skins.

She donned her brown, baggy trousers, and topped them with a blue, beaded vest. Over all she slung her sheepskin jacket for protection from the chill of the morning. Lastly, she tugged on her leather boots.

The boots were new, made from the best hide, beaten, and softened. They were a deep brown colour, decorated with diamond designs. How she loved the look and feel of them.

Glancing back at her sleeping sisters, she pushed past the blanket cover. On tiptoe, she stole across the yurt, willing nobody to call her for some task or other. The strong light outside, and the chilly breeze accompanying it, made her eyes water.

Once outside, it was only a few moments before her black pony, Storm, noticed her. He was nearby, snuffling the frost-covered coarse grass, yet to be thawed by morning sun. Storm trotted over to her and pushed his nose in her hand, wheedling for titbits.

Merthaylis had no need of saddle or bridle; she had been raised to ride bareback from childhood. Storm raised his front left hoof to give her a stepping purchase as she vaulted on to his back. With one hand wrapped in his floating mane, and her knees talking to the pony, she was away.

She rode towards the light, now making swift encroachments on the shadows of the night. The distant hills to the east were dark blue blurs – their glistening peaks showed they were topped with snow. When gleams of sunlight traced across their crags, so the spires turned a deep rose colour, quickly changing to orange. Watching the changing hues of the landscape, Merthaylis urged Storm to canter.

As her pony's hooves thrummed across the plain, they startled many a small creature, just waking to face the morning. A flight of geese rose into the air, honking and complaining, their long legs trailing behind them, as if loathe to leave the ground.

Merthaylis gave Storm his head and they settled down into a steady gallop, putting a long distance between herself and the sleeping clan. It was good to be on her own, and out in the crisp morning air.

She leant down close to Storm's neck murmuring endearments in his ear. He had been her pony since she was a small child, barely able to walk. Over the years they had developed a rapport, which conveyed feelings without any words or movements needed.

With a toss of his head, Storm broke his gait, slowing their flight to a more peaceable momentum. Straightening up, Merthaylis snuffed the scents of crushed grass and the swelter of her pony. Her thoughts strayed back to the news, her father, the headman, gave her last night, while they were sitting around the fire.

Always imposing, her father's large, lean body, with its hidden strength, was frightening enough, without his deep, reverberating voice. In her mind's eye, she revisited last night's scene.

There was her father, sprawled out upon his sheepskin seat, on a higher ledge than hers, or his subjects. The firelight, and the sparks from a falling log, reflected her father's precious red goblet as he sipped at his after-dinner wine. What he said resonated in her head, pounding in her brain, like Storm's thundering hooves.

'You are now 13 child, and already a young woman. No more are you to play with the children, while flaunting your youth to the young men.

'You bear the blood of the chieftains in your veins, and as of today this will be proclaimed for all to see who dare. I have designed your heritage. The priestesses have been summoned.' Merthaylis had known this would happen, sooner or later, but day-by-day had hoped to postpone the moment.

With hesitant fingers, she took the piece of leather her father held out. Despairingly, she inspected the markings, burned in the leather, then blackened in with charcoal. The number of marks had filled her with horror.

Each arm was to bear a coiled snake with its tail etched in her armpit, its body curling around her arm, and the head resting on the back of her hand. Her breasts would be circled with spiralling concentric circles ending in darkened nipples.

Rising from her groin, stretching over her stomach was a wolf with a snarling face, its jaws snapping below her breasts. As if those riffs were not enough, covering her whole back would be a phoenix, rising from flames; the totem of the clan.

Her father must love her very much to inflict so much pain on her, he must think her brave and worthy, to be able to withstand so much suffering. She remembered how he had looked, sitting above her in the firelight.

He had smiled at her, while his eyes, full of love and expectation, were unwaveringly fixed upon her face. His red woollen cloak had been thrust back, showing what a fine man he still was. Grieving for her deceased mother had not impaired his good looks.

Why did he not find another wife to bear the riffs? In her heart she knew it was her duty, but could she bear the outcome? Once the riffs were done, she would wear nothing on her upper body except a sleeveless bolero when she was inside the yurt.

No man would touch her on fear of death; all eyes would be lowered in deference. In future, her noble blood would be proclaimed, by the riffs on her body.

Storm was starting to slow, so Merthaylis calmed him to a walk, then allowed him to crop some special grass they often found in a certain spot beside a stream of icy purling water. She slid down and wandered aimlessly towards the water, pushing through crackling bushes.

The little stream was surrounded with small trees and furzy bush. It was in a place she liked to hide. There were few places on the open plain where one could escape the searching icy fingers of the wind.

She lay on the bank, looking for fish, but the sounds of her boots must have disturbed them, for there were no shadows in the water. She rolled over and looked at the clouds swirling across the sky, and let her fingers dangle in the snowmelt.

Her future stretched before her like a patterned tapestry. Commencing today, when the priestesses began their work. If they were skilful and caused no infection, she might live. She had known this to be her fate from early childhood.

The ruling family had to prove their women were strong, and also brave enough to bear the next ruling chief. Depending on the outcome and if her riffs were clean, she would be married. If she had daughters, their riffs would include the Phoenix as well as their father's totem. Sons had their totems tattooed on their inner wrists. Only the husbands of a Horse Lady, like her father, had the full tattoo on their backs.

She remembered the huge wolf on her mother's back. Her mother had been a brave and gentle woman, with protective hands and loving eyes.

In her mind Merthaylis sent her mother greetings, as the vision of her lovely face drifted into her consciousness. Her mother, Thaylis, had farewelled her on the day the main beam of the yurt fell across her breast, while she lay sleeping. She was the only person inside at that time in spring, everyone else was out rounding up the herds.

Thaylis had been a strong chieftain, much loved by all the clans ruled by the major Horse Lord. Her judgements had been fair. She always listened patiently to all those wanting her advice. The clans had flourished under her leadership. Her children were bereft by her untimely death, and now Merthaylis was to lead the clans.

The sound of horse's hooves drumming across the plain aroused Merthaylis from her reverie. A band of horsemen swept into sight around the bend in the stream. They crossed the rivulet, making the water splash up around their horses' withers.

The bright sun caught the water as it sprinkled, cascading in rainbows, back to the stream.

Hot from running, the horses wished to drink. Merthaylis saw the horsemen included her father and brothers. They made the horses swirl in circles to prevent them gorging in the water.

'What are you doing, Merthaylis?' her father asked sternly.

'She's waiting for her lover!' laughed her elder brother Borin. He was 17. Soon, he would be married to Muria, Horse Lord as chieftain near the mountains. His future father-in-law had asked for him already.

Borin's dark red hair was flowing away from his face in the wind, leaving his features outlined against the morning sky. His face was well-proportioned. Good looks ran in the family. He pushed his huge black stallion out of the water, and leant down to grin at his sister.

Merthaylis stood up, shading her eyes with her hand, and watched him with dislike. Borin's brown eyes had flashed with flecks of red, indicating he was about to tease her. His handsome, sardonic face never appeared to be worried. He was always teasing her. She would be glad when he was gone.

Ignoring Borin and his silly remarks, she replied to her father's question.

'I've been saying goodbye to Storm.'

Andreas swung off his stallion and looped his reins around the limb of a nearby tree, then came and squatted besides her, crouching by the stream. He nodded his head in Borin's direction, thus dismissing him. Swinging his horse's head around, Borin moved to join the other men, further down the stream.

'You're not going to lose Storm, you know. You just won't be riding him much longer. When you have your riffs you will be given a bigger horse. Then you can let one of the other girls take over Storm.'

'I don't want another horse!' Suddenly Merthaylis burst into tears.

Her younger brother, Redd, came up behind them. He put his arms around Merthaylis and gave her a hug, making her breathless.

'You will be too heavy for Storm soon, Merth. You wouldn't like to be a burden for him, would you?'

She turned and put her head against his brown leather coat. Redd, just 16, always knew the right thing to say.

Her father stood up impatiently. Andreas had known Merthaylis would react badly to news of her initiation from the moment he lost his wife.

'Go now, child. The priestesses have come. Redd, you take her home. The rest of us will continue with our hunting. Hopefully, we will return with some game this evening.'

He strode to his horse, gathered the reins and waved to the rest to follow him. With the jingle of tack accompanying the soft thuds of hooves in the long grass, they cantered out on to the plain.

Redd smiled at her, then gave her a little push.

'Go catch Storm,' he instructed. Merthaylis stumbled to where Storm was waiting in the clump of special grass. The day seemed dull through her tear-filled eyes. The pony lurched against her, and she threw her arms around his glossy neck, smelling the sweet nut aroma of his shining coat.

'Who shall I share you with?' Merthaylis whispered. Suddenly the images of her sisters swam before her eyes; she, however, hated them both.

Redd rode around a clump of trees astride his chestnut. He gave his sister a commiserating glance, then beckoned her to follow him. Merthaylis mounted and they rode together across the plain. Redd was well-aware his sister was in no hurry to meet the priestesses, so he held the horses at walking pace. He kept up a steady stream of small talk as they rode, trying to distract Merthaylis from what was before her. Glancing at her every now and then, he saw she was recovering some composure, but it was taking a huge amount of will power.

He turned to smile at her, and was rewarded with a tremulous grin. Merthaylis looked at her younger brother, whose usually merry brown eyes were now clouded with worry. She stared, as if she would never see his light brown curls and happy face again.

Three women, aged 20-23, were grouped inside the yurt as the riders approached. Redd and Merthaylis knew they were priestesses because their abbreviated leather vests, worn above full-length divided woollen skirts, displayed the riffs of their clans. Indeed, their riffs indicated that they were younger daughters of ruling chiefs. They were destined to remain as priestesses unless their older sister died and then they became her successor. They were talking to each other, their braids glinting in the sunlight.

Suma, the oldest of the priestesses, spoke quietly to the others, then stepped towards Merthaylis, who was standing outside, uncertain. Redd kissed his sister and wished her good luck.

'I'll take Storm to pasture for you,' he said. 'You go now.' He gave her a little push towards the yurt.

'Well, Merthaylis!' said Suma. 'Your father has summoned us to start on your riffs. Have you eaten today?'

Merthaylis shook her head as the thought of food made her gorge rise.

'No?' Suma slipped an arm around her shoulders. 'That's good. The poppy will work more efficiently on an empty stomach. It will settle that queasiness, too.'

Tria and Feta, the younger priestesses, led the way behind the yurt. Merthaylis was surprised to find a small tent erected there. It had an even smaller one in the shadow behind it.

'This is where we shall live for the next few weeks,' Tria called over her shoulder. Her face changed completely when she smiled, as if lit by an inner glow. Suma guided Merthaylis into the smaller of the two tents. There was a padded mat stretched out on the floor with a stuffed mattress in the middle of it. Merthaylis realised that the mat was for the women to kneel and sit on, while the mattress, covered with soft cloths, was for her.

Feta, the smallest and roundest of the priestesses, knelt down beside the mattress and started to pray. Suma helped Merthaylis take off her jacket and her beaded vest, then indicated she was to lie on the mattress.

Tria passed Suma a tray, holding the riff sticks and some bottles, and then joined Feta in prayer.

Trembling with fear and cold, Merthaylis watched, as Suma lit braziers around the tent. A sweet, heavy perfume filled the air when the smoke rose from the incense, as it caught alight.

Please my Lady give me strength, Merthaylis thought. *I must not show the Phoenix can be frightened, nor that I am a coward, and not fit to lead the clan.*

'Drink!' commanded Suma, holding out a cup. 'The Phoenix will rise again.'

The drink of the poppy sent Merthaylis into ecstasy, blurring the agony caused by the riff sticks. She remained in the tent for the whole of the riff making. The priestesses lived in the larger tent, making sure one of them was with her, night and day.

Occasionally, she was delirious, and at times entered a state of grace. Once or twice, she left her body and hovered over the tent. When thus suspended she saw how the designs were appearing, and also saw the tolerance and patience of the priestesses.

In her drugged dreams she met the Phoenix, and saw his beauty. Proud and fierce, majestic in the spirit world, she travelled with him through time and space, drifting through the void. Burrowed in the downy feathers of his golden chest, she had no fear. He spoke of courage and her future, giving advice from countless chieftains of her ancestral line, whose spirit faces drifted past in swirling coloured mist. She gazed on them in awe.

Her visitations with the Wolf, given to her by her mother's clan, were happy times. The Wolf was an old friend from her childhood, and when he was with her, so were the soft hands of her mother. Always at the end of day, on the verge of sleep, the soft cooling pads of the priestess, the laving touch of the tongue of the Wolf, and her mother's gentle hands, were all inextricably intermingled.

Another recurring dream aroused interest in her future. An unknown man, someone she had never met, always featured in these visions. He was tall and fair with an angular, handsome face. His blue eyes followed her movements. She would have liked to see him smile but he never did; he seemed to always be searching for something.

Occasionally she wakened in the night to find Andreas standing at the flap of the tent, gazing in at her. Once he spoke.

'You are doing well, daughter. You will be a worthy mother of my grandchildren.' He entered the tent and leaned towards the mattress. He ran his fingers over the newly-raised skin on her arm, then nodded his approval.

As she drifted off to sleep again, Merthaylis wondered if he had chosen her husband already. What would he be like? Could she bear to have a stranger thrusting between her legs, as the other women described, like a stallion with a mare? More pain and blood. Would there be delight too? Or would her soul drain away in hopelessness with her lost virginity?

One morning Suma covered her from chin to toe with a red blanket. This usually only covered her at night.

'You are to have a visitor,' Suma told her. 'I know it is unusual, but I have prayed to Mut and permission has been granted.'

Borin entered the tent, then dropped to one knee beside her. He was wearing new clothes of tooled green leather, and he had a woollen cloak with a fur-lined hood slung over his shoulder. He had taken off his boots at the tent flap, but she could see them. They were knee-high riding boots of soft red leather, covered with intricate designs.

'How are you?' he asked. 'I can see from your face, you have lost a lot of weight.' His lean face showed concern. *This is the first time he has ever worried about me*, she thought.

'I survive,' she answered tiredly. 'Are you going?'

He nodded assent. 'The Bear clan has sent for me. Muria has completed her riffs.'

Merthaylis remembered Muria. When the Horse Lords had gathered for the Autumn Festival, Muria had been there with her clan.

In her mind's eye Merthaylis pictured a tall, willowy girl with long, blonde braids. Her fine, delicately-boned face had been serious, as she overheard the gossip of the other girls. She had seemed a careful child who was listening to things better left unsaid. At that time her slender body had shown no signs of burgeoning womanhood.

Merthaylis hoped Muria's riffs had been accomplished without that fragile beauty spoiled, or her spirit damaged.

'Did you know where you were going, or that it was Muria's father who had chosen you at the Festival?' She gazed at her brother, as he knelt beside her.

Borin closed his eyes before he answered. Merthaylis realised he was picturing Muria and the encounter at the fair.

'Not then,' he replied. 'No one said anything to me then. I didn't think I would be powerful enough to have a clan of my own.'

'Be kind to her,' Merthaylis entreated. Without thinking, she stretched out and grasped his hand. Borin's other hand covered hers, but not before he had seen the black, striking snake emblazoned on the back of her hand.

'Great Mut, forgive me!' Borin put his face down on the blanket. Merthaylis clenched his fingers between hers. Relaxing, she put her hand on his dark red hair. 'No harm comes from this. The Lady has given her permission. Are you pleased with Muria and her clan?'

He recovered, then sat back on his heels.

'I suppose I am,' he muttered. He gazed out of the tent flap, purposefully not looking at her.

Merthaylis pulled her hand back. 'I don't know who is coming here, but I do hope he will be kind, think of the needs of others, and be caring towards the animals.'

She pulled a face at him, then added, 'I'm sure this is all Muria will need, too. Go with the Lady.'

Borin bent and kissed her. He gave her a tear-filled glance, and then rapidly left the tent.

As she listened to him pulling on his new boots and heard his receding footsteps, she wondered if she would ever see him again. Probably she would, she consoled herself.

He would be there when the Horse Lords gathered again for the Autumn Fair. He would have taken the Phoenix to the Bear and his eldest daughter would wear the Phoenix on her stomach and the Bear on her back.

Merthaylis wondered which totem her children would wear. Soon the ceremonial standards would have to be re-woven.

The tent flap moved again, and Suma entered, bringing her some warm milk and a honey cake.

'He has gone, then?' she questioned, raising her eyebrow as she spoke. 'Soon it will be young Redd's turn.'

A wave of misery swept over Merthaylis. Perhaps no clan would choose Redd for their Horse Lord. If not chosen, he would stay by her and give her the support she knew she would need. She knew she shouldn't wish for such a thing, but if Redd were snatched away, there would be no buffer between her and destiny. She longed for Redd's comforting arms now.

She sat up on her mattress and reached for the cake and milk. As she moved she watched the snakes writhe on her arms, shifting with her muscle movement. Who would want to comfort her now? Who would hug her as the leader of the Phoenix Clan?

Chapter Two

The men leaned against the balcony and gazed out over the city.

'As there are pirates in their waters, one of you will escort the Kordovans home,' King Joseph was saying.

'It will have to be Lex,' Troy gave his older brother a push.

'I shall decide.' His father gave his lanky, blond-haired son a stern glance. 'I cannot send a galley into their territorial waters, so whoever goes will have to be content with merchant vessel, which, of course, will attract pirates.'

Lex continued to admire the view while listening to his father.

The palace was built on a hill, which overlooked the city of Devron. The city had not been planned, but had grown as each house had been built next to its neighbour. In spite of this, the houses were spacious and set in their own gardens. Their pink roofs, when viewed from the balcony, dotted throughout the lush greenery, making a pretty carpet stretching out to the sea.

Near the port the shops were more closely clustered, while narrow alleyways led the way down to the ships. It was a peaceful scene. Out at sea a huge sailing ship was tacking towards the harbour.

'What else are you doing today, father?' Troy asked. He turned and looked at his father, while holding his hair out of the way.

'I shall be having audiences this morning. As you know, this afternoon I shall be busy with the Ambassador. You could help me there. Would you like to show his daughter round the city?'

'I should think that is more the kind of job for Lex,' said Troy, not pleased at the prospect of losing his freedom.

'Oh no! I have my own business to attend to. Anyway, I have to be at the meeting with father. If the daughter is anything like the mother, you might like the work,' Lex said, giving him a grin, and a friendly shove.

The brothers were good friends. Lex was a smaller, darker version of Troy. He was the first born, so was heir to the throne.

Slightly disconsolate, still green about the gills from this morning's hangover, Troy duly presented himself at the ambassadorial suite during the afternoon. He was admitted to a sumptuous salon, resplendent with peacock blue walls; the silvery, filigree furniture carefully arranged on a dark, blue carpet.

He was invited to sit down by the dour butler.

'The ladies are expecting you, and will be with you shortly, Sir.' Glancing round, Troy wondered if his moleskin trousers, yellow shirt, and brown, velvet doublet would be sufficiently elegant, for which seemed now, to be a grand occasion. Shrugging his shoulders, he settled himself on a spindly chair.

The stern butler offered him a choice selection of refreshments. He considered, then declined. However he did accept a glass of a golden wine, which effervesced in the goblet, already misted on the outside with chill.

On inquiring where it came from, he was informed it was a speciality from Kordova, made from grapes, which were unique to that area. The wine was tangy, yet spicy, although too viscous for his taste; nevertheless, he enjoyed it while waiting.

As the wine began to mollify his latent headache, Troy crossed his legs and prepared for a long wait. Thinking about the events of the previous evening brought a faint, ironic grin to his previously annoyed countenance.

He had enjoyed himself at the masked ball; his friends had been in fine fettle, and they had finished the evening by putting Lex's squire into the main fountain in the town centre. Lex would not be pleased if he found out, however. The squire, Jocelyn, was a good sport and probably would not mention it.

The butler loomed into view at his shoulder. The man had moved so quietly on the thick carpet Troy had not noticed him before he spoke.

'Lady Lesla will receive you now my Lord.'

Following the butler's portly frame, Troy found himself being ushered into a stark room with white walls. The furniture was alabaster, while the windows were draped in white tulle.

The windows were open, and the room conveyed a feeling of lightness and air. There was an elusive perfume, tantalising him, until he tracked it down to a small brazier burning steadfastly on the hearth.

Troy was becoming restive having finished the wine, when a door opened and three women came in. Lady Lesla was a buxom beauty with brown hair and deep black eyes.

Attired in a yellow over garment with trailing sleeves, the neckline of her low cut, pale cream undergarment was decorated with topazes. Her hair was dressed high and offset her regal features. The low cut garments displayed her flawless skin and superbly columned neck.

Troy was taken aback by the allure of this mature woman, though he made the customary greetings. This is a powerful woman, he thought, I wonder if the daughter is as strong?

Lady Lesla smiled at him. 'I hoped we were going to meet the other prince. May I present my daughter, Delia?'

Troy turned to face the other woman who was standing to one side. Imperious, flashing, brown eyes, almost enveloped by lashes so long, they caressed their bearer's cheeks, met his. Every glance from Delia was a challenge.

She was wearing a dress of similar cut and style to that of her mother's, but in rich, burgundy velvet. Her trailing sleeves were decorated with tiny, silver bells around the cuffs; they tinkled as she moved. Because her cleavage was so low, she was exposing hints of ivory breasts.

Troy kept his gaze on her face, yet he was aware of a luscious body underlying the burgundy-coloured garment, which revealed lissom waves, rippling in the fabric as she moved.

'Lady Delia, with your mother's permission and your acceptance, I have the honour of showing you and your companion, the town. You wish to go shopping, I believe?'

The doll-like image of the fairy princess was instantly shattered when she spoke.

'You are late! We have been ready for an hour. Have you a carriage? I intend to have many parcels.' Her husky voice was imperative, and irritated.

'The streets are too steep and too narrow for a carriage, my Lady. I have acquired two carrying chairs, called sedans, which no doubt will be sufficient for yourselves and your shopping. Shall we proceed?'

She swept out of the room, flouncing her full skirt, while twirling her matching brolly in a brusque fashion. With a slight shrug of her grey, neatly-clad shoulders, her smaller companion followed her.

Delia's mother moved to Troy's side and laid a hand on his arm. 'I'm afraid my daughter is a trifle fractious,' she confided.

'The weather does not suit her. She wishes to purchase something more appropriate for the ball this evening. She claims all her clothes are too heavy as we have come from a cooler climate.

'Thank you for your decision to accompany them, I hope you have a happy afternoon.'

Troy trailed alongside the sedans, feeling quite out of sorts. This presumptuous girl had her mother persuaded to her way of thinking. Thank Mut it was only for one afternoon! As he handed them both in and out of the covered sedans his thoughts were elsewhere, mainly with his horses.

Delia gave him haughty glances, then as these failed to arouse him from his contemplation, she finally waved an outfit at him.

His attention recalled, Troy peered in the boxes. 'My Lady, if you wear this, I am sure you will be the belle of the ball.' He gave her a glance under lowered lids, with a faint smile on his lips.

'Don't be stupid! That is an undergarment! Have you no taste?' She stamped her foot in annoyance, making all the bells on her sleeves jingle and bounce. 'How can I trust, you are taking me to the best couturiers? What are the most fashionable colours in mode at the moment?'

Impatient and out of temper, Troy pushed away the fripperies and caught her by the arm.

'Lady Delia, I do not set myself up as an arbiter of fashion, nor do I follow all the whims of the court. I know my sister and her friends visit these shops, often. Perhaps you would wish a dressmaker to make something to your taste?'

'No, no! That would take too long. However, I shall need to buy some intricate belts and some jewellery, to offset these plain gowns, with some matching ribbons for my hair, of course.'

Troy gazed at her in horror. He knew the shops where these things were readily available were a distance away.

They went through winding dirty streets, which were so narrow, their half-timbered houses leaned across the alley way to almost touch each other. The streets were dark, almost impenetrable, gloomy passages.

Using a silk handkerchief, which he had fortunately found in his pocket, Troy wiped his face and hands, while surveying his dirty boots.

'Come on, Delia. Those places are a long way down towards the docks. Let us rest awhile in the shade and have a cooling drink, first.'

She stood uncertainly beside her sedan, twirling her parasol. 'All right, my Lord, we shall have a short rest.'

Delia's face was flushed with the heat. In the full glare of the afternoon's sun, with the burgundy dress clinging to her figure, more of her was revealed than should be seen in the street. Troy was aware of the appreciative glances from the sedan bearers, and knew they were also amused, as their elegant lord was being made a monkey of at last.

Troy told them to take the sedans behind an inn close at hand and to have a drink themselves. He warned them that if they lost the parcels, he would ensure they spent the rest of their miserable lives in the mines, that is, if they had any years left after he had finished with them.

His hand under her elbow, Troy escorted Delia into the inn. She moved well, and attracted many an admiring glance. Troy settled her at a table with her friend, Amelia, and repaired to the old, scratched bar.

He was often a customer here, and was well-known.

'A bit early in the day, for you isn't it, Prince Troy? Do you wish your usual?' The hotelier was round and red-faced with a cheery smile above the green apron, which covered his broad chest. He had a matching cloth, which he was using to polish the glasses.

'Far too early, thank you, Stephen. I am running nursemaid to those wenches over there. We'll have some cold lemonade please.'

'I'll bring it to your table.'

Thanking him, Troy turned and started to push his way through the crowd, hampered by the oak settles and solid tables scattered around the room. Barking his shin twice on ill-placed furniture did little for his temper.

When he reached the corner where he had left Delia, he found to his chagrin she was entertaining a group of young men, one of them his squire, Anton. Troy made his way towards them.

'Troy, you young dog! You have been hiding that luscious maiden from us. Did you intend to keep her all to yourself?' Trojan D'Auton's voice was loud, deep and husky, and also right in Troy's ear.

Extremely tall with languid good looks, Trojan was one of Troy's usual companions. His finicky manners and long, fair hair disguised an amused nature. He had the ability to extricate himself from most of his escapades by using guile and charm.

'Not at all, Trojan. In fact I find her exceedingly tedious, not to my taste, by any means. I have been named chaperone for the afternoon, whilst she indulges her desire to shop until she drops. Are you going to the ball this evening?'

'It is my intention, but who knows what fascinating enterprise might deter me? Does your lady intend to grace it with her presence?'

'That is the main purpose of this expedition.' Suddenly, wearying of this whole affair, Troy beckoned Anton to his side. Slight and dark, Anton had not been in Troy's service for only a few months, and was eager to please.

Grasping both men by their arms, Troy pulled them towards his person, then dropped his voice.

'It is political to keep her happy, my father desires it. I have stomached enough shopping for one day. She wishes to go down to the harbour booths to make further purchases. I beseech you, if you love me at all, take her there and stand guard as my proxy. I shall make some excuse.'

Anton shrugged his shoulders, then nodded. 'As you wish, my Lord. The lady must finish what she has started. I shall see she comes to no harm.' He shifted his sword in its scabbard, making a soft slithery sound.

Trojan slung a nonchalant arm over Troy's shoulder, then contributed, 'I am not armed my Lord, but no doubt I can entertain the lady with a few pleasant comments. I shall guide her away from those around her, fear not.'

After making excuses to Delia, assuring her that important matters of state needed his attention, Troy then expounded on the capabilities of Anton and Trojan.

'I am sure these gentlemen will look after me. They will probably be more considerate of my wishes than you have been,' she said. Delia gave Troy one of her steely glances, then turned the full force of her beaming smile on Trojan, while grasping Anton's hand.

Passing the landlord who was pushing through the crowd with the lemonade and glasses held high on a silver tray, Troy complimented him on his swiftness and requested the price be added to his slate.

Taking the steps up to the palace two at a time, he felt the responsibility of Delia roll off his shoulders, like slipping off a heavy cloak. He hurried to his rooms, discarding clothing on the way. Soon, attired in his riding gear, he was making his way to the stables.

The winding corridors in the palace threaded from his suite of rooms overlooking the town with airy balconies and resplendent hangings towards the rear of the building where the kitchens, outhouses and stables were situated in the shadow of the mountains.

On his way from his room to the stables Troy passed the open door of his father's library. The King had made this room, which was situated on the north side of the palace, his own domain.

Large windows from floor to ceiling, accompanied by huge skylights running in strips across a covered airy balcony, gave the room light and air in all weathers. The walls were lined with books and maps; the furniture was made of polished wood. His father, ensconced in his favourite leather chair, waved to Troy as he passed the open doorway.

'You called, my Liege?' Troy hesitated by the door, eager to be gone.

'I did, come in! You have returned early from your duties. Has the Ambassador's daughter finished her shopping?'

Joseph surveyed his son with a discerning eye; again his instructions had not been followed to conclusion. Though Joesph was fond of him, he also realised it was time Troy grew up and learnt he was judged by his behaviour.

Troy slumped down on a stool beside his father, irritation showing in every line of his body.

'I persuaded Trojan to carry on for me. Anton is with them, too. I found that girl distressingly annoying.'

His father looked at his younger son with an expression of mingled annoyance and amusement.

'It takes one to know one, so they say. You will escort them back to Kordova, when they return home,' he said.

Joseph raised a thin, brown hand on which to rest his chin. The black, silk sleeve of his jacket slid down his arm. He stretched his legs, clothed in neatly tailored grey trousers, out in front of him, and appeared perfectly relaxed.

'Me!'

'You! You will go as my representative to discuss the agreement with Kordova about the wood. I shall expect you to be polite to the Ambassador and his family, and of course be respectful to their King.'

Troy persuaded and wheedled, giving excuses as to why it was imperative for him to stay in Devron, offering Lex as an alternative representative, but it was so much wasted air. His father was determined he should go, and what was more, was equally adamant Troy should be courteous and use his intelligence to obtain some good trades.

When he finally escaped, he knew his fate was decided. Thudding down the dim corridor continuing on his way to the stables, his face was flushed with fury. He leapt down the stairs three at a time and charged across the courtyard into the dimness of the cool barn. Throwing himself down on a pile of straw near the door, he considered the situation.

As his anger cooled, he realised he would only have to put up with the silly girl while they were on board ship. When Kordova was reached, his dealings would be with the King. On consideration he would be involved with the court dignitaries and officials dealing with the wood. Lady Delia would not be his responsibility after she reached her home.

Feeling slightly happier, he got up, picked straw from his black leather riding clothes, stretched, and moved over to where his favourite mare was stabled.

Aware of Troy's moods and actions, Pertrand, his groom, moved forward from the rear of the stables carrying riding tack. A group of young men, who had been dicing around a barrel at the side of the stables, noticed the movement.

Troy nodded to Pertrand and held his hand out for his mare's bridle. She thrust her head forward in eagerness, investigating his hand, then nuzzled round his pockets, hoping for a treat. Calling over his shoulder, he announced, 'Juliette needs to stretch her legs, who wishes for a gallop?'

With whoops and catcalls, his friends readied their mounts. The horses were as anxious as their riders to have a run. All this excitement and noise strung their nerves higher, so it was a few minutes before all were saddled up and prepared to move.

Troy sat on Juliette's narrow back as she crabbed and sidestepped in the yard, waiting for the last of the group to emerge from the stable.

He stroked Juliette's arched, ebony neck, her coat-like warm satin under his hand. She shifted to the left with impatience, and he gentled her while giving a chuckle of appreciation of her mood. At last they were ready.

The Prince shouldered into the front of the group and then led the way down a narrow track between dark grey stone walls, which led to the plain, in front of a flat-topped mountain at the rear of the town.

With the land so mountainous, there were few places where the horses could gallop freely. In front of this mountain was one, and the other was along the coastline, depending on the incoming tide.

With tails streaming from the speed of their passage, the horses raced across the dry stubble of the plateau.

Troy headed for the distant mountains, which raised their dark, blue peaks against the myriad colours of the late afternoon sky. Reaching the foothills, the forest air was cooler where the great trees stretched down to meet the plain.

Easing up the mad caper, Troy reined in, to allow Juliette to rest a little, then they threaded their way through stands of pine, interspersed with the occasional gnarled oak.

Now they were travelling at a more reasonable pace with the horses blowing, their steamy breath outlined in front of them against the dark green trees. Pertrand permitted his stallion to draw up beside Juliette, and the pair moved companionably along the forest path.

'Juliette is ready to be mated again. My chestnut here has a strong chest and a good bloodline. It is a pity he is so small.'

Troy cast an eye over the other's horse. It was well-proportioned, but lacked that eternal spark essential for good breeding.

'A good thought, Pertrand. He is probably the best of a poor bunch. A pity we can't import a pure-blooded stallion. I should like to improve the herd. They are too skinny and too rangy for my liking. They do their best, but some fresh lifelines in the pool would give them a boost.

'Imagine Juliette's strength and spirit coupled with a barrel chest and strong withers. One reads of them in books, but never have I seen one.'

Pertrand had a knowing look on his long, saturnine face.

'What do you know about them? They are bred in some backward island community, so I have heard. The people breed them for their strength and stamina. It is just what we need – organise half a dozen!'

'I'm sorry, Lord, it can't be done. The horses look magnificent animals and have all the attributes you mentioned. However, they never come on the market. Only culls are sold outside their land, and they have been gelded.'

Patting Juliette's neck, Troy signalled to his retinue to turn back. 'Where did you see them?' he asked, his face alive with interest.

'In my youth I crossed *The Dark Ocean* and visited Dishnigar. I saw the Strevian horses there in the market. The Horse Lords bring them down from their high country for the spring fairs. They are magnificent animals, bred for speed.'

'No hope for me, then!' Troy smiled at the groom. 'I shall not be going there. My father intends me to visit Kordova shortly.'

'Before the yearly gathering, my Lord?'

'Probably. I shall miss the races. You will have to ride Juliette for me.'

'Wouldn't you prefer Lord Trojan to ride for you, my Prince?'

'Trojan's, too lanky for Juliette, and he saws his horse's mouths. I would prefer you to ride her if she will let you. She has her own opinions about what she likes. We should go faster now. I shall be in trouble if I am late for this ball!'

Raising his arm, as he dug his heels gently into Juliette's sides, he waved the returning group to a gallop across the darkening plain.

Julliette started to slow as the ground became rocky. Troy gave her to Pertrand when they reached the stables. As he made his way back into the palace, he felt happily tired. He was pleased to find a repast left in his room. He had a drink of beer, followed by a crusty bread and some tasty cheese, and then made his way to the bath.

Chapter Three

Dishnigar was a deep-water harbour port. The original fishing village, settled in the centre of the curve of the bay, had been surrounded over the centuries with warehouses and stores.

Beyond them, as progress and trade had increased, large family houses had been built. Of necessity, these were erected on cliff faces and over hangs, as most of the flat land had already been claimed. Because of this, the locals referred to the two areas of the town as the Tops and the Flats.

The Flats belonged to the fishermen, the servants, the traders and their families. Their houses were poor affairs with thatched roofs over wattle and daub, occasionally interspersed with slate-covered stone buildings. The houses had been built around open squares, often with a well in the centre. Fresh water came from the cliffs behind, where the streams diverted, then filtered down from higher ground. Each square belonged to people with similar trades, the largest being the one that belonged to the slavers. Their square was surrounded by grim barracks, which were assigned to both keepers and slaves. In the main part of the area was a roped-off dais where the wares were displayed, bid for and sold.

The horse traders' square was encompassed by big barn like stables. Each side of the stables was partitioned off, all sections being carefully tagged and each stall numbered. The horses were kept separate so there would be no fighting. The festering bite, or injury from a vicious kick, could bring down the price of an animal by half, at least.

Business was brisk in this square, with people coming from all over the continent, bringing fodder, trading animals, purchasing tack, while gazing in wonder at the Strevian beauties.

Up in the Tops, living in the houses of the wealthy, were ships captains, doctors, lawyers, well-to-do businessmen, politicians, and those who made their living by buying and selling human cargo.

Few of the slaves remained in Dishnigar. Most were transported out to other seaports. Some of the unfortunate ones went to the inland mines, while others were taken to farms and plantations in the interior.

As the city had developed around the deep water of the harbour, tides had small effect on trade. In consequence, water traffic was continuous, day and night. The cliffs were full of caves and caverns, many of them open to the passage of the sea.

Interspersed throughout the cliffs were lanes and steps, some caused by rifts in the land, others man-made, and while the constant wear of water had resulted in unusual fissures.

As a result of this veritable cornucopia of hiding places and secret tunnels, Dishnigar was the heart of the smuggling trade.

Goods could be brought into a sea cavern at dead of night and not be seen again until they reached their market, either in the city, or far beyond the cliffs and mountains, reaching the other lands of the vast island, which was a continent.

Seated on a bench in a dark corner of the bar in *The Endless Tankard*, which was situated on the sea front, was a burly figure. His massive body showed no sign of fat, muscles rippled under his brown surcoat when he lifted his drink. His dark eyes kept constant watch on the comings and goings in the taproom.

It was early evening and the crowd had not yet gathered for the evening of gambling, boozing and roistering. Watching Dolly swaying around the tables as she brought his evening meal, his eyes lit with amusement.

'What have you got for me tonight, girl?'

'The best we have, Sir. I have brought some fine chicken in spices, and rice, with a bottle of red to wash down the cheese. Compliments from Jade, she is taken with your special delivery.'

'I'm not surprised, I felt like keeping it for myself!' He smiled at Dolly, then gave her a friendly push as she unloaded the tray. 'Would you like to come away with me, Doll? You must be sick of this musty old pub.'

She tossed her thick, brown curls, while running her hands over the creases in her apron.

'How silly do you think I am Ricci? The moment you tired of me, I would be given to your men. I have a good job here with my Da and I know where I am sleeping of a night, and I can choose alone, or who is with me. This pub will be mine one day. Peace of mind keeps a body healthy.' With that she turned away and sauntered back to the kitchen.

The chicken was good and he enjoyed it. Finishing his meal with the cheese and wine, he kept an eye on the doorway, stiffening when The Watch loomed inside, then relaxing when they moved off down the street.

A little while later another figure entered. A small, slight man pushed open the door, looked around, then sidled up to the man sitting on the bench in the corner and sat down beside him. He looked at the wine the burly figure had in front of him and licked his lips. This produced a grin from Ricci, as he raised his glass again. After some time had passed, he set down his glass and spoke.

'How are you, Tom? You look as if you are up to no good, moving so shifty-like. Is it you 'The Watch' are looking for?'

'No way, Ricci.' The stranger gave a grin, showing broken, browning teeth in his deeply tanned face. His taut fingers were tapping on the tabletop, until in despair, Ricci shoved a glass of wine his way.

'They are looking for a runaway girl. Probably some of Jade's bitches didn't like her style. They don't want any new, pretty ones hogging the custom, you know.'

'What are you here for, then? I'm sure it is not for the pleasure of my company.'

'I am keeping out of the way, I must admit. Big Jacques is looking for me for my gaming debts, but that is not the reason I am here. I'm bringing you a message.'

'I was expecting one, but I didn't connect it with you. I suppose you are getting paid for this?'

'A little,' Tom admitted. 'I have to keep body and soul together.'

'I can't think why. Where is this message?'

Tom slid a scrap of paper across the table. Ricci lifted it to the light from the lantern in the corner, then grunted with satisfaction, having read the contents.

'What does it say, Ricci? I can't read, you see.'

'Well, ain't that a shame. Perhaps that's why you are such a perfect messenger. You should set yourself up in business. You could have as your motto, *'It is for me to bring and you to know.'* Ricci patted the little man on the shoulder, then swung away from the bench, lifted his leg over it and stood up, towering over the smaller man who was still sitting down.

'You stay there, Tom and finish the wine. I don't want you spying on me, or following me.'

Ricci moved towards the door, hailing the landlord as he went. 'I'll be back later on, Stu. Make sure you have a bed for me, will you? Make it nice and clean with a flagon of ale in the room, I'll probably be back late.'

'Of course, of course. The tap boy sleeps by the door; I'll make sure he lets you in. Good night, Sir.'

Dolly's father watched him go with an interested look on his face, then swung around to pay attention to his other customers.

Outside the streets were slick with rain. Ricci pulled his cloak around him, hiding the cluster of throwing knives in the heavy belt around his waist. A pale moon glinting behind shifting storm clouds caused the cobbles and slates to glisten in the wet.

Ricci turned to his left and started a steady climb up the cliff road, his boots sliding at times in the loose gravel. The houses that he passed were shuttered, with only a faint flicker of light showing here and there, gleaming through cracks in the boarding. Occasional travellers passed him, but mostly the street was empty. The effort of climbing soon warmed him, and he was glad of the land breeze coming from the rift in the cliffs.

This opening in the cliffs gave the wind passage to the sea, and also gave the late afternoon sun access to a spreading plateau of land that jutted slightly out over the harbour.

A large house built in the grand style with glazed windows and turrets, dominated this prime piece of land. The stone building had balconies on all four sides on the third floor. Because of this, sunlight could be enjoyed all day long, especially when the city of Dishnigar was stranded in gloom from early afternoon, as the shadows descended from the cliffs.

The balcony facing the sea was partially enclosed to contain a bird loft. Message pigeons fluttered and cooed there, resting between their onerous flights.

The west balcony overlooked the road that connected Dishnigar with the rest of the land, a passage forging across the rift, often lined with convoys of wagons hauling cargoes of contraband, interspersed with those carrying legitimate goods.

The southern balcony gave a good view of entrances to the caverns and caves, otherwise hidden from sight by the grim cliffs.

Under the house, the basement was where the work was done. Everything needed by those in the house could be made there, a virtual village in its entirety. Bread was baked, horses were shoed, arms were forged and grain was stored.

Below the basement a veritable warren of passageways, storage rooms and sleeping quarters extended down into the depths of the cliff. These were then connected to the sea caverns by ladders or steps and in some cases by wide passages, where goods could be shifted by cart.

Towards this house, The Eyrie, as the populace of Dishnigar called it, Ricci made his way. He reached the juncture where the main road swung to the right, to lead up towards the rift, then turning, he followed the smaller road to the left. A high rock wall surrounded the house. The entrance had large iron gates, with a watchman sitting by his lantern.

'Good evening, Sir,' the watchman greeted, eyeing Ricci with suspicion.

'Good evening. The Eagle has requested my presence.'

'Tonight's watch word?' countered the watchman.

'Eyas.'

'That'll do.'

The gate swung open with a creak. Ricci re-wrapped his cloak against the gusting wind when the material threatened to enshroud him as he made his way across the sward towards the house outlined in the distance.

The Eagle was sitting in the dining room holding conversation with this evening's dinner guests. Every evening, the house had a variety of people as guests, from all walks of life in the community. This way The Eagle kept a finger on deals and differences.

Her name was Essa Esse. She had started life as the daughter of a young skivvy who was in the service of the chief justice of Dishnigar. The workings of the law had fascinated her, and she had twisted it to her advantage throughout her long life, using her position and her charms to become educated in litigation. Now she was mistress of The Eyrie and all that it entailed.

Like a spider in her web, she trailed her gossamer through every shady deal, or every smart move that occurred in the city, and beyond.

Tonight at her table, an unusually small group was gathered. There was the chief of the city police, an eminent judge, some visitors from beyond the cliffs, and a young girl.

The girl was delicate, pretty in a thin-boned way, with long, almost white, blonde hair. She was dressed demurely in a navy dress of heavy linen, contrasting with her translucent skin. Her big blue eyes looked worried, as well they might have been, in this unusual company.

The fact that the watch was now searching for the girl in the city, did not disturb her hostess. When one was under the protection of Madame Esse, she was in charge of one's fate.

Essa had not made up her mind about the girl, as yet. She could turn the girl over to The Watch, demand ransom from her parents, give her back to Jade, sell her to any of her other guests, or as the idea was just forming, keep her to become her heiress, as she had no appropriate living kin.

A bird-like little woman now, Essa always dressed in flowing, covering black. Well into middle-age, her claw like hands covered with rings and thick veins toyed with the cutlery. Her deep-set green eyes watched her guests speculatively, shooting penetrating glances around the room, while musing *about* the girl.

The young woman had good manners and displayed excellent breeding, although she must be aware of her predicament. Perhaps time would alter her dismayed attitude, which was now so distressingly obvious, as she twisted her napkin in her lap.

'I shall change her name of course, she decided, *I'll think of something suitable.'*

A tall man, suddenly interrupted her thoughts.

'Madame Esse,' Dogan began. He was sitting down the table on her left, and raised his deep voice to gain her attention.

'Have you heard there is a run away girl in the city? Madam Jade is annoyed to lose a valuable member of her trade. The Watch is out searching for the girl as we speak.' With a curious glance his eyes slid knowingly to the girl across the table.

'Chief Dogan, I was unaware your interest was involved with every waif loose in the city. Aren't there more worrisome people with whom you can occupy your time? Cut throats, smugglers, and murderers?

'Of course, My Lady, there are many of them, but the reward for this young woman is manifestly higher. My men need incentive to do their work properly.'

'I'm sure they are paid adequately, however,' she slipped a diamond ring from her finger, one of an ostentatious number, then slid it across the damask towards him.

'Perhaps this will be reimbursement for the noble men out in the rain.'

Without having incriminated herself in any way, she felt she had won freedom for the girl at little cost.

Dogan picked up the ring, and after inspecting it carefully, he slipped it into his pocket.

'Madam, you are most generous. I'm sure my men will search thoroughly, in all the correct places.' Their eyes met in understanding, each with a slight smile on their inscrutable faces.

The butler cleared his throat to gain Essa's attention. She leaned back in her chair to hear what he had to impart.

'My lady, there is a man in the foyer who says you have requested him to attend you.'

'Of course! I was expecting him to call this evening. Please show him in.'

Ricci followed the butler into the candlelit room aware he had gained the attention of everyone seated there, including the Chief of Police. Many of the people dining with Essa were old acquaintances, with whom he exchanged greetings as he was shown to a place made ready for him on Essa's right.

'Have you eaten?' she asked, raising dark eyebrows in inquiry.

'Thank you Ma'am, I ate at *"The Endless Tankard.'* However a drop of something warm won't come amiss. It is very cold outside.'

When he had been served some of Essa's best brandy, he settled in his chair and waited for her to begin.

'I agree about the weather,' she nodded. 'My birds do not like this wet and cold. I have been receiving messages still, although it has been windy for my passage birds. I received a message this afternoon, in fact, despite the blustery conditions.'

His gaze shifted from the golden liquid, catching her meaningful look. 'Does the flight of this bird have any consequence for me, my lady?'

'It might well do so. I hear one of the other landlords has set off.' She picked up an envelope which had been lying beside her plate and handed it to him.

'Here are your instructions. My concern is for the one mentioned only. If others join the game they will be for you to deal with. This will be extra recompense for you. When the work is completed send me news as to what has transpired. I have been waiting for this for many years.'

Later that night, as she sat by the fire in her bedroom, Essa considered the outcome of the evening. Ricci had taken the envelope, and her instructions would now have been read, so he would have started pulling the enterprise together in his mind.

The blonde girl had been bedded down comfortably for the night, and was securely guarded. The police chief had gone on his way happy, having been introduced to Madame Esse's great niece. The girl had shown little surprise at being presented as such. Essa had hopes for her now. She seemed to accept Essa's schemes without question.

Her thoughts turned to the past, when she would have been about the same age as this girl was now. In the service of the chief justice, she had travelled north to Orphur, the main city of the northern kingdom of Hast. She had met a handsome young man during the festivities to celebrate the coming of age of the Prince of Hast.

The young man, who was in the retinue of the king of Devronia, had been charming and swept her off her feet. It was not until much later she found out he was a scion of the royal house and could be in line for the throne. On her return to Dishnigar she gave birth to a son.

Shortly after the baby had been kidnapped, and nothing more had been heard for many years. On the death of the chief justice, she had found among his papers, some information, which led to her child being in line for the succession to Devronia's throne.

Over the years she had followed the affairs of Devronia with great interest, albeit with difficulty, as the Dark Ocean spread wide and deep between the two countries. Perhaps now her plans could reach fruition.

She snuffed out her candle and slipped into bed, relaxing her tired muscles and sore old bones. Tomorrow there would be more interest in her day. A shipment of wood to be used for shoring up the caverns was waiting in the harbour.

Hidden within the wood were concealed packets of fine quality hashish, and there should also be some emeralds and aquamarines from the far south. These had been secreted in the wood by her agent in Kordova. She considered having a necklace made for the girl. Those aquamarines would suit her colouring.

Chapter Four

The day before Merthaylis would have her 15th birthday she sat on her mattress in the small tent surrounded by priestesses. The filtered sunlight from the drawn screen covering the tent flap, made strange patterns on their faces, bars of light and streaks of shadow, giving them a look of difference which she had not seen before. The air in the tent was cool and smelt of incense and herbs.

Merthaylis looked around carefully; she must remember every crease and fold of the place where she had come to adulthood. She had survived her riff-making. Some portions of her skin were still slightly puffy and inflamed, but time would smooth and soothe them.

Tria was behind her, re-plaiting and ornamenting her braids with feathers and brightly coloured beads. Feta was on her knees before her, finishing oiling her body, her hands lingering on The Wolf as she bid farewell. Merthaylis watched Suma pack the utensils of her trade, painstakingly cleaning sticks and stoppering bottles, putting them away with care and precision.

'I must thank you all for bearing with my cowardice,' Merthaylis ventured. 'Through your nurturing and kindness and the wishes of the Goddess, I have been permitted to survive!'

Suma raised her head from what she was doing, sweeping her dark hair away from her face with the back of her hand. Her gaze met Merthaylis' with gravity and compassion.

'No one is brave when the riff sticks for one's tattoos approach,' Suma said. 'You bore it well, at no time did we have to tie you down or stifle your screams. Our thanks to you, Leader of the Phoenix; you made our work easy for us. You have two sisters, I believe?'

Merthaylis nodded in assent. 'They are younger than I,' she returned.

'Well then, we shall return to give them their riffs when they are older. They are lucky you have become The Totem. Their suffering will be minor.' She smiled at Merthaylis, then nodded her head in a delicate gesture of respect.

Goodbye Merthaylis, Merth mused. She had often wondered how her mother had felt, when becoming an adult. She had been denied the part of her name which had belonged to her mother. Thaylissandra could only be Thaylis to her daughter.

There was movement outside the tent and the sound of harness; the priestesses' horses had been brought from pasture.

'We must go now,' Tria said regretfully, 'as it is, we shall be hard pressed to reach the mountains before dark.'

She gave Merthaylis a hug. 'Be strong Lady Merth! I know you will be worthy.'

There were tears on Feta's cheeks as she also bid Merth goodbye. The women swung heavy brown cloaks over their beaded vests, gathered their belongings and slipped quietly out of the tent.

Merth sat impassively, listening to the hoof beats die away. So it was over, and now the real testing time was to begin. How competent was she, and how good her judgement? Her mother's face came to mind, with the Wolf image hovering behind her. She had been highly respected by all, and her decisions had been impartial.

If I can remember to do as Thaylis would have done, Merth thought to herself, *I will have my toes pointing along the straight road*. Comforted, while feeling the presence of the Wolf still with her, she rose.

On a bench just inside the door were her new clothes, received from Andreas, shortly before the priestesses had left.

Merth was anxious to find out what the women of the clan had made for her. The intricacies of the ornamentation should reveal how well the women thought of their new clan leader.

There were three outfits on the bench, all of the same design, but in different colours. Their sleeveless, loose jackets, which would reach just below her breasts, were beautifully decorated with beads and seeds.

One jacket was mostly violet, verging on deep purple; another a brilliant green, while the third was a glowing midnight blue. The trousers, which accompanied them, were padded, embossed, and wonderfully embroidered. When on, they covered her legs, but barely reached her hips, so her riffs could be displayed to their best advantage.

There were three pairs of matching soft leather boots underneath the bench. Last of all, she found a magnificent padded riding jacket, with a fur-lined hood. At least her bare skin would not be exposed to the elements; she gave a wry grin as she picked it up.

Donning the violet outfit, which she thought would complement her colouring, she composed herself to wait until sundown. She knew that preparations would be being made for her welcome into adulthood in the big yurt.

Whiling away her time, waiting to be summoned, she considered her sisters. Merthsandra, her twin, born some hours later than herself, would not celebrate her birthday on this night when Merth became The Riffed One. Merth decided she would arrange a simple ceremony for her, later in the month.

Merthsandra would need a special moment for her own dignity. Her younger sister, Merthsalla would be the lucky one where Merth's pony, Storm, was concerned.

Merthsalla was a good horsewoman at the age of 10. The pony she had learnt to ride on was old enough now, to be put out to pasture, to be kept as a family pet. Who knew, perhaps Merth would provide a small rider for him, herself. Her thoughts returned to her twin.

Although they were twins, she and her sister were not identical. Where Merthaylis was curvy and light brown, Merthsandra had a slim, fair beauty. Where Merth had shunned male friendship, being shy, and preferring her brother Redd's stoic, quiet reassurance, her sister flirted with all of the boys, and even the men took notice of her.

I shall have trouble with her, Merth mused, *and she will not be content being second when I am clan leader. She will make trouble for me, even if she does not intend to.*

She pictured her sister's smiling face, with a provocative tilt to her head, emphasising the thick lashes surrounding the fetching grey eyes, which was the usual pose she liked to hold. *It would have been simpler if she had been the eldest.* Merth lifted her head as she heard a faint sound outside the tent.

The tent flap moved and Redd's face appeared in the opening.

'Are you ready? The sun has gone to his mountain home and everyone is starving!'

Laughing, she surged to her feet, aware of a wave of hunger she had previously ignored.

'Aye, I am ready!' She slipped her hand into his companionably, smiling into his trustworthy face.

Redd waited behind when she entered the yurt, taking the quilted jacket from her, to hang it on the pole placed especially for that purpose, just inside the tent flap. It would remain there, a symbol to show whether she was in residence or not.

He remembered his mother's jacket, with the leaping wolf depicted on its back, hanging there during his childhood.

As he hung Merth's coat upon the peg he admired the Phoenix soaring out of embroidered flames, which rose from the bottom of the hem. His father would be pleased with the workmanship.

Merth walked with deliberation toward the group around the fire. As she approached, all eyes were cast down, yet she was aware of the stolen glances of curiosity as the work of the priestesses was assessed.

Amid murmurs of approval and welcome, she made her way to the new white sheepskin arranged on the bench beside her father's chair. Seating herself beside him, she leaned across and put her hand on his arm.

'Well, father, are you pleased with me?'

For answer, he leaned forward to fill a cut glass goblet, similar to his with dark red, ruby wine.

'A toast to The Totem, the leader of The Horse Lords!' His voice rang out over the low toned chatter in the yurt, and there was a scramble to refill mugs and glasses.

Amid cries of 'The Totem!' 'The Riffed One'! 'The Leader of the Horse Lords!' all sprang to their feet to drink her health and to their own hoped for prosperity. Now the Phoenix would rise again, and who knew how many foals this would bring to birth this year?

The flickering lights cast deep shadows in the corners of the yurt. With feet made silent on the thick woven mats, slaves hurried to replenish jugs and dishes.

The tents of the Horse Lords were not an evil place to be, if one had to be a slave. All lived in the same surroundings, and food and drink was there for everyone. Freed slaves often chose to stay on living their life in the yurt, finding the easy atmosphere less threatening than the life they had lived previously.

As the evening progressed and the food removed, a sense of anticipation settled around the tent and people arranged themselves in comfortable groups, facing the centre.

Merth rose from her bench, the light gleaming on her burnished body, outlining the coloured riffs, which shifted as she moved. She beckoned to the sitar player, seated in the shadows.

He struck up a soft, lilting melody, which had traces of melancholy, slowly crescending through longing to expectancy, finishing with determined chords, which were then accompanied by the drummer. His drums provoked the crowd to stamping feet.

In the centre of the room, outlined by the fire, Merth started to gyrate to the dance of the Totem Master. Her mother had taught her the movements when she was small. Latterly, she had had tuition from a wandering gypsy folk when they had camped by at a gathering.

The vibrant dancer who helped her, had given her assurance and grace she was unaware she possessed. Swirling, gliding, twisting, her body a painted canvas spinning over her flying feet, she soon had the clan clapping and shouting in her praise.

She brought her exhibition of prowess to a close by plucking a sword from the scabbard of one of the men standing by, and using it in her routine, finishing with the sword held high. Holding the last cutting flourish, she poised in silent stillness.

The uproar of clapping and stamping died away as she turned to return the sword, then go to her seat, breathless. Merthsandra pushed her way to her side and put her arms around her twin.

'How did you learn to dance like that? How I wish it were me! Will you teach me, or will you be too big-headed, now you are The Totem?'

'If I have time I will, gladly.' Merth smiled at her, looking up at her fair beauty. Merthsandra tossed her head as she pushed away, her face twisted with annoyance and upset.

Merth watched her sister join her friends, worried, yet aware she could not alter anything. *She will have to forge forward herself*, she considered, as the golden head disappeared into a welcoming group. *It is not my fault I am the eldest.*

Her father nodded to her as she returned. 'Well done, Lady Merth. I think this is a fit beginning to establish your chieftainship. More wine for the lady!' he called.

Conversation drifted to other topics. Two riders who were having a discussion about a saddle distracted her father. One was the son of the original owner; the other was best friend to the man.

Merth listened intently to her father's questioning. Swirling the ruby liquid in her glass, now a match for his, she lifted her head and gave judgement.

'I well remember the day Dayle promised the saddle to Hansa,' she recalled. 'It was to repay a debt. Dayle promised Hansa the saddle, if he helped him bring his herd down from the top shoulder, as a storm was bringing snow and it would take too long to do it on his own.'

Turning to the young horseman she added, 'Norsa, your honour depends on Hansa. The saddle belongs to him in repayment.'

Her father agreed, his black eyes shining in the reflected firelight, as he nodded his head.

'A good judgement, Horse Lady.'

Norsa, the young rider, hung his head and retired to the side wall of the yurt. Watching him go, Merth realised she had gained an enemy on the first day of her riffing. She shrugged her shoulders and glanced around.

The rest of the clan seemed to be happy and contented. Some were sitting talking, while others were enjoying the evening dancing.

Her eyes rested on Redd who was pushing his way through the crowd, coming towards her. Feeling full of love for him she stretched out her hand to grasp his hand in hers.

Smiling, though with his eyes downcast, he dropped at her feet then put his head on her knee. She placed her hand on his curls, pleased with his presence. His dark brown riding gear suited his colouring.

As usual, his words were what she needed to hear.

'The Phoenix has risen in strength from its pyre. Tomorrow you should choose a new mount.'

'Yes,' Andreas agreed. 'I have three or four for you to have a look at. Do you want a stallion or a mare?'

Merth would have preferred a mare, but felt her position demanded a stallion, preferably one no one else could ride.

'A partially trained stallion, I should think. That will keep me busy for a while! You choose one for me, father.'

The horse her father brought to the yurt in the early morning, seemed part of the mist himself. His coat was a glistening silvery grey, while his flowing tail and mane were black and silver mixed. He was not enormous, but every movement showed an intractable edginess. His delicate build was revealed by long tapering legs, yet bulk could be found in bulging muscles, particularly in his shoulders. His neck arched when she attempted to pat him, then he reared with nostrils flaring.

Before the week was out she had named him Sythe. This suited the way he moved through the grasses and also his attitude to life. His cutting approach to all around him was not inclined to win him many friends. Then followed months of wooing him, intermingled with arduous training for both of

49

them. Sythe had been harshly treated for his bad temper when he was younger, and had no intention of being mastered by anyone. Every morning she greeted him with carrots and sweet grasses. The day he allowed her on his back was a moment filled with joy.

Before the finish of winter, they had come to an understanding. Working with him in partnership, loving and trusting, she trained him eventually to do what she wanted, because he wished to please her. By the beginning of spring he was as tractable as Storm, yet woe betide anyone else who hoped to rope him.

While she had been training him, Merth had done her duties from the back of a steady mare, who she now returned to the herd where they roamed free on the grasslands. Sythe would have liked to go to the herd too, fancying his chances to fight for the leadership, but instead he obeyed the pressure of Merth's knees and returned to the camp.

The air was scented with spring flowers, as they opened their faces to the warmth of the early morning sun. Merth encouraged Sythe to a smooth canter, which ate up the distance over the rolling plains.

As she rode, she considered her duties for the day. Traders had come last night, so their goods had to be inspected and haggled over this morning.

The evening meal had to be planned, and the supplies had to be distributed to the cooks.

The foal with the poulticed leg would need his liniment renewed. He was improving, but had not recovered from his fall, as yet. Then her smaller siblings needed their lessons; perhaps by the afternoon she might have some time for herself.

Slowing to a trot as they reached the encampment, Merth leant forward to whisper into Sythe's silken ears. He whickered in return, nudging her shoulder as she slid to the ground. She released him from the high-pommelled, red leather saddle, then rubbed him down with a wisp of grass.

Turning, he trotted away to join the small group of working animals nearby. Some were tethered, like the traders skinny mules, some were hobbled, but Sythe and the other riders' horses roamed free. Merth knew her appearance, or a whistle, would bring him to her side.

Entering the yurt, she slung her jacket on its pole inside the entrance way, and approached the main living area. Ramesh, the trader, had been busy, she saw. His men had spread their wares on blankets to one side of the cooking fire. He greeted her in accepted fashion, eyes lowered, with his right hand gesturing towards her, with his fingers joined.

'I await your pleasure, Phoenix Lady.' His voice was well modulated, soothing honey with a lift of amusement and pleasure in the tones. He had no trouble with the language as he had spent many years amongst the horse people. She glanced at him, daring his mockery, but there was none.

He was attired in brown leather trousers and jerkin, with a thick, yellow, woven, under garment, which complemented his amber eyes, though its purpose was to keep in warmth. His brown hair was streaked with grey. How many springs had he travelled this way, she wondered? She remembered him dealing with her mother many times.

'Well, Ramesh, let us see what we can afford.'

She chose bolts of felt like cloth of varying hues, then some hides and beads. Moving on, she found blocks of salt, cakes of sweet smelling soap, and some bags of sugar.

After she had purchased some extra flour, she decided what she had was sufficient, and was about to finish her dealing. Suddenly, he surprised her by rolling out some amethyst velvet on the rug in front of her.

'Your women would make a fine skirt for The Riffed One for the wedding,' he cajoled.

'What wedding?' Caught by surprise, the question was more a growl than words.

'On my travels, I learnt The Eagle greets the Phoenix, oh clan leader!'

Merth's face became pinched and lost colour, with her features chiselled in her distress. With an involuntary gasp, she recoiled as if he had struck her. Lifting the heavy velvet in both hands, she buried her face in it, hiding her expression from anyone brave enough to look.

'In that case, I shall purchase this, then, trader,' she stated calmly, as she lowered the material, her expression inscrutable with no sign of perturbation, although her soul in torment, fluttered for escape.

The day stretched interminably. She instructed servants and family, taught the children, practised with the whip until her body ran with sweat, bathed in the stream, settled to needlework, occupied herself preserving wild berries, and still her father did not come back from his hunting.

At length, when all was ready for the evening meal, with the lights lit and the fires giving forth a warm welcome, she heard the clop of hoofs and the jangle of harness. Standing by the entrance, she ushered home the hunters. They had meat, plenty for many days, and were pleased with their day's work, chatting and jibing each other over the events of the chase.

She maintained her calm and composure until the meal was finished, and her father was ensconced in his favourite chair, with his henchmen around him.

A dice game they were playing was fast deteriorating into a swallow's nest of argument and laughter, Andreas drew back from the heckling, leaving Redd in charge, creating an area of peace around his chair.

'Well, my Lord,' she began, conversationally, 'your day was lucky, so it seems?' Carefully, she refilled his special goblet, watching the wine deepen to ruby as it filled the glass.

'Yes,' he agreed, 'the deer were kind today, and kept their bargain.'

'I hear a bargain has been struck before today.' The trader tells me eagles fly, and stoop.'

He raised his head from his wine, meeting her eyes over the rim of his goblet, level with her, where she stood beside his chair. His black eyes flamed with red lights when he understood to what she was referring.

'The trader speaks too soon, but speaks the truth. I have summoned the Eagle!'

Rage and ignominy flushed through her. She grasped the wine flask so hard she feared it would break. With difficulty, she forced herself to turn and replace it on the table. Swinging round to face her father, she ground speech from between gritted teeth.

'Surely, I should have been first to know?'

'Does it matter when you know? The result will be the same. I am sorry, Merth, I intended to tell you when Daresh returns from message taking. The Eagle Lord will be here for the night of the full moon. This gives you time to prepare the feast and whatever else is needed.'

'When did you make the choice?' she asked, worry in her voice.

'I'm surprised you had not guessed – at the Autumn Gathering. Though now I think of it, your interest at the time dwelt on dogs and their puppies.'

While at the festival she had traded a filly for two large hounds, Boris and Borland, who accompanied her wherever she went when away from the camp, except when she had been training, or they had been commanded not to do so.

'I was a little girl, then,' she reminded him.

'Well now you are a woman, and you need a man to support you in your clan leading. Remember, you are Totem of all the clans, not just ours. It is time you are settled with a mate. The Phoenix must be reborn again.' His expression changed as he glanced at the unruly mob of youngsters.

'Speak to Merthsandra. Her behaviour is wanton!'

Pushing through the group of young men, who on the whole drew back in respect, not wishing to anger The Totem, she leant forward and grasped her twin's arm.

'Enough! You have them all besotted with your charms. Anything further and honour will be lost.'

Merthsandra glared at her in hate, her heavily-fringed eyes, which were delineated with a thick line of kohl, were stubborn and sultry. Recognising the sparks deep in her sister's eyes, Merth let go of her arm, realising there would be a backlash for this chastisement. She murmured, 'Your father calls for you.'

'He will growl and then tell me to make miles and miles of wool for carpet.'

She tossed her head with annoyance, setting all her beads and silver tokens attached to the ends of her braids glinting, and shining in the light. Nonetheless, she approached Andreas, albeit unwillingly, then sank down beside his chair.

'Child, do you wish to join the priestesses in the mountains?' Her eyes widened in horror at the thought.

'No, my Lord. I have no calling for that destiny.'

'What then will become of you, if you bring dishonour to the Phoenix? Leave the men alone. After your sister's nuptials I shall find a suitable man to help herd the horses, whilst bedding you.'

Merthsandra looked at Merth who was engaged in conversation with Redd, apparently discussing remedies for Boris, who had favoured his right front paw when returning from the hunt.

'That one will never be wed, no suitor will be good enough.'

'You are wrong. The Eagle Lord will be here for the wedding on the night of the full moon. I wish you to welcome the guests when they arrive.'

Realising Merth's new husband would bring a retinue, her sister thought about fresh faces to draw into her net. She brightened her mood, grimacing appreciatively at this idea, then returned her father's smile, though grudgingly.

'I shall need my riffs before I marry,' she reminded him.

'There will be no time before the night of the full moon. However, arrangements can be made to call the priestesses; it won't take so long for you as it did for your sister. I might make a match for you during the wedding.'

The days passed quickly for Merth as she made ready for guests, and the second most important day of her life.

The yurt fairly bristled with activity while food was prepared, clothes designed and sewn, bedding made and everything within the yurt washed or refurbished.

She was used to being in charge now, and the older women and the slaves responded to her kind courtesy and sympathetic manner. Her every wish was their desire too, as they strove to please her.

Outside, activity was just as frantic for the men. Messages were sent inviting guests to the wedding, food bought or hunted, wood to be chopped, and all this on top of the everyday jobs of supervising and working with the herds.

Redd seemed to be busy every moment of the day. When he returned to the yurt, he sank down with the others, seeming in a stupor by the fire, while planning the work load for the coming day.

In the evenings Merth was sequestered by the women of the clan, family and slave alike, trying on the violet skirt, while examining the stitching of the beautifully embossed flowers, fawns, horses, owls and eagles, or diamond patterns outlined in silver thread and beaded crystal.

Every female member of the clan added her own design, and the skirt became heavier every day. The cropped open jacket which accompanied the skirt was so adorned it stood by itself, as stiff as heavy brocade. Her purple and red riffs rose from the low slung skirt as though they were extensions of it, while the snarling face of the wolf sat just below her breasts.

At night when the yurt was full of sleeping bodies, Merth lying on her mattress, could feel the wolf's shaggy coat beneath her hand. This was a great comfort, and she was always surprised, and a trifle dismayed when she woke in the morning to find an empty space. Her dreams were full of the slim boy with the blond hair, who often stood beside the wolf in her nightly visions. She wondered if this was whom she was to marry.

The day before the full moon finally arrived. All was ready, the fires were banked and the dishes stacked. Clean rugs were spread on the floor, and all wooden furniture, sparse though it was, had been polished until all the surfaces gleamed.

Not only Merth was attired in new clothes, though her knee-high purple boots of soft hide were certainly the most valued.

The day started with a luxurious bath, in the big tub, kept for the purpose, the water having been heated during the night for this formal occasion. Then she was massaged with sweet smelling unguents. Her nails were carefully manicured with black varnish, disguising all the hard work she was always in the midst of participating.

Finally attired in her amethyst skirt, with the matching waistcoat demurely clasped with a large silver horse's head brooch, just for this occasion, she filled a tankard with mead and then sat with it beside the fire.

Her father and the other riders were restless, drinking and gaming, as the time passed while they waited for their guests. Redd, accompanied by six of the younger men, had ridden out to form a welcome guard for his future brother in law and his entourage.

At last there was the sound of galloping hoofs. Within a cloud of dust a party of horsemen could be seen as they charged across the plain approaching the yurt. In the middle of the group, the Eagle banner, gold on red, could be seen fluttering in the breeze of their passing.

Casting dignity away as she jumped up, anticipation mixed with dismay, Merth hesitated, then strode outside, with her heart beating in her throat like a trapped sparrow. She watched the approaching riders with such trepidation, she felt her feet were bound to the ground.

Andreas and the rest of the riders tramped outside and stood behind her, ready to give welcome to the visitors. Andreas threw an arm around Merth's shoulders. 'I have a good eye for horseflesh, daughter, what think you of Jerain?'

His voice had humour in it and she was glad of the comfort of his touch, though it was carelessly done, and not too gentle. 'Look yonder, then tell me what you think.'

In the centre of the group, beneath the fluttering flag, was a youth of not more than 18. He had red flowing locks, merging on auburn; his skin was lightly tanned, contrasted by straight brown brows. He looked tall and strong. She could see even his legs were well-shaped, not bowed like most riders, having spent their lives on horseback from childhood. He was wearing a crimson shirt covered by a laced black leather vest.

The Eagle rose in red and gold across his back; the whole work embossed with gold. Soft black boots reached his knees, where, they joined black pants. They met with the edge of his flowing cloak, now casually draped over one shoulder.

She met the gaze of forceful, laughing, hazel eyes, and was compelled to smile back. She was impressed with his horsemanship, as the skittish black stallion he was riding came to a sudden halt, then turned away towards the picket line.

'What do you think?' Andreas still questioned, his arm resting across her shoulders.

She turned towards him and smiled, though tremulously, her eyes serious and anxious.

'I think he will be suitable, this Eagle Horse Lord,' Merth answered quietly. She reached up and gave Andreas a hug, then went back inside the yurt to make sure all was in readiness, while the men outside greeted each other and the horses were attended. *It had been too much to hope for, that her future husband resembled the man in her dreams*, she thought.

Jerain swung from the horse's back, tossing the reins over a silver peg attached to the front of his saddle, placed there for this purpose. His horse could now have freedom, yet would not get entangled in the reins. His second led the horse away for water and a brisk rub down.

Swaggering slightly, using the black cloak for full effect, Jerain approached the yurt. He had been too far away, and too occupied with his riding, to discern what Merth was like previously, but now looked round for her with an appraising glance, and found she had disappeared.

Chapter Five

Standing in the prow of the merchant vessel engaged by his father to transport the Kordovans home, Troy watched the dolphins leaping in the bow wave of the ship. He was entranced by these graceful animals, and was also amazed at their speed and skill. It was early afternoon, a week after the day they had set sail. He grimaced as he thought of the flurry and upset caused by Delia the afternoon she had been shown her cabin.

She had complained about being confined in a horsebox, had stamped her feet and then burst into tears. This was when she realised she had to share with her lady companion, Amelia. Troy was about to tell her what he thought of her behaviour, but was forestalled by D'Auton, who quickly soothed her temper, by producing some wine. Then he had said that with Amelia present, he would be able to visit with her often. Her stormy countenance had become calmer and Delia immediately started to organise the arrangement of her trunks.

Trojan D'Auton had taken Troy's arm and had guided him away towards the bow.

'Now, my Prince, did you not wish the other evening, that I instruct you in Kordovan?'

Troy assented. 'It is not that they do not speak our language well, I only wish to be able to understand what they say between themselves, in case there is any dirty dealing over the timber.'

Trojan laughed. 'I'm sure there will be some shady characters at the Kordovan court. If they think you cannot understand them you might catch them off guard, for sure. As well as this, remember the Kordovan princesses might not have the command of the language our friend Delia does.'

'Friend!' Troy spluttered much to Trojan's amusement. 'That hussy! For all her beauty and expensive clothes, she could drive me to drink.'

'That wouldn't be hard.' Trojan grinned as he teased, 'I thought you made a striking pair at the ball.'

The memory of the ball, a few evenings before they left, was too much for Troy. Delia, attired in a silver sheath with a crimson belt, and crimson ribbons in her hair, had been the belle of the ball, particularly as her gown was cut so low it amazed him how it stayed up. She had also been wearing a collar of rubies worth a king's ransom.

She had pursued Troy all evening, filling his card in every available space. He had tried to explain to her that etiquette did not work that way, but to no avail.

In the end he had made his escape, complaining of a headache, passing her off to Trojan and Anton, much to their entertainment. He had determined to keep out of her way on the voyage, as much as was possible. His Kordovan lessons might aid him in this respect, his mood lightened at the thought.

'Well, Trojan, let us get started, no time like the present.' He was surprised when the indolent Trojan turned into a first-rate scholar, producing books and texts, complete with papers and stylus. He even had a small blackboard for quick delineations to prove his points. There was certainly more to this languid young man than Troy had at first appreciated.

'Where did you gain all this information, Trojan? You are a veritable storehouse of Kordovan trivia. Is the language really so flowery and convoluted as you make it out?'

'My mother was Kordovan, and I spent my childhood there. I doubt very much if things have changed whilst I have resided in Devron.'

They spent the rest of the afternoon discussing the language of Kordova and the differences in structure to that of Devronian.

So their days continued, with all spare time devoted to their studies or in sword practise. Delia and Amelia came to find them occasionally, but they were usually on their own, while Anton shepherded the two girls.

One afternoon, as he was so immersed in his study, Troy did not notice the change in the weather. Only when a wave larger than the others invaded the bow, then slid away through the scuppers, was he aware of how great a change there had been.

The erstwhile calm blue sea was now grey and turbulent, with white caps dancing on the tops of the waves. The tide was running strongly and the large, cumbersome merchant vessel was having difficulty with a strong cross wind.

Getting out of the way of the sudden activity on the deck, Trojan and Troy gathered up their equipment and retreated to the cabin, which they were sharing.

Water sloshed against the closed portholes with sufficient strength to make a hard blow against the thickened glass. Troy was glad the portholes were shut and firmly bolted. Glancing at his timepiece he realised they had spent the whole afternoon studying.

'Come my friend, time to stop. Will you share a glass with me?' So saying he stepped across, or rather staggered, to where the cut glass decanters were firmly enclosed in a brass harness, which restricted them against the vagaries of the ship. Trojan was not averse to join him and they were soon ensconced in chairs with the decanter between them and glasses in their hands.

'This is starting to be a bad one,' Trojan said, as the ship lurched forward and down, while loose objects scuttled across the cabin floor.

'I hope the Captain knows what he is doing. He should bring the bow around to face the wind and ride out the storm, with sea anchors out. We certainly don't need all this canvas now.'

As if on cue, the sails came flapping down, while below the anchor chains could be heard rattling down to sea.

'I wonder how Delia and Amelia are liking the exigencies of the weather.' Troy gave Trojan a conspiratorial glance, and they both laughed.

As it happened, Delia and Amelia were well-organised. Both had accepted a remedy for seasickness from the attentive Anton, and were now strapped in their bunks.

Unbeknown to the girls, Anton had administered a variety of herbs in their potion. This had the effect of causing relaxation and soporific dreams. He had finished off the dregs of the potion himself, then retired to his own small cabin, which he shared with the chief officer.

Lying on his bunk, he dreamed of Delia. Her regal attitude and imperative tongue gave him no worries. Underneath it all, he understood, her demeanour was mainly caused by insecurity, and beneath the bad behaviour was a kind and gentle heart.

All the time she had been away from Kordova she had been acting a part; aping the ladies at the court in Devron, insisting on her rights as an ambassadorial visitor.

Anton thought she had finished with this pretence and was now returning to her natural sweet self while on board ship. In his dream they wandered hand-in-hand through a darkened wood, whispering endearments, while the sunlight made dapples through the gently tossing leaves.

During the night the storm worsened. Huge breakers hit the vessel broadside, and most of the extraneous deck cargo stored outside was swept away. The rigging had been damaged, and what sails remained aloft were cut to streamers, which flapped and cracked in the continuing wind.

The scene, which greeted the sailors in an early, uneasy dawn, was desolate indeed. Lines were strung around the ship so that those assisting in the clean up had something to steady themselves by, or if needs be, to cling to.

Surprising everyone, Troy was one of the first to escape from his spirit fumed cabin, to help the sailors where he could.

While casting a broken spar overboard, he was held fast in his tracks by overhearing a string of foul oaths emitting from the lips of the captain.

'What on Erm can be disturbing you, Sir? Surely the damage can be rectified?'

'It is not the damage, boy! Look over there!'

Following the captain's pointing hand, Troy was just able to discern two long, lean shapes in the heaving water, disappearing then re-emerging, depending on the rise and fall of the still agitated waves.

'God's teeth, they are galleys! What does this mean, captain?'

'They are rovers; that's what it means! We are a sitting duck with no sails raised. They are coming here purposefully to strip us bare.'

'I must get my sword and wake Trojan and Anton.' Troy turned to the companionway, ready to dash away and arm himself.

'There is not any point, my prince. There are far too many of those blaggards on one of those ships, never mind two! My men won't fight them; they will be terrified. If you young men are the only ones putting up any resistance, you will be cut down in moments. The best thing is to give in without a fight.'

The usually blustering captain was looking tired and haggard.

'What about the girls? What about Delia's parents?'

'They will be the reason for the attack, most probably. A tidy ransom they will produce, you will be an extra bonus.'

'We must warn the others so they can be prepared.'

Shortly, they were gathered in a small group below the mast. Troy had ordered the women to collect their jewellery; taking off rings and earrings, in particular. Delia refused to do anything of the sort, tossing her head defiantly.

Troy shrugged his shoulders. 'Wear your rings then, my Lady. If they won't come off easily, I'm sure a cutlass will sever your fingers without any trouble. I suppose earlobes can be stitched.'

With an even expression, Delia contributed the rest of her ornaments into the small casket at Anton's feet.

Taking the lead, Troy divested himself of swords and knives, though he retained the two throwing knives concealed in secret pockets in his boots. The other men all laid their weapons down with rueful expressions. The captain stood at the rail where the first of the raiders was about to make contact.

On closer inspection, they saw that the galleys that had ranged up alongside their hapless ship were long and lean, with banks of oars protruding from their lower decks. They had little superstructure, apart from a few tent like contrivances, both fore and aft.

The men scattered about the decks were arrayed in motley clothing. Some had no shoes; others wore thigh high boots. Most clothing was brightly coloured, though dirty and often torn; all had swords, or fierce looking, curved knives.

'I see you intend to be sensible,' the pirate captain called. He turned and shouted to his men.

'Prepare a boarding party!'

While this was being assembled Troy had time to study the man. He was dressed in a dark brown velvet suit, cross-laced over his chest. His thigh high boots were well worn and dark in colour. He had a black bandanna on his head, from which escaped long, black, greasy curls. For all his bulky stature, he exuded power. His large figure was taut with muscle.

An old sabre gash, starting at the bridge of his nose, gave a white scar across the tanned skin, stretching to the bottom of his left ear. He had throwing knives stuck in his belt, and looked competent enough to be able to use them with deadly accuracy; obviously not a man to be ignored.

After a gangplank had linked both ships, he sauntered across and approached the group by the mast. He gave them an engaging smile and before presenting himself, dropped a sweeping bow to the ladies.

'Well met, Mr Ambassador. I am the captain of *The Dark Dart* which you can see yonder. My name is Ambry, and my friend Petric, who is captain of our sister ship, *The Dark Mistress*, will be here shortly. We have come to escort you on your way!'

'How do you know me? How did you know I am on this ship? I am the King of Kordova's Ambassador, please leave!' Peter Ambrosius sounded weak and effete even to his own ears. He hated to think how his statement had sounded to this pirate.

'Oh we know who you are, noble lord! We have been watching for your vessel. We were warned the moment you left the port of Devron. A sloop, which was following you contacted us, and we have been trailing you ever since. We had to wait until you left Devronia, of course. Now to business.'

Troy stepped forward. 'As my father's representative, I demand you leave our waters and stop harassing our guests! Remove your ships!'

'Well!' Ambry gave him a wry smile, resting his hand on the hilt of one of his ornamented knives, 'and who are you, my young Lord?'

'I am Prince Troy of Devronia, and swift retribution will come to you, once my father hears of this outrage.'

'Well then, he won't learn of it, will he?'

Trojan surged forward beside Troy.

'As soon as we reach port we will inform our King!'

'Another young bully boy! The port where you are going, people won't worry. Ah, here comes Petric.'

While they were talking another gangplank had been placed against their ship, and Luke Petric strode ponderously across it. Petric was wearing a yellow shirt with ruffles and had an ostrich feather in his hat. These trimmings looked incongruous with his darkly bearded face and his massive, burly body.

'I see the birds are in the coop, friend Ambry, have you decided how we shall separate them?'

At these words, Delia rushed to her mother and was enfolded in her arms. Lesla soothed her with calm murmurings to strengthen her resolve. Amelia stood beside them grasping Anton's hand.

The girls had lost all their burgeoning bravery, gained by being treated as young ladies of the court. They were now reduced to tears and in need of re-assurance by their elders.

Peter Ambrosius was shaking with temper and horror. Delia, his pride and delight, was in danger and there was nothing he could do. Lady Lesla was white, but composed.

'We must do as these people say,' she whispered to Delia. 'We must be brave until we are rescued. Keep your chins up until we are to be ransomed. The fleets from both countries will be out hounding them. We must stick together and support each other while we can.'

Ambry and Luke Petric were still discussing what they were going to do.

'I bow to your extra years,' Petric joked.

'I will give you the lighter task. I will escort the Ambassador and his wife to Kordova, treating them with all kindness. I shall stay out of the harbour until the ransom has been paid. I might ask for some pretty maidens to be included with the gold, to comfort my lonely days at sea.'

His dark eyes flashed amusement, when he heard the exclamations of surprise and horror issuing from the close knit group in front of him.

He was admiring the luscious Lady Lesla, who, although looking distraught, was still a striking woman. Thinking about keeping her husband cabin bound, while entertaining the lady, he gave a shout of laughter. He considered himself a lady's man for all his brawn and bulk.

Petric intended her no harm, but thought a little dalliance would pass away the time on his trip to Kordova. All thoughts of his other mistresses had been forgotten.

Ricci Ambry was well-aware of the lascivious glint in Petric's eye. He knew his old friend well – they had served on the same ship together before they took to pirating. Thinking about what they were about to do, his face turned grim as he came to the business in hand.

'I shall take the younger members of the party then, on this small jaunt to Dishnigar. I'm sure I shall find plenty to occupy them there.'

He swung round to smile at Delia, his teeth gleaming in his straggly beard. 'I see you have been sensible already, and have collected your belongings. Well, what are we waiting for? Step this way.'

His eyes flicked to the members of his crew who were standing in a line against the rail, while keeping the Captain and his crew under duress. They were a dirty unappetising group, brandishing pistols and swords. Ambry raised his voice to a louder growl.

'You will stay on board here, and make sure this hulk keeps up with *The Dark Mistress*. You will know how to deal with the crew on the voyage. Who knows, by the time you reach

Kordova, you might have persuaded some of them to join us? Mr Jones, take charge!'

There was laughter amongst his men, and a few muttered 'Aye, aye, Sir.'

Swinging round, Ambry spoke to the other pirate.

'Follow us to Dishnigar Luke. Bring this tub of lard along as booty. I realise it will hamper your progress, so I shall wait in Dishnigar harbour for you, after I have completed the business. I have no doubt Madame will have a good deal to say.'

'What business is that?' demanded Trojan. His handsome face looking gaunt, strained and white under his newly-acquired tan.

Ambry strolled towards him, looking up at the taller man, then suddenly hit him in the stomach with the hilt of his knife. As Trojan bent over double, clutching his abdomen, Ambry followed his first action with a swift chop to the jaw. Trojan reeled back, then collapsed on the deck.

'In future, you will speak when you are spoken to, and you address me with respect. However, I will tell you that the slave markets in Dishnigar pay high prices for such aristocrats, as you young people appear to be.

'Now to the ships! You younger ones can go first. We shall be away before Petric has loaded his cargo.'

'This is monstrous!' Troy spoke over his shoulder as he was helping Trojan to his feet. 'You will never get away with this! The whole Devronian fleet will hound you down. Don't think it won't be noticed that we are missing!'

'They were lost at sea in the storm, of course! This happened before our ships parted, after we had rescued you and your wife from the water.' He leered at Peter Ambrosius, then added, 'don't you forget this story either, or you might never see these young ladies again!' Ambry stood smiling, tapping his knife against his teeth.

'This is the story we shall put about. All we found was some floating debris. Enough of this! Clay, come here, will you?'

'Aye, aye, Captain!' Clay was nearly seven feet tall and built with such muscle structure that his height was not obvious.

Clothed in a dark blue jacket and cut off trousers, he almost passed for smartly dressed. However, when one looked at his face, which was covered with a strong beard, yet showing missing teeth, and also sporting a black eye, turning an ugly green, the illusion quickly vanished.

He was second-in-command of *The Black Dart* and was carrying an evil-looking whip, which he cracked behind Delia. He looked ominously at the prisoners and then said one word.

'Move!'

When they hesitated, he indicated the plank holding the two ships together.

Troy helped Trojan across the slippery plank, then turned to help Delia. The ships were still heaving in the aftermath of the storm, and their steps were hesitant and fearful, as waves surged up between the hulls.

Anton was helping Amelia who had been left with the small amount of luggage the girls had been able to gather. The jewels had already disappeared.

Delia's parents were being hustled off across the deck towards *The Dark Mistress* urged on by Petric. Lady Lesla was in tears and Delia's father was angry and distraught.

'You will pay for this,' he gritted at Petric, 'if a hair of my daughter's head is harmed!'

Petric gave him an obscene grin. 'If anything happens to her, I don't think it will be her hair that is harmed! I advise you to forget about your daughter and her friends.

'I doubt very much if you will either see or hear of them again. Once they reach Dishnigar, Ambry will dispose of them quickly.' Lady Lesla gave a smothered gasp.

'What you have to do is compose yourselves, ready to write your pleas for ransom for when we reach Kardova. The higher the price, the quicker you will gain your freedom.' So saying, he gave Peter Ambrosious a shove to help him on his way across the plank, then he swung Lesla up in his brawny arms and carried her on to the adjoining deck.

The ships drifted apart and *The Dark Dart* turned swiftly and pulled away from the other vessels. Delia and Amelia were bustled below decks, while the young men remonstrated and tried to accompany them. Ambry arrested their impetus by putting his leg across the companionway.

'Oh no, you don't. I have something more interesting for you three cavaliers. When we reach Dishnigar I expect you to be worthy merchandise for me to sell. You won't gain those attributes dallying with young ladies in cabins. Come with me.'

Looking at each other in despair, Troy, Trojan and Anton followed reluctantly.

Glancing across the merchant ship Anton gestured to attract the attention of the others. *The Dark Mistress* could be seen taking Delia's parents back to Kordova. She was making good speed and was pulling away from them fast.

Troy said a prayer for them, hoping there would be no retribution for them to endure, when they reached civilisation with all the bad news.

Their worst premonitions were soon fulfilled. Clay took them to the slave benches and found two – one which was empty, and one with a poor soul struggling by himself. In their excitement, anger and fear, their conversation was monosyllabic and tense. Clay cut across what talk there was, flicking the cat on the bench.

'Strip to the waist,' he advised. 'It is hard to keep dry here, and the cat flays your clothes.' He gave a grin to see their dismay.

The narrow bench was constantly awash with sea spray entering from the oar port. Their shackles hampered their movements, but with encouragement from Clay's weighted thongs, they soon picked up the rhythm of the other oars in their bank.

To begin with they put too much effort in their strokes, tiring themselves and causing unnecessary feathering and lost strokes, then Trojan took them in hand and after a half hour they were able to keep the steady beat of the bank.

They found if they worked as a team, one had a slight rest every third stroke.

When it became time to change shifts their relief was evident. Troy thought every muscle in his body had never been tested before. He was surprised Trojan showed no ill-effects and Anton seemed to thrive on the activity. Trailing their shackles they followed the other men into the hold.

The foetid air smacked them as they descended. The slung hammocks had already been assigned to the benches, so there was no argument as to which they should occupy.

Watching the other slaves, Troy realised they would soon dispense with their trousers for loincloths.

Food, such as it was, was distributed to them in their hammocks, and each seat was given a job. Swilling the faeces from below the hammocks into the bilges was the worst job. Troy devoutly hoped their turn would take some days to come.

Anton was despatched to collect their rations of black bread and bean soup, which was being distributed by some junior cooks. Troy and Anton were soon fast asleep, worn out by the unexpected exercise.

Trojan was uncomfortable and lay considering their predicament, his mind running over what had happened during the day and wondering if they could have prevented it.

He had a feeling that there was more to this abduction than had been previously thought.

He finally composed himself for sleep, then found he had a problem. He was too large for his hammock, and when he turned trying to make himself fit he was deposited on the greasy, smelly deck.

Eventually, he found he could rest as long as his legs stuck out, resting on the bottom of Troy's equally unstable, string contraption.

Troy, who had been woken by his contortions, watched his struggle, and the final outcome.

'Playing footsy is one thing, but this is ridiculous,' was his comment, sourly muttered, before closing his eyes.

Delia and Amelia had been assigned jobs too. They had been given some old, blunt scissors, and were instructed by Ambry to open their trunks and slice up their gowns and petticoats to make a stock of neat bandages.

'When we are in battle,' he informed them, 'the surgeon is always short of material for swabs, pads and bandages. Your work will be worthwhile.'

Delia looked at her trunk of billowing petticoats, glowing in a variety of hues, with dismay. 'I shall have nothing to wear!' she wailed.

'Don't worry,' Ambry laughed. 'When we reach Dishnigar you will be lucky to wear a breech clout! The purchasers wish to see the goods they are buying.' Grinning at the consternation on her face he continued on his way to the bridge, well-pleased at the outcome of this affair.

After another eight hours had passed, the men were returned to the rowing benches. The first week of the journey was the worst.

Aching bones, salt drenched skin, cracking around their mouths, the constant rub of the wooden seat, and the galling of the shackles, made every movement painful. Then the continual work started to trim away fat, leaving them strong, lean and lethal.

Skin transformed by the sun, wind and sea, became tough and golden bronzed. Their bleached hair set them apart from the other men in the hold. Trojan was amused to hear them called barbarians.

To pass the time on the rowing benches the Kordovan lessons were continued. In a short while Troy and Anton could understand a little Kordovan, and could make their needs known in the language.

'Will we ever get a chance to practise our skills, I wonder?' Troy questioned. 'I doubt we shall ever see Kordova.'

Trojan stretched his legs, momentarily stopping rowing as he shifted on his seat, earning himself a baleful look from the overseer. 'Kordova is not that far from Dishnigar. Most likely some form of Kordovan is spoken there. The merchant classes probably understand it.'

Next morning as they were moving toward the rowing benches a commotion could be heard on deck. There was the sound of running feet, and excited voices were calling to one another.

'What is happening?' Anton asked, screwing his head around, trying to look up the companionway.

'Land has been sighted,' one of the other rowers returned. 'We must be half a day away from Dishnigar.'

The wind was now blowing steadily in the right direction so the sails were raised. Resting on their oars the men watched the land approach. In this mild semitropical zone, the shore looked lush and dark green. Behind the fertile strip a range of large mountains loomed in the distance.

The land looked attractive, and Troy could not wait to get off the stinking ship, no matter what the future might hold.

Much later, Ambry passed, on his way to speak to the first mate. Acting as if he had just recalled their presence, he halted and then waved to Clay to loosen their shackles.

'Well, my fine lords, one of my first jobs will be to find a suitable escort to take you ashore.

'Get on deck now where we have some buckets of seawater, a few of those thrown over you should sweeten you up.'

Blinking their way up the ladder from the darkness below, Troy and Trojan were unprepared when they were doused with cold water. Anton missed the brunt of it, being the last to emerge. A sailor handed them some coarse soap, and soon they felt wetter, if not much cleaner.

Inspecting the others, with their thin bronzed bodies, sporting straggly beards, and covered in various festering sores, Troy realised he must look just the same. He ran his hands down his chest, dismayed at his thinness, every rib stood out, ready to be counted. He looked at his legs, they looked like a runner's.

'What do we look like?' he commented. 'They won't get much money for us!' However, it was great being out in the fresh air again.

They moved to the rail, watching the increased activity as the ship approached the harbour. The attractive landscape had been by passed, and now huge gloomy cliffs came down to the water.

Dishnigar must be a busy port, Troy thought, watching tall schooners turning before the wind, jostling to gain precedence to enter the tranquil water of the harbour.

The black flag tumbled down above them, and up went the yellow and green striped flag denoting a trader out of Dishnigar. Taking their turn, they crossed through the harbour passage.

The thick stone walls on either side were covered in moss and mildew. Anton pointed to pigeons who had made nests in the harbour walls, completely oblivious to all the activity streaming along below them.

Emerging through the rock tunnel, the ship entered the harbour's still waters. Bumboats plied their trade, fishing smacks were readying to set out on the tide, coastal shipping were dropping anchor, tying up at the dock.

The bigger ships had barges unloading their cargo from where they were berthed at one side of the port. There was so much activity going on, Troy did not know where to direct his gaze.

The bright water glittered and danced in the sunlight, belying the fact it was extremely dirty with dropped ballast, drained bilges, streaks of seaweed and the other effluvia produced by so much shipping.

Cormorants gathered on posts, trailing their wings to dry in bedraggled poses, while sea birds uttered guttural cries as they swirled and glided overhead. The thick air wafted the spices carried by the barges which were ferrying their loads across to shore, while from the land itself came an off shore breeze. This smelt of an exciting mixture of tropical flowers, and the pungent acrid aroma of a seaside town.

The Dark Dart dropped anchor eventually, and the occupants of the bumboats, plying their wares, immediately bombarded the sides of the boat. Trojan looked over the side to be instantly confronted with the sight of luscious oranges.

Having no money, all he could do was look. Then he remembered he still had his earrings, hidden under his mop of long blond hair, so far unseen by Captain Ambry.

After some haggling, he exchanged a dozen oranges for one golden hoop. They set in to devour the fruit without a word; unaware until this moment their need was so great.

Anton appropriated two of the tangy fruit to take down to Amelia and Delia, where they were still incarcerated in their cabin. The sailor who was guarding them was loath to let him pass to begin with, but finally allowed him to enter.

Amelia stuck her thumb in her orange and sucked noisily. Delia ate hers more elegantly, having peeled and segmented it. Just as she had finished the Captain strode in, banging the cabin door against the wall as he entered.

Instinctively, the girls shrank together, huddled against a bunk.

'Now, young ladies, out on deck with you. There are buckets and soap up there. Get clean, then put these on.' He held out a couple of white muslin shifts, which were transparent in the sunlight.

'Why can't we wear our own clothes?' Delia demanded bravely, although her lower lip was trembling and she was on the verge of tears.

'All slaves wear the same,' was the terse reply, as Ambry bundled them out of the door. Anton followed them up to the deck.

Squinting in the strong sunlight, the girls staggered across the deck after having been hurried along by Ambry thrusting his palms in the middle of their backs.

Amelia tripped, slipped and landed on her knees in a puddle, knocking over a pail as she did so. Troy was in time to grab Delia before she suffered the same mischance.

When the girls realised they were supposed to wash in front of the crew and their travelling companions, they were horrified.

Troy and Trojan saved their blushes by holding up a tarpaulin for them to hide away from prying eyes, much to the chagrin of the crew, who emitted catcalls and boos, with odd remarks like, 'Wait until you're on the block, won't be so high and mighty then!'

After the girls finally finished and had crept around their temporary shelter, they looked entirely different. Although moderately clean, with their hair unbound and slicked back, with the formless shifts replacing their pretty clothes, they looked dull and uninspiring. That was quickly changed.

With a look of enjoyment, Ambry picked up a couple of buckets of water and drenched them both. The transformation was amazing. The muslin became extremely transparent when wet, and clung to every curve.

'Keep them like that,' Ambry growled at a passing cabin boy. 'If their clothes are dry before we reach the market, you will feel the lash!'

It was a sad and sorry little group, which climbed down the rope ladder on their way to the town. The sailors who rowed the little boat towards the shore could not keep their eyes off the two girls. Poor Anton came in for some ribald comments as well, when sailors saw his eyes and fair skin, just a boy after all, in these circumstances.

The harbour wall with its encrustation of seaweed and barnacles approached too soon for their liking. Once up the rusty iron rail set in the stone of the harbour, they were unceremoniously pushed into line.

Delia was crying openly now, and Amelia was standing white-faced and baleful, as they were each tethered by one wrist to a long line.

Strung together, like geese going to market, they started to trek into town. Troy was glad of his boots. All the men had footwear, but the girls were bare-footed. As their skin was soft from lack of use, they were soon complaining of cut feet. Their cries were overlooked.

Ambry strode ahead, pushing through the throng of people who had gathered to watch them pass. He had his hand on his cutlass, easing it out of his belt, then pushing it back. Six of his crew surrounded the captives, all armed with knives and swords.

Troy was first in line. He held his head up, thrusting out his chin. His clenched teeth made his muscles bunch along his jaw. Glancing to right and left, looking at the people in the crowd, he understood there would be no help from any of them. Some of them were obviously enjoying the spectacle of the captives' plight.

A cheer went up as the cabin boy came running with a bucket of seawater, which he dumped unceremoniously over the girls. Trojan collected some of it as well, as he was trying to help Delia walk over the lumpy cobblestones, and Amelia was walking behind him.

'Thank you, my friend,' he called to the cabin boy. 'I was getting quite overheated.'

Finally they crossed a square, leaving the narrow, fetid street behind. Troy had the impression that shops surrounded the square on all sides, then he saw the shops were just stands from where people called their wares.

The buildings surrounding the square were dark and gloomy. At the far side were large wooden gates, which allowed entry to the slave quarters, shortly these clanged together behind them.

They were separated. The girls were pushed into a long dormitory, while the men were left in the main hall. Fortunately there were only a few in the hall, so each was able to find a sleeping board without having to fight.

Chapter Six

'Good Day Andreas. I have come as commanded to promulgate your wishes for the Phoenix.' Jerain stood straight and tall, looking Andreas in the eye as an equal.

Andreas grasped his arm, then pulled him towards him. He gestured towards the yurt, with an expansive wave, wearing a smile of friendship on his face.

Jerain strode forward with his black cloak swung over one shoulder. He grasped the entrance flap, hesitated a moment, then pulled it aside.

Merth was standing just inside, gaining courage to greet him, trembling with nervousness and anticipation.

She had just gained enough assurance to step forward, when he entered, and was now blocking out the sun with his size.

When Jerain saw her in front of him, he dropped to his knees, then clasped both her hands in his.

'I see I have found a paragon, whose riffs are excelled only by her beauty. The Phoenix will rise again!'

She glanced at him under lowered lids, a small smile lifting the corners of her mouth. She dropped her hands after urging him to his feet, although he did not want to rise.

After pulling him up, she turned away, reaching for a well wishing cup of mead, for him to slake his thirst. As she held out the cup he grasped her lower arms, pinioning her in front of him.

Merth felt the feeling of his hands as icy bands on her wrists. Knowing that at all times the clan mistress must meet challenge, she did not drop her eyes, but stared into his with as much discrimination as he had shown, although she had to strain her neck to meet his tawny glance.

'Welcome, Eagle Lord,' she murmured, again presenting the cup, with the glimmer of a faint smile still twitching the corners of her mouth. 'Please stay standing and partake of this, a fitting end to your journey.'

As he complied, she was able to discern his nose was straight, over a full mouth with all visible teeth present.

Merth beckoned the women to greet their guests now pushing into the yurt, following Jerain to his wedding. The women came with mead and ale, the tension of the first meeting over.

Watching from the side, Merth was amused as she spied Merthsandra filtering through the group, topping up empty goblets.

She was wearing a cropped, yellow velvet top, heavily beaded, with a flowing divided skirt of the same material, tucked into doeskin boots. Her eyes were large and luminous, the kohl accenting their grey glints with silver. Her sinuous movements were carefully coordinated, and were coupled with slight, almost absent minded touches which she bestowed along with the mead, making her presence as heady as the drink she bestowed.

Laughing and teasing, everywhere she went there was a stir, as her shaken blonde hair reflected silver from tinkling beads and bells, attracting the light to her long locks.

As she happened to pass her sister, Merth was aware Merthsandra had raided her perfume store. She wafted a heavy scent of musk every time she moved.

By now all the visitors and friends had entered the yurt and the sun was going down.

The slaves and the female members of the household had been well-schooled by Merth, and the food arrived with little waiting. Andreas had purchased special wine to complement the meal, and the ubiquitous beer was there for all.

Merth invited Jerain to sit beside her on her quilted bench. She was too embarrassed to look at him, and kept her eyes cast down firmly on the food, yet she was aware of his every breath, and quivered at his nearness.

She ensured he tasted all the delicacies, most of which she had prepared herself, occasionally popping a special treat into his mouth, glancing at his firm lips as she did so.

All the while the meal was partaken, Andreas carried on a conversation with Jerain about the journey he had just completed.

Finally everyone was satiated. Even the dogs were content to doze around under the tables, or around the fire, heads on paws, contemplating full stomachs.

A flute, played by Redd, commenced a haunting melody. On cue, Merth rose, shedding her amethyst top, revealing the mastery of the priestesses' work. Someone tossed more brands on the fire, and this produced a flickering backdrop for Merth's artistry.

The dancing flames outlined, yet hid, giving an air of mystery to her movements. Picking up her whip, she moved into an empty space in front of the dais, having kicked off her boots before she left her seat. Then began the marriage ceremony, the only time she would be visible to all.

She danced with the whip, making it curl around her body, twist in the air, crack with resounding force as she flexed her wrist, then falling, it snaked around her feet.

As the tempo of the flute speeded, she swung the whip above her head in cracking arcs, all the while performing an erotic dance, usually attributed to the ploy of enticing whores.

The men whistled and stamped, enjoying her prowess as much as her beautiful body, while admiring the riffs, which stood out in vivid contrast to her pale brown skin.

Eyes glazed, her body one sinuous movement, she seemed as if she had given the whip life. During the past months of arduous exercise, she had grown and had thinned down.

The leather thong slid up her leg, around her torso, finally being brought down her arm, intermingling with the snake delineated there.

At length, she approached the dais, and with one quick movement, flicked the curling thong around Jerain's wrist. Casually, she pulled the quirt, causing him to lean forward, then stand up. Shortening the length, she gathered him to her, until they were standing face to face.

Raising her head, she stared into his hazel eyes, which were bright with flashing golden glints, gleaming in the firelight. Poised, she waited, her breath coming quickly from the effort, by which she had exercised her ritual.

Slowly, he bent his head to kiss her. His lips were sensual, and tasted of a mixture salt and wine.

The uproar in the tent clamoured in her ears. She could hear Andreas calling for more wine, and heard the flute, now joined by other instruments, commence a lively tune which soon had most dancing. Wearily she dropped the whip, allowing Jerain to free himself.

Realising that she was shaking, as if weak from illness, she allowed him to guide her to her seat.

He sat with his arm around her, after she had donned her jacket, his face close to hers, until they were given fresh goblets.

Sipping his wine, savouring the moment, he stretched his long legs out in front of them.

'Put on your boots, Clan Leader, then we may dance. I would not want to stamp on those pretty feet.'

His eyes were on her shapely feet and the neat ankles, protruding from the folds of the amethyst skirt. Complying, she slipped on her boots and they rose to dance. Then there followed an evening of wild music and frenetic dancing.

Merth danced with every man in the gathering as custom declared, but always returned to the strong arms, whose touch she recognised already.

An evening to remember, was followed by a night of passion, unanticipated in her wildest dreams. He was a skilled lover, and set to please her, while on her part she was willing and eager to learn.

She had thought she would be embarrassed in the crowded yurt, but once ensconced behind the heavy wool curtain raised for the occasion, they found themselves in an oasis of calm.

He was gentle, but still hurt her, yet as her passion rose she was impatient to try again. He was not the man in her dreams, who was so gentle and persuasive, but he was her husband and in her arms. Perhaps, the golden lover did not exist.

When she awoke the next day, her new life had begun. She was surprised to find her head on his shoulder, and she was able to study his profile to store in her memory, while he still slept.

His straight eyebrows nearly met across a jutting nose. His sensitive mouth enticed her fingers to flutter across his firm lips with just a butterfly touch.

Without awakening him, she rose, made her way quickly to the stream, to allow the tinkling water to refresh her body.

Afterwards, it was time to chase the cooks to clean up, and prepare the morning meal. By the time Jerain awoke, she had already exercised the dogs while riding Sythe, with her cloak streaming in the wind.

Suffering from the effects of too much alcohol the previous night, Jerain awoke with a thick head, and a mouth so dry he felt his tongue would never work again.

Merth pushed aside the heavy curtain, bringing him chicken soup, fresh mare's milk and some bread and honey. First however, she presented him with a bowl of ice cold spring water, scented with the fresh herbs she had gathered on her ride.

He took it in both hands and gulped from it thirstily, then started to devour his breakfast.

'Aren't you eating, Clan Leader?' His hazel eyes were smiling at her, as she straddled the bed, looking down at him.

'I have already breakfasted,' she replied, 'my days start early.' Unaccountably, she felt suddenly shy, and retired to a stool at the bedside.

'I have arranged for the new totems to be made,' she told him. 'As you came with red and black, I assumed that is how you want them to be.'

He nodded in assent; his mouth was full of bread and honey.

'That pleases me then, as I had remembered your colours from the banners at the fair.'

After swallowing his mouthful, he gave her a cheeky grin.

'Are you sure you need a Lord?' he teased. 'You seem to have everything in hand.' He grabbed her wrist, inspecting the intricate detail of the snake on her arm.

'If the Phoenix was to rise, I had to be mated honourably. My father did not wish to be dominated by the Wolf, after my mother died.'

'I see; that is why there was the unseemly haste. We must give him his Phoenix granddaughter, if we can.'

So saying, he stood, brushing off crumbs, and then wandered away through the tent toward the stream; his handsome bronzed face wearing an ironical grin.

As Merth watched him go, tall and shapely, she decided her father had made an unusually good choice.

Merth was not the only one watching him wend his way to the stream. Merthsandra sat in the sunlight brushing out her beautiful hair, apparently unaware of where Jerain was going, yet watching his progress in her treasured hand mirror.

When he returned, Merth had the banners ready for his inspection. Her needlewomen had assisted in their making, though she had done most of the intricate work herself.

The long thin banners lent themselves to the two emblems. At the bottom rose the golden Phoenix in its bed of coals, emblazoned with red, orange and golden flames, while above soared the Eagle, black against a red sky, its talons not quite touching the Phoenix crest.

Jerain was impressed with the workmanship, which had created such beautiful artefacts. He complimented Merth, then sought out all the other women who had contributed to the banners, to offer them praise, thanks and good wishes.

His grace and charm won all their hearts. The tribe gathered that afternoon to watch their new emblems raised on the poles in front of the yurt. Everyone was appreciative of the display.

When the hunting party left later that day, Jerain among them, one of the new banners flew from the pole sunk in the socket of the saddle, where the banner carrier held it, fluttering bravely in the wind.

Merthsandra watched the party of horsemen thundering across the plain. She was sitting on a saddle outside the yurt plaiting a silver and gold band to put in her hair.

She had considered the members of Jerain's riders and had found them wanting. They were certainly taken with her beauty.

They were overawed by her sensuousness, and would probably make urgent bed mates, but none of them had the ability to raise her anticipation with a word or gesture.

No doubt her father had already made an arrangement with someone plain and solid.

At least none of the horsemen was in his dotage. She sighed and stood up, stretching her lissom body, before entering the yurt to continue with the daily tasks.

Finding Merth seated at a table, measuring out dried fruit in preparation for the evening meal, Merthsandra sat contemplatively beside her, casually pushing her sister's dog under the table with her foot.

'Move over, Boris! You're getting bigger by the minute! Why hasn't he gone hunting with the others?'

Merth bent and ran her hand over Boris's shoulder. 'He has a strain. I thought a poultice and some rest would do him good.' She received an appreciative lick before Boris rested his huge head upon her knee.

'You spoil your animals,' Merthsandra commented, picking up a handful of raisins and eating them.

'Leave the fruit alone. I had already weighed that.'

Merthsandra filched some dates, then ducked from her sister's flailing arm.

'You're far too serious,' she laughed. 'If this is what it is like to be married, perhaps I should stay single.' She flicked a glance at Merth, her face avid with curiosity. 'What is he like, this Eagle Lord, then?'

Colour rose under Merth's tan, as she felt her sister giggle beside her on the bench.

'I don't compare,' she answered, tilting her chin defiantly.

'You mean you have nothing to compare him with.' Merthsandra nudged her meaningfully with her elbow. Then she slid off the bench to involve Boris in a play fight, slapping, teasing and tickling, until he was panting.

Suddenly, the big hound raised his ears, jumped up and trotted to the open tent flap. He stood there, barking and growling, with his hackles raised.

The two girls exchanged glances, then followed the dog to the entrance, intrigued as to why he was making such a disturbance.

Coming towards them across the plain was a tinker's troupe. There were four caravans, each pulled by a plodding horse, while surrounding them were gaily-dressed riders, both male and female. Following the caravans, herded by boys and dogs, were a flock of sheep and some scrawny goats.

'These are the tinkers who came last year,' Merthsandra remarked. 'I remember that yellow stallion. I quite fancied his rider.'

'You were too young last year to be fancying anyone,' Merth retorted, still squirming from the embarrassment Merthsandra had made her feel earlier.

Having told Boris to be quiet and to sit inside, Merth welcomed the travellers and said that the Phoenix would allow them to camp down by the second stream, where they had been last year.

When they were settled, she continued, perhaps they would like to join The Totem and her family for the evening meal and the following festivities.

An older woman with greying hair and rosy cheeks accepted the offer with pleasure. Obviously, a life on the road had done nothing but good for Meg Mellison.

Some weeks later, Andreas was tethering culls on grazing lines. He had some of the riders helping him, but preferred to choose which of the animals to sell himself.

This involved selecting the horses, catching them, staking them out, then inspecting them for age, and general good health. He had no wish to start the trek to Borin's yurt with stock that might falter on the way. Apart from the loss of revenue, he hated having to deal with sick animals, particularly if they had to be put down. Giving the last of the 20 that he had chosen a pat on its rump, he whistled up Borland.

The hound had been worth four riders at least, working way out on the plain gathering horses. It was a pity he had not had Boris as well, they would have done the job more quickly. Merth had insisted on keeping Boris by her, saying his injury still needed rest.

Ensuring the horses were all in reach of the stream and had available grass, Andreas turned towards the camp. He was looking forward to his trip to Borin's enclosure on the following day. He missed Borin's companionship when working and hunting, though Redd was slowly taking his place.

Trotting across the plain, followed by his riders, with Borland racing in front, Andreas noticed the gipsy encampment, down by the second stream.

He remembered the family had been invited to visit with the gipsies that evening. It was their summer festival, when marriages were arranged and challenges given. He felt too tired to bother with the festival, but knew honour demanded he joined in the party.

He had decided to let Borin sell the horses himself. Previously, Andreas had taken the stock all the way to Dishnigar, and had done the trading personally.

Now Borin was herding further across the plain, it suited Andreas to take the animals to Borin and then he could complete the trek, taking some of his culls as well.

Easing his back in the saddle, Andreas was pleased this arrangement had been made. Days of trekking and herding would be too much effort this year.

His mind shifted to Merthsandra, an arrangement had to be made for her. He knew she was flirting with the young gipsy who rode the yellow stallion, but he also guessed the gipsy life would be too hard for Merthsandra to choose. She would want her own yurt and would want to be in charge of her own destiny.

He had hoped an arrangement could have been made with one of Jerain's riders, but apparently none was suitable in Merthsandra's eyes. They were all either too young or too uninteresting. Jerain seemed to have fitted in well, Andreas mused. He did his share of the work, got on well with the other riders, and Merth appeared to be happy.

He would take Merthsandra with him to Borin's yurt and he would leave her there for a while with Borin's new wife, he decided. While she was there, someone might catch her eye.

She was lucky to be the younger twin, so she could make her own choice of a mate. If necessary, Borin's wife could arrange for Merthsandra's riffs to be done. It was not as if she would be clan leader like her sister.

That evening, just before the sun was setting, now throwing long golden fingers of light across the purpled shadows from the mountains on the plain, the clan made their way to the second stream to accept the invitation from the gipsy encampment. Presents of food and wine were brought, and Meg Mellison made much of the bounty from the yurt.

She ushered her guests to sit on blankets arranged near an enormous bonfire, where the gipsies were roasting lambs on a spit.

After the beer had been passed around and good wishes toasted, a gipsy with gold rings in his ears started to play a stringed instrument.

The sound was high and wavery, but soon other instruments joined in, and the evening developed into a happy occasion with much laughter and ribald jokes.

The leader of the gipsies, Sligo Mellison, offered Andreas more beer. Andreas proffered his tankard to be re-filled, then made a complementary remark about the bevy of throwing knives stuck in Sligo's green sash.

'Yes,' Sligo agreed, 'they are very fine. They were made in Jaddanna, in the far north. We were performing for the great Jada at the palace. Part of the payment we received, were these chased knives. I practise with them often, but rarely use them with purpose in mind.'

'In my time I have thrown a few knives,' Andreas said. 'The balance is important, and also how well the haft sits in the hand. Of course, a good knife thrower takes great care of his weapons.'

Sligo pulled out one of the knives and passed it to Andreas. Andreas examined it carefully, weighing it in his hand and nodding.

'You know what you are doing,' Sligo commented, with a flash of white teeth in his darkly saturnine face. 'How about a challenge?'

After some bickering and input from bystanders, it was decided to use a pole at the edge of the stream as a target. Having marked a distance deemed acceptable to both men, a line was drawn in the dust. The gipsies and the guests from the yurt lined up on both sides of the throwing area, with much bantering and betting taking place.

Both men had a few ranging shots and then the competition began.

Andreas did not feel too confident as it was a while since he had thrown a knife, and they were not his knives, however he was ready to try, if only to provide some amusement for the gathering. After they had competed for a while Sligo was well ahead.

Deciding to give himself more impetus, Andreas pushed back against the bushes to find more room. His boot caught in a fallen log, which was concealed behind him, in the undergrowth. Grasping the knife tightly, he staggered back and fell. He lay there in pain, as family and friends came to see what had occurred.

Merth looked at her father's whitened, strained face and called for a healer. She took the knife out of his clenched fist and handed it back to Sligo, who was standing anxiously at her side. He leant forward as if he was going to help Andreas to rise, but Merth demurred.

'No, Sligo, let him lie. We must let the healer look at him before we move him. Who knows what damage we could make worse.'

Patras, the healer, arrived pushing through the group, while carrying his leather satchel of herbs and potions in front of him. He had been working with the children in the gipsy encampment, cleaning small cuts and bruises while talking to them about different herbs, and asking them if they knew any places to gather particular ones where he had not been. He was a young man who had taken over the position of herd healer when his grandmother, who had served in that position, had died.

His grandmother had raised him when his parents had been killed in the mountains by an avalanche. They had been out looking for strayed horses and were the only people there.

Patras took his job seriously and had gained knowledge by studying. He had been apprenticed for some years to the chief healer in Orphur, coming back to the yurt when his grandmother was failing. He examined Andreas carefully, and then announced Andreas had torn ligaments in his leg. A stretcher would be needed to carry him back to the yurt.

Jerain flung off his big cloak, and by using it and a few poles, a sling was improvised, sufficient to enable Andreas to be carried back home. The party came to a quick closure, as most of the guests followed the father of their leader back to the yurt.

Patras settled Andreas in his sleeping quarters, then put poultices on his knee. Later, he bound it up with bandages soaked in herbs. He gave Andreas a potion to help ease the pain, then turned and smiled at Merth.

'It will be a while before your father will be on a horse again. He must rest with poultices and massage, and do the exercises I shall prescribe for him.'

'What rubbish!' Andreas said hotly. 'I shall be fine tomorrow. I have to take the culls to Borin's yurt, so he can sell them at the horse fair in Dishnigar.'

'If you put too much pressure on those ligaments now, your knee will never heal properly,' Patras said quietly. 'It is your choice if you want to spend your old age crippled.'

'You will stay in the yurt,' Merth stated firmly, catching her father's eye and looking at him sternly. 'Jerain can take the culls to Borin. They have not met yet, and it will be a good opportunity.'

'I was taking Merthsandra with me,' Andreas said brusquely. 'I thought she might find a husband there.'

Merth hid the disquieting lurch this news had given her stomach. She had been well-aware of the interest Merthsandra was displaying towards Jerain; she also had a nasty feeling the flirtation was reciprocated.

Merth had no illusions about the beauty of her sister, or of her unscrupulous behaviour. Merthsandra would take what she wanted, no matter what the cost. '*It cannot be helped*,' Merth told herself, '*fate will follow its own course.*'

'That will be fine,' she announced aloud, forcing a smile. 'Merthsandra will be able to help Jerain with the herd, and she will also be able to show him the way to Borin's yurt. I must gather some gifts for you to take to Muria.' She turned to Merthsandra who was seated at the foot of the bed, on the sheepskins on which her father lay.

Merthsandra nodded hastily, disguising the look of anticipation this turn of events had aroused.

'I shall come and help,' she declared, jumping to her feet.' Patras will look after father.'

Redd slid into the spot at the foot of the bed vacated by his sister. He and Patras were good friends. He watched Patras moving the pillows to ease Andreas's knee.

'How long do you think he will be laid up?' he asked the healer.

'A couple of weeks, at least,' Patras answered. 'We must get the swelling down, and ease the pain before he starts moving around. Then he will need to do some quiet exercise. No riding for a while, I'm afraid.'

Andreas did not like being discussed as if he were not there. He shifted impatiently.

'You will have to look after the herds, you know.' He glared at Redd with annoyance.

'I shall do whatever you wish,' Redd replied, 'as long as you do what Patras wants you to do. Jerain will have his hands full taking the culls to market. By the time he gets back you should be up and about again. Can we have some wine, Patras?'

'I don't see why we shouldn't. It might help the potion to ease the pain. Is there anything else you would like?' he asked Andreas.

'I would like to be shifted to the main living area tomorrow.' Andreas said. 'Then I can keep an eye on what is happening. Apart from that, I suppose I should look at the accounts. That is something I can do if I have to stay still.'

'Not tonight,' Patras averred. 'Tonight you must rest. Redd and I will stay to make you do so!'

A passing slave, who had been sent to bring wine, came into the Lord's sleeping chamber. He passed the wine he was carrying to Redd and then the glasses.

'The Totem needs your advice, young master.' He indicated the way he had come.

'I shall see her soon,' Redd promised, as he poured the wine. Later, he found his way to where Merth was sitting; surrounded by various articles she had purchased from the trader.

'Which of these bracelets do you think would suit Muria?' she asked.

Redd picked up a silver bangle studded with topazes.

'This should suit her fair beauty,' he smiled at her. 'You have good taste. How do you think Merthsandra will behave?'

Redd's eyes glanced across the yurt to where Merthsandra was busily packing bags, getting ready for the journey.

'As long as she has her own way, and has the current man she fancies trailing after her, she will be charming.'

'Yes,' Merth agreed. She sighed and shrugged her shoulders in despair. 'As long as it is not my man on the end of her tether. We are just getting into partnership, I don't want Merthsandra to come between us, but there is little I can do.'

Redd looked at her in concern. 'Have you told him?'

'Have I told him what?'

'That you are puking every morning on your way to the stream.'

'Who told you that?' she lifted her head and looked at him in surprise.

'No one needed to tell me, I have seen you myself. Perhaps if you tell him before they set out on the journey to Borin, he might feel more inclined to remain faithful.'

'If he is going to stray with Merthsandra, and she wants him, it will happen. I have decided not to worry about it.

I shall wait and see what has occurred when they come back. I have enough to worry over, with father on his back, the yurt and herds to run, as well as throwing up all the time.'

'I will help,' Redd gave her a hug. 'Father will be like a stallion with a bee in its ear. He wants his bed by the cooking area so he can keep a watch on us. I shall take the herds out to their new pasture tomorrow. Can Boris come with Borland, now? Has his strain healed?'

'Yes, he can go, he is wishing to be free.' She patted Boris, as his ears lifted to his name.

When Jerain joined her in their sleeping quarters that evening, Merth was close to tears. She was thinking she had only just got used to him in her bed, and now he had to leave. Jerain ran his hands down her back, sliding his comforting fingers through her silky hair.

'Don't worry. I shall be back before the autumn. I know it will seem a long time to be apart, but we can look forward to being together again.'

'I have news for you now, before you go.' She looked at him searchingly, wondering what his reaction would be. He looked very young and oddly vulnerable, a boy given a man's tasks.

'Oh? Were you going to tell me Merthsandra is coming with me? Andreas has told me already. I shall look after her, you don't need to worry about that.'

Merth broke into a fit of giggles. 'No, I'm sure you will look after her well,' she gasped. 'I should imagine it would be you who will need a guard! No, something else, different entirely. When you come back I shall be well on the way with our first child.'

Jerain's hazel eyes gleamed with delight. He gathered her up in his embrace, kissing her until she was short of breath. Laughing with pleasure, he finally released her.

'How do you know? Will it be a boy? Are you happy about it?'

'I am pleased it has happened so Andreas can stop plaguing me, especially if it is a girl, but happy I am not sure. I was looking forward to going riding with you, having some fun, perhaps visit other lands.

'Now I shall be tied to the herds, the baby and the yurt without you. I shall have to look after father too. He will only want me to care for him.'

She put her face on his shoulder. Comforting her with endearments and kisses, Jerain fondled her into relaxation, and the night passed in passion.

Next morning, when they were loading up the baggage mules, Merth was again feeling disconsolate. Her usual cheery face was drawn into grim lines from anxiety and jealousy.

She snuggled into her heavy jacket with her hair tucked inside the high collar, glad of the protection it afforded from the icy morning air.

Sythe came up behind her and whickered in her ear. Turning she buried her face in his silvery grey coat, gaining comfort from his warmth. He wants to be going with the others, she thought, that makes two of us.

She was still feeling ill from her morning sickness, which often lasted all day. Instead of putting on weight she was getting thinner and tenser.

Merthsandra, on the other hand, was full of gaiety. She flashed her eyes, tossed her blonde hair, and managed to arrange herself in seemingly unassumed, provocative poses.

She had a piebald, mettlesome mare, called Thunder, who needed a firm hand. Her mare was nipping at Jerain's stallion, Jet. Merthsandra called the riders to help her move the mare away, her voice rising in mock dismay.

Merth knew Merthsandra had complete control of the animal. She was using the occasion as a ploy to attract attention, particularly from Jerain, who was standing near trying to harness Jet.

Finally they were ready. The party consisted of Jerain, Merthsandra and six of the riders, the rest being wanted to care for the main herd and do the hunting, particularly with Andreas being laid up.

Redd made certain everyone was well kitted out, ensuring that bedrolls and water bottles were all in place. He would have liked to go with Jerain, if only to see Borin and his new wife.

He also enjoyed Jerain's company, they had formed a firm relationship and the travel would have been a pleasure together. He realised he had to stay and take care of the heavy work at the camp. Merth would have plenty to do and would need his help.

Jerain came to Merth where she was standing by the door flap, having shooed Sythe back to the other horses belonging to the remaining riders. Jerain enclosed her in a bear hug.

'I shall miss you so much,' he breathed into her scented hair. 'Take care of our future, our Phoenix Lady.'

'Come back safe.' Merth ran her fingers tenderly down the side of his face, putting the imprint in her memory. Tears brimmed in her eyes but were not allowed to fall. He had raised his arm in his black cloak against the tent side, giving them a shadow of privacy away from the gazes of the curious. He kissed her fervently.

Merth responded, as if this would be the last time she would see him. She felt his body, firm and hard, pressing against hers and carved the pressure on her mind forever. He smelt of salt and horse, bound together with the indefinable essence of himself, so dear to her.

At last he dragged himself away. He leant inside the yurt to give farewell to Andreas, and then strode to Jet, waiting patiently with the rest of the party.

Merthsandra waved to Merth with an annoying grin on her pretty face, while making Thunder kick and cavort, then rear up, before setting off at a sedate trot at Jerain's heels.

Merth stood and watched them until they were out of sight, feeling more miserable than she had ever felt. Andreas called to her peevishly, and she returned inside to help him with his pillows, yet again.

Andreas was restless in body and in spirit. He studied Merth as she tended him. When she leaned forward to shift the pillow that rested behind his head, he grasped her arm and pulled her down to him to give her a hug.

'You are strong, Merth, you will overcome whatever happens. It is possible your worries are not needed. They will go and come back, successful and unharmed.' Her eyes met his, so alike in their dark direct gaze.

'Things will never be the same, my father. I fear Merthsandra will entrap him on the way. If he succumbs to her wiles and takes her, then your grandchild will be fatherless. The Totem cannot have an unfaithful mate.'

'A grandchild? Well, that is something to look forward to! As for the other, who knows? It is in the hands of Mut. These feelings occupy our thoughts, but in the length of time fate sets its seal on all of us.'

After she had settled him for the morning, Merth took Sythe to the spot by the stream where she used to go with Storm. Sythe was happy to crop the sweet grasses, while she let the rippling stream soothe her turbulent thoughts.

Her mind drifted back to the nights of love with Jerain. Remembering her tension the first night he came to her, she shivered in the warm sunshine.

His touches had been as soft as silk sliding over her body. His gentleness had raised her to desire, a feeling she had never experienced. She had pushed against him, demanding more and more.

He had traced around the concentric circles on her breasts until he had found the nipples. Her breasts had become taut and hard, the nipples thrusting against his teasing fingers.

Raised to ecstasy, she had been boneless in his hands, yet he had not forced her further, until she had caught his hand and placed it down below her snarling wolf. Then he had consummated their marriage, while she had run her fingers over his velvet back, astounded at the strength of his loins.

Their mating had become a thing of wonder, entrancing her thoughts and feelings night and day, and now it could be over. She rolled over in the soft grass and allowed herself to cry and cry.

Chapter Seven

Jara ben Jada fidgeted restlessly as he lay on a pile of silk cushions. The day was more humid than usual, although sea air filtered past the decorated, marble filigree wall of his audience chamber, bringing the tang of the ocean.

Through ornate arches he could see the dolphin fountains in the inner courtyard, as they spouted myriad rainbows of perfumed water, which gushed steadily from their mouths, unceasingly cooling the air with drifting vapour.

The sunlight was too bright there, for him to appreciate the wonderful blooms surrounding the pool, so carefully tended by the gardeners.

Jara motioned to the slaves to wave their feathered fans with more enthusiasm. His silk robe was sticking to his skin again. He tossed aside the sheaf of documents recently presented to him by his vizier, then clapped his hands petulantly.

When his body servant appeared, he demanded cold towels for his face and hands, and more chilled fruit juice. When his needs were catered for, he waved to his minister to open the doors to allow in his subjects who had brought today's petitions.

Was there no end to the needs of his people, he wondered? Such petty nonsense they brought before him for judgement. His days were filled with inanities. He watched the group of people filing in to the chamber with a jaundiced eye, while tapping an irascible toe in its silken slipper.

He had been leader of his populace for two rounds of seasons now, after his father, Drus ben Jada, had come to such an untimely end. He thought with longing for his carefree life when his father had been alive, riding, wenching, carousing all night long. Now he was penned up in this room for the greater half of his days, and was discussing affairs of state for most of his nights.

'Present the first petitioner,' he growled at the vizier, between his teeth.

An old lady hobbled towards the dais, stopping at the end of the blue carpet, before the marble steps began. He nodded at her impatiently, while running his hands through his luxuriant black hair, having loosed it around his shoulders while he had been waiting, hoping to catch a cooling breeze.

'Eminence,' she wavered, having just managed to descend to her rheumatic knees, with the help of a court official. 'My livelihood depends upon my chickens. I sell fowls in the markets, and my eggs are renowned for their freshness. Yesterday, some young louts broke through my fences and my chickens scattered up into the bushes. What am I to do?'

'Can't you call them down by offering to feed them?'

'I have no grain left for them, my lord, I have given them the last. I was going to buy some in the market for exchange of eggs and some plump pullets, today!'

Jara was a kind man, who bore every trouble on his shoulders. He looked at this poor old granny, who could barely walk, never mind climb trees, with compassion.

He motioned to his scribe.

'Ensure this woman gets a couple of bushels of grain from the granary, and send two of the scullery boys with her. They can chase the chickens back home after they have mended the fences. They should take some lathes and hammer and nails with them.'

Jara nodded graciously as the poor old woman staggered to her feet, full of praise for his kindness.

'Next,' called the vizier, wiping his brow with a large red handkerchief, which he kept in a pocket of his voluminous robe, especially for these occasions.

Following the old woman, there were two pretty dancing girls.

Although Jara ben Jada had many wives, and even more concubines, he was still not averse to seeing more beautiful girls. His attention perked up. Straightening himself he gave the beauties his undivided attention.

'What is this all about?'

The girls were similar in looks and build, and both wore swirling skirts with a small band around their breasts. Even though it was still early in the morning, their faces were made up, enhancing their youthful beauty.

One of them stepped forward to make obeisance to The Jada.

'Oh mighty one, my sister and I do an act with burning batons. The man who supplies us with oil has put the price up ten times what it is worth.

'He says we must sleep with him if we are to buy the special material at the proper price. We are professional performers, not some street sluts for him to put his greasy hands on!'

'This is extortion,' said Jara. 'Bring the man forward.'

A merchant dressed in flowing white robes approached the dais. He was overweight, with a balding head, and sporting golden rings in his ears and on his pudgy fingers. His face was screwed up with anger, and he poked forward a large bulbous nose. He started to remonstrate with the girls before he came to the end of the blue carpet.

'Great One, these girls have made up this story. It is true I import the slow burning oil from afar. It is expensive, and the price has gone up. I am a married man and have no need for their favours.'

Jara selected a piece of fruit from a dish, then chewed on it thoughtfully.

'I think we can cut out the middleman,' he remarked to the dancers. 'Scribe, find out where the oil comes from. These girls can perform for my court once every moon, for the price of the oil. Make sure they have a ready supply for their needs.'

The oil merchant was voluble in his protests, sinking to his knees, trying to speak while making obeisance. Jara ben Jada waved to the guards to escort him from the chamber. As he was dragged away, he was still maintaining his innocence.

'Next.'

The court officials had been infiltrating the crowd of petitioners, asking questions, accepting bribes, arbitrarily pushing supplicants forward, only finding someone else with a needier cause and an open purse to promote in line. Others were waiting for extra recompense from those who wished to approach their ruler quickly.

In the general hubbub, a quiet person was often overlooked. Sheer persistence at times resulted in one able to reach the end of the carpet, and such was the case of the next litigant to approach Jara ben Jada.

He was a tall man who had not grown old without affliction, and was now bent over with frailty; he supported his weakened frame with a stick. Although weighed down with age and obvious pain, he was adamant and faced the court with a determined mien and a steely eye.

Following his imposing presence was a middle-aged man with a sulky expression, who was explaining to an usher how he did not need to be at court, but should be at home mending his property.

'Tell me about it,' Jara ben Jada said to the older man. 'No, you don't need to kneel,' as the grandfather commenced gathering his white robes ready to make obeisance.

Straightening up, the old man gave Jara ben Jada a little bow.

'My Lord, I purchased my property over 20 years ago. This man is my next door neighbour. As soon as I had started to live in my home I measured my property carefully, then built a stout fence to keep my neighbour's goats from coming to eat my vegetables.

'He agreed to this, and even paid for some of it. He painted his side of the fence when my wife and I painted ours. Just recently he started to knock the fence down. When I remonstrated with him, he said it was in the wrong place.

'Day by day, he has shifted the fence on to my property. This has taken many seasons, and often there are holes in the fence where he has not replaced the boards.

'When he does put the fence up, he has moved it no more than the size of my thumb to the first knuckle. In the big storm, part of the fence fell down because he had loosened it, and now he does nothing about it. I have lost income from my garden, as the goats have destroyed my crop. What am I to do?'

'What do you have to say?' Jara ben Jada asked the other participant, while gazing at him curiously.

'Sire, he put the fence up when I was away from home, selling my goats. He put it in the wrong place.

'I have no time to be mending fences, as I have to look after my herd. They jump up on my roof and I have to mend the holes they make. It is an on going problem.'

Jara selected a grape and popped it into his mouth with a thoughtful expression.

'This is a difficult decision I must make. I must think about it.' There was silence while he ate another grape.

'Now, you have been remiss in the mending of this fence for some time, and you have caused inconvenience to this old man, who has done you no harm.

'You accepted the fence when it was first erected, and apparently it has been there for many years, so it was all right then. If you have moved it only a little, it could not have been too far from where you think it should have been.

'This is my judgment. For every moon you do not work on the fence in future, you will give your neighbour a kid. He will then be able to start his own goat herd to recompense him for his vegetable plot.

'When the fence is finished and stands firm, we shall consider the bargain completed. My overseer will visit the property once a moon, to make sure my wishes are carried out. So be it.'

Both men bowed to the dais then mingled in the crowd. Their problem had been sorted, but neither had come to terms with the decision, nor had their disgruntlement eased.

Jara ben Jada cast his eye over the milling throng of humanity filling his court room. Everyone was trying to catch his attention except for one man who stood by the entrance way, talking to the guards in the doorway. He wore the attire adopted by the cattle herders from the far plains, below the mountains to the south.

Few of these herders ventured into Jaddanna. They were more at home with their cattle, wandering over the remote vastness of the plains. The cattle herder was dressed in leather breeches topped by a flowing garment, shielding his face and head.

All that could be seen of his face were his eyes, as the rest of his head was swathed in the dark green material. The guards were not going to let him pass into the court, either he had not presented enough money, or they thought he was armed, or because his appearance was too unkempt.

Turning to his adviser, Jada commanded, 'Go and fetch that man to me. He must have a good reason to have travelled so far to speak to me.'

In due course the cattle herder stood at the end of the carpet.

'Greetings, great king. May the sun and moon shine on you.' Piercing black eyes surveyed Jara over the top of the muslin.

'Not both together, I hope,' Jara smiled. 'What brings you here? You have made a great journey, by the look of you,' *and by the smell*, Jara thought, catching a whiff of horse, dung, dust and sweat.

'The grasses and the crops fail, Your Eminence.'

'So I have heard.' Jara ben Jada gestured for him to continue.

'The cattle are hungry and close to dying from lack of water. We have to shift them from place to place to find water and food. Every day there is no rain, the thunder heads gather but nothing falls. The clouds sweep over the mountains and the rain must fall on the plains on the other side.'

'Your name?' Jara interrupted, holding up his hand.

'I am Habon, Sire. I am chief of the Makkan tribe.'

'Well Habon, what do you think is the reason for this drought? Has it happened before?'

'No, Eminence. We think the pattern of the weather has changed. There has been a shift in the climate. What can we do? The country depends on our herds to save it from starvation.'

Jara mused on the situation. Although surrounded on three sides by water, Jaddanna was not benefiting from the sea, apart from the bounty gained by the fishing fleets.

The mountains in the south offered an insurmountable barrier. No one had scaled the mountains, let alone taken cattle over them. The cattle herder raised a timorous hand to distract him from his cogitation.

'There is hope, Eminence. Last week there was a cataclysm in the mountains. A big earthquake brought part of a gorge tumbling down. There is now a gap through the chain.

'My brothers and I climbed through and saw the lush grasses on the next plain, but this is the land of the Horse Lords.'

'Can the cattle be herded through this gap?'

'Yes, Lord. The ground is rough, but not impossible. Yet we fear the Horse Lords, and we would not want to trespass on their lands.'

Jara understood this, knowing of the fierceness of the Horse Lords and their violent reputation. He shifted again on his cushions, feeling the temperature becoming even more unpleasant. He longed for his bath. It was close to midday and his wives would be ready to attend to his needs.

Although approaching middle-age, he was a virile man with healthy appetites.

'I shall consult with my advisers and will give you audience tomorrow. We will find an answer to this problem, never fear. Have you a place to stay over night?'

'Your Eminence, I came by horse, and I have slept by my animals on the way.'

Jara clicked his fingers to attract his Vizier's attention.

'Give this man, Habon, some coin, so he can find a hostelry for himself and his horses during his stay in the city. He has brought valuable information and I do not wish him to suffer more distress.'

Habon bowed to The Jada, then accompanied the Vizier to receive his monies.

Jara signalled to the slave standing by the big brass gong in the corner.

From his desk, the Vizier announced, 'The audience is over for the day, all supplicants must present themselves again tomorrow.'

When the gong reverberated, the assembled people made obeisance to their Jada, then shuffled towards the door.

They slowly started to empty the chamber, disgruntled and unhappy because their cases had not been heard. Yet tomorrow was another day, and they would present themselves with their pleas again, although they would probably have to give more money to the wily court employees, rapacious as they were.

Jara uncurled his legs, stood and stretched. He kicked the cushions out of his way, then sauntered to the entrance of his private chambers. The fan wavers heaved sighs of relief when they let the cumbersome fans fall to the ground.

As soon as they left the royal platform, it was immediately occupied by two more slaves, who pummelled the cushions, swept and dusted, then removed the remains of Jara ben Jada's fruit and drink tray, now swathed in soggy towels.

Walking to his bath, Jara dropped clothes as he went. Soon he was embraced by cool water, faintly-perfumed, and two of his favourite wives were massaging his shoulders and feet to ease his tension.

After his afternoon rest, dressed in loose cotton tunic and pants, he repaired to his council chamber. When he was seated comfortably at his desk, with a cool sea breeze coming through the open doorway, he sent for his vizier, and his younger brother, Jast.

Jast had a quick mind and he could often solve Jara's problems. Solomon, the vizier, was perspicacious and gave good advice. They both had the good of the country at heart, rather than their own advancement.

Jast, however, was not eager to be Jast ben Jada, he was quite happy for his brother to bear the brunt of the position. He enjoyed being in charge of the army. He spent his days in drills, swordplay and horse riding. In consequence, he was hard and fit, much to Jara's annoyance. Although he was very fond of his brother, Jara regretted losing his own wilder youth.

When both men were settled, and drinks had been served, Jara explained to Jast the reason for the meeting. He explained about the famine the herds were suffering, and finished by showing a solution.

'There has been an earthquake in the mountains and a god given pass has been formed. Apparently it is large enough for us to send the cattle through. What do you think?'

Jast rubbed his short black beard as he considered. 'Will you inform the Horse Lords?'

'I would have to. However, we can't wait for permission, the cattle are starving.'

'The Grey River cuts the Horse Lord's lands,' the vizier interposed. 'Perhaps they are not using the northern plains at the moment.'

'We shall have to give them recompense.' Jara was frowning as he pondered the problem.

'What have we got to offer them?' Jast inquired, his bright eyes flicking from one man to the other.

'We can face that when we get to it,' the vizier replied, brushing his robe with an impatient air. 'First we have to gain permission to graze our herds on their lands.'

Jast leaned forward and put his glass on the table with a thump.

'I shall organise the army to track across the pass first. When we have established a base, and can guard the herders and their beasts, then the cattle can be driven in. It will be difficult for the Horse Lords to attack us then.'

'Hopefully, they will not want to attack,' Jara interposed. 'I would like a peaceful settlement. Yet, your idea has merit. It would be good if the army is in charge. I will send an embassy to the Horse Lords. Will you arrange that?' He lifted an eyebrow at the vizier, who nodded in assent.

'Yes, Lord, I will put that in motion. I will arrange for a party, with horses and baggage, plus guards. I think they should sail to Orphur firstly.

'From there, they can circumnavigate the mountains, and will be able to ride unimpeded to the southern camps of the Horse Lords. I believe the chief Horse Lord is always a woman.

Perhaps we should send some suitable presents with our embassy?'

Jara glanced at him with a smile. 'Fripperies, you mean? By all means, civilise the natives. Why not?'

'We have another worry.' Jast tapped on the table to gain attention, his thin, agile fingers, making a tattoo of sound. 'When the army is established in the northern part of the plain over the mountains, how will the cattle herders know when to come, and where to come?'

The cattle herders were nomad families, similar to the Horse Lords. Each family looked after their own herd and wandered where they willed. Jara considered this for a moment or two, then came to a decision. His worried frown lightened, and he sat back in his chair, at ease. He gestured to the vizier with his glass.

'Solomon, there are many tradeless young men loafing around in the bazaars, with little to do, except get into mischief.

'Why do we not band them together, give them horses, rations, and a uniform? Give them a title, let us call them scouts, and put them on the payroll. They can each band with a herd, and lead them to the pass.

'Once on the northern plain they can then liaise with you, Jast, and you will then know the whereabouts of each herd, and how they are faring.

'This will remove a nuisance from Jaddanna, and solve our problem in the field. Something else for you to apply your skills, my friend!'

The vizier grimaced at this backhanded compliment, but agreed the plan was possible, and asserted he would commence collecting equipment and young men in the morning.

'These riffraff will need training, Excellence. I doubt if any have had any dealings with horses, let alone have had the opportunity to ride.

'They will have to have lessons, and they will also have to learn how to look after their animals, otherwise the whole scheme will be in shambles. This will take some coin, you understand?'

Jara sighed. 'It will be silvos well spent. Get them a banner to carry, too. It will make them feel more important to be on The Jada's business. My stable master should be able to install some pride in them, he terrifies me!'

The others both laughed. The stern rigidity of the stable master was well known to all, but his thoughts were only for the well being of his horses.

'What have we missed?' JadaJara inquired, raising the expressive eyebrow in query.

'All cooking fires must be carefully guarded. We don't need the dry grasses in the arid pastures set alight, causing a stampede.' The vizier slid his hands into his sleeves, a habit he had when he was worried.

'What about the pass?' Jast was thinking ahead. His thin face was eager with excitement at the prospect of mobilising the army.

'Of course, when my men enter there, they will be able to shift boulders and scree to make a suitable track for the cattle. What if some of the boulders are too large, and block the way for four-legged beasts?'

'Easy!' Jara replied. 'You will take four of the imperial elephants with you. They are getting lazy and bored with so little to do. They are working elephants and the mahouts will have the pass cleared quickly, they won't have to go any further.

'When the army passes through, the mahouts will bring the elephants back to their enclosure, ready for their next job. I shall want them for future processions. Mut help me, they are hairy, uncomfortable beasts, with minds of their own. Still, they will make a good job of this clearing of the pass.'

'This is going to be a big operation,' the vizier stated, 'and it will take some time to accomplish.' He looked at Jara with a doubtful expression on his usually calm face.

'It will work out, you will see. The first thing is to get the army mobilised, and the next is to get the elephants on the move. Unfortunately I shall not be able to join you, Jast. As you will be the next ben Jada it will be an excellent opportunity for you to practise being in command. You will be in charge of the whole operation.'

Fine points were discussed during the evening. When they went to bed, each felt they had found some solutions to the difficulty.

The next day dawned no cooler. Jara sat in dour stillness on his bank of cushions, too distressed to fidget. He could feel runnels of sweat sliding down the inside of his royal, blue robe, congealing in puddles around his waist, hidden by the golden sash swathed around his middle. A slave holding damp towels, dabbed occasionally at his face, removing excess moisture from his stately mien.

Solomon, the vizier, hovered near by. He was less distressed, as his gown was of lighter material, but he was still glad of the comfort provided by today's white handkerchief, already reduced to a sodden twist.

He raised a weary hand to wave said handkerchief, which should have fluttered, but was now a sad rag, in the direction of the gong, that now reverberated through the chamber.

'His Majesty, Jara ben Jada will now hold court,' the vizier announced in a ringing tone.

The bronzed doors at the other end of the room swung open and the supplicants surged forward.

When the room was filled and the chatter had died down, the vizier spoke again.

'Let Habon, chief of the Makkan, come forward.'

Habon came from the back of the crowd to prostrate himself at the edge of the blue carpet.

Jara gestured for him to remain upright. 'Was your accommodation adequate?' he asked.

'Truly, Sire. I was well-looked after.'

'Good. A decision has been made. Hopefully, this will settle your difficulties. I shall send envoys to the Horse Lord in Strevia to inform her we wish to use their land above the Grey River, until our grazing has replenished. I hope we can manage this peacefully.

'In case they demur, I am sending part of the army to make a base camp there. They will be in the charge of my brother, Jast, and he will be in control of the operation.

Scouts are to be sent to each herder to tell them where to find the pass and when to move their herds. Let us hope the army and the royal elephants will have been able to make the pass useable.'

'Elephants, Eminence? I have never seen one.'

'They are large beasts who will be able to shift boulders, God willing.'

'My Lord!'

'The army will be ready to march in about five days' time. You may go home and inform as many of the chiefs you can find, then tell them what is happening.

'Oh, I shall be sending wagons of fodder and barrels of water, throughout our dry plains, so the animals will have enough sustenance to be able to make the long trek.

'Make a note of that, scribe. It is important to arrange for this immediately.' Jara looked at the tribesman and saw he had ceased trembling.

'This pleases you, Habon?'

The tribesman bowed to his ruler. 'This should save many lives, Eminence.'

'You must realise this can only be a temporary measure, I'm afraid. When our grasses have recovered we must come back. We must not inconvenience the Strevians.'

'Even if it is only a short relief it will be worth it, Sire.'

'Go then, and let us make a start.'

Habon retreated back down the carpet, a look of relief on what could be seen of his craggy face.

'I hope we are doing the right thing,' Jara murmured to Solomon. 'Have we got the delegates organised yet?'

'They will set sail tomorrow, Lord. There is a young noble lord, and your son, Drun, who wished to accompany him.'

'It will be good for Drun to have some adventure. He has been uneasy and restless for a while. He can be charming if he wishes, and might just be the person to state our case without offending anyone. Well done. How about the scouts?'

'A proclamation was made in the market place this morning. In answer to that, the courtyard in front of the stables is full of young men wishing to sign up for the enlistment. The stable master has sent to the estates for suitable beasts.'

'You seem to have everything under control. I will have Drun to my chambers this evening to give him my final instructions.'

'Your will, My Lord.'

A flickering oil lamp cast traces of golden filigree across the white marble floor.

The moon's soft light gave luminescence to the areas near the open windows, which were shielded in white bead drapes, framed by oval arches.

In the shadows of the room, incense smoked and swirled, gusting, carried by the breeze, which was drifting through the open door.

The bead curtains containing the room from the night, had not prevented a moth from entering. It zoomed round the lamp, insistent on its frenzied dance with death.

Jara lay in a lounging chair, clothed in cotton, content and peaceful now the heat of the day had passed. His eyes shifted to the bead curtain as it rattled against the door jamb.

'You may enter, I am alone.'

He raised his hand in welcome as Drun crossed through the curtain, making a formal greeting to his father as he did so. He was dressed in a fitted jacket and trousers of a dark green cloth, simple, but elegant. His soft slippers made no sound as he approached his father, then he sank on an ottoman, tucking his slippers under him.

His 18 years had given him height, and width to his shoulders. He had a broad chest that tapered down past slim hips, to the legs of an athlete. His black wavy hair was shoulder length and he sported a neatly trimmed beard. His movements were graceful, well-balanced, and he studied his father with an eager, alert air.

Jara looked at him with a slight smile, *a boy to be proud of*, he thought.

'Are you ready for your journey, tomorrow?' he inquired.

'Yes, father. Our baggage has been embarked and our guards are ready. We shall sail with the tide in the morning. We have decided not to take the horses, but shall purchase some in Orphur.'

'You are stopping in Orphur? You should pay a visit of courtesy to the Prince there. He is a young man like yourself, and will probably entertain you royally. Do not linger there though. My embassy must arrive at the Horse Lord's encampment as soon as possible.'

'We shall travel with all speed, father.'

'What do you know of the people of Strevia?'

'I know they breed wonderful horses, that they live in leather tents, and that they wander from place to place. Barbarians, are they not?'

'I have not met one, my son, but I believe the actual leader is the Horse Lady, often referred to as the Horse Lord. She is also named The Totem, or The Riffed One, and is considered above all others. What gifts are you taking?'

'A trunk full of dresses and scarves, some beaded slippers trimmed with gold, marble ornaments and some embroidered friezes, perfume bottles, silver dishes and other small trinkets. I can't bring them all to mind at the moment.'

'Do not think these people are naive natives to be charmed by silken snobbery. They live a hard life, and will be a proud and stubborn people. They have not survived out on the plains for generations without skills and traditions. Be careful how you tread, and treat them with respect.

'Remember, we want something from them. They will not want to let us use their land; it is their livelihood. You are my representative, do not show arrogance. Be polite.'

'I shall try to remember, father!' Drun looked perturbed and a trifle disconsolate as his visions of a spree at the expense of the people of the plains disappeared into fond memory.

'Make sure you have warm cloaks and leather boots,' his father continued. 'Down there in the southern plains it will be cold at this time of year, particularly at night.

'I think you should take a healer with you. Who knows what might happen to you on the journey and the food of the Horse Lords may not be to your liking.

'You should organise your healer tonight so he can join you on your ship tomorrow morning.' Jara thought for a moment, then smiled.

'I know. Take Chun with you. He comes from Keshia, down on the western coast. He should know what herbs are to be found on the plains, so he can supplement his medicaments.

'He might like to leave you later, to visit his friends where the Grey River reaches the sea, a good opportunity for him. You could let him take a couple of guards. They can sail back to Jaddanna later, following the coast. Have you bid farewell to your mother?'

Although Jara had many wives and concubines, his first wife was the love of his heart. He knew this second son was her idol. Anise would worry about him all the time he was absent.

'I visited her apartments before I came here father. She wished me well and gave me this.' He produced a golden amulet from under his jacket, where it hung suspended around his neck on a chain.

'It is a token to keep me safe, I believe.'

Suddenly he looked young and vulnerable, as the enormity of his enterprise overcame him.

'You will be fine,' his father assured him, patting him on the back as they both stood up.

'I hear you have a steady companion and some fine guards. If you have difficulties, discuss the problems with the other men. Don't take all the responsibilities yourself.'

Pulling Drun into a hard embrace, Jara was hiding his worry while bidding him goodbye. 'Go with Mut, my son, and use your sense. I look forward to your return.'

Drun returned his father's hug, then turned and slipped out past the bead curtain, letting in another importunate moth as he did so.

Jara heard him chatting with the guards in the courtyard as he carried on his way. Returning to his lounging chair, Jara lifted a hookah to his lips, calming his anxious thoughts with cooling smoke. *His sons had to grow and gain experience*, he thought, *how else could they follow in his footsteps?*

Chapter Eight

The little yacht tacked in the light breeze. She was pushing up the Devronian coast, jaunty, now the wind had freshened.

A young man, stood in her bow, was enjoying the salt spray flung up by the waves, and the feeling of urgency thrumming through the hull. He had spent most of the voyage in the sparse cabin, banished there by inclement weather.

Firstly, a storm came, which tossed the little boat about like a twig in a river, then secondly, there were banks of fog, which made everything clammy to the touch. Now, the sun was kind and the air invigorating.

The competent crew had finished the journey with excellent seamanship, and ahead the town of Devron could be seen. The pink roofs were catching the light of the setting sun, giving the town a rosy glow. High on the hill, the palace was evident.

As he looked forward to going there with his dispatches, he clutched the message satchel more firmly under his arm. The bow of the little yacht turned toward the harbour entrance; she was gliding steadily now, surrounded by a flock of gulls come to bid them welcome, while squawking hopefully for scraps. When he looked down into the clear water, shoals of fish could be seen, while lower in the depths large dark shapes streaked in and out of vision.

King Joseph was sitting in his favourite chair on the balcony, also enjoying the evening. He fondled his spaniel's ears absently, as Flick leaned against his knee.

'*No more biscuits,*' he murmured, *'you're an old fraud, with your cupboard love.*' He was watching the yacht enter the harbour, and noticed it was flying the Kordovan flag. *I wonder who that is?* It is possible they are bringing news about the timber, he concluded to himself.

The yacht disappeared behind the buildings, which seemed to be poking their roofs into the darkening sky, as the evening drew to a close.

He rose, and then made his way to the study, where he found Lex leaning over the large table in the middle of the room, intent on studying drawings and ship designs.

'What are you doing, boy? Are these the designs of the new ships? They look very sleek. I wonder how seaworthy they are.'

'Hello, Father. Yes, they have just been delivered. When we get the wood we shall be able to enlarge the fleet.

'I know we have three seaworthy galleys and two three masters, but they are getting old and need refurbishing.

'We must always have vessels that are seaworthy so we can protect the merchant ships and the fishing fleet from pirates.'

King Joseph sat down at the table and they spent a pleasant hour discussing the designs, exclaiming over new features and radical innovations.

'Are there sufficient funds in the treasury for all of this?' Lex inquired wistfully.

'We will do it one at a time,' his father replied. 'A fast galley to begin with, two would be better, if we can manage it. This would mean our ships could hunt in a pack.

'If we can stop the attacks on the merchant ships we could charge an escort service for foreign vessels, which would raise some revenue. I wonder how Troy is getting on purchasing the timber?'

The seneschal walked into the room, carrying a message envelope on his tray.

'My Liege, this dispatch has just arrived by special courier from Kordova. The messenger said it was imperative for you to see it as soon as possible.'

Joseph reached for the envelope and inspected the seal.

'It is from the Prince of Kordova. I wonder what he wants.' With that, he opened the packet and commenced to read.

'Good Lord, father, what is wrong?'

Unable to speak, Joseph passed the missive over to his son.

Lex read quickly, his face paling, as he understood what the writing portended.

'Troy has been kidnapped! The ship they were in has been taken!'

He jumped to his feet, and took the document closer to the light to enable him to study it more closely.

'Even the Ambassador and Lady Lesla suffered indignity at the hands of the pirates, though they were allowed to be ransomed. Delia and Amelia were taken, as well as the men! This is dreadful.'

They gazed at each other in horror; Lex had crushed the document in his fist, involuntarily.

'Where will they take them?' Joseph gasped. His heart was thudding wildly, and he had a sudden pain in his chest.

'They'll take them to the other continent, no doubt, or to an out of the way island. Dishnigar would be the best bet, I should think, to the slave pens there.'

The thought of Troy losing his freedom was too much for Joseph.

'You will have to tell your mother, I cannot do it.'

'I shall tell her when we have started getting the ships ready to go to search for him.'

Lex strode to the fireplace, stabbing his finger on the bell push to summon a servant. He stood in front of the fire with his face a mask of anger, his jaw clenched in a grim line.

When the seneschal reappeared he was looking frightened and anxious, as soon as he saw the Prince's face.

'Please send for my father's medical adviser, and also send for the three captains of the galleys in the harbour. As well as these, if the messenger from Kordova is still in the palace, I would like to see him. If he has left he must be found in the morning.'

The king's personal physician soon arrived, having been told that Joseph was seriously-ill and needed instant attention.

After the king had been examined, everyone was relieved to know his condition had been the result of shock, and that he would be recovered after a good night's rest.

His valet helped Joseph to bed, while servants lit lights, and started a cheery fire in the hearth in his bedroom. He was sitting up sipping a hot posset when Lex entered the room.

Lex studied his father's face with concern. He was pleased to see Joseph's face had regained some colour and he was looking more relaxed. Flick, who was ensconced at the foot of the bed, thumped his tail as Lex approached the bedside.

'Any news?' Joseph inquired, putting down his mug.

'Nothing new,' Lex returned. 'The messenger will be found in the morning. I'm expecting Downs, Smart and Gregory to arrive shortly. I intend to set things in motion this evening, the least time wasted the better.

'I have told mother, by the way. She was very calm, and seemed sure we would rescue him, I have dire misgivings myself.

'Dakana is a large continent to search, and goodness knows how many islands there are, to search in the southern seas. He could have been taken anywhere.'

'I'm coming with you, you know.' King Joseph looked at his eldest son with determination on his face.

'I thought you would have this silly idea! How shall I look after to you in the middle of a battle with pirates?'

'I'm quite capable of looking after myself. I am neither decrepit, nor incapable. I will not interfere with the running of the galleys, but I will sit in on the battle plans.

'Your mother and sister can look after Devronia for the length of time we shall be at sea.'

'If this is the case, you will bring your valet and your medical adviser, then. I don't want to be king before my time.

'Mother is coming to see you, by the way. She was going to get dressed when I saw her; she had gone to bed early and was going to have supper in bed.'

'I would like some supper now. Arrange for a light meal to be sent here, would you? Your mother might like to share it with me. Thank you for telling her, Lex. I couldn't bear to give her such terrible news.'

A light tap on the door heralded the coming of Queen Marie. She was wearing a navy evening robe of satin, embroidered with a pattern of silver swans. Her dark hair only slightly silvered, swung in a long plait down her back. She slipped to the bedside, and sat beside her husband, leaning forward to embrace him.

'Oh Joe, what has happened to our boy?' He kissed her gently, then waved a hand at Lex, still standing by the bed.

'Lex knows as much as I do. All we have been told is that all trace of him has gone, even to the ship he was on.' He then told her what had occurred concerning the Kardovan Ambassador and his wife.

Lex left his parents consoling each other, and stamped down the dimly lit corridors to the study. At every corner and at every passageway, a soldier came to attention. The news of something of importance happening had travelled through the palace like a flaming torch. He ignored the palace guards, concentrating on his thoughts.

On reaching the study, Lex arranged himself at the head of the large table, after having retrieved the documents strewn about, and stored them carefully in the safe. He sat staring at the glistening expanse of the polished table, unaware of its sheen.

In his mind he was seeing Troy, his younger brother, always ready to enter into any scheme Lex could devise, with his blond hair, long then, always in his eyes.

He followed his growth through teenage years, when Troy had rebelled at being the younger sibling. He did not want to be king, but neither did he want to be the second son, with only a princedom to be his lot in life. Now, just as he was settling into adulthood, it had all been ripped away from him.

Lex grieved for his younger brother with a fury, which tightened a band around his heart.

The door opened, and the seneschal looked around it,

'Your visitors are here, my prince.'

'Send them in,' Lex commanded. 'I have been waiting long enough.'

The three men who entered, masters of the galleys, were all looking expectant and slightly apprehensive. Apart from their expressions, they were vastly different.

Captain Austin Downs was the oldest of the three men. He was portly, with a ruddy complexion, wearing his uniform of well-cut, navy serge. His curly grey hair was cropped close to his head, yet showed the imprint of his cap, which he now carried under one arm. His companions were dressed for shore leave.

The first one to enter after Austin, was Jack Smart. He was a man in his early thirties. He was wearing black trousers tucked into calf length boots, topped by a full sleeved, white shirt. His black hair was also cut closely to his head, receding slightly at his forehead. He had an alert air and a handsome face, which attracted many a female glance.

The last to enter was Bill Gregory. He had risen to his position through the ranks, and had a swashbuckling air of direct authority. He wore knee-high boots with dark red trousers and a frogged jacket over a lacy shirt.

'Please sit down, gentlemen. We have much to discuss.' Lex pulled a decanter of port towards him then filled four glasses.

'The pirates have attacked again. They have kidnapped at least five people, one of them my brother, Troy, and have ransomed the Kordovan Ambassador and his wife for an incalculable amount of money and treasure. Not only that, they have taken the ship the passengers were travelling in.'

'Where did this happen?' Bill was the first to speak. His voice was deep and hoarse from years of instructing from the bridge.

'Outside our territorial waters, on the way to Kordova.'

'How many ships were involved?' The higher pitch of Jack's voice, came from the other end of the table.

'I can't be sure of that, but I believe two. One was to take the Ambassador to Kordova, and the other, who knows where?'

'Didn't the Kordovans do anything?' inquired Austin filling his pipe.

'They tried to follow, but lost the two ships that were outside Kordova harbour in the mist.'

'We don't have much to work on.' Jack crossed his legs while sipping on his port.

Lex propped his head on his hands, elbows on the table, suddenly tired.

'No, we don't.'

'Down in that area, I'd reckon its Ambry and his mate, Petric.' Bill pushed away from the table and started to pace, puffing on a cigar.

'They are free booters, out of Dishnigar. They think all of the southern seas are good pickings for them.

'Apart from Dishnigar, they have many settlements on islands down to the south. Their ships are fast galleys, *The Dark Mistress*, and The *Dark Dart*. They are nasty bits of work, so I have heard, both of them.'

'You don't think it is our local boys?' Smart contributed. 'They might know more about what is happening in Devron, and have ideas above their station?'

Lex shook his head. 'Too far to the south, I should guess.'

Austin rose to inspect a chart, which hung on the far wall of the chamber. Using a pointer he had picked up by the map, he surmised where the initial attack might have taken place.

'If they sailed to Dishnigar from here some weeks ago, they will have unloaded their cargo by now.' He put his pipe in his pocket.

'I realise that.' Lex looked at the older man with a stony expression fixed on his lean face. 'We shall still search for the devils. If it is only to find out where they have sold their prisoners.'

Gregory stopped pacing, put his hands on the table and leaned on them.

'When are you intending to leave?' he asked.

'As soon as we can get ready,' Lex replied. 'We must assemble stores and troops, and prepare for a lengthy voyage. I don't expect they will be hanging around for us to find them.'

'Who goes?' demanded Smart.

'I have been considering that.' Lex ran a hand across his forehead, pushing at his headache.

'One galley must stay here to keep the local lads at bay. The merchant vessels and the fishing fleet must still be protected, and one of you must do that and be in charge of the rest of the navy, while I am gone.'

Downs returned to the table and raised his hand. 'I will volunteer to be the one to stay. The *Aranda* is slower and heavier, not only that, she has a deeper draught. You will want manoeuvrability in strange waters, popping in and out of coves to look for hidden vessels.'

'Thank you Austin for making that decision for me.' Lex nodded in respect to the older man. 'In that case, we don't have to keep you here. Make your way to your ship and keep our fleet safe.'

The three men who were left congregated at one end of the large table and Lex refilled their glasses. There was palpable tension in the room, which had increased as soon as Downs had left.

'I have an added trouble,' Lex confided. 'The King intends to come with us, no matter what reasons I give to the contrary.'

'His Majesty must never be in danger!' Bill lifted his head in concern.

'That is undeniable, but it also means we shall have to curtail our activities. We shall board *The Aurora* with you, Jack,' Lex continued.

'That will give Bill here, free rein on *The Astora*. In the morning I shall interview the messenger from Kordova. He may have information, or he may just have been sent with the dispatches, we shall see.'

'We should make straight for Dishnigar,' Bill said firmly. 'I have reasons for this. It is a harbour where the pirates are likely to hold out, the slave market is there, and we should talk to Essa Esse. She keeps a finger on the pulse of the city; little happens there that escapes her notice.

'A formidable woman, we shall have to be careful or we could have assassins in our beds.'

Lex ran his hands over his face, tiredly. 'Well, gentlemen, we are decided. We shall sail in two days' time.

Make all the arrangements you wish.'

The two captains rose from the table, their swords clattering against the polished table legs. As they strode across the glistening floor, their heavy boots resounded loudly.

After he had sent a manservant to usher the captains out of the palace, the seneschal came to ask Lex if he needed anything. 'You would like a light supper perhaps, my lord?'

'No, thank you, James. I'm too tense to eat. I intend to speak to their majesties, to let them know what has been decided, and then I will make my way to bed.

'Oh, would you send Jocelyn, my squire, to my sister early in the morning, please? She will have to know what is happening. She will have to take over the affairs of state with my mother, while the King and I are absent. Who knows how long this affair will take, or what will be the outcome.'

His parents were glad to see him and agreed with what had been proposed.

When he finally got to bed, Lex found it difficult to sleep, as pictures of what Troy might be suffering kept imaging across his mind. His imagination was vivid, and did nothing to relieve his distress.

Shortly after Lex had breakfasted, with Flick making his presence known, he did have one piece of disturbing news.

Apparently, after the Ambassador and his wife had been safely returned to Kordova, and the ransom had been paid, the prize ship, *The Lady*, and *The Dark Mistress* had left the environs of Kordova. Although a search had been sent out after them, they had not been discovered.

Later that week, Lady Lesla had disappeared. There was no trace of either her, or of her maid. A trunk of clothes had also been removed.

There had been much speculation about the lady, some thought she had left in shame for having led the country into such a predicament, while others thought she had set off to find Delia, but no one really knew.

Lex gave the messenger returned dispatches, then sent him on his way. He called for more coffee, then waited for his sister, Sophie, to appear.

She lived on her estate outside Devron, where she raised unusual breeds of animals. She would come after the usual morning chores were completed. From where he was seated,

Lex could see the road she would ride on, so he was ready to welcome her when she arrived.

Sophie was a competent person, very like her brothers in looks. Her honey-coloured hair was tied up in a bunch of ringlets, setting off her shapely, clean-cut neck. Her blue eyes were full of worry when she greeted Lex.

He told her all that had happened, and then sprang the news she and her mother were going to be left in charge of the country.

'Mother and I can't arrange a table-setting together amiably, how will we administer the palace, let alone the country? Anyway, I can't leave my animals.' She tapped her riding whip against her boot impatiently, eager to be off.

Lex looked at his sister with annoyance. He loved her dearly, yet her stubbornness always riled. She leaned to consider what would suit her best.

'Mother will take charge of running the palace. You must be in a position to be in charge of the exchequer, and to see to the smooth running of public facilities.

'Make sure all services are kept working, organise the incoming of merchandise and the transportation of outgoing goods.

'Listen to petitions and ensure law and order. I'm sure you have competent grooms on your estate, give one of them the ultimate responsibility. This is no light task I have set you to be dismissed so summarily.'

Sophie put the riding whip under her arm, then put her hands in her breeches' pockets.

'What else, do you want, Oh High and Mighty One?'

'You will have to contend with petition day and night, separate squabbles between the lands, judge on fighting in the poorer quarter, and maintain law and order.

'I have informed the ministers to bring all problems to you, as temporary ruler. You will just have to cope. Troy must come first. Not only are you being a damned annoyance, I have father on my hands!'

'Have I any help?' she asked plaintively, seeing he was in earnest, looking all of her 17 years.

'Downs will run the harbour and the shipping.

'He is a steady reliable man. You can always go to him for advice. General Masters is in charge of the army. He will provide soldiers for whatever enterprise you might want them for, putting down uprisings, bands of robbers from the highlands, whatever.

'Solomon will do most of the ordering and decision-making, but you have to be definite, the country has to have a strong ruler.'

Her bottom lip came out in a pout, and then she threw her hands in the air.

'You have been trained all your life for this! Why don't you stay? I could go to sea!'

'You would probably do a good job, I agree, but can you manage father?'

'I can't manage mother, let alone father. Why do you think I live away from the palace?'

'Well then, we do as I suggest. I think you should start by having Austin bring the bills of lading. Our ships must keep on time to honour our agreements.'

'Oh, all right!' She swung away from him, then stamped about, hitting her boot with the whip as she walked, though there was a gleam in her eye. She was rising to the challenge, and after all nothing had ever been as interesting as this.

Mollified, she helped herself to coffee, then finding she was hungry, sat down to help herself to breakfast, which had not yet been cleared away. Flick came to beg at her knee, always hopeful for some special little extra titbit.

'What an old scrounge you are!' She gave him a few scraps from her plate.

'Well, someone is pleased to have you back in the palace,' Lex smiled at her across the table. 'I thought he might have been put on a diet with father absent, but I see that will not be the case.'

She returned his smile, then Lex rose to go and arrange with his squire what they would find necessary to take with them aboard the galley.

Two days later, before dawn, the galleys left Devron. They slipped out of the harbour with barely a splash, the only sound of their passing the muffled drumbeats of their timekeepers.

These ships did not employ slaves for their oars; the oarsmen were part of the navy and were well-paid. They took pride in their strength and ability, and could earn bonuses when asked to stretch their strokes.

Each galley had ten heavily-armed and armoured soldiers assigned to its crew. They formed part of the fighting force which would come into action when they boarded enemy ships, after they had been crippled by ramming attacks.

A heavily-weighted ladder with handrails was slung across between the ships in order to let the soldiers board the ship being attacked.

Although the galleys carried masts for sailing, when the wind was in the right direction, they fought under oars.

Enemy ships were crippled after ramming, by smashing off their oars, then the soldiers could board, while the dozen archers in the rigging could pick off their foes from the safety of their own deck.

The most-skilled of the sailors were those who steered by the two large rudders at the rear of the ship.

There were watches kept on the galley.

The men had time for rest and relaxation, a mess deck and sleeping area were shared in the centre of the craft. Above the oars were tiny cabins for guests and officers.

Lex and Joseph were sharing one of these two narrow bunks with a sea chest between them. It was all the space available.

Lex spent most of his time on deck, or on the bridge of *The Aurora* with the captain. He had known Jack for many years, and they had always been comfortable in each other's company.

Jack had the galley running to the drumbeat, everything was calm and orderly. The soldiers in the charge of their officers, were either at sword practice, or cleaning their weapons, and the sailors ran the ship without question.

Soon the open sea was all that could be seen. When they had pulled away from the land the huge square sail had been raised, and the oarsmen were able to take a well-needed rest.

Lex had listened to the scream of the winches, and had then watched the enormous sail flap above him, before billowing out to chase down the channel. The waves slapped against the prow, sending streams of water past the bow.

'How are you feeling?' asked Smart.

'I'm fine,' Lex replied. 'I understand father might be a bit squeamish, though. He was lying down looking green when I last saw him.'

'He will recover quickly,' Jack said. 'A few days at sea will get him used to the motion. It is brave of him to come, I think.'

'He is anxious about Troy.' Lex frowned, thinking about his younger brother. 'It's eating him away that he sent Troy on that voyage, and now we can't do much about it.'

'We will do what we can,' Jack replied. *The Astora* is keeping up well.' He had turned and was looking at the other galley with its white sail masking most of the vessel.

'A good team,' Lex commented, looking at the other galley. 'Only what we expected, of course.'

The sun had risen fully now, and the waves danced in the morning light. The rolling swells of the dark blue sea erupted in frothy white tops, which caught the sun's gleams, to refract shining rainbows of spray.

It pleased Lex to feel they were doing something at last. Dishnigar was getting closer by the minute.

The Aurora moved smoothly through the ocean, its ram jutting out above the prow, well clear of the water. If it came to having to use the ram on an enemy ship, there was a mechanism installed, which when used, enabled the seamen to detach the ram from the galley, so the oarsmen could then manoeuvre to the side of the other craft.

Huge ropes were wound around the outside of the galley, giving strength to amidships; these ropes had been braided together in the same fashion as a girl's hair would be plaited, then fastened to huge stanchions placed at either end of the deck.

The oarsmen sat above these restraining ropes on rowing benches. The height of the benches was adjusted to the length of the oar, and the ability of its wielder. Naturally, the stronger men were assigned the longer oars, and each rower was situated in a place that suited his skill and physique.

Lex stood under the huge sail as it billowed out above him, with the tarred sheets creaking and groaning. He leaned over the side and admired the oarsmen sitting chatting to each other, getting up and doing stretches, or refreshing themselves from the water barrels, and was thankful that such men wished to be in the navy.

Chapter Nine

Amelia awoke just as the steely light of dawn was filtering through the black bars of the slave quarter windows. She shivered, clutching the sparse cotton sheet which was all the comfort she had been given.

Her glance around the dormitory revealed that all her companions were still asleep, including Delia, who had cried herself to sleep. She was now hunched in a ball, with her sheet wrapped tightly around her. Her dark hair was spread like a fan on the cot behind her.

I have always been the quiet follower, Amelia thought. Her position as Delia's lady in waiting was subservient, as custom demanded.

The younger daughter of a minor lord, Amelia had enjoyed the opportunity of visiting the court at Devron. Now their circumstances had changed irredeemably, and both of them had an unknowable fate, with only themselves to rely on.

She rose, wrapped the material around her, and went to sit by the bars, tucking her bare legs under her to conserve as much body heat as possible. They had been in the slave pens for a week now, but this was the day when their fates would be decided. She wondered how the men were getting on.

Troy had been foolish, she reflected, *making such a fuss when they arrived.* He had demanded to see the Devronian Ambassador, not realising there was no such embassy in Dishnigar. He had then tried to break free, and had been severely beaten.

She could still remember the sound of the lash, a soft sodden sound, as the whip had risen and fallen, risen and fallen. Troy had made no sound, but had stood erect with his hands tied high, his body quivering and jumping.

Later, she had heard he would have had vinegar poured into his wounds, which would then be covered with paper to help them heal.

No matter what had been done, the mark of the lash would show he was a recalcitrant slave, and his merchandise would be spoiled. It would also mean who ever bought him would not value him enough to treat him kindly. Trojan and Anton would have helped him all they could, she supposed.

So far, she and her companions had been fairly well treated. There was plenty of plain food and there were washing facilities. Their only clothes were the muslin sacks they had been given, and the other girls incarcerated with them wore the same.

Most of them were very young. Some had been stolen, like herself, but most had been sold to the Slave Master by their parents. This was an aspect of life that astounded her.

Her parents had always been kind to her, in their off-hand way. They were only interested in her older brothers, and really considered her an encumbrance who they would have to marry off. They would not need to worry about that now.

Delia woke and came to sit beside her. Delia's face was white, and her eyes red-rimmed from weeping.

'What are you doing?' she asked plaintively.

'Thinking about what will happen today. I wonder if we will be sold together?'

Delia looked at her, horror struck. 'You don't think they will separate us, do you? I won't survive without you! You are the strong one of us two!'

'No, I am not stronger, just different in my outlook. In my life I have had to face more reality than you have had. You will be all right. Remember, charm will get you better treatment. Don't answer back and do as you are told.'

She put her arms around Delia and held her tightly. Delia seemed to be a little, frightened girl again, living in a nightmare.

'I will try to look after you,' Amelia whispered. 'Just be brave and accept what must happen. Who knows, later on we might be found and rescued. Here, let me fetch a cloth for your face, and then we should comb our hair. The better we look, the higher the price. No one will damage something they have paid good money for.'

The other girls were stirring now and they all clustered around Amelia. She had proved to be the one they all turned to for advice and comfort. Soon she had raised a few weak smiles from her companions, and even a slightly ironic one, from Delia. The door clanged and their breakfast was brought in by a surly warder.

'Food for the condemned,' the woman said with a sneer. 'Make the most of it. Who knows where the next meal will be, or what it will be?'

Delia was looking at Amelia with new eyes. Before, she had considered her companion as a foil for her own wit and beauty.

She had been a quiet, brown-haired, grey-eyed cipher, contrasting with her own flashing eyes and wondrous looks. Someone she could gossip with about clothes and men. She had never considered Amelia's feelings or wishes, and had often expected her to fit in with her own flighty schemes.

She has always been a person in her own right, she thought, *but I have never seen it. Now, when I could really make her my friend, we are likely to be separated.*

The men had similar treatment in their enclosure.

Trojan and Anton had found a corner where they could pile two of their thin mattresses together, so Troy could lie on his stomach.

After the agony of the vinegar being splashed over his raw back by an unfeeling guard, Troy had relapsed into unconsciousness.

Days later, when he came out of his stupor, his back was a mass of suppurating sores, and he kept fainting again and again, with the pain.

Trojan and Anton kept watch over him, taking turns to bathe his back; this was all they could do to help him. Finally, on the day of the auction, their pleas for a healer had been answered. A busy, fussy, little man was shown into the pen, carrying his herbs and potion bag. After he had examined Troy he declared he was unfit to be sold.

'I shall come every second day to dress his wounds, but it will take some days for the fever to abate, and then weeks for the wounds to heal.'

'But we are to be sold today,' Trojan said, worry and despair making his voice croak. His long, blond hair hung in straggles and he had a scrappy beard on his usually clean-shaven face.

'Yon fellow should have thought of all this before he made such a nuisance of himself. There is nothing more I can do.' With that the healer departed.

Trojan and Anton looked at each other in dismay. The next time Troy returned to consciousness they would not be there.

There was nothing to be done. The slave auction was held once a month. Troy would be kept in the pen for another month, while they would have gone, who knew where?

Outside the square was filling up with people. Some had come out of indiscriminate curiosity, but others were genuine buyers. There were farmers looking for hands.

Meanwhile, a surly overseer from the mines had already entered the pen and had inspected the men standing in a coffle. He had examined their bodies, felt their muscles and had even looked at their teeth.

Trojan pretended to have a twisted hand and walked with a profound limp. Anton had been overlooked; he was not physically mature, as yet. All the men were terrified of the mining overseer, with his cruel eyes and probing hands. He had pushed Troy with his boot.

'I'll look for this one next time round,' he promised, with an evil grin. 'I might add to his decorations.'

Essa Esse stood back in the shade of a verandah. She examined each man carefully as they entered the block, one by one. Most were for the farms or mines, though occasionally one was taken by a wealthy buyer, for a body servant or for a scribe.

She discussed the merchandise with Jade, who was standing nearby. When it was Anton's turn to be put on the block, they were talking about a scandal in the town, which had interested them, and Jade missed out on purchasing him. Anton had been spoken for by a swarthy man wrapped up in layers of thick wool scarves and sweaters, topped by a heavy cloak.

'Has the boy gone?' Jade cried. 'I could have had many customers for him, so young and handsome. Who bought him?'

'The Jaddannese who buys for the palace,' Essa answered. 'He would have been out of your range. That man never cares how many silvos he pays.'

An iron collar was fitted quickly around Anton's neck, and the chain attached to it, handed to his purchaser.

Trojan stepped forward onto the platform. His limp had gone, but although his height made him impressive, and he held his head up while looking the crowd in the eye, his usual debonair resilience had disappeared.

'I need a body servant for my niece,' Essa said. 'Don't you bid against me Jade, he would be too long for any of your beds.'

Drifting in and out of consciousness, Troy was occasionally aware of his surroundings. In his dream state, he found arms reaching for him, while comforting hands reached to soothe, but always the hands became covered with writhing snakes and he drew back from the shadowy figure of a wolf, which over rode the proffered comfort.

The tongue of the wolf eased his pain, and allowed him deeper sleep, but when he woke he disliked the idea of his dreams being so invaded. He missed the reassuring presence of Trojan and Anton, but fortunately a young boy who had a twisted ankle had been slipped some coin by Anton, to make sure Troy had water, and was as comfortable as possible.

The situation was worse for Troy than for the others in the pen. His nose was pressed into the mouldy, smelly mattress, which also had the odour of old urine, mixed with other olfactory delights. He had never passed a night away from his quarters in the palace or shooting lodges, until he had boarded ship. That had seemed like an adventure, this was definitely not.

He wondered what had happened to the others. In a way he felt responsible for them, but could not think what he could have done differently, in the circumstances.

When the healer came again, he suffered the ministrations without a sound, though the peeling away of the old dressings was agony. He held on tightly to the edge of the dirty mattress until it was over, then swooned into oblivion again.

Amelia was next on the block, she had been held until the last. People had been wanting to view her lovely figure and composed mien, but did not have much opportunity to see her charms. As soon as she appeared the swarthy, cloaked gentleman had bid an exorbitant price for her.

Jade had barely opened her mouth to bid, when she realised so many silvos was way beyond her bargaining price. She had to be content with the younger girls she had already bought, convincing herself she had the better bargain, as they would be easily trained.

Shackled, but without the ignominious iron collar, Amelia was bundled away into a closed carriage. She was thankfully pleased she did not have to walk in the coffle with the other purchases the factor had procured.

Stumbling into the carriage, she was surprised she was not alone, as there was a shrouded figure in one corner away from the light. When she sat down the figure turned to look at her, and to her amazement proved to be Anton.

'How did you get here?' she gasped, as she was flung back in the seat, when the carriage started moving with a jolt, without any warning, then stopped again just as suddenly.

'Our buyer decided I was too pretty a boy, so I might be a distraction for his handlers. I have been put here to keep them away from temptation, and also for my own good.'

'I am so glad you are here, I should have hated to be on my own, not knowing where I was, by myself. Who has bought us, and where are we going, do you know?'

'I heard the soldiers talking, we are going in a caravan to Keshia. From there we are going somewhere by boat.

I wish I knew what has happened to Trojan and Delia.'

'They were taken by an old crone, all dressed in black. If she is nobility, Trojan must be my brother. Is Troy all right?'

'He is still in the pen, though he is getting a healer. They will keep him there until the next auction.' Anton sighed, and looked out of the window.

On the seat of the carriage there was an old, grey blanket similar to the one Anton was wrapped in. Amelia swathed it around herself, and then sat down again, close to Anton, huddling up to him for warmth. The shackles on her ankles clanked every time she moved.

By the activity they could see and hear outside, it seemed they were getting ready to move. Dust permeated the air, and the horses stamped and whickered. There were other animals making strange noises, grunts and spits, sometimes it sounded as if they were gargling in bad temper.

Anton craned his neck but could not see the animals. He therefore surmised they were camels, which were carrying packs for the journey. The slaves clinked their chains, the drovers cracked their whips and they were off.

When the carriage began moving again, they found the motion was uncomfortable, but Amelia was thankful she did not have to walk. They found some flasks of water under the seat, and soon Amelia started to feel slightly human again.

All Anton could think about was how Troy had looked when he left him. He was lying on his side with his eyes closed.

The warders had hustled Anton away, and he had no time to comfort, or to say farewell. He crunched up further into his ball in the corner, and hoped the stoic Amelia had not noticed the odd tear he had shed.

Trojan had followed his captor up the steep streets, tripping over the cobbles when the other man had pulled his rope. He felt like a cow being taken to the slaughterhouse, and endeavoured to keep up, so there was no tension on the rope. The cobbles gave way to the dusty road. He was glad he had managed to retain his boots.

Shortly they were passed by an exotic-looking caravan. The outriders, with spirited horses, were all wrapped up in blue covering cloaks, heavily dressed because of the cold. They carried curved scimitars and looked ferocious.

In amongst the carriages and carts were huge beasts, laden down with supplies and packs. Their accoutrements were bright with red, swinging tassels and ornamentation in their harnesses.

131

Trojan had never seen a camel, but supposed that was what these smelly animals were. Their riders guided the beasts with ropes through their noses. There were bullock carts too, making heavy going of the steep hill, with the big, white bullocks slipping as they strained against their halters.

In the centre of the caravan were the slave coffles. Trojan looked at both groups as best as he could, being tugged along himself, but there was no sign of Amelia or Anton, though he did give a sad wave to some of the men he had struck up acquaintance with in their sleeping quarters.

The caravan turned towards the right, to go through the gap, but Trojan's gaoler pulled him to the left, towards the huge walls surrounding an imposing looking building.

Once inside, he was ushered to a bathing area, then told tersely to bathe and shave, as his mistress would want to see him shortly. He was given a suit of dark grey serge, which was warm but itchy.

The upstanding collar of the jacket covered the iron around his neck, hiding it from view. He was given a meal of bread and cheese, washed down with thin beer, and told to wait in an anteroom until his mistress called.

He was left alone, as if no one in his position would attempt to escape. *Not yet, anyway*, Trojan thought grimly, *but there will be opportunities*. He knew escaped slaves had summary justice.

A thin, short and bird-like woman entered the room, well into middle-age, she was dressed in black with ornate jet embroidery. She stared at Trojan with piercing dark eyes.

'So, my purchase is clean and tidy.' She looked him up and down as one would a horse in a market. 'What is your name?'

'Trojan D'Auton, Duke of Desra, at your service, My Lady.' He swept her a bow, an ironic smile on his handsome, laconic face.

'Mistress will suffice, what can you do?'

'I can read and write, I speak Kardovan, I can ride and shoot, little else I'm afraid.'

'H'm. I have an adopted niece, Eyas. She will need a lackey to serve her whims. You will escort, and guard her. I want her tutored in the ways and etiquette of the courts.

'If you lay a finger on her, your head will be severed from your shoulders and slung into the sea by that long hair. Get it tied in a queue, by the way; we don't want it in the soup.

'I'm sure you have other skills so far unmentioned, they will come to my knowledge as time passes. You will dine early, then wait at table.

'I expect you to remember, then relate to me, anything of interest my guests have to say each night. The beaten slave, still in the pens, who is he?'

'Prince Troy of Ardarth, Mistress.'

'A fine catch for the slave master. Is he the heir to the throne?'

'No, Mistress. His elder brother, Prince Lex of Rhodia, is the heir.'

'He is a young man, then? No use to me, what a shame!'

She sat for a while in silence, staring out of the window at the sea, running her jet beads through her fingers. Her gaze shifted to Trojan, patiently waiting on her orders.

'Go find Eyas, and tell her you are her man servant. I'm sure she will find something to occupy you.'

Trojan bowed, then left the room, closing the door quietly behind him. The corridor stretched from left to right, and he had no idea which way to go.

A good opportunity to explore, he thought, setting off to the left, as he had been taken to the room he had just vacated from the right. His boots made no sound on the thickly carpeted floor.

Essa continued to sit in her chair after he had gone. *The boy in the slave market was no kin of hers, then*, she thought, *although he would be Joseph's son*. She would have to wait for another opportunity to arrive before she put her plans into action.

Ambry had left port, she had seen his vessel leave, and she had no way to contact him. She could wait a little longer; after all, she had waited over 20 years.

Trojan tapped on each door before glancing in. Every room seemed to be a bedroom, until he came to the end of the corridor.

When he opened that door he was confronted by a sunny sitting room, with a light breeze gusting through it, lifting the flimsy curtains beside an open window.

Inside, sitting on a divan near the window were two girls. To his amazement, one of them was Delia.

As soon as she saw who was at the door, Delia jumped up and dashed across the floor, throwing herself into his arms.

'Trojan! What are you doing here?'

'I am the Lady Eyas' tutor, guard and general factotum,' he replied, putting her down on her feet and surveying her.

She was demurely clad in a dark, high collared dress, with no ornamentation. Her hair was tied back and she looked better than when he had last seen her in the slave muslin.

'Well, that makes two of us, because I am her lady's maid.' They turned together to look at Eyas who was still sitting on the divan.

A faint flush of colour came to the ivory cheeks of the tall, slender girl, dressed in flamboyant, red satin, although she gave the impression of composure, with her hands clasped on her knee.

'Please come and sit down, both of you.' Her voice was softly modulated, though slightly husky, lower in tone than one would expect. Looking at Trojan she continued to speak.

'Welcome, yes, I am Eyas, the adopted niece of Madame Esse, though why she should have taken me under her wing and tutelage, I have no idea. As you were, so was I captured for the slave market.

'I come from Keshia. I was fortunate to escape the clutches of Madame Jade in the city and was wandering the streets of Dishnigar. I was bundled into a carriage and brought here. I have been presented to all and sundry as Essa's niece, but I really don't know her at all. It is all very strange.'

Trojan was admiring her long, nearly white hair, and this reminded him of his instructions.

'Well,' he said, 'it seems as if we are all in this together. Delia, would you plait my hair for me, please? Apparently I am to wear it in a queue.'

He sat down on a low stool for Delia to be able to reach his head. He was facing Eyas who had remained seated on the divan. Her movements were elegant and her features aristocratic. Her pale blue eyes, under arched golden eyebrows surveyed them with amusement.

'Is your name really Eyas?' he asked.

'Of course not. Eyas means a young eagle, and it is a fancy of Essa's. However, it suits me well enough, seeing as how we live in The Eyrie.'

'Who are you, then?' Delia demanded, raising her face from the thick plait of blond hair in her hands.

'I am the daughter of the President of Ghat. My name is Estelle Edwuard. I was riding in the park with my friends, when we were set upon by bandits. All of my party was killed, but I was to be ransomed.

'Unfortunately, my captors were attacked by another band of raiders from a pirate ship. We were all brought to Dishnigar and sold in the slave market.

'Jade bought me. She would not listen to my plight, even though my father would pay a huge amount of silvos to get me back. She said when she had finished with me I would be earning her much more, in steady income.

'Before that night was over, I had managed to squeeze through a broken trapdoor in the floor, which I had discovered under my bed. It led to an outside privy, from which I made my escape.

'She didn't recognise me here, I don't think. She paid the slaver good coin for me, and will be feeling hard done by.'

'What an adventure!' Delia admired the other girl for her fortitude and stoic behaviour.

'We must make plans,' Trojan said. 'Firstly, we must get to know the layout of The Eyrie, and the routines of the guards. Our best bet will be to leave by sea.

'We shall have to explore all avenues of escape. This will take time and patience, as no one must know we intend to make a run for it.

'We will act out our parts. Eyas will be the dutiful niece, and I the careful watchdog. As for you, Delia, start your duties by rustling us up some tea.'

Trojan jumped up and started to examine the walls, looking for hidden exits. He pushed and pulled every ornate bit of plaster and rapped on all the panels, all to no avail. Eyas watched him with interest.

Delia looked at the ceiling for help, then threw up her hands, turned around and made for the door, on her way to the kitchens in the bowels of the house.

'Essa would not have made things easy for me, by giving me a bolt hole, I don't think. Come and sit down and tell me your story.'

Trojan had just finished relating their miserable journey, when Delia staggered in, bearing a tray loaded with tea and cakes. She thumped the tray down on a table and sat down with a bump.

'Those things are heavy. You can do it next time, Trojan.'

'No', he countered, 'it will help you to strengthen your muscles. You both are going to do a good deal of exercise.

'I'm not wanting to make a dangerous escape, followed by a long journey with two women who can't keep up with me. We shall start with balancing exercises after we have had tea. You are going to learn to fight as well.

'I will not always be around to defend you. We shall not attempt to leave here until you can both look after yourselves, run, climb, ride, and have instinctive self-preservation. I see I shall be busy.'

'At least it will pass the time,' Delia remarked, picking up the heavy teapot. 'I didn't realise maids were so strong.'

Later that evening, standing behind Eyas' chair at dinner, in the gloomy dining room, Trojan cast his eye over the strange mixture of guests at Essa's table.

On either side of Essa were two sea captains, still in uniform.

The Kingdom of Ghat had a large navy, and in a whispered conversation with Eyas, he found these were sailors she had never seen at Keshia, though their uniform of dark blue serge with silver epaulets, seemed to be correct.

There were four merchants on the left of the table, discussing the importation of goods, and the difficulties of keeping grain dry in such a damp climate.

A silversmith, to the right of one of the sea captains, was involved in a conversation with a blacksmith, about the properties of metal.

Seated below them, was a man swathed in a long, black robe, who was trying to bribe a lowly clerk from the council to sign some papers he had, stuffed in a leather bag attached to his waist. The clerk kept glancing at Essa, waiting for her attention to be distracted.

Next to Eyas was an elderly woman who sat sternly upright, and spoke very little. Eyas had tried to make conversation, but every opening had been rebuffed. To Eyas' right was a young lawyer, who was employed by Essa, and to his right, surprise, surprise, was Ambry.

He had returned from a short journey to an outlying island where he had some stores. He had slipped up the cavern stairs and had arrived at the table just as the meal was beginning. He caught Trojan's eye and bowed in ironic greeting. Trojan had nodded in reply, after all Ambry might be useful in the future.

'Who is that?' Eyas asked, her pale eyes glancing at Ambry with curiosity.

'He is one of the pirates who captured us.'

'Strange company Essa keeps. I wonder why these captains are here?'

'Not for the good of Ghat, I should think. Wearing a uniform does not mean you are not a pirate. They are probably lining their pockets with some deal with Essa.'

The evening dragged on. The food was good and Trojan was kept busy by the butler, changing and re-filling glasses. As he bent beside Ambry to top up his glass, Ambry gave him a dig in the ribs.

'You did all right for yourself, then?'

'It could have been worse,' Trojan admitted. 'What are you doing here? I would have thought this would be too dull for you.'

'Oh, Essa is an old friend of mine.' Ambry raised his glass in toast to Essa. 'We do many a business deal for both our benefits.'

Moving around the table and glancing over the clerk's shoulder, Trojan saw he was scribbling his name on a deal of sale underneath the table. The dark robed priest took it quickly and returned it to his pouch, while removing gold coins from his waistband with the other hand, to give to the clerk surreptitiously.

The elderly lady finally broke silence.

'Tell your Aunt I agree,' she snapped. She rose, gave a short bow to the table, and then sailed out of the room without a backward glance.

'What was that all about?' Eyas marvelled. The young lawyer to her right leaned forward.

'Madame intends to breed some fine hounds for tracking. Mistress Long has a fine stud male. She has been arranging stud fees with The Eagle. They must have made some arrangement during dinner about the price.'

After the guests had departed, Essa called Trojan into her sitting room. It was a small room decorated in pink, with chunky furniture set around the fireplace. She leaned back in her favourite chair and waved him towards a stool.

'You have been standing long enough. Tell me what you have learned.' She listened to his recount of the activities at the table with an impassive face.

'That fool of a clerk has sold the last piece of free land to the Abbey. I bet he got more for it than the councillors will see. Mistress Alla came to terms about her dog, then? Good, I shall make a fortune when the pups are trained to track. Ambry has returned, I see. I have another job for him. I'll call him in the morning. What were the merchants talking about?'

'Shipping grain.'

'Go to bed, boy. I have arranged a pallet for you in Eyas' ante-chamber.'

Trojan found his way along the empty corridors until he found an open door, through which he could hear the girls talking. Delia had spent a lonely evening waiting for the others to come back from dinner.

Closing the door to the bedroom, Trojan fell on the pallet in the far corner of the small chamber. It had been a long day and tomorrow promised to be just as arduous.

Chapter Ten

Borin scrabbled in his saddlebag to find a thong to tie back his auburn hair, which was being whipped across his face by the wind.

The herd of culls trotted ahead, 40 in all, kept well bunched by the riders. It would soon be time to catch and tether them again, as another day passed towards a misty dusk from blinding sunlight.

The wind, which had risen since evening approached, was a nuisance, as it would make the fires for the evening meal gust and billow; it would also make the horses restless on their picket line.

Having tied his hair back, he rode on. He was considering the journey that they had been making. Borin had been looking forward to seeing his father again, and had been desirous of showing off the yurts and the lush plains he had inherited from his wedding to Muria.

He had been none too pleased to see Merthsandra in the party, when they had arrived with the horses. Meeting Jerain had been a pleasure, they had immediately found they were kindred spirits, and he was delighted to hear Merth was with child.

Still, he was ill at ease about the camaraderie so well established, between Merthsandra and Jerain. He had noticed Jerain kept well away from Merthsandra whenever they made camp. He kept close to Borin, and made sure Merthsandra was bedded down with the couple of women riders, who were also wives of some of the men in the team.

Borin remembered how his little sister had taken the news she was going to be the chieftain. She had not been ready to leave her childhood, for all her ability and winning ways. He had visited her when she was having her riffs done, to tell her he was leaving to become Lord of the Bear. She had been concerned about his teasing nature, and had warned him to be kind to Muria. He hoped Jerain was faithful to Merth, not that he could do much about it.

However, Merthsandra made sure she rode beside Jerain, and kept close by, whenever they stopped during the day. Borin was accustomed to her using her wiles, and her beauty, on every man she met, but felt she was going too deep this time, for his comfort. He shifted restlessly in his saddle, knowing how this flirtation would affect Merth, who appeared to be really in love with her wedded husband. She would be unable to stop her sister's bad behaviour.

Realising he was lagging behind, Borin kicked Cloud into a gallop to catch up. When he reached the others, he indicated a small valley in the shadow of the mountains, which would make a fine camping site.

There was a narrow pass into the valley, formed by towering rocks at the entrance, while the mountains reared up at either side of the enclosure. They herded the horses through the rocky entrance, then set about bedding them down for the night, before they started making camp.

When they were ready to wash up in a nearby stream and the fires were started; Jerain came by where Borin was rubbing down Cloud. He was carrying his saddle and looked tired and dusty.

'We have covered a good distance today, without much trouble,' he greeted Borin. 'How long do you intend to stay here?'

'A day and a night, anyway. The horses need to graze and have a rest, and I could do with one, myself!'

'Good! I have a broken strap I must mend. You have some fine beasts in your herd. Do you usually get a good price?'

'I don't know how we shall go. Andreas usually does the bargaining. Muria will not be well pleased if I don't bring back all the things that she wants from Dishnigar. I have been given a list, so we had better drive hard bargains.'

His wedding had been a great success, and Muria was all a wife should be. Her blonde beauty never failed to amaze him. *How had he been so lucky to be her chosen one?*

He had followed Merth's advice and had been kind and thoughtful, which was slightly out of character, he laughed to himself, but it had won Muria round, and now they had established a firm, loving bond.

Merthsandra came towards them, dragging her cloak in the dust, while tripping over blankets, clutched tightly in her arms.

'Come and help me,' she called to Jerain. 'I'm going to drop everything soon.'

He put down his saddle and went to relieve her of her load. She purposely tripped, as soon as he was close to her, and they both fell over into the pile of blankets. Jerain extricated himself carefully, then helped her fold the blankets into a more manageable bundle.

Returning to Borin he laughed. 'How she can be so clumsy when she is so balanced and supple, defies me.'

'Don't trust her a thumb's length,' Borin returned. 'She always has hidden motives, rather than what you expect her to be doing. I know my sister very well. We don't want to call the priestesses out here, do we?'

He continued to groom his horse, thinking about the inevitability of what he was sure would happen. He hoped Jerain would keep Merthsandra at arm's length, at least until they reached Dishnigar. He did not want to play the heavy brother and have to send her home in disgrace, before they even reached the city.

The evening was cold, made even colder by the wind tunnelling down the valley, striking chill to animals and people alike. A guard was set, and after grouping around the fires for a while, most moved to sleeping bags early.

Towards the middle of the night Borin was roused from sleep by a feeling of uneasiness. Pretending to roll in his slumber, he cast an eye over the sleeping camp, squinting in the faint moonlight.

The horses were up and restless, pulling at their tethers. The fires had died down to dull embers, but it was still difficult to see past them to the tether lines beyond. Then came the unmistakable sound of the chink of a spur on rock.

Borin slid his sword out of its scabbard with his left before he rose, then grabbed his throwing knife in his right hand. He prodded Jerain with the pommel of his sword. Jerain lifted his head a fraction, with his eyes wide open.

'Bandits!' Borin whispered.

Quickly they moved around the group, crawling on hands and knees, while wakening the other riders.

Borin nodded towards the valley entrance and they all slipped away like shadows, leaving the camp behind. Borin gestured for the group to come closer.

'When they are ready they will chase the horses out,' he murmured. 'Let them go, we can get them back later, after our attack!' They spread out across the opening into the valley, weapons ready.

Suddenly there was a loud whoop, making the horses start to thunder down the valley floor. The horse thieves were a little way behind, as they had to release their mounts, then jump astride them.

Hating to do it, but knowing it had to be done, Borin crouched beside the path and swung his sword at the galloping hooves of the first thief's mount. Screaming, the horse fell, throwing his rider and blocking the pass.

Changing sword for knife, Borin approached the fallen rider, who was already on his feet with his sword and knife extended.

Block, parry, counter thrust, jump out of the way, with this going through his mind, Borin dropped into a sideways stance, with his body turned away from his opponent's sword, while his own sword was ready for the coming rush.

They closed and he whipped his opponent's thrusting sword away with his dagger, then tried to use his own sword on the outstretched arm; however the other swung with a quick side step, and raised his dagger again.

Retreating, Borin slashed with his sword and nicked the dagger arm, then backhanded his sword into the fast moving sword arm, coming towards him. Both weapons clattered to the ground, and he was able to stab a killing blow to the throat.

Panting, he looked around to find the others had despatched four more. Apart from Jerain having a nick in his upper leg, only one rider was seriously hurt.

Borin looked at Ben in sorrow, as he knelt beside the boy, supporting his head while holding a flask to his lips.

The young rider of only 14 years had belonged to Muria's yurt. He had begged to go with Borin, wanting the adventure, and wishing to see Dishnigar. Now he was lying in the mud of the valley, while his life's blood flowed from a huge cut in his neck.

The sword thrust had nearly severed his head from his body, and his jugular spilt blood. As Borin held him, the boy's eyes fixed in a glassy stare and he heaved a final sigh, then lay still.

They wrapped him in a blanket, then brought spades from the muleteers. The riders dug a shallow grave, not wanting to leave him lying on the ground, in case wild animals found him.

They had soon piled rocks to build a cairn, then Borin realised it was up to him to send Ben on his journey to Mut. Hastily, he recalled the words Andreas spoke on these occasions, and then all the riders bowed their heads and sang a hymn, praising the young rider to the Goddess.

Standing by the grave, Borin looked at the corpses scattered near.

'Leave these scum until the morning,' he ordered. 'Back to the camp and let us find what has happened to our guard!'

The moon slid behind the scudding clouds, and it was difficult to find their way back. Those who were without boots now felt the hard, chilly ground though they had not been aware of pain, before, or during, the action.

The women were awake, having been roused by the shouts and screams of battle, and then by the search for spades. They were huddled together by the dull fires, with knives and stabbing swords in hand. They looked with apprehension as the first group of riders came into view, then relief flooded their features as they realised who was coming. Merthsandra was the first to move. She ran to Jerain and flung her arms around his neck, hugging him with abandon.

'Oh, I was so worried, I nearly came to find you!'

His leg gave way under her extra weight, and then she was supporting him, looking in concern at the seeping blood running down his left leg.

'You have been badly injured! Come to the fire.'

Jerain examined his leg.

'It isn't bad, only a surface cut. I'm all right.'

'Get it washed and bound,' Borin said. 'It might get infected, let her see to it.'

Jerain gave in with bad grace, and soon Merthsandra had cleaned and bound his leg, and had brought his sleeping furs to keep the night's chill away.

Most of the rest of the night passed in discussion and everyone had to repeat his story.

The guard had been found unconscious, tied and gagged. He had been surprised by a stealthy attack, when someone had jumped down on him from behind.

'They knew the terrain,' Jerain commented. 'This valley is probably their hunting ground. We shall have to set more guards in the future.'

In the morning they struck camp and were glad to be leaving the gloomy valley. Borin divided their company into three. He assigned the least competent riders to bury the horse thieves. He sent the women and the cooks to butcher the fallen horse in the pass, and then to continue slowly the way they were travelling.

While the third group, consisting of himself, Jerain, Merthsandra and the more competent riders, had the task of herding up the culls and catching up with the rest of the party. They collected the riderless horses of the thieves as well. They turned out to be ordinary hacks, which could be sold in the market, or could be used as baggage animals on their return journey.

The sensible mules had not bolted with the horses, but had remained in the valley cropping sweet grasses.

It took most of the morning to round up the culls. The trained riding horses, including Cloud, Thunder and Jet, had returned to the whistles of their owners, but the wild horses led them way out into the plains, and had to be driven back in a herd.

Merthsandra proved her worth by encouraging her mare to provoke and dance, then sent her leading, with tail and mane flying; the others finally gathered together and allowed Thunder to lead them.

By the time the sun was at its height, they had all gathered together at a riverbank, where the horses were pegged out, and camp set up. In a way the thieves had done them a favour, as they now had more animals than they had started with, and they also had juicy meat sizzling on the fire.

Merthsandra made great play of caring for Jerain, ending up by massaging his leg muscles, where he had been holding them cramped, against the pain in his thigh. Her deft hands brought relief, and her closeness allowed him to admire her beauty. Her face was flushed in the firelight and the flames accentuated the highlights in the swirls of golden hair, hanging loosely from a dropping, golden ribbon, now fluttering around her face.

'You are a strange family,' he remarked. 'There is Merth, berry brown, with dark hair, while you are blonde, Redd has brown curls, and the little ones are both fair. How has this come about?'

'I suppose it is because our clan has always sought mates from afar to strengthen our breed. Merth and I are twins, but not identical. Although Andreas is so dark, his mother was from a tribe to the far south, where the skins are fairer. Thaylis, our mother, had red hair. Does that answer your question?'

'It's like horse-breeding, I suppose,' Jerain answered. 'Merth's horse, Sythe, is a beautiful animal. I would like some offspring from him. I hope she allows it. I wonder what our child will be like?'

'Child?' Merthsandra queried. Sitting back on her haunches, she surveyed him with surprise.

'Didn't she tell you? When we get back she will be well on her way with her pregnancy. She tells me it will be a girl.'

Merthsandra rose, then making an excuse, went to the river to wash the unguent from her hands. Another one to step between her and the Totem! Her face twisted in anger. She would have to change her plans; no way would she ever be Horse Lady now, no matter how many men vowed to follow her.

She rid herself of her annoyance by grooming her horse, and soon her face had returned to its usual amused expression, as she flirted with the riders who were occupied with similar tasks.

Jerain's horse would let no one near it, so Jerain had to get up and tend to it himself. They stayed by the river for the rest of the day and for that evening, being careful to set guards in a position where they could not be ambushed.

However, apart from a pack of marauding wolves, which were soon chased off with flaming brands, the night passed peacefully enough.

They were early on their way next morning. The party spent weeks passing through countryside, which now had cottages, and then small towns.

The land was predominantly farmed, and on occasion, thickly-wooded. This gave respite to their journey across the open plains. The last camp was made on the outskirts of the city, just before they were to cross the mountain pass.

When they settled around the fire that evening, Borin announced their mode of progress would have to be altered.

'Each rider will now have a string of horses to look after.' He pulled a bundle of rope towards him, then started hacking at it with his knife. When others saw what he was doing, they joined in too.

'Make halters for the culls, then attach leading reins to them. I should imagine we each will have between two or three animals to lead.

'The roads from here are narrow, and there will be other people coming and going, with carts and suchlike. Only take on what you can handle.

147

'If needed we can leave some animals here with a guard, and return for them later. I don't want us to get into fights, or any sort of trouble, because we can't control our teams.'

Discussion followed, as everyone had different opinions as to how to go about entering the city.

Next morning Jerain and Borin demonstrated how they wanted the horses harnessed. The culls were used to being staked out and were easily haltered if two riders came up on either side and a third person slipped on the halter. Merthsandra exhibited skill and finesse, and soon three animals were ready to be put on leading reins.

Setting off was more difficult, as the horses were inclined to buck or stall, getting in the way of each other, or in the path of the following string. In the end, Borin called a halt.

'We shall camp here for another day, sort out who is taking which horses and arrange an order of passage, so we know who we are following. Let us have a break now, then we will have a practice this afternoon.'

It was decided to let Borin lead, and Jerain was to come last, but in front of the muleteers and their well-behaved animals.

The horses recovered from the thieves were the most badly-behaved. They were willing to nip, kick, or rear, as soon as anyone approached them, obviously they had no trust in humans. At one point, Borin considered letting them go, then decided on stringing them out at the rear of the lines, and this worked better, as there was no one near for them to kick.

Merthsandra enjoyed watching the scenery as they passed. There were farmsteads, surrounded with crops, and some had fields with animals out to graze. She admired pretty cottages at the roadside, and wondered what it would be like to live in one place all the time, behind stone walls.

Many of the inhabitants came to their doors to watch the horses go by.

Reaching a crossroads they turned west towards the cliffs approaching Dishnigar. The horses clattered through the stony pass. Suddenly, the city was spread before them, the road dropping down steeply. Beyond the city was the sea, boats bobbed in the harbour, and a big galley could be seen, heading for the shore with oars dipping in automatic unison, sweeping the waves.

Merthsandra had never seen so many buildings all in one place, and the sea was something she had never been able to imagine. Sitting on Thunder, holding her leading reins firmly, she turned and hailed Jerain who was following her.

'Is all that water drinkable?'

'No, silly. Sea water is salty!'

'What is its purpose, then?'

He gave her a grin. 'Home for the sea creatures, I suppose.'

Borin started to lead them down the track, going slowly so his string of horses was able to keep footing on the gravel road. Merthsandra counted to 30 before she followed him, and then the riders behind her began their counts. Some horses slipped and staggered on the way down, but none fell, and the strings reached the bottom of the incline with little incident.

Going slowly, Jerain watched the mules plodding along behind him. They were sure-footed, but looked tired, although their packs were lighter now the journey was nearly over. He promised himself he would find a good spot for them and some fine substantial food.

He knew the horses would be well taken care of, as they were the purpose of the trip. They were in good condition, having been well fed on their journey and having been examined every evening for strains or hoof problems. *They should bring a good price*, he thought. He would be able to tell Merth and Andreas the news he had succeeded in his task, as well as Andreas would have done himself.

Entering the Tops gave them a view of the fine houses situated at the summit of the cliffs. They had imposing gates and long drives, with trees planted around the varied structures of their estates.

Each homestead was different, but all were imposing, their grandeur displaying the affluence of their owners. Merthsandra could not make up her mind whether she would like to live in such opulence, or whether she would prefer the freedom of the plains.

The road was still steep with many turns and corners. However, when one large corner had been passed, the shingly surface gave way to a cobbled path, and the incline lessened.

Here, the houses were smaller and closer together, the roofs thatched or shingled, and the houses shabbier with only mullioned panes for windows.

The horses attracted attention here as their passing was amplified by the clatter they made on the cobbles, in the enclosed space. More and more people appeared in the streets. Some came out to stare and pass comment while others were going about their daily business.

Often, the horses had to pause as a laden cart, or carriage came towards them, or a big dray blocked the way in front of them. Dogs came barking, yapping at their heels, while small bare-footed children ran alongside, waving sticks and hallooing.

All of this activity made the half wild horses nervous, and many of the riders had trouble with their strings. Of course, Merthsandra, showing superb horsemanship, had her bunch well under control.

Borin led the way to the Horse Square, which luckily was not too far away once they had entered the Flats. When the mules had joined them in the centre of the square, Borin dismounted and handed his reins to Jerain.

'Look after these for me, would you? I'll go and find the Horse Master, or whoever is in charge here.'

He did not have to go far, as the Horse Master was standing outside his office, waiting to talk to whoever had brought such fine animals into the square. He was a large man with grey hair, who held out his hand as Borin approached.

'Good day to you. I suppose these are from Strevia. Where is Andreas, he must have something to do with these beauties?'

'Good day Master Ennett. I am Andreas's son, Borin. We have met before when I was younger. Andreas has had an accident, so it has come to me to bring the string. Can we stable them?'

Master Ennett waved them to the right of the square.

'There should be enough stalls over there. When you have done, let me know the numbers you have filled, and which are for sale. Then Jon, here, can go and put a ticket on the stalls, so we will know which ones buyers may look at. We wouldn't want yon stallion sold, now would we?'

Borin shook his head in agreement. He thanked the Horse Master for his consideration before returning to where the others were waiting. He led the way into the long, cool building, which held stalls down either side of the entire length of the stable.

Borin went down the full length before he started putting his string into the stalls, so there was room for the rest to follow him in. There were other entrances to the building, and at the far end, a ramp, beside a set of stairs, led up to where straw and fodder were kept.

Way above, a fenced walk had been built so prospective buyers could survey the horses from different angles, rather than just over the stall door.

Ventilation and light came from shuttered windows in the roof. Ostlers and stableboys were assigned to the stalls, and the whole building had an atmosphere of quiet, pleasant efficiency.

The stalls were all clean and ready for occupancy, with good fodder in the mangers, buckets of water, and clean straw underfoot.

'This is worthwhile, isn't it?' Jerain commented, as he unfastened his string, preparatory to entering them into their stalls.

'I hope we can find somewhere as suitable,' Borin returned, rubbing down his first charge.

'I want a bath and a comfortable bed,' Merthsandra came to join them. 'Do you know where to go?'

'There is a hostelry called *The Endless Tankard* down by the harbour. It is pretty rough, but the beds are clean and the food is good. Shall we try there first?

If it is full I'm sure there are other places, but they will probably be more expensive.' Jerain shrugged his shoulders, meaning you decide.

It took most of the afternoon to get the horses watered and groomed. The stable staff were willing to help but each rider preferred to supervise the well-being of the animals in his, or her, charge. Jerain made sure the muleteers had a corner in a barn nearby, where they and their mules could be comfortable.

The muleteers were given the charge of the packs and the harnesses, as they were staying with their animals. Some of the riders promised to relieve them for a couple of hours so the muleteers could have a beer and look at the Flats and the harbour area.

It was getting dark when they finally left the Horse Square, and set off for the harbour.

Merthsandra slid her hand into Jerain's as they walked along the cobbled street.

'I need to hold on to you,' she said, smiling up at him, 'my boots keep sliding on these funny stones.' He looked at her smiling at him, and saw the gleam in her eye.

'Borin might look back,' he whispered softly while squeezing her hand.

'He is not my keeper,' she retorted, dropping Jerain's hand while snuggling up under his arm. He pushed her away gently.

'No, but he is my brother-in-law,' he reminded her.

She tossed her head, the yellow hair flying loose around her shoulders, then turned and joined the riders following behind. She soon had them all in fits of laughter, and in the end, Josh, one of the bigger riders, ended up by giving her a lift on his back.

The harbour came into sight at the end of the road. They stood at the edge of the quay and looked down into the water's gloomy depths. The shadows of the houses behind them, made the water look darker than it really was.

Boats bumped against the bollards as the water surged back and forth, gulls screamed as they swung passed, gliding on the evening breeze in search of their last meal before nesting time.

Someone was playing a pipe on one of the merchant ships anchored further out in the bay and the sound was amplified as it drifted across the water with a melancholy cadence. Jerain shivered in the cool wind, while looking at the various crafts moored in front of him.

The smells of the harbour were astringent; unused to such on the open plain, he found them unsettling. He wondered what it would be like to live one's life on the sea at the mercy of wind and wave. He kicked a small stone into the water, then stood watching the ripples it had made, as they slowly expanded into circles.

Life is like that, he thought, *one thing leads to another, and who knows what will happen tomorrow?*

Turning away from the water, with its melancholy mood, he followed the others slowly, watching Merthsandra, who was still teasing the riders. She was playing a game of follow my lead, running along the edge of the harbour, and then jumping in and out of boats, making them bump and rock.

She followed that by throwing stones in the water; while her golden head flamed, as she tossed it in the gleams of the dying sun. Her laughter, as she watched the riders slip and slither, pealed around the harbour, echoing across the water.

Jerain caught up with them as they were entering *The Endless Tankard*. The inn was much bigger than he had expected.

The owner of the hostelry, whose name was Stu Bard, was a portly, darkly, handsome man, with a green baize apron wrapped around his middle. He was polishing the bar when they entered, and looked up with a smile.

Putting his cloth away, he picked up some tankards.

'Welcome to the inn. Is it rooms you are wanting, or just a drink and a meal?'

'The lot!' Borin answered. 'A drink first, and then we will wash up before we have a meal.'

'Is it possible to have a bath?' Merthsandra pushed to the front of the riders, then gave the inn keeper a winning smile.

'Of course, my lady, a bath it shall be.' He turned to the kitchen door. 'Doll!' he called. 'Get the potboy to fill the baths in the wash house, please. Hot water, if we have some.'

His daughter appeared around the kitchen door, her cheery face red with effort. She nodded at Merthsandra. 'You are lucky,' she said. 'I have just heated the water up. Joe is filling the baths now. Come with me.'

Merthsandra and the two female riders followed Doll's bobbing brown ringlets as she led the way around the back through the kitchen.

'We might as well sit down and have a few drinks,' Jerain grumbled. 'She'll take forever in that wash house, prinking and prissing. Will you have enough rooms for all of us?' he asked, turning to the landlord.

'There are rooms upstairs for those who must have them,' returned Stu. 'We also have a bunkroom out the back. It is cheaper by far, and has more comfort there, for men who are used to living as they wish.'

It was settled, then and there. Borin and Jerain would share; Merthsandra would have a closet of her own, while the married riders would have their own quarters, with everyone else in the bunkhouse.

Stu slid frothing tankards of dark brown ale along the bar for Dolly to collect and deliver to the waiting riders who were seated around a big, plank table in the centre of the room.

Soon the plainsmen were happily-relaxed, chatting to each other about the journey though there were also many quiet moments as they remembered the untimely death of Ben, who had been a favourite with everyone who had met him.

Before they retired to bed, Borin wandered over to stand beside the bar. He was looking lean and fit, attractive in his boots and riding gear, with his auburn hair glinting in the candlelight. Now it was washed and waving again, he attracted Dolly's attention.

She came over to ask him if there was something he needed, her lissom body attracting many an appreciative glance from the watching riders and from the other occupants of the bar. Borin smiled at her, then ordered another tankard. As he slid the coins towards her when he received his beer, he asked her a question.

'Are most people employed around here?'

She glanced at the throng of people in the bar and nodded.

'Yes, these are fisherfolk and local craftsmen. Why do you ask?'

'I lost a rider on our way here. We were ambushed over night. I was thinking that with a man short I shall be stretched in the spring, what with foaling and bigger herds. I was hoping to hire someone.'

'You won't get city boys to want to go out on the plains, I'm afraid. Someone who is not used to horses wouldn't be much use to you, anyway. Why don't you try at the Slave Market? There won't be an auction for another month, though.

'There are a few men there at the moment. Most are old codgers or layabouts, but I heard there was one young man there who had tried to escape. He is scarred from being beaten, but is strong and fit now.'

'That is a good idea. I'll go down and talk to the slave master in the morning. I wonder how much he wants for him?'

'Not much,' Dolly replied, 'I should think they will be glad to get rid of him, the nuisance he has been making.'

'Well, at least it sounds as if he is active,' Borin replied. 'There is nowhere to run to out on the plains.' He gave Dolly an extra coin, then returned to the riders, well-pleased with the conversation.

Chapter Eleven

Andreas sat in the sunshine, watching Merth groom Sythe. The stallion's coat glistened like silver, shining under the ministrations of the last soft brush, which was covered by a silk cloth.

Merth had to stand on a box to reach up around the back of Sythe's ears, though most of the time he dropped his head to suffer the blandishment of her caresses.

Andreas flexed his knee, which was still stiff and painful, but now, at last, it did allow him to move around. *Young Patras has done a good job*, he mused. Merth had been a hard taskmaster, insisting on him following Patras's advice, yet it had all been worthwhile. Soon he would be back riding again, and in charge of his life.

Merth gave Sythe a final pat, and with a whicker, he trotted off towards the other horses gathered near the yurt, lifting his feet with precision. Gathering up her cleaning tackle, then dropping it into the box she had been standing on, Merth brought it over to where Andreas was sitting.

'You're not going to curry me, are you?'

She smiled at her father, and he noticed she was looking a trifle pale, and there were dark circles under her eyes.

'Aren't you well, girl?'

'Just restless and uneasy. Your grandchild makes life difficult. I'm thinking of going to the mountains for a day or two. Perhaps the seeress can give me some advice.' She glanced at Andreas to see what effect this announcement would have on him.

'Well,' he replied, 'your mother used to go there on occasion. When she returned, she always seemed to be calmer and happier. How about asking Patras? Couldn't he give you a potion?'

'Patras is lovely, and he has aided me in many ways, but this is more of a spiritual trouble, rather than physical. I think the seeress will be more helpful.'

'Well then, you must leave. When will you go? It is a fair distance to the mountains in the east.'

'I intend to go tomorrow. I shall leave early in the morning and I shall take one of the riders with me. He can look after the horses while I am in the cave.'

Andreas nodded. 'Take Rolf with you. He knows the way and he can always be trusted and relied upon. He can make camp and have a meal ready for you, when your visit is over.

'Take the dogs. I won't worry so much about you if you have Rolf, that devil Sythe, and Boris and Borland. Redd will look after things here, and Patras, no doubt, will fuss over me like a broody hen!'

She patted his arm, then rose to go to help with the evening meal. 'Thank you, father for being understanding.'

He continued to sit in the late sunshine after she had gone inside. He knew what was troubling her. It could only be about Merthsandra and Jerain; worry about the coming baby; and apprehension about what she would do once her fears were realised.

He hoped the seeress could help put her distress at rest, but doubted it. Karma would not, no matter how many incantations were said, or to which Goddess was prayed.

He wished his wife were still in the world as she would have known what to do with these recalcitrant daughters. Jerain was weak as far as Merthsandra was concerned; he would be like soft leather in her hands, in time.

His thoughts shifted to Merth's coming trip. Rolf was a sensible, older man. He was quiet, thought deeply, and was not prone to taking rash chances. He would protect Merth from bandits and wandering wolf packs. With the help of the fighting stallion and the two big dogs, The Totem might as well have a posse of a dozen armed guards.

Merth and Rolf were ready to begin their trek early in the misty morning. Merth had spent the previous evening readying supplies, and deciding what to take on the packhorse, which Rolf would lead.

He had readily agreed to escort her, and was quite looking forward to doing something different from every day herding. She had appreciated his eagerness and his enthusiastic smile, as the trip she was intending could have been with someone surly, which would have increased her tension, high enough as it was.

With the dogs bounding around them and the packhorse on a leading rein held by Rolf, they trotted away from the yurt towards the distant mountain range.

The air was full of the smell of the grasses, as the horses were trampling them under their hooves. Larks were singing high in the sky, too far above for Merth to see them. In the distance she could hear the occasional bark of a fox, busy about its daily business.

Merth was wearing her green outfit with her big jacket. She had also added a snug leather hat, which controlled her hair, as she had left it loose, mainly to keep her ears warm.

Rolf was attired in his usual riding gear of leather jerkin and pants. His horse, named Star, was a big chestnut mare, with a white patch on her forehead. She was quite happy to follow Sythe as he forged ahead. A good-natured animal, she whickered encouragement to the gelding, Flit, who was carrying their belongings as he trotted behind.

They made good progress over the open plain. The day was breezy, though sunny, and cool enough to allow pleasant riding. They stopped by streams a couple of times during the journey, giving the horses a well earned rest, while they had something to eat, and were able to stretch their legs.

The dogs instantly found shade under small, sheltering trees growing on the banks of the rivulets. There had been little stirring amongst the grasses; they had disturbed a fox during the afternoon and had seen an occasional rabbit, but there had been no sign of coyote, or the wolf packs they had dreaded meeting.

As evening drew near, they were approaching the foothills of the mountains. Entering the trees, the air instantly felt cooler.

Leading the way, Merth set Sythe on a forest track, which would wind towards the dwelling of the seeress. Her heart started to beat faster as her anxiety grew.

Would the seeress welcome her and give her advice, or would she have to turn back without a seeing? No one could be sure whether the seeress would deign to cast the stones – She was a fickle lady, who made her own decisions.

They came to a fork in the path, and Merth took the one to the left, knowing the one to the right led to the small village where the priestesses lived. She wondered if they were at home, or off somewhere doing riffs for some clan leader. She ran her hand over the wolf on her stomach, gaining a feeling of comfort and strength from the essence of her mother's totem.

They came to a turn in the path, and beside it was a dell, a little lower than the roadway. There was soft grass growing there, as the trees had not encroached onto this particular spot.

'A good place to camp,' Rolf declared, trotting down into the glen. 'You see to the horses, and I will get a fire going. Look, someone has made a fire pit already. This must be a place where travellers often stop.'

Merth wondered where travellers would be going on this deserted road. She decided the seeress would have a stream of visitors, not just her.

She attended to the packhorse first, as he needed to lose his load, and the things he was carrying would be wanted through the night. Flit gave himself a shake, then trotted off to have a roll in the soft grass, before he allowed himself to be picketed out.

Merth gave him a quick rub down, then found the packet of oats he had been carrying. Rolf had got the fire going and had gone to a nearby stream for water while she attended to Star and Sythe. Sythe had his nose in the oats as soon as his bridle was off, and she had to push him away to save some for Star, and Flit.

She arranged the bedrolls at the side of the fire with their backs to the wind, then saw to feeding the dogs, who had been roaming and investigating every ditch and tree trunk.

They were in their bedrolls early, the fire had died down to embers, but they were snug and warm. Boris was at Merth's back, while Borland was curled up in front of her.

Rolf complained about unfair advantages, but although she agreed, with the dogs fidgeting, scratching and sniffling, the extra warmth was not worth the disturbed sleep. During the night there was some baying in the forest leading to both dogs sitting up, ears pricked, growling quietly, and on alert. However, whatever it was soon moved away leaving them in peace.

In the early morning Merth rose, and after a trip to the stream, had the fire going again with water heating for an early breakfast.

'What happens today?' Rolf inquired, leaning on an elbow, sipping his drink.

'I shall go to see the seeress. You can do a bit of fishing down in the stream. The dogs will guard the camp.

I shall be back by nightfall, I should think.'

'Don't you want me to come with you?'

'No. I shall be all right on my own with Sythe. You get us some fresh fish.'

She dearly wanted to be on her own, as she wanted to arrange her thoughts before she met the seeress. She had only taken Rolf with her, because Andreas had insisted she do so. It was not that she disliked him, only that he intruded on her thoughts by his presence.

Sythe was quite willing to be on the move again. The dogs wanted to come with her, but were firmly told to stay with Rolf and guard the camp.

The trail wound steeply up the mountainside, with the trees close together, crowding in to the narrow path. The day was cold and mist drifted through the heavy boughs, soon her clothes were sodden, from water falling off the overhanging branches.

The path was stony now, and had deep ruts, often crossed with runnels from smaller streams. Towards mid-afternoon she had to dismount and lead Sythe as the incline was so steep, then when the path entered a narrow ravine she had to picket and leave him.

The sides of the ravine closed in, holding the pathway in a crack of confined space of misty gloom. Shivering, she stepped through the water, which had now become a slippery torrent. As she lifted her head to look ahead, she saw the seeress' cave.

The entrance was covered with a hide, but faint light could be seen glistening at the sides. Crunching on the pebbles, Merth finally reached the opening. She was looking for some way to announce her presence, when a skinny hand shot out of the side of the hide and grasped her wrist.

'Come in, Merth,' a croaky voice uttered, almost in her ear. 'I have been expecting you for some days now.'

Merth started with surprise, then peered at the seeress, who was ushering her into the warm cave. It was lit with wall sconces, which flickered and jumped from the draught coming through the doorway. Around the roomy area there were braziers against the walls, well placed away from anything flammable, while in the centre there was a hearthstone.

The seeress had little, apart from a bed, a table and a couple of rickety chairs, but the floor had been covered with soft hides and rugs. The resin in the hearth spluttered and crackled, but also gave out a tangy aroma, and the atmosphere in the cave was clean and pleasant.

Merth sank into one of the chairs with a sigh of relief, and looked at her hostess who was standing by the table.

She was much younger than Merth had expected, in early middle-age, with an oval face, surrounded with dark, curly hair. She wore a heavy, dark green skirt and vest, with a brown leather jacket pulled on top. She was wearing felt slippers, but solid boots were placed neatly by the cave entrance.

'You've come for a reading, then, young Merth? What can I tell The Totem of the Horse Lords?' The seeress looked at her quizzically, a slight smile lifting the corners of her thin lips.

Merth folded her hands together in her lap, composing herself to confide her feelings and fears.

'My questions are of the future,' she said quietly. 'The honour of The Totem is the honour of The Horse Lords. I must be prepared for circumstances, which will affect me, but are not yet conceived.'

The seeress pulled a shallow, silver tray towards her. From a pewter jug she poured a viscous, dark liquid into the dish. She waited for the substance to settle. It seethed about in turmoil, as if it were quicksilver, then settled to lie flat and still. Murmuring an invocation, she bent over and gazed at the black surface of the dish.

Merth stayed where she was, sitting quietly in the chair. The seeress stood staring at the black, glassy surface for an inordinate length of time. Merth listened to the fire crackling, and heard sleepy birds croaking as they made ready for bed. Finally, the seeress gave a sigh, and lifted her head.

'You are not only the Totem, my dear, you are a nexus, holding the threads of many lives. Yes, your sister, Merthsandra will betray you, but in the end, her fickle behaviour might change. Much is happening in the country, and the paths of many strangers lead to you.

'You are worried about the success of the trip to Dishnigar – they will return with good news. Be strong in spirit and have a giving heart, this will bring you good friends and peace in times of need.'

'My child?' Merth queried, her eyes liquid with anxiety.

'Will be a daughter, as strong and as healthy as you would wish.' The seeress moved from the table and sat in the chair beside the open fire. Swinging a kettle over the leaping flames she began to prepare a tisane, selecting her leaves carefully from a bundle by her side.

'We shall have a cup of heart's desire, and then you can gossip with me, now the hard work is over.'

As Merth was leaving a short while later, the seeress grasped her hand in her two skinny ones.

'One word, my dear, before you leave. Look for blond hair and blue eyes, tall, well featured, and so regal.'

'That will be difficult,' Merth returned. 'There are none such out on the plains.' Yet in her mind she could see him, a vision from her dreaming.

Sythe was pleased to hear her returning footsteps. He pulled at his picket and made a little hurumph noise, blowing in her ear. They picked their way carefully in the gloom, and made the return journey much more quickly than they had come.

Rolf had a fine fire going, and there was fresh trout simmering in a pan over the burning cinders. Boris and Borland bounded up, giving Sythe annoyance as they rushed and jumped around him.

Soon they were all settled near the fire, enjoying their evening meal. Rolf related how he had caught his fish, and then asked Merth how she had fared. She told him she had learned little, as the priestess had been ambivalent in her seeing, but it had all seemed to be positive, though she had learnt nothing definite, except that the horses seemed to fetch a good price.

Next morning, as the early morning sunlight was sweeping across the plains in front of them, they trotted out of the trees. Delighted to be returning home from her mission, Merth luxuriated in the sun streaming on her body.

The late summer grasses, thick with grains were interspersed with bright red poppies, nodding their heads in the early morning breeze. The ground was firm and dry, making the hooves of the horses raise little clouds of dust, which increased in size as the day wore on.

Shading her eyes, Merth noticed a group of travellers far ahead. She had become aware of them because of the large cloud of dust hovering behind them as they travelled in their view, over the grasses.

'It looks as if one of them is lagging behind,' Rolf remarked. The single individual could now be plainly seen, outlined on a grassy knoll, as the rest of his party disappeared, over the skyline.

Slowly Rolf and Merth gained on the lone individual.

As they approached, they could see the reason for his laggardness; his horse was lame.

On reaching him, Merth called out.

'Good traveller, you seem to have a problem. Where are you heading?'

The rider had stopped. He turned in the saddle to survey them as they trotted towards him. He looked at them warily, with his hand hovering over his knife hilt, ready to draw in defence if need be. His bay horse was standing, head down, with its left forefoot held off the ground.

Rolf slid off Star, then attached Flit's leading rein to the pommel of his saddle; when he was sure Star knew to stand, he walked through the grasses to the other man.

'No need to be so wary, we are just travellers like yourself. Perhaps we can help.'

The rider finally cracked a sour smile, then slid off the bay to greet the others. He was tall, with dark skin and eyes, and the smile showed flashing white teeth. Dressed appropriately for the plains, with good boots and buckskin trousers, he had wrapped a thick cloth around his head and upper torso. His knife was an unusual curved shape, and he had it stuck through a dark green sash tied around his waist.

'Greetings.' He bent at the waist in a perfunctory bow. 'As you can see, I am soon to be stranded in this demon destroyed desert!'

'Oh, come now!' Merth expostulated, 'the open plains should not be so maligned. Granted there are no dwellings, and not much visible game to the untrained eye, but it is home to us. Who are you and where are you trying to go?'

'I am Rahadir Dun, a companion of Prince Drun from Jaddanna. We are an entourage on a mission to contact the accursed Horse Lord.

'We have been travelling across this land for days since we left Orphur. The horses we hired are not fit to travel so far, as you can see!'

He indicated his own animal, which was still standing in the same position.

'We are not sure where this leader of the horse clans lives, but have been following directions we received in Orphur. I wish I had stayed there. I have no interest in this desolate place, or its savage lord. I feel no good will come of this.'

'Who is your leader again, and what is your mission?'

Merth could hardly grind the words out, while trying to appear pleasant.

'The leader of our party is The High Prince from Jaddanna. His father, Jara ben Jada, may he live forever, is the high lord of Jaddanna. We wish to ask grazing, to the north, for our cattle, as they are dying from the drought.

'The barbarian Horse Lady must be wooed to allow this, if she has any wit or honour. I suppose she can barely rub sticks together to make fire, let alone treat with a civilised nation.'

'Is that so?' Merth questioned, kicking Rolf in the back of his knee, as the Jaddannese turned to look at his horse.

'Well, Rahadir, we had better have a look at that hoof.' Rolf raised his hands, palms up at his sides, while giving Merth an ironic grin. He moved to the bay and lifted the painful hoof.

As soon as he saw the trouble, he made a sharp sound of dismay. There was a small sharp stone wedged in the quick.

'There, there, girl, we'll soon have this feeling better.' Soothing and gentling the mare, he quickly extricated the stone with the point of his knife.

Returning to his saddlebag, he found a pot of soothing cream, which healed and also had a dulling effect. Merth had asked Patras to make this cream using leaves she found on the plains, from a recipe of her mother's, and all the riders had a pot.

After filling the hoof with the medicament, Rolf bound it tight with some twine, having placed a light covering of leather to make a sturdy pad to protect the painful area. The mare was given a drink, and soon was munching happily on a carrot, Merth had found in her pack.

Determinedly, Merth started unloading what was left of the equipment Flit was carrying, mainly bedding, now.

Turning to the Jaddannese, she said, 'You can ride our packhorse, and we will put our gear on your mare. It won't be such a trial for her on her sore leg.'

He looked at her imperiously, with a frown on his face. 'I will not ride that inferior animal. Riding this mare was bad enough. It was because I was late for the muster when we chose our animals. Now I will ride that handsome grey. You can ride the packhorse, woman!'

Rolf rose from his knees by the bedrolls where he was sorting them, ready to lighten the load for the mare. Before he intervened, Merth signalled to him to be quiet.

'Well, my lord, if that is your wish,' she agreed, a small flicker of amusement in her brown eyes.

Rahadir strode towards Sythe and put a hand out to grab his reins. Sythe erupted in a blur of motion. Teeth snapping, eyes rolling, he reared, bringing his flailing hooves down a finger's length away from Rahadir, while letting out a whinny of outrage. Wheeling, he wandered away, out of reach.

Rahadir, who had staggered back out of the way, tripped over a tussock and sat down with a bump, glaring at Sythe, who was now peacefully cropping grass.

'That hellion needs his spirit broken. I'll buy him off you. How many silvos? I'll train him with whip and knife!'

'He is not for sale, and you will keep away from him. You ride the packhorse, or we will leave you out here on the plains, taking the mare with us.' Merth was not playing games; her dark eyes met his in a fiery glare.

After he had acquiesced, with ill grace, they set off at a slow pace, giving the injured mare opportunity for rests, every now and then.

Rolf berated Rahadir for having ridden her with such an injury. He replied in anger, that in his country, horses were looked after by servants, and there was always an extra one, in case there was a difficulty. He knew nothing about the well-being of such creatures.

'Ignorance and barbarity, then?' Merth asked, looking at him askance, and that was the end of that conversation.

Borland and Boris chased around them, occasionally dashing away on the hunt for some small creature. Before they reached their home plains, Rolf had five rabbits and a partridge, cleaned and in his game bag.

Rahadir watched him working on the last rabbit.

'Why are you bothering doing that?' he asked impatiently. 'Shouldn't we be carrying on?'

'It is good food, and will be added to our meal when we reach the yurt. The dogs earn their keep, and give us good meat.'

'You don't expect me, or the Prince, for that matter, to eat something caught by a dog, do you?'

'If you don't want it, you can provide your own, or do without,' was the reply. Rolf put the last carcass in the bag, then mounted Star with a chuckle of amusement.

Soon the lights around the yurt could be seen in the gathering dusk. People were working outside, tethering horses; feeding chickens, catching goats, cleaning tackle.

Merth noticed a group of strange horses had been picketed away from the yurt. Riders belonging to the yurt were tending them; there were no sign of the people who had been riding them.

'I shall see to the horses, Rolf. You take our guest into the Horse Lord. Introduce him to Andreas, and make him welcome. I shall be inside shortly.' She waited for the men to dismount, then led the horses away to the stream.

When the animals were contented, Merth had a quick wash, slipped quietly into the yurt through a side entrance, and made her way to her sleeping quarters. There she changed into her amethyst clothes, donned the bracelets and the amethyst necklace inherited from her mother, then combed out her hair, which she decorated with strings of pearls, beads and feathers. Holding herself proudly, she pulled back the curtain and made a grand entrance.

The visitors were clustered around Andreas and did not notice her at first. The people of the Horse Clan recognised her demeanour, and quiet fell on the assembly. The visitors turned to find everyone with head bowed, noting their obeisance to the Horse Lady. Merth walked steadily across the yurt, reaching Andreas' side without acknowledging the presence of the newcomers.

'Greetings, Horse Lady,' Andreas smiled. 'I hope your journey was successful?'

'In some ways, father. Who are these people?'

'This is Prince Drun from Jaddanna, who has been sent on a mission to find us by his father, The Jada.'

Merth turned and cast her eye over the assembled group, finally lingering on Rahadir.

'This one, I have already met. Introduce your lord to me, Rahadir.'

'My Prince, this lady must be the Horse Lady, though I did not realise her importance when I met her on the plain.' His face was suffused with anger and embarrassment. 'My Lady, may I introduce Prince Drun from Jaddanna.'

Merth sat on the sheepskin. She raised her eyes and gave Drun a cool glance. 'You may make obeisance,' she informed him.

Dressed in black leathers, with his head covering secured by a band of opals, Drun looked the epitome of a northern prince. For a moment he seemed nonplussed, unused to being in the role of supplicant. Then, with a gesture of compliance, he sank to one knee before Merth, with head bowed.

'Horse Lady,' he murmured.

'You have permission to call me Merth. Come, sit beside me, Prince of Jaddanna,' she concurred. 'Be welcome in our yurt. Your journey must have been long and arduous. Bring refreshments for our guests,' she called.

Immediately, a line of waiting slaves came forward, bringing wash cloths and towels, glasses and wine, followed by others bearing sweetmeats and delicacies on silver salvers.

The companions and guards who accompanied the prince settled down on carpets laid beside where he was seated. Soon the yurt was filled with chatter, while food was prepared for the evening meal.

'We shall discuss our business after we have finished our meal,' Merth pronounced. 'Tell me about your country. I have heard many wondrous stories about the greatness of Jaddanna.'

For most of the evening, Drun regaled Merth and Andreas with stories about the desert land he lived in. He described the marble palace, the beggars, the colourful houses with their palm treed gardens, and with their water lilied pools in the centres of the houses.

'A charming city, no doubt,' Merth commented, as they completed their meal. Having rinsed her hands and dried them on a towel offered by a friend, she flicked her first fingernail with her thumbnail. Instantly she was flanked by Boris and Borland, who leant against her legs.

Merth made an impressive sight with her regalia, letting her hands rest on the hounds' heads; the snakes writhing down her forearms, finishing in striking heads on the backs of her hands to complete the picture.

'Now, Prince Drun, I think it is time for you to state your business.'

Drun shifted uneasily, remembering his father's words about being pleasant.

'We wish to bring our herds over the mountains to the plains above the Grey River. We plead you allow this, as our land is dry and the cattle are dying.'

'How do I know this will be only a temporary measure? Perhaps it is a ploy to gain territory.'

'Horse Lady, I assure you that will not happen. Our army and our herds will return to our lands when the drought has lifted.'

'Army?'

'Only for protection, and for helping the herders look after their animals safely.'

'When will this happen?'

'I'm afraid we are there already. We were in a parlous state, with the herds dying, so it had to be done quickly.'

'So, I have an army camped on our northern plains? You think I should accept that, without query?'

'I have brought some gifts,' Drun waved to his entourage to bring forward the heap of packages lying by the tent flap.

Merth made no comment as she watched the contents of the packages strewn before her. When the last parcel had been opened, she pushed the nearest garment with her boot.

'So you think these baubles will be sufficient recompense for a savage, barbarian woman?' She lifted her chin and gazed over his head.

Feeling the tension in her legs and alerted by the tone of her voice, Borin and Borland emitted low growls. Borland threw in a snarl as well. Drun moved back from the glittering teeth, so close to his knee.

'These are only gifts, my lady. My father   is willing to stand by any agreement we make, to ensure a peaceful treaty. My mission is to make sure you understand why we had to move early, and to respectfully ask your permission to stay until the drought has broken.'

'You may retire now. Arrangements have been made for you in a separate tent, to the right side of the yurt, down by the stream. I shall discuss this proposal with my father and my brother. You may come and speak with me again, in the morning.'

At that moment Redd entered the main tent flap. He had been with Patras, tending the mare with the damaged hoof.

'Merth,' he called, 'what idiot rode that mare so far with a stone in her hoof?'

'An ignorant one,' Merth replied, giving Rahadir a grin without humour, where he stood beside Drun.

Drun noticed the family resemblance between Merth and Redd. 'Is this the young Horse Lord?' he queried, hoping for more sense from a man, 'or is it your father?'

'I am the Horse Lord of all the plains, including what lies beyond the Grey River,' Merth stated, categorically. She rose and swept away, followed by her hounds, leaving the Jaddannese to make their own way to their tent.

Servants came to clear away the gifts, putting them carefully into leather boxes, for future distribution.

Later that evening, Merth, Redd, and Andreas gathered together to discuss the proposition. Andreas was astounded at the arrogance, which had enabled the northern people to enter their plains, without even informing them they were doing so. He was all for raising the clans to go and drive the strangers back over the mountains to where they belonged.

'That would not be politic,' Merth declared. 'They will be well established now, and have an army to defend them. It would be bloody slaughter and we would be the losers. What we should be doing is thinking about how we can put this to our advantage. What is it that would help us most?'

'I have an idea,' Redd contributed. 'Often when our dry season is upon us, we too have to search for lush grasses. They have an army at stand down, let us put it to work. How about putting canals along the northern plain, with irrigation ditches, so the land is watered from the river?'

Merth's eyes lit up with the thought.

'Of course, there must be some sort of pumping system which we can shut off when the ground becomes too wet, an excellent thought! Father, do you agree?'

Andreas muttered and grumbled, shifting his leg. It pained him in the evening, and he spent time sitting in his chair rather than going to bed, where he was more aware of the aching joint.

'It would be an advantage to have all year grazing where we wanted to be, rather than having to move all the time,' he finally admitted. 'How do we know the agreement will be substantiated?'

'Easily,' Redd put in. 'We shall keep Drun and Rahadir here as hostages, and then they can find out how barbaric we can be. Then when the work is completed, we will allow them to return.'

Merth thought this was a great scheme and clapped her hands to compliment him. Redd blushed to the roots of his hair with pleasure. Merth was rarely overt with her enthusiasm about anything.

'You will speak with them in the morning?' Andreas was impressed with the idea and wanted to implement it immediately. He was already picturing fields of waving grass in the dry season.

'In the late afternoon,' Merth stated. 'They can make their arrangements before the pigeons fly. We will keep them in suspense for a few hours.'

Next day Merth sat in full regalia, with the amethyst skirt spread over the sheepskin rug. She had her hands on her knees, displaying her snakes, attracting glancing eyes, from all about her.

When the Jaddannese entourage entered, Prince Drun came towards her, followed by Rahadir, while the rest of the party stayed a few strides away.

'Greetings, Horse Lady. Have you reached a decision?' Drun nodded his head in a perfunctory manner, showing impatience, added to the annoyance of having been kept waiting.

'Good riding, Prince Drun,' Merth tapped her whip, which she never used, on the side of her highly polished boot.

'Do sit down, as this is likely to take some time.' She indicated the carpets to the side of the sheepskin bench. Showing ill grace, Drun finally sank down in his allotted space.

Merth started the conversation by outlining what had already happened, and then continued by explaining how the Jaddannese could make reparation, by irrigating both sides of the plains, to the advantage of both peoples.

'Of course,' she continued, 'we must have some surety that this will be done.

'Therefore I propose that Rahadir and yourself, stay here with us, while your soldiers and your companions repair to Jaddanna, to ask The Jada for this to be implemented.

'When the work is completed we shall take you back to Jaddanna, inspecting the progress of the irrigation on the way.'

Speechless, Rahadir looked up in horror.

Drun was not so tongue-tied. 'This cannot be! The work will take months, if not years! I can't be incarcerated in this wilderness for all that time.' He jumped to his feet, beckoning his soldiers. 'We will leave now!'

Merth smiled sweetly, as she rang a small bronze bell by her side. Immediately, riders and Horse Lords surged into the yurt. Within moments the visiting party was surrounded with armed tribesmen arrayed around the walls.

'I don't think so,' Merth remarked. 'Instruct your fellows to pack and leave. The sooner they leave the quicker the work will be started, and your days with us will be less. Accommodation has been made here for you, in the yurt.

Discuss this with your nobles.' To that end Drun and Rahadir rejoined the group.

A young man, small in stature, with high cheekbones and oval eyes approached Drun. 'Speak, Chun the healer.'

'My Prince, I might be able to improve this mess we are in. I come from the city to the west. It is where my family live, in the seaport of Keshia.

'Would you allow us to travel there, rather than returning to Orphur? I feel sure we would be able to hire a fast dhow from there, and be able to make our way up the coast to Jaddanna more expedite.'

'Do that! Drun agreed. 'In fact, my father has given permission for you to go there, so it will be excellent for all our party to go. The sooner you leave and the message delivered, the less time Rahadir and I will have to stay here.'

Merth smiled, still tapping her boot, amused at their discomfiture.

'We shall have to entertain you, my lords. Perhaps some hunting and fishing?

'You could learn how to make our barbarian floor coverings? Who knows? You might like our lifestyle in the end.'

Chapter Twelve

The galley edged along the coastline, nudging into rocky coves, slipping quietly through the water as the waves slapped against the sun drenched shores.

The two men doing soundings were constantly busy, the only murmur being their repeated calling of the water's depths. Those up in the rigging added their comments, when they spotted rocks hidden under the rolling waves.

The search along the coast was getting monotonous. Lex desired action. His impatience was mounting, fed with his vivid imagination as to what might be happening to Troy.

Joseph was grumpy. He wanted to take charge of the ship, and resented being foiled by the captain, who was suave, courteous and adamant. He spent hours in the chart room, laboriously studying the Southern Ocean.

Lex was involved with the charts and was studying the coastline carefully. He had decided to leave the sailing to the sailors.

Rounding a headland they noticed a narrow fissure in the cliff. The lookout's attention had been drawn to it by a flock of sea birds diving for fish in the entrance.

The captain was all for carrying on, but Lex insisted they investigate. Grumbling, the captain, still thinking it was a waste of time, set the galley on course for the inlet. Jack Smart then flagged a message to the other galley to wait at the mouth of the opening.

The deep fissure ran straight for some 100 yards, then turned sharply to the left. A small hamlet of patched up huts came into view on the coastline, and anchored in the middle of the inlet was their ship, which had been captured.

'Isn't that *The Lady*?' Lex asked the captain.

'By Mut it is! I wonder what she is doing here.'

As the galley approached the shore some ragged figures came from the ramshackle huts, crowding down to the water line and raising a faint cheer.

After some manoeuvring, the galley was grounded on the sandy beach, and Lex, with a few of the crew, descended to wade through the water to talk to the stranded seamen.

When the initial welcomes were over, their story came out. The crew had been taken to Kordova by the buccaneers, and had then set off with a pirate crew aboard, to go to Dishnigar, following the black ship. However, they had been intercepted by a cutter, which obviously brought news not to the pirates' liking.

The Lady had been bundled into this cove with no escape for the men, as the escarpments were too steep to climb. The sails had been taken from the ship, and its crew had been abandoned by the pirates.

After the pirates had stripped the ship of anything of value, they had transferred to *The Dark Mistress*.

Returning to the galley, Lex held conference with the captain and the first mate. After a lengthy discussion, they decided to take the sailing ship with them, when they had outfitted it from their own stores.

That evening they had a big bonfire on the beach, and the captain broke out some rum. They spent a joyful evening, as the survivors were delighted they were to be rescued. There was a stream in the cove, but their diet had been seaweed, shellfish, and any fish they had been able to catch.

It took a couple of days to outfit the ship, and then the small fleet set sail. This time they were heading for Dishnigar, not knowing whether Troy had been taken there.

'Why do you think the pirates were in such a hurry to leave?' Lex asked the appointed leader of the survivors, a grizzled seaman with gold earrings and gapped teeth.

He sucked his teeth then spat on the sandy shore, carefully avoiding Lex's boots.

'Yon Petric was taken up with his new whore. They had heard the Devron navy was coming for them, and he didn't want to lose his booty, or his beauty, is what I surmise. He was mighty quick to get rid of us, as we were holding him up. He wanted to get out of these waters as quick as he could. Fair sotted with the woman he was.'

'What was she like?' Lex asked idly.

'You must know her, the flirty, buxom, dark woman, with the big breasts and the flashing eyes. She was on the ship when we sailed from Devron.'

'The ambassador's wife?' Lex was astonished.

'Aye, that's the one. He got the ransom and all was going well, when blow me down, if he didn't turn around, leaving us to wait for him, and off he goes to the south of the island to pick her up. They had made an assignation and she was there waiting for him. Fair smitten with the dashing pirate, she was.'

'Wonders never cease to astound me! A fair stir that must have made in Kordova!' Lex was chuckling, thinking about how carefully Delia had been guarded. Perhaps there was more reason for it, than had appeared.

'Well, it looks as if Petric has got away to set up house with his floosy. We will continue with our original plan, our task is to find Ambry, Troy and Dishnigar. Prepare to sail!' Smart smothered a giggle.

With much screeching of halyards and flapping of the huge sail, *The Lady* set off, with *The Aurora* coming behind.

For all its bad treatment the sailing ship was sound, and easily kept up with the galleys, as there was a favourable wind. Lex watched her blustering through the billows, still looking smart for all her ills.

'I wonder what possessed him to abandon such a prize? She would be a fine adage for any pirate fleet.'

'Perhaps he has just left her here in safe keeping, intending to pick her up on his return journey?'

'That will be the price of it. Keep a weather eye for a strange galley, Lookout!'

'Aye, aye, Sir.'

They rounded the headland and were soon in deeper waters. With a following wind they sped across the ocean. Although they travelled at speed, there was no sign of any other vessel until they saw a faint line of land on the horizon to the east. Then fishing vessels could be seen near the coast.

'Where will you go when you reach Dishnigar?' Smart asked Lex, as they leant against the rail.

'I hear there is a Madame Esse there who virtually runs the port. I suppose I should make courteous advances to her first. Then I suppose we will scour the slave pens in search of Troy.'

Joseph came up on deck in time to hear the ending of this conversation.

'Mistress Esse? I would prefer it if you keep away from her.' He looked worried, in fact, his face had blanched. He reached out a hand to find a pile of rope to sit upon.

'What is the matter, father? You look as if you have seen a passed spirit!'

'Metaphorically, I suppose I might have done, Lex. I wish to have a quiet word with you, perhaps the cabin would be suitable?'

Amiably, Lex accompanied the King back to the cabin they both shared.

Joseph sat on his bunk and looked at his eldest son with an inscrutable look on his face. 'This Madame Esse might cause us trouble, Lex.'

'How is that? I have never heard of the woman before.'

Joseph now looked embarrassed. He could barely look at Lex, and sat with his arms folded, staring into space. Lex looked at his father in surprise; he had never seen him so riled up.

'Spit it out,' he said, impatient to find out what was happening on deck.

Joseph shifted uncomfortably, crossing and re-crossing his legs, staring at his ankles. It took him a time before he could force himself to speak.

'Years ago, when I was a young adjutant, Prince of Rhodia, as you are now, I met this Essa Esse.

'In those days she was not a powerful woman, but a pretty, young girl, at the court in Orphur. She was in the train of an important lawyer from Dishnigar.

'We had a fling, and some time later I heard she had had a child. You are that boy.

'I had you kidnapped and brought you to court. Your mother could not conceive at that time, and we decided to bring you up as ours.

'No one knows about this except Essa, Marie and the nurse who looked after you, and me of course.'

Lex looked at his father in stultified horror. His world had crumbled around him in the space of a few words.

'So, this means I am not the heir! Troy is the real future King of Devronia?'

'No! I have named you heir, and you have been adopted. You are still the heir, but Troy is your mother's son.'

Lex was looking at his father with fresh consideration. *This fussy, old stick must have had some spirit when he was younger*, he mused. Then he gathered his thoughts and tried to adapt to the new situation.

'So this is why I am smaller and darker; I often wondered why. We shall meet this Madame Esse, no doubt. I wonder if she will be inclined to help us?

'I had better be careful, who knows what plans she might have, a woman scorned, remember?'

'It wasn't like that! I was just a foolish boy myself, at the time. She was very attractive and vivacious, it was all I could do to tear myself away from her company.'

'I must think about this. Excuse me, your highness.' When Lex spoke, his tone was cold and remote. He rose, bowed formally to his father, before leaving the cabin, wanting to feel the wind and spume on his face.

His thoughts spun in all directions. He remembered his childhood when he had thought his mother had favoured Troy in unexplainable ways. He thought of the future when he would be acting a lie. The galley was inexorably approaching Dishnigar, where perhaps his Karma awaited him.

His solitary figure had an air of despair, as he stood grasping the ropes in the bow, with wind and wave streaming over him. No matter how he looked at it, the situation could not be altered.

What would he do if Troy could not be found? He gazed at the water sluicing through the scuppers, and considered joining it as it slid into the sea. Despair was a feeling he had never experienced, and he found it totally overwhelming.

When he finally turned to continue his work, the carefree, young prince had been lost forever.

Unaware of Lex's state of mind, the captain joined him as he had paused, in his stride across the deck. Smart laid a hand on the prince's arm.

'Look, my prince, the cliffs of Dishnigar approach. We should be in the harbour within the hour.'

Lex looked at the steep crags, with the sea sweeping up their forbidding sides. The narrow entrance channel appeared to vanish in gloom, as the glancing sun could not penetrate the massive stone.

'Is this a deep-water harbour?' Lex inquired, tersely. When this had been confirmed he advised the captain to inform the king of their imminent arrival.

'Please send Jocelyn to our cabin, I shall bathe and change before we disembark.' It was a relief to find the cabin empty, as Joseph had gone to look at the port, now easily seen.

Soaking in the hot, soapy water did disperse his misery a little. Jocelyn arrived with hot towels and a truculent visage.

'What were you doing, standing out there in the cold for so long? You will be lucky if you don't catch a fever!' He helped Lex dry, then change into more suitable garb for a visiting dignitary. However, while he was helping fasten his prince's gleaming boots he felt he had to speak again.

'What is wrong? You seem to have lost all your spunk?'

'I've been thinking of calling off my engagement to the Lady Enid. Times change, and until I find Troy I don't need any more encumbrances.' Lex gazed at the tips of his boots with a gloomy expression.

Jocelyn, was a tall, thin lad, with spindly arms and legs. He gestured by waving his arms, and giving a shoulder shrug.

'You never wanted to marry her anyway. It was a political arrangement to please her father, your father's friend. Your wishes were never considered.'

'By Mut, they will be now!' Lex swore, with a thump of his fist.

He strode out of the cabin and on to the upper deck, with Jocelyn hurrying behind.

'Captain, are we ready to disembark?'

'Nearly, my prince, we are heading to a berth at the southern end of the harbour.'

As soon as the gangplank rattled down, Lex was ready to charge ashore. His father appeared at his elbow, grasping his arm in remonstration.

'Lex, what are you about? Let us go together, then I can present you to Madame Esse.'

'What title will you give me?' Lex's face was drawn in grim lines, his skin white with fury under his tan.

'You are my son, and my heir. I shall introduce you as Prince of Rhodia!'

'I'm not sure I want to be heir apparent now, father. It all seems to be a farcical amount of unnecessary trouble. Let us find Troy, and then I shall decide. After all, the bastard line bans me from being king.'

Jocelyn, who had overheard this conversation, hurried ahead across the gangplank, then asked sailors on the quay for directions to an ostler's. He trotted across the cobbles in the direction indicated, musing on what he had heard.

So, he thought, *Lex has good reason not to want the Lady Enid pushed on him for convenience sake. He won't want to please anyone now, least of all the King.*

On reaching the stables, he hired sufficient horses for Lex and his honour guard, and a carriage for Joseph. By the time everyone had assembled in the yard the horses were ready.

Joseph and Lex had been standing to one side, studying the scene around them. The ostler's stable was close to the quay, and seemed to have little to recommend it.

The low-roofed buildings were built of stone, and the cobbled passages around them were strewn with refuse. The people who could be seen on the streets, all seemed to be fisher folk; the smell of fish in the air was overpowering.

However, when the horses were led out, they were well-fed and carefully groomed.

'We shall need a lad for a guide,' Jocelyn told one of the grooms.

'Where do you wish to go, my lord?'

'I believe the establishment is known as the Eyrie. I hear it is a large house on the edge of the cliff. Is this information correct?'

The lanky stableman's blue eyes became round with surprise. 'Well then,' he said, 'you must be visiting Madame Esse. Is she expecting you?'

'How could she be expecting us? We have only just arrived!' Lex exclaimed impatiently.

'Oh, Madame has many ways of keeping her finger on the pulse of Dishnigar,' was the reply. 'If you are not admitted this morning, you could return for dinner this evening. I would advise you send her a message before you try a second time.'

'What rubbish!' Joseph growled. 'Will she keep the King of Devronia waiting?'

'She would keep The Lord of Angels waiting, if she was of a mind to, Sir,' was the reply. 'Anyway, how can we tell you are a king?'

With a grim laugh, Lex swung up on his horse, signalled to the stable boy sitting on his old nag, to lead the way. The whole cavalcade set off, clattering under the arched gateway, trotting noisily over the cobbles.

Joseph had climbed into the carriage bringing up the rear, with its wheels grinding across the bumpy tracks.

The carriage was musty, and its leather straps smelt of mould, though the seats seemed clean enough. It was chilly in the carriage, but the rugs smelt, so he refrained from trying them.

Joseph sat in the lumpy equipage in a state of apprehension, an unusual feeling for one whom was usually in charge of everything around him.

In his mind he pictured the vivacious apparition who had charmed all his senses all those years ago. He should have sent for her, he thought, when he was younger. He could have established her as his mistress when he became king. It would have been possible to have kept her a secret from his queen.

He shifted uncomfortably as the carriage swung around a corner, and his retainer hurried to adjust his cushions. They were leaving the lower town, and were now starting up a steep gradient. The road surface was more suited to the horses and the carriage became slightly less uncomfortable.

Riding at the front of the group, Lex looked around at the palatial buildings, which were now coming into view. Judging from her neighbours, this Madame Esse must have a substantial fortune.

He had imagined someone like a pirate's mistress to be his mother, but now realised this was not the case. His pulses quickened, thinking about this mysterious stranger who had suddenly turned out to be his blood kin.

As Jocelyn was riding at Lex's side, he became bold enough to ask.

'Where are we going, Lex?'

Lex had difficulty in deciding what to answer.

He glanced at his squire, encountering a questing gaze from bold, green eyes.

'We are going to meet a mysterious lady, who might know what has happened to Troy. Not only that, she is also an old friend of my father's, and she is my newly-discovered mother. Does that answer your question?'

Jocelyn's horse veered away into some bushes, as he pulled in the reins with surprise.

When he returned to Lex's side he ventured to carry on the conversation.

'Is the lady of the Keshian royal family, my lord?'

'No royalty involved,' Lex replied. 'Probably a bastard, like myself.'

This closed Jocelyn's mouth as surely as if he had been gagged.

The stable boy led them off to the left when they reached a fork in the steep road. Upon reaching some impressive doors in a massive stone wall, he rang a bell by pulling on a rope.

An enormous guard appeared, when the gate swung open.

'Madame Esse is in conference, today,' he announced. 'She has sent you word that you are to dine with her this evening. The password will be 'fledgling.' Four gentlemen will be expected, your guards will wait here.' So saying, he turned on his heel and the gate banged shut behind him.

Lex turned his horse and ambled up to the carriage where Joseph was just getting out.

'Don't bother, we shall have to come back this evening. We have been invited to dinner.'

Before his father could answer, Lex had started trotting his horse along the stony driveway. It took a while to turn the carriage around and by the time Joseph had started the journey back, Lex was well out of sight.

Having watched them turn away, so obviously despondent, Essa tucked her spyglasses under her arm as the carriage trundled out of sight.

'So!' she breathed, rubbing her hands to refute their chill, then turning away from the balcony, she entered her bedroom and walked to her dressing table to put the glasses away. 'I set a sprat to catch a mackerel and caught a whale.'

Surveying herself in the mirror, she thought, *I wonder if he bears any resemblance to me?* Smiling at her image, admiring her upright stance and air of confidence, she wondered, *Joseph has aged. Being a king must be hard work. I wonder what his wife is like?*

She moved to her chair, sat and rang a handbell, then requested the answering maid to send Eyas and her body servants to attend her.

A few minutes later there was a light knock on the door and Eyas entered, followed by Delia and Trojan.

'Good morning, my lady.' Eyas looked at her levelly, through her heavily-lashed, sapphire eyes. 'You called for us Madame Esse? Can we do something for you?'

'I wished to tell you the King of Devronia and his elder son will be dining with us tonight. Please make yourself presentable.

Glancing at Trojan, she said, 'You of course will serve the wine as usual. I would like to know why they are really here.'

183

Trojan bowed. 'Lady Essa, they will be here for us, and also for the young prince, Troy.'

'Well, they shall find you, much to their loss. You madam, will stay in your room.'

Delia was about to protest, then thought better of it.

Gaining the livery stables, Lex ordered the carriage and riding horses for the evening, then returned to the galley.

Finding Smart ensconced at the main table waiting for lunch, while studying a chart of the harbour, Lex joined him with a tankard of ale. Having slaked his thirst, and with his temper slightly mollified, he asked, 'Captain, what do you know about this Madame Esse?'

'I have never met the lady, but the shipping lanes abound with rumours in which her name often figures. Apparently she was a great beauty when she was younger, sufficiently so, to turn crowned heads. She travelled a good deal and made many contacts.

'Using her intuition, and having a vast amount of knowledge, has enabled her to build her empire. She is devious and sagacious. According to gossip, she runs this town and harbour from her dinner table. Her fortune is reputedly massive.'

'Did she never marry?'

'No. There was some talk of a hidden romance, but she has remained single; she lives a solitary life. Recently she has established her niece in the Eyrie. She is to take up the reins when the lady retires from the fray, so I have heard. She will be a wealthy young woman, from all of the accounts.'

A commotion on the deck alerted them to the arrival of King Joseph. Stewards hurried to make arrangements to serve lunch.

After the meal Lex decided to have a wander around the town while his father was taking a rest in their cabin. Feeling restless, angry and disconsolate, he strolled around the narrow streets investigating the small shops and stalls.

Coming across the slave market, he stood at the entrance surveying the selling block and the gloomy buildings surrounding the square. A young boy passing by glanced at Lex's well-polished boots and carefully cut clothes.

'There won't be another auction for another three weeks, young sir.' This was volunteered in good humour by the boy. He had a cheery open countenance, and seemed willing to talk.

'Are there any slaves in the buildings?' Lex slipped a quarter silvo along the railing he was leaning on, pushing it towards the scruffy lad.

Grabbing the coin with a whoop, the boy startled a flock of seagulls, which were settled on the roofs of the building. He came and stood beside Lex, companionably leaning against the railing.

'There are one or two boys of about my age there,' he volunteered.

'What do you want them for? They ain't pretty, and they're a lacklustre lot, sold to the market by their parents, when they turned out to be layabouts without any skills.'

'Definitely not what I am looking for,' Lex replied. 'What do you do?'

'I'm Ambry's new cabin boy, Dan Hurd. We sail tomorrow.'

'Who is Ambry?'

'Don't you know Ambry? Captain Ambry is the top buccaneer around these parts. His ship, *The Dark Dart*, is in the harbour.' Dan spat over the bar with disgust.

'So it is. Have you been to sea before?'

'Course I have, lots of times, see yer.' With that the cabin boy sauntered away.

Lex continued on his way, glancing down noisome alleys, meandering through narrow streets, missing muddy puddles that would ruin his boots, and avoiding overhangs which dripped dirty water down on to the cobbled streets.

There were people about, all wrapped up well against the cold. The women had shawls and aprons, and many of them had a strong odour of fish about their persons.

Lex was careful to let no loiterer near him, and kept a tight hold on his money pouch, with the other hand grasping the hilt of his dagger. Turning a corner he came upon another square.

This one had a well in the centre, and the buildings looked well-cared for, unlike those of the slave market, these buildings were made of wood. He realised he had reached the fabled horse market when he saw a couple of geldings led out to trot around, showing their paces to a prospective buyer who was standing by the well.

Lex walked across the square to the centre, being careful to keep out of the way of the horses.

'Good day to you!'

'Are these the famous Strevian horses?'

'Yes, my Lord. Aren't they just the beauties? I have been sent to purchase one for my mistress' niece and I can't choose between them. My mistress is Madame Esse, and she won't stand for second rate!' He frowned at the two horses, screwing up his eyes.

Lex regarded the other man with interest. He was elderly and displaying the bowed legs of an inveterate stableman.

'You must be Madame Esse's head groom?' he speculated.

'Indeed, I am, Sir. Jim Sawsay is my name. Are you visiting Dishnigar, my lord?'

'Oh, just passing through, my galley is in the harbour. What does Madame's niece look like?'

'The lady Eyas is a real beauty.' Sawsay's brown eyes lit up as he spoke. She is tall with a slender figure, and her hair is like white silk.'

'Well then,' Lex countered, 'your choice is made. Take the bay horse with the long blond tail; he will compliment your lady.'

'Of course! Why didn't I think of that?' Sawsay chuckled with pleasure, nodded to Lex, and strode off to the office to make his purchase, well-pleased with the decision.

Gazing at the remaining black horse, which was now being led back to the stable, Lex was overcome with the desire to purchase it.

The Strevian horses were all that he had heard – handsome, sleek, and spirited animals. They would be a joy to ride. He knew, however, it would not be fair to the animal to have it confined in the belly of the galley, for who could tell how long?

He decided, then and there, when this journey looking for Troy was over, he would return to Dishnigar to the horse fair to choose some of these lovely creatures to take back to Devron.

He waved to Sawsay, as astride the bay with its tail pluming behind it, he trotted out of the square on his way home with his purchase.

That evening, Lex, Joseph, Jocelyn and Captain Smart presented themselves again outside the gate of the Eyrie. They had come unescorted, not wishing to leave men waiting for them in the cold. There seemed no reason for them to be guarded, as there was no threat to their persons.

Joseph had elected to ride, having had enough of the bumpy carriage, so they were all able to proceed to the house together. Servants came to lead their mounts away, and a footman was there to escort them to the dining room. They were shown to seats near the head of the table.

The small jet chair, with a high back, situated at the table top, was vacant, as also was the seat to its right side. Various people already seated along the length of the table viewed the newcomers with interest. A low murmur of excited talk buzzed around the room, giving an air of expectancy amongst the waiting people.

Joseph sipped from a water glass, suddenly overcome with a feeling of anxiety and unease. Should he be exposing himself and Lex to the vagaries of this woman, who was such an unknown quantity?

Jack Smart nudged his elbow. 'See that man seated at the far end of the table? That is Ambry, Madame's tame buccaneer.'

'Not so tame, I should think,' Lex commented, sitting on Smart's other side. He glanced at the burly figure sporting throwing knives in a belt. Their bone handles outlined against his brown velvet jacket.

Ambry turned at that moment, the candlelight catching the white scar on the left side of his face. He inclined his head towards Lex in amusement, his dark eyes glinting across the table length with a look of slight mockery. He then continued his conversation with the dark-haired woman sitting at his side.

The double doors behind the empty chairs swung open, and two women entered the room. Madame Esse greeted her guests in general.

'Good evening, everyone. Please remain seated. Eyas and I are slightly late, I'm afraid.' So saying, she ushered the girl to her chair, then seated herself at the head of the table, while her eyes scanned the faces in front of her. When they finally came to rest on Lex, she gave a small smile.

She noted his quick movements, his ready smile, the way he gave attention to those about him. She was watching his deft hand movements, so like her own, as he discussed a topic of interest with his neighbour.

'Well, well!' she murmured, 'the pigeon has come home to roost!' Her gaze shifted to Joseph, who was scarlet with embarrassment, half-standing from his chair.

'Relax, King of Devronia. We shall let bygones be bygones.'

Lex sat stunned, unable to speak, with his mouth dry and his fists clenched. The woman at the head of the table, petite, yet stern, bore the countenance he saw every day in his mirror. Every nuance of expression, every shift of head, lift of eyebrow, or tilt of chin, was his own. Forcing himself to take care, he took a deep breath, then shifted his gaze to the other newcomer to the table.

Eyas sat in languid beauty, unaware of how arresting she looked. Her long, white blonde hair, hung in loose waves over her shoulders. She was wearing ice blue silk, which shimmered in the candlelight.

Her perfect face and swanlike neck, were complimented with a single rope of pearls. The pearls were replicated by flashing teeth when she smiled at the person sitting opposite to her. Lex was smitten.

When she turned and smiled at him and their eyes met, he felt quite faint with the rush of emotion. Here were his future and his past, brought together without his expectation of having either. He looked at Eyas with his heart shining in his eyes, his pulse had quickened and he started to blush.

'What is the matter with you?' Smart asked, kicking him under the table. 'You look as if you are about to pass out!'

'I need a drink, that's all.'

Smart turned and beckoned to a footman who was circling the table, filling glasses with wine. Then it was his turn to have a shock.

'Trojan D'Auton! What are you doing here?'

Trojan came over and grasped Jack's hand before filling their glasses.

'I am a slave of Madame Esse's. Delia and I were bought to be body servants to the Lady Eyas. Good evening, King Joseph, Prince Lex!'

'Delia is here, too?' Lex gasped with incredulity.

'I'm sorry to say so, Sir. You won't see her; she is not allowed to attend the dinners.'

Joseph listened to this, his face hardening as he made up his mind.

'Madame Esse! Essa! I must purchase this footman and your lady's maid!'

Essa stared at him with contempt on her face.

'Oh Joseph, don't be so silly. You will never get anything of mine, again. The slaves are not for sale. Why don't you eat your dinner? The salmon is particularly fine.'

'But he is the Duke of Desra, and Delia is the Kardovan ambassador's daughter!'

'Not now, they are not. I purchased them perfectly legally in the slave market in Dishnigar. You are not in Devron now, my king, or, for that matter, in Orphur. Please continue!' She turned to her other guests with a smile.

Shrugging his shoulders, Trojan was about to continue on pouring wine, but with a restraining hand, Jocelyn caught his sleeve. As Trojan bent to ask why he was being held, Jocelyn slipped a bag of gold coins into Trojan's pocket.

'For emergencies, my friend,' he whispered, then indicated he needed his glass to be refilled.

As they were about to depart when the evening had ended, they were waiting in the hall for their horses to be brought round. Essa was waving goodbye to departing guests, then beckoned their party into a side chamber. She caught Lex by the hand and then pulled him towards a large candelabra, so the light fell on his face.

'You are aware who I am, young prince?' she inquired, looking at him steadfastly.

Lex was nonplussed, but equal to the question. 'Yes, Madame Esse. You are my father's long lost love, and my lady mother. I have recently learnt of my parentage and I am delighted to meet you! Of course my colouring could not be from Devron.'

'Well done!' was her reply. 'I wanted to meet you. I am pleased to see the resemblance. Perhaps you will visit me at a more auspicious time?'

She turned to Joseph and grasped both of his hands in hers.

'I bear you no ill will, now. What occurred all those years ago is past.

'Unfortunately, I have no idea what has happened to your younger son, apart from the fact he was in the slave market and has since been sold. I will make inquiries, but I doubt any records have been kept, as there has been no legal auction recently.

'The boy will have been sold to a passing trader and no record kept. I do know he is not in Dishnigar. Your best idea would be to sail to Keshia, where the traders go. I wish you good fortune in your search. I know how it feels to lose a son. Good night to you all.'

With that, she turned away and swept out of the room, with her head held high.

'What about Trojan and Delia?' Lex demanded.

'I don't think we could get them, even if we attacked the town. She is playing by the rules of the law here.' Joseph shook his head in dismay, and they proceeded to where their horses were waiting.

Delia sat in the window seat surveying the guests departing after dinner. She had spent a long, lonely evening kicking her heels, waiting for the others to return. She watched Lex and King Joseph with their small party mount and trot away. She with a glint had waved through the mullioned window, but no one had looked up, or paid her any attention.

Finally the door opened, and Eyas appeared.

'Well?' Delia demanded, noticing her sparkling eyes and pink cheeks. Eyas had more animation than Delia had ever seen her have.

Eyas came and knelt on the window seat beside Delia, searching the grounds below with an eager expression on her face.

'Do you know the prince?' she asked turning to look at Delia.

'Mercy, Lex, do you mean? Yes, of course I do. He is not much fun. Yet his brother, Troy, has a deal more spunk.'

'Is he married?'

'No. I do believe he has some sort of arrangement set up by his father, but nothing has come of it so far.'

'I intend to wed him,' Eyas stated calmly.

'Who?' asked Trojan from the doorway.

'Prince Lex!' Delia told him, turning with a chuckle.

'If that is the case, we shall have to make further efforts to ensure our escape. The King can't take us. Essa refuses to part with us.

'We have two choices, the trade route, or take our chances by sea. Perhaps Ambry would take a run to Keshia if we can find enough to lure him, even against Essa's wishes.'

The next morning the royal party assembled in the captain's cabin for a consultation. Lex was all for setting out on horseback along the road to Keshia, hoping to catch the slaver who apparently had taken Troy with the rest of the slaves.

Smart had no intention of leaving his galley in the harbour in Dishnigar, and considered it a foolish scheme, as they really had no surety as to where Troy had been taken.

King Joseph did not wish to admit it, but felt the long ride on horseback would be too much for his ailing body.

It was decided, therefore, by general consensus, to sail around the coast to Keshia. This would take longer, but would get them there with less stress. They might also manage to come across the pirate galleys in the open sea. Ambry was untouchable in his own home harbour.

Furious that the decision had gone against his wishes, Lex called Jocelyn to go out for a walk along the harbour. Jocelyn was quite happy to get off the ship. When they reached *The Endless Tankard* he suggested they should go in for an ale or two. Nothing loath, Lex agreed, and they were soon settled at a table to one side of the room with Dolly in attendance. They refused a meal – although the aromas permeating from the open kitchen door were delicious – knowing food would be waiting for them when they returned to the ship.

Jocelyn was admiring Dolly, teasing her about her glorious curls. He asked her if she put her hair up in rags every night, much to her chagrin.

'I'll let you know these curls are natural,' she protested, tossing her head so the ringlets bounced.

The door opened and Ambry entered the tavern. 'Well. Doll, my back is turned and you find yourself another suitor.' He smiled at her, but his glance was steely when he turned towards the other men.

Seizing the opportunity, Lex rose. 'Captain Ambry, a word with you. Do you have any idea what has happened to The Prince of Ardarth? He was on your ship, so I hear.'

'He was booty won by me fairly on the high seas. I sold him legally to the slave master, who would put him up for auction.

'Mind you he had made a fool of himself, so he had to be chastised, so I doubt if the slave master made such a good bargain.

'Who knows who bought such damaged goods? Good day to you, Sir!' With that, Ambry called Doll over to his usual corner, by the window, and ordered his luncheon.

'I've had enough of this,' Lex growled. 'Finish your drink and we'll go. I don't want to be in the same room as that blaggart!'

Jocelyn gulped his last mouthful and stood up. He caught Doll's eye as she was passing. He found she was quite ready to return his glance with a smile in her eye, she watched the two

young men leave, admiring the taller of the two. He walked
with a swagger that she found quite entrancing.

Chapter Thirteen

Amelia and Anton squeezed together, both trying to look out of the small window in the door of the vehicle. It seemed the cavalcade was approaching a big city, perhaps their incarceration in this hot, smelly contraption was soon to be over.

'Look at that!' gasped Amelia, as they rolled past a magnificent building with sloping roofs nearly reaching to the ground. It was covered in sparkling green tiles edged in gold. This was only the first of many such, all bright, clean and beautifully maintained.

The surrounding gardens were full of flowering shrubs, with peacocks parading through the bushes, while ducks and swans sailed majestically among flowering lilies on the ponds and lakes.

'This must be Keshia,' Anton rubbed the crick in his neck. He had been bending, looking out of the small gap which was really there to allow the guards to look inside, rather than for them to look out. 'I wonder if we shall be staying here?'

The further they were taken to the centre of the town, the more ornate the buildings became.

Amelia noticed that the people who were crowding the streets were of an olive complexion. They all wore long trailing garments, both men and women, in an array of a complexity of colours.

The women had their lustrous black hair piled high upon their heads. These styles were decorated with pearls and ornaments; each person with his or her own style, to compliment clothes.

The pavements were full of tables and chairs, where people could sit to chat, drink or gossip. Each pavement was covered with an awning to protect the populace from rain or sun. These were all decorated in stripes, or stippled in bright colours, giving a festive air to the streets.

Clumps of trees had been planted in the centres of the roads, and there were babies with their nurses, dogs on leads, or left to roam, while children played, as they waited for their parents.

Still looking out of the window, Amelia watched the passing scene with avid curiosity.

'I don't think you want to be a slave here, Anton. Look at those poor men pulling carts.' Anton shook his head vigorously, when he saw them; they were so emaciated. Bending his head, he sniffed when the salt tang he smelt replaced the town by the sea.

The caravan of traders and slaves pulled up in a large field which had obviously been designated for this purpose as there were washing facilities, ablutions, firepits provided for cooking, and running water pumped along small canals.

In due time, a guard came to release them, allowing them to relieve themselves and stretch their legs. They were then permitted to join a queue to get a bowl of thin gruel like stew, eked out with a piece of stale bread.

After this sumptuous meal, they were replaced in their box, with no reply to any of their questions.

Early next morning, just as dawn was breaking, their door was flung open, and the slaver who had bought them stood outside, surrounded with half a dozen guards.

'Out!' was his command.

Glad to obey, Amelia was the first to descend the steps, feeling chilly in the cold dawn with just her thin muslin dress, as her blanket had been stripped from her and thrown back into the caravan. Anton followed, even more skimpily attired, in his boots and loincloth.

The merchant slaver looked at his tally sheet; then marked them off. He held out chains to two of the guards, with wrist shackles attached.

'Take these two beauties down to the harbour. *The Golden Guinea* will be flying the royal standard of Jaddanna. Put them aboard and get a chit from the purser to show you have delivered them.

' I don't want that devil, the chief eunuch from the court, saying I didn't deliver the goods he has paid for, though how these two can be of such importance, I don't know.'

Shackled together, they were hurried along by their erstwhile guards. They went through the market, then down narrow streets leading to the harbour. It was breakfast time and the smells made them ravenous.

After boarding the ship, waiting at the dock, they were escorted to the chief purser. He was a large man wearing uniform, which was bulging at the seams, while on his head he wore a green silk turban. Gold chains hung in profusion around his neck.

'Who have we here?' he asked, accepting the chit, which was becoming soiled with clutching and handling.

'Oh! Just slaves for the palace. Unshackle them, they don't need chains when on this ship and under my eye. My boys will keep a close watch on them.'

Amelia and Anton were quickly hurried out of sight into a cabin reserved for the purpose of holding recalcitrant slaves. It was well below deck and had a heavy lock on the door, but they were surprised to find washing water and food awaiting them.

Shortly the door opened, and a slight man with a thin moustache gazed at them. He went away and then returned, bearing suitable clothes to replace their rags.

Anton had trousers and a shirt, while Amelia had a voluminous dark green gown, which covered most of her, except for her arms. The material was soft and pleasant to wear. After using a comb and brush, which she had found near the washing bowl, she started to feel human again.

Shortly, there were sounds of the huge hawsers being unfastened, and the rattling sounds of the enormous anchors being reeled in. The activity on the deck changed from milling crowds to concise precision as the officers took over the ship and in an orderly fashion, gave the crew commands to set sail.

Amelia nursed her scratched and bruised feet. Anton had been wearing his boots so he hadn't suffered from the walk as she had had.

She sat thinking. *Nothing she could do at present would alter her intended future, so she should make the most of the moment.* Anton came to sit beside her. He held her hand.

'Well, the next part of our journey has begun. Let us hope they keep us together. I wonder where Troy and the others are now?' he said.

The door swung open and the same man who had brought their clothes stood there.

'My name is Amul,' he told them. 'I have been assigned to look after you by the purser until we reach Jaddanna. Is there anything you need?'

Anton introduced Amelia, then shook hands with the steward.

'We will need fresh air and some exercise occasionally,' he replied.

'Yes, you may go up on deck when we have left the harbour. I can't be responsible for you not going over the side while we are still in reach of land.'

'Do you know what is to become of us?' Amelia asked, her lip quivering at last.

'No,' Amul replied, 'except you are to go to the palace.'

They had to be content with this. Amelia asked Amul for a pair of scissors and soon had Anton's hair neatened. Reflecting on the stylists who had taken care of Delia and herself, she was forced to chuckle.

Life on board the ship was peaceful for them, and they had time to recover their health after the dreadful journey they had had in the caravan. However, a couple of days later, Amelia demurred when offered a stroll on the deck.

'I'm afraid my feet are too sore,' she confided to Anton.

Glancing down when she lifted the hem of her green gown, he was horrified to see her feet, which were swollen, scratched and bruised from their march to the ship.

'Amul, what can we do?' he demanded from the steward, who was patiently waiting for them to follow him.

Amul came forward and carefully examined her feet.

'I have heard there is a healer on board. Wait here and I will find him and fetch him to see you. I think he is in a party of soldiers and gentlemen returning to court.' So saying, he left them and dashed away.

Anton came and sat beside Amelia and put a comforting arm around her shoulders. 'You should have said something before,' he scolded.

'I didn't want to make a fuss,' she replied. 'We don't know what to expect after we have been so badly treated.'

Not long after Amul returned, bringing a young man with him. He was of slight build, but handsome, with an oval face and high cheekbones. He was dressed in a long yellow tunic edged in green, with tight trousers to match.

His dark hair was plaited out of his way.

He gave a slight smile when his eyes met Amelia's grey ones.

'I hear you are in need of help. My name is Chun Gar.

'I come from Keshia, but I am in the employ of the great Jada, so I am returning to the palace after visiting my family. I have trained as a healer in both, Jaddanna and Keshia.'

Amelia introduced herself and then Anton, before showing Chun her feet.

He was kind and gentle, and soon she had swallowed a soothing potion and had a balm smothered over her bruises.

While they were talking, Amelia found she was much attracted to this young man, with his liquid, soothing voice and kind eyes. She involved Anton in their conversation, explaining how they had become partners in grief. Chun listened carefully to their miserable tale of how they had been entrapped into slavery.

'The Great Jada is kind,' he told them, 'who knows, he might set you free?'

'Who knows?' Anton agreed. 'We were purposefully selected from all the others at the auction, and have been treated with reasonable kindness in comparison with the other unfortunates, though for what reason we can only suppose.'

Chun met Anton's troubled gaze and gave him a reassuring smile.

'I shall speak to The Jada on your behalf. As long as we are dealing with him, and not his wilful sons, we should get good attention. Do not fret. I shall keep watch for you while you are aboard *The Golden Guinea.*

'I am travelling with the prince's guard and we will go straight to The Jada. We are returning to the palace after a mission to the Horse Lords, so I will have the ear of The Jada as soon as we reach the city.'

'Is the prince in your party?' asked Amelia.

Chun laughed. 'Unfortunately not. He has been detained by the Horse Lady, at her pleasure.'

'You would like her,' he added. 'She is a creature of wild spirit and mixed gentleness, some of the qualities I think you must possess.'

Amelia smiled and blushed. 'You think more highly of me, than I deserve, Sir,' she replied.

'Time will get us acquainted,' he declared. 'We have many weeks of travel ahead of us, until we reach the city. I'm sure we shall have some games of chess and other occupations, to pass the time most pleasantly.'

He nodded to Anton, then left the cabin, while calling to Amul to fetch them a cooling drink, and to bring some more pillows so Amelia could rest her bruised feet on them.

Later that day they were moved to a cabin, which opened on the deck, and had portholes through which blew sea breezes. On questioning Amul, they found the healer had arranged the change, giving their health as needful reason for their new circumstances.

During the weeks that followed *The Golden Guinea* travelled slowly through the tropics in balmy weather, which made every day of the journey a delight. Chun introduced them to the other members of his party and Amelia soon became a firm favourite.

Anton also became popular when the soldiers discovered he was a trained swordsman. Immediately, duelling swords were produced and Anton started taking regular lessons under a striped awning on the deck. Soon he was taking lessons every day, and the practice sessions attracted a small crowd of onlookers.

Anton regained his agility and strength, which had been lost during the time spent in the caravan. Their hopes and expectations rose as they were treated so well by their new friends.

As Amelia was the only girl in the party, she was never short of a companion. She had eyes for only the one, though. Her face lit up with delight whenever Chun came into view, as her heart gave a leap with emotion. Her feelings were reciprocated, as he was charmed with this quiet, doe-eyed girl, who seemed at the mercy of an unkind *karma*.

He thought he knew she was destined to become a member of someone's *harem*, or worse, a high-class whore. He ensured that both Amelia and Anton had everything they needed, including sea chests abandoned by previous travellers.

Amelia soon found herself the proud possessor of various flimsy garments of varying hues, sizes and styles. To her delight, she also found a pair of red leather boots, which laced up to just below her knees. They were slightly big, but were a wonderful find, hidden right at the bottom of an old sea chest.

One morning when they came on deck they were surprised to see there were ominous, dark clouds massing in the west.

'The temperature is dropping, we are in for a storm,' Chun declared.

That afternoon the huge, floating palace started rocking and bucking. The passengers were all sent to their cabins and the hatches were closed. Amelia heard the cries of seagulls, and sat by her porthole watching the birds soar past as they were carried by the wind.

'We must be close to the land,' she said, turning to look at Anton, stretched out on his bunk. 'I don't think the birds would venture far out to sea in winds like this.'

'I think we have been following the coast line all the time,' he replied. 'Just that we were too far out to sea.'

That evening there was great activity among the ship's crew. The sails were reefed and sea anchors were put out, yet the wind was so strong, the mighty vessel continued to drive to the east. During the night Amelia, the only girl in the party, was tapping on their cabin door.

'I want the door open, what will happen to us?'

'What do you think?' Anton retorted.

'Are we sinking?'

'No, no. Don't worry.' Chun entered the cabin and sat besides Amelia, putting a comforting arm around her shoulders. 'We are aground on a sandbank. There is no structural damage, but the Bosun thinks we shall have to wait until the next high tide before we can be pulled off, and that is in another month.

'I said I had to take my message to The Jada before that, and the reply was we would have to take the boats ashore at low tide.'

'Good,' Anton broke in.

'So in the morning we must get the horses ashore, probably by swimming them. Get yourselves all packed up and we will take you with us. Come on deck at first light. I must organise stores and equipment so I am busy now, but I shall see you then.'

'Can you ride?' Anton asked. 'You will need riding britches.' They both burst out laughing.

'In a fashion,' Amelia said. 'I'm not an expert, but I don't fall off easily. What do you think we should take?' She indicated the open sea chests with their contents strewn around the cabin.

'A selection,' was Anton's answer. 'We will need light things for the day and warm things for the night. Something special for when we reach the city.'

They wrapped up their belongings in small parcels suitable for placing on a packhorse.

When Amul arrived, bringing their breakfast, they thanked him for all his kindness and asked if he wanted to come with them. He thanked them for the suggestion but said he couldn't as his family relied on the monies sent from his wages as his job as steward.

As soon as they had gobbled up their breakfasts, Anton and Amelia shouldered their packs and went on deck to find Chun surrounded by his travelling companions, who all welcomed them like old friends.

Amelia stood to one side of the bustle on deck and gazed at the view. The ship was stranded on a series of sandbanks, which looked like stepping stones up to the beach. The waves were rough in the bay, with white tops curling around the shifting sand.

Above the beach a cliff path led up to massive, sandstone cliffs outlined against the sky. These were so looming and impressive that they cut off any further sight of what the land might be like behind them. The sky though was a dull, metallic colour, with faint gleams of sunshine just penetrating the heavy clouds.

A ramp was lowered from the deck to the firm sand, and the horses were brought up on deck. These were the horses who had made the journey from Orphur, and they had been on board ship before, on trips across the Grey River. They were small, hardy and well-trained.

Chun was very attached to his mare, Astar, and she greeted him affectionately. She was a brown beauty, with a black, flowing tail. Having encouragement from Chun, she was the first to lead the way down the ramp. Soon they were all assembled on the hard-packed sand. The wind had dropped and the tide had ebbed, so their progress was not hindered by the weather.

As they trekked across the sandbanks, the horses on occasion had to be encouraged to swim beside the small boats which the Bosun had provided, to carry their luggage to the shore.

Anton helped with the horses, but Amelia stayed in one of the boats, keeping as dry as she could. She had her new boots laced around her neck, ensuring the leather was out of the seawater as much as possible.

Eventually, they reached dry land. Amelia gave a sigh of relief as she helped unload the boats and watched the horses shaking and stamping, pleased to be away from the sea and the unstable ground.

The men, who were not moving stores or looking after horses, helped turn the boats around and gave a hand to shoving them off.

The oarsmen started to pull and they were soon on their way back to the distant sandbank, where *The Golden Guinea* could be seen, outlined by the setting sun. It had taken a whole day for them to complete their passage to the shore, having had to wait on a sandbank for the tide to rise and abate during the middle of the day.

Chun called the company together.

'We will move up the beach, I think, to reach the tree line. Everyone collect firewood on the way, so we can build a bonfire to cook an evening meal.

'We will find a spot for the horses to graze; somewhere over near that fresh spring trickling water on to the beach would be good.

'We can leave the packs piled up here, above the high water line, until tomorrow, unless there is something people particularly want.'

With one accord, the group turned and started climbing the beach toward the spot where running water could be seen. Before the night was fully dark, they had set up camp and were sitting around the fire awaiting a fine stew, which was bubbling over the coals.

Chun had a map of the coastline, which he had scrounged off the Bosun on *The Golden Guinea*. He was studying it by the flickering light of the fire, when Amelia came and sank down beside him.

'We have quite a distance to go,' he confided, grasping her hand. 'Our way may be beset with bandits and wild animals.'

Amelia looked over her shoulder at the thick foliage growing on the cliff-face behind her. 'What kind of wild animals?' she queried, while a shiver of apprehension ran tingling down her spine.

'Well, there might be lions or jackals in the dry lands. Worse would be two-legged predators. There are sure to be bandits, many of them could be sailors who have been marooned on these shores.'

'We are lucky to have Anton and the soldiers then. His training will come into good use.' She then asked Chun what his duties were at court, hoping to take her mind off the dangers they were in. He explained his main function was to maintain the well-being of the Jara and his family.

Anton joined them and the evening passed in desultory conversation, mainly about the journey, which lay ahead of them. Chun showed them his map and outlined the route they were about to take.

Large cliffs stretched around the bulge of headlands lying to the north. These would give them firm-footing and a clear view, as long as there were no more storms, until they had to turn inwards to the west, as they progressed towards Jaddanna. Their main worry would be to keep a steady supply of fresh water for themselves and their horses.

Before they retired for the night, Chun called the company together. While he was waiting for them to assemble, Anton noted the slight man was showing signs of strain. He had changed from his healer gowns for travelling, and now wore trousers and shirt the same as the others.

Without his robes he seemed younger and more vulnerable, Anton thought. He smiled at his friend and made a sign showing Chun had all his support.

Chun watched the party gather, considering what he was about to say. As the soldiers and companions he had been travelling with had left their leaders on the plains, as next in rank he had assumed command.

Now, Chun assigned guard duties and chores, ensuring that all worked for the common good in a variety of tasks. Each evening Amelia was to assist with cooking, and Anton was to engage a member of the party in arms practise.

All agreed that those not delegated duty in the evenings, should practise with their weapons, even if not Anton's designated opponent, as who knew what might lie ahead of them?

Chun had no difficulty with the soldiers, as they were used to taking orders, but some of the prince's officers were recalcitrant about washing dishes and digging latrines, never mind about grooming horses; they grumbled to each other and gesticulated.

Chun stood up and moved a few steps away from the group, striding up the side of the cliff path until he could be seen by all.

'We are stranded on a beach away from civilisation. If you are not willing to contribute your share of the work, perhaps you would care to leave us.

'You could make your own way, or you could return to the ship and await rescue. I will expect your decisions in the morning.' So saying, he dropped down without further discussion and made his way to his sleeping bag after calling out goodnight.

As he thought, in the morning each member of the prince's party came to apologise, and after they had finished their breakfast, the group started their journey.

The first sortie up the cliff proved hazardous, but the horses were sure-footed and no one fell, though there were one or two anxious moments as the sandy path was crumbly.

Amelia enjoyed the exercise in the open air. She had chosen a small, brown mare with dainty hooves. A biddable little creature, her big, brown eyes had won Amelia's heart. One of the pack horses, which the soldiers had brought from their trip to the plains, she had been overlooked, rather than cruelly-treated. Her name was Tam, and Amelia was delighted with her.

At mid-day they stopped to give the horses a rest and to have a meal from their saddlebags themselves. As she was leaving for the shelter of some nearby bushes, Amelia bemoaned to herself, what a pity it was she was the only female member of the party. Another woman would have been company in these circumstances. In fact, as she pushed further into the greenery, she suddenly felt quite alone.

Her thoughts betrayed an inner desire to return to her home, and the picture of her parent's house in Kordova rose to her inner eye. *I wish I never left the island, off adventuring with Delia*, she thought. *If we had not gone to Devron we would have missed the pirates, and none of this would have happened.* A few tears gathered, and her eyes felt tight and hot.

'I am not going to cry,' she announced aloud, 'that will only make me feel worse!'

As she was returning from her sojourn in the bushes, she saw a flicker of motion at the side of the path. Then her eye was caught by a movement in the grass, beyond her feet. Involuntarily, she jumped to the side, just as a large snake struck the ground where her feet had been. The huge body slithered by and disappeared into the undergrowth on the other side of the path. There was now no sign it had been there at all. She had uttered a cry of surprise, which had attracted members of the party, including Chun, to dash to her rescue.

When she had explained what had happened, one of the soldiers named Todda, searched the grasses where Amelia had said the snake had come from. In a short while he emerged, carrying something.

'It was a King Cobra,' he exclaimed. 'You were very fortunate, as they are angry and upset when they have just shed skin. Not only that, they strike at anything that moves as they feel threatened because they don't see so well at such a time.'

Chun consoled Amelia, who was still white and shaking. 'In future,' he said, 'if you have a call of nature, you take one of the soldiers with you to protect you from dangers.'

Amelia assented, saying she would not be so silly again. She was glad to return to her mare, feeling secure in the presence of her sharp teeth and flying hooves.

Later, she had a look at the snake's skin, and was impressed with its beauty and design, though death stalked in its fascination.

Anton sank down beside her. 'You should have called me to go,' he growled.

'I am aware of that,' she answered. 'Foolishly, the thought I might be in danger never occurred to me. Let us forget about it.'

'Listen to me! I will come into good use.'

She nodded and squeezed his hand, then turned to ask Chun what supplies they had.

Anton joined them and the evening passed in desultory conversation, mainly about the journey, which lay ahead of them. Chun showed them his map and outlined the route they were about to take.

Large cliffs stretched around the bulge of headlands lying to the north. These would give them firm footing and a clear view, as long as there were no more storms, until they had to turn inwards to the west coast, while hawks flew over the land.

Every now and then they could see the wrecks of ships stuck mouldering in the sandbanks near the sea. They all looked as if they had been there many years. Anton wondered what had happened to the sailors who had been on those ships. There seemed to be no sign of habitation anywhere in view. The day passed and the sun lowered in the sky, and then they started to see shadows in the scruffy grass.

Calling out so all could hear, Chun announced, 'we should stop at the next suitable place. Todda, ride ahead and look for a track down to the beach. Let us hope you can find fresh water.'

Todda kicked his horse into a canter and was soon far ahead. When they caught up with him, he had found a small rivulet, which was emptying over the cliff on to a beach far below. There was also an overgrown path, which meandered down the side of the cliff.

'I have been down for most of the way,' he said. 'We will have to be careful, going down, stay close to the cliff side, but I do think it is man-made.'

One by one, they set foot on the narrow cliff path, leading their horses, as they were resisting setting out on the crumbling ground.

Todda and Anton went first, followed by Amelia and Chun, with the rest of the party bringing up the rear.

On reaching the beach, Anton was surprised to see some broken-down sheds, huddled together, at the foot of the cliff. There was no smoke from the huts, and they seemed to be abandoned. As they approached, they smelled why, before their eyes registered what they were seeing.

The occupants were stretched out corpses in front of their doors. Some were reaching for knives, while others were lying in a group of bodies, where they had crumpled together in life. Their animals were stretched about them.

Amelia was sick with horror as she understood she was a witness to a past murder. The tracks around the sheds showed the movement of people dragging bundles.

'They have been murdered and robbed,' Chun announced, after he had ventured into the three huts. He looked hollow-eyed, with his face drawn grim and tight-jawed.

'They were surprised at their daily work. I wonder where the robbers are, and what was needed so badly, to cause such slaughter?'

Anton was the first to understand what was necessary. 'We must bury them in the sand. We will not be able to rest here, with all of this about us. Let us look in the huts for shovels, or spades.'

The gruesome task took time. While the soldiers and their companions dug pits and moved the corpses, Amelia had taken the horses to water, and had then picketed them out. She found some oats and had started to curry their mounts, when Anton found her.

'The job is done,' he told her. 'They were just ordinary fisherfolk by the looks of it. Perhaps they were smugglers who were hiding too much contraband.

'We have decided to make camp at the other end of the beach. No one wants to be in these huts during the night.'

Amelia was glad to be sleeping in the open air. Anton helped her with the rest of the horses, and then they made their way to the beginnings of the camp being organised by Chun.

He raised a hand as he saw them coming towards him. 'Let us hope whoever did this is now far away,' he said. 'Otherwise, the smoke from our fire might attract them here.'

Amelia drew her shawl around her shoulders more closely, her eyes wide with apprehension as she gazed at the towering cliffs.

Chapter Fourteen

The bay gelding, with its floating, white tail and silky mane, was a delight to Eyas. She spent much time in the stables, cosseting and admiring him.

Eyas had learned to ride under Trojan's stern tutelage, and was now a competent horse-woman. After much thought, she had called her horse Sultan, and he had blossomed with her careful treatment, not to mention the delicacies she brought to the stables to delight him.

Delia had also learned to ride. She had understood it was something she needed to do, and impatiently wanted to get on with it, treating it more as a duty than a pleasure.

Trojan had been careful to ensure the horses Delia rode were biddable, and would not arouse her ire, not wanting her to be deposited on her admirable bottom too many times. She had proved to be a competent horse-woman to his surprise.

He was still considering the best way for them to make their escape. The long journey to Keshia on horseback would strain their riding abilities and their constitutions, but they would have only themselves to rely on.

The other option was to engage a ship's' captain, possibly Ambry, to give them passage to the same destination. This would be quicker, but it meant they had to put their trust in others, and it also would probably take all of their funds.

Trojan had spent hours tracking the paths down through the tunnels and sewers under the house and could easily find his own way down to the cavern, where the contraband came in. Leaving the Eyrie that way would be no problem.

He lay on his back in the long grass of the riding meadow, beside the Eyrie, gazing at the sky. Trojan watched an eagle soaring overhead – it was using the wind funnels on the top of the cliffs to maintain its height.

As he was watching, the eagle plummeted from the sky, swooping on a flight of pigeons making their way to their home under the eaves. The pigeons scattered and escaped, bringing their messages safely into Madame's pigeon loft.

I wonder what devious plot she is up to now, he mused. The pounding of hooves approaching across the grass distracted his thoughts. He sat up and waved to the girls as they dismounted; then he joined them to help tie their horses to a fence nearby.

'You are quite capable now,' he complimented Delia, admiring her bright eyes and flushed cheeks.

'What do you expect?' she retorted. 'You have forced us on these animals day after day!'

Eyas led them to where Trojan had been sitting, then sank down on the soft grass, beckoning him to join her.

'I have made up my mind,' she said, looking at him levelly.

'What about?'

'I am not going with you. You owe Madame nothing – either of you – as she bought you both for a purpose. She rescued me from the brothel, and from the streets. She has given me fine clothes, a good home and a future.'

Eyas gave him an apologetic smile, 'I couldn't leave Sultan, anyway. I shall stay here and be her adopted niece.

'I think she is really a lonely person and I might give her some company. Perhaps we shall be able to meet again when you are both returned to your lives.

'I will help you make your escape. How do you want to go?'

'I think by sea. Although we have spent time for you both to learn to ride and how to manage weapons, the safer route would be purchasing our passage on a vessel.

'If we left by road, Esse could not only claim us as escaped slaves but could call us horse-thieves as well. What hope would we have then?'

'You are probably right. Do you want me to speak to Ambry for you, or would you rather hire a fishing smack?'

'I have been considering it. I think Ambry is the better bet. He is in and out of the harbour all the time, and Essa doesn't seem to know when he will be here or not. Probably it would be better if you spoke to him; I would be too obvious.

'What would a bound, indentured slave want with a sea captain, unless it was for something devious?

'You think of a reason why you need to speak to him, something he can get from Keshia for you. Then if he wants to know where he is going, it will be to the right place.'

She nodded in agreement, while running her hands over the soft grass in the meadow. She plucked a piece, and put it between her teeth, sucking on the sweet sap.

'You'll get worms doing that.'

She was horrified, but did not show it, tossing her long, blonde hair in disdain when he laughed at her.

Delia returned from giving the horses sugar lumps. 'Why are you both sitting down?'

'Come!' Trojan called. 'Take this dagger away from me!'

Delia flung herself on top of him, holding a small dagger, which she had produced from her sleeve, already presented at his throat. She menaced him with a wild gleam in her eye.

He rolled over, holding both her arms spread-eagled on the ground. 'No good,' he said. 'You must keep out of my reach, and certainly come up under my arm, if you are going to be that close.'

The lesson continued, while Eyas watched them, glad it was not her involved in the rough and tumble. She would miss them when they left– they were good companions, yet she was pleased with the decision she had made. Getting up she went to stroke Sultan, his coat glossy in the sunshine.

Looking out to sea Eyas saw *The Dark Dart* nearing the harbour. She watched as the sails came down. The sounds of pulleys and the squeal of metal as the anchor slid deep came carried on the breeze.

A small boat was lowered and then rowed across the harbour towards the cavern below *The Eyrie*.

He will dine with us tonight, she thought. *I wonder what I can ask him to bring me from Keshia? A rope of pearls for Madame, perhaps, or a bolt of silk for a new dress? I could do with some new clothes.*

Delia did not seem to care that all she possessed were her two slave dresses and a pair of men's pants for her riding practice. She wondered what Delia had been like when she was free.

They will both have to be properly clothed before they leave, she mused. *I will have to organise that too. Delia might fit some of my dresses, but they will be too long.*

I'll tell Essa I want some alterations made, and while the woman is going back and forth, she can purchase some suitable jackets and cloaks for Trojan. I shall sell my jewellery to pay for this work; lucky I have been given so many trinkets from people who want me to use my influence with Essa to gain what they want.

The others joined her, and then they turned the horses back to the stables. Trojan and Delia were still arguing about tactics. Delia was flushed, her hair had come loose and her eyes were flashing. Trojan looked slightly amused, his sardonic looks and leisurely horsemanship, giving more fuel to Delia's annoyance.

When they reached their apartment, Eyas immediately asked a servant to summon a seamstress from The Flats.

As the afternoon was to be spent going through clothes and selecting jewellery, Trojan made himself scarce. He wandered down through the kitchen and then into the cellars, exploring the passages further. It was dark and gloomy under the house. The corridors and steps were lit with flickering rush lights, just giving a sufficient glow for one to find the way.

The place smelt of burning straw, mould and rat droppings. If he stood still he could hear the rats squeaking and scratching in the heaps of mouldy rags and rubbish abandoned in the cellars. There was some straw, which had been spread to absorb the moisture dripping down the walls and dropping off the ceilings.

Coming down a flight of crooked stairs, he saw the shadows of two people dancing in the shifting light outlined on the wall in front of him. Their heads were together as they were involved in conversation.

'We set sail the day after tomorrow with the evening tide', he heard Ambry's unmistakable, gruff voice say. 'I am having stores loaded now.

'I have a message to do for Madame in Keshia, so I can deliver your order for the opium for Jade then. After that I am going further north, to see what pickings can be found in The Bay of Storms.

'When I come back I will pick up Jade's parcel. I'll send young Dan around later on today. Tell her she can trust him with the silvos, but I will count them to the very last one.'

'I'll do that, captain. Mistress Jade will be pleased. She was expecting a package coming down from the north, but it seems to be a long time coming. It is strange, as Timmo is usually very dependable. Mistress Jade needs a constant supply when trade is brisk.'

Trojan turned and climbed the stairs, slipping into a side passage at the top. He flattened himself against the wall, while listening to Ambry's heavy footsteps pass him by.

Trojan followed more slowly, making sure Ambry was unaware of his presence. When he reached the main corridor he turned off towards the silversmith's cavern. It was always well-lit and cheery there, and he had made friends with one of the armourers, who now hailed him with a smile.

'What can I do for you today, Trojan?'

'I have some knives which need sharpening,' Trojan returned. 'I can't pay for the job though.'

'Never mind. I'll slip them on to the butcher's bill,' Leff returned, giving him a wide grin.

Soon the whirr of the whetstone forbid conversation. When they were finished, Leff handed Trojan the knives, then beckoned him over towards a shelf on the wall behind his bench.

'I have been tempering some new steel,' he said, lifting up a thin sword. 'I would like your opinion. You have done some duelling and some sword fighting in the past, haven't you?' Trojan assented with a nod.

'Then take this please and try it. I don't want it back but just want to know your opinion and whether it is worth making more.'

'I can't accept this!' Trojan exclaimed, though his eyes glistened with pleasure. He hefted the sword and made a few exploratory passes. 'The balance is just right, so is the length!'

'There, you see, it was made for you. Should I make some more?'

'Of course!' Trojan went to hand the weapon back, but Leff would have none of it.

'Look, I made it for you; accept it with good grace. From now on, I shall accept orders knowing they will be fine. You have done me a favour.'

Smuggling the sword back to Eyas' quarters was a problem. In the end, he slid it up the back of his shirt, held by the band of his trousers, and leant against the wall whenever anyone passed by.

'Why are you looking like a ramrod?' Delia demanded suspiciously. She was standing on a table while Eyas measured the hem of a skirt she was wearing.

'Because of this!' Trojan slid the sword out of his shirt, nicking his neck on the sharp blade as he did so.

The girls were all attention, clothes forgotten, and soon Eyas had the bleeding stopped and a bandage tied around the cut.

'We shall have to do something about those collars,' she observed. 'It might have saved you from doing yourself more injury, but otherwise it is a definite disadvantage.'

Delia touched hers, always hidden by the high collars of her dresses.

'Madame keeps the keys in a small drawer in a tallboy in her bedroom. There are at least half a dozen all the same. I will borrow one while she is talking to her guests as they are leaving this evening.

'We will unfasten the collars, then put the key back. You must continue wearing the collars until you finally escape, as someone might notice their absence.'

'It will be wonderful to be able to take this horrid thing off.' Delia jumped down from the table now Eyas had completed her measuring.

'It is no worse than a Lord's torc,' Trojan commented. 'I hardly notice the thing. I will need a scabbard for the sword, though.'

'I'll put my mind to it,' Eyas promised. 'I think I know where I can find one. Here, put this on.' She pulled a leather jacket out from behind a settle where it had been hidden. Trojan hurriedly put the sword down on the settle out of harm's way, before complying.

That evening the dinner party was smaller than usual. Eyas was thankful when she saw Ambry seated in his normal place, chatting to Jade. He was in an expansive mood and gesticulated as he talked, obviously explaining something devious to her.

'I have a commission for the captain.' Eyas murmured to Essa as they rose from the table. 'I won't be a moment.'

'Oh! What about?'

'Never you mind! You will find out soon enough when he returns to harbour.'

Eyas met Essa's eyes with a mischievous smile.

She beckoned to Ambry as he was walking past.

'Captain Ambry! A favour from you!' She drew him aside, keeping well out of earshot of the rest of the gathering.

'What can I do for you, my lady?' He eyed her beauty speculatively.

'I have two boons to ask. I have some friends who are eloping. They are hidden at the moment, and wish passage to Keshia. Have you a free cabin on your next trip?'

'How lucky you are! I am going to Keshia the day after tomorrow.'

'Well then, it is arranged. Send Dan to me when they are to alight. If he guides them to their cabin and then serves their meals and sees to their wants, only he will see them and only he will know they are aboard. We can then all pretend we know nothing of them. Oh, here!' She slid the heavy bag of gold out of her waistband and into his palm.

'The other boon?' he queried, raising an ironic eyebrow.

'Oh yes, the other commission. Would you buy Madame a double rope of black pearls for me please? I shall pay for them when you return. Only the best quality, mind!'

'At your service, my lady! Now, who are these passengers I am not taking aboard *The Dark Dart*?'

'It is better if you neither know them, nor see them, as then her father will not bring war galleys to hold us accountable.'

'I see you are gaining wily ways and weasel words from your Aunt, My Lady. I shall endeavour to fulfil your commissions.' He slid the gold into the voluminous pocket of his jacket, having hefted it experimentally, and listened to it clink.

Eyas strolled back to the table and nodded to Essa as she was returning from the door where she had been chatting to Jade, who was waiting for Ambry to escort her back to town.

Eyas wished Essa good night and mounted the stairs to her room without a backward glance. In no aspect of her demeanour did she betray her inward terror and trembling nerves.

Delia heard her footsteps and hurried to open the door.

'Well?' she demanded, 'did you see him? Have you done it?'

'Let me in!' Eyas exclaimed, pushing past her, to collapse on a chair. 'Yes, and yes! Now it is up to you two to complete the charade. What will happen to me when you leave, bears no thought!'

'Oh! I hadn't considered that!' Delia's eyes were wide with worry and concern. 'Perhaps we should tie you up?'

'It might come to that,' Eyas gritted, fanning herself with her hand.

The two girls continued to talk and plan while they waited for Trojan to return from his duties.

He had had not much to report to Madame Esse. All her schemes were working well and there appeared little afoot she was not aware of. Mistress Alla was pleased to have the promise of the free gift of one of Essa's puppies and was honoured to be asked to help with their training.

She had informed the Abbot that with her help, Dishnigar would soon hold the monopoly for the finest tracking dogs. In return the Abbot had told her the Abbey had purchased excellent land overlooking the harbour for a very good price from the city council. He intended to build a mill there, as there was a stream running through the property.

Not only that, as it was on a headland, there was plenty of wind suitable for a windmill. He had expanded on his theme, explaining that when the mill was built they would have a bakery as well. Then, he had carried on, people would bring their food there to be cooked for a price after they had bought their flour.

'Never mind all that,' Delia spluttered, when he related to them the evening's happenings after he had slumped on the window seat, worn out from his evening's work.

'What about us? Was anything said?'

'Oh yes,' he replied, 'but nothing to worry about.' He smiled at Eyas. 'You did well with Ambry. Madame stopped him before he left and asked him what you wanted.

'He told her you had given him a commission to buy her a present and that was all he was going to say. I was holding my breath, I can tell you! I was wondering what we would do if he told her our plans.

'Are we all set for our journey, the day after tomorrow?'

Eyas nodded. 'Dan will come to get you when it is time for you to go aboard. He will take you to your cabin and will see to your needs. Ambry doesn't have to see you until you choose, if at all. Certainly not until after you have sailed.'

'Of course he could take us into slavery again!' Delia was apprehensive about the outcome of the situation.

'There is that possibility,' Eyas agreed. 'If that happens I will track you down, never fear. I doubt if Ambry will, because he will know I will have no further dealings with him, if that is the case.

'He must stay honest with me, if I am going to inherit the Eyrie and the businesses. It wouldn't be worth his while to fall out of favour with me.'

Delia flung her arms around Eyas and gave her a hug. 'When this is all over we shall return to see you,' she promised. 'You have done so much for us with little thought for yourself.'

'Yes,' Trojan said. 'I shall take you back to Devronia, to stay with me at court and then on to my estates at Desra. We shall have parties, balls, go hunting, anything you like.'

'I shall look forward to the prospect,' Eyas said gravely, 'but let us spend the rest of the time we have together, enjoying each other's company while we plot your escape. Nothing must be overlooked in our preparation. At the same time our days must be as usual, so signalling nothing is amiss.'

Time passed slowly, but finally they were perched uncomfortably on the fronts of their chairs, waiting for the summoning tap on the door. Eyas looked them over critically.

They were both wearing soft boots to the knee, with thick trousers tucked inside them. Their heads were covered with loose hoods, attached to voluminous dark brown cloaks, covering warm jackets.

Little could be seen of their faces, but what could be seen was covered with light masks disguising their features. Their belongings were tied together in cloth bundles, which were easy to carry.

Trojan had his treasured sword hidden under his cloak, while Delia had a knife stuck through the waistband of her pants.

It is the best I can do, Eyas thought, giving them an approving nod.

Everyone started, when the expected tap finally came on the door. Eyas embraced them both, then motioned them to the doorway.

'Keep safe,' she breathed, 'remember to keep your faces covered.' She gave Delia a little push towards the door.

Trojan kissed her hand. 'I shall return,' he promised. 'Thank you for all your help and understanding.' He swept up the bundles hampered by his sword, but finally negotiated everything. 'If we have to fight to get off this hulk, we will.'

'Why should we want to?' Delia was looking puzzled. 'Didn't you hear? Out there is a ship from Devron!'

He stood in the doorway with his burdens. Delia had already started off down the dimly-lit passageway, following the lead of Dan, who was eager to leave the house and get back on board the ship.

'Wait!' Trojan whispered crossly, 'you can carry some of these.' He pushed a couple of parcels into Delia's hands to her surprise. She was all ready to protest till she saw the steely glint in his eyes over the top of his mask.

Making little noise in the rush-strewn passages, they made their way through the servants' quarters of the Eyrie until they reached the kitchens. At this time of night the kitchens were empty, the servants abed, and the fires banked until morning. Delia helped herself to some little cakes displayed on a side table, left over from the sweet course at dinner. She collected them all into a napkin and crammed them into her pocket.

'My favourites!' she told Trojan, squashing one into her mouth, then licking her fingers to taste every last sugary morsel.

'Let us hope it is not the last thing you eat,' he retorted. 'Holding us up while you stuff yourself.' This set her off with the giggles. Her laughter was infectious and soon Dan was chuckling as well.

They staggered down the next flight of stairs, while Delia clasped her bundles tightly as she slid down the curve of the wall, hardly able to stagger as she was full of subdued hysterical laughter, having stood on the bottom of her cloak and nearly pitched down the stairs.

There was a growing rumbling sound in the passage below them, accompanied with a screeching sound. Dan turned and pushed Delia into a side passage, then reached out and pulled Trojan beside him.

'I don't think The Eagle would like us to view her contraband,' he whispered. 'Just stay still until the brandy and the baccy has passed us by.' He put his finger to his nose, then nodded at them conspiratorially.

'The least we know, the less accountable,' he added. When the noise had dwindled into the distance, he allowed them to proceed.

They emerged on to a jetty in a cavern below the cliffs. The only light, which gleamed on the black oily water, came from faint rush lights, stuck in iron sconces, flickering in the night breeze. There were a few rowboats attached to the jetty, bumping against the planking with the movement of the water. Dan pulled one close to the side and held it against the wood. Faintly, in the poor light, Trojan could make out *The Dark Dart* painted on the hull.

'Here we are again!' he murmured to Delia. She responded by pulling her cloak around her more closely, while ensuring her hood covered what could be seen of her face. They climbed into the rowboat and settled themselves. Delia sat in the prow, while Dan and Trojan took up the oars.

The small boat made little noise as they set off across the cavern. After they had exited through a gloomy tunnel, the water was much choppier. Delia clutched the sides of the boat as the prow rose and fell with the surge of the tide. A cold wind blew in from the west and the men had difficulty making progress against both wind and tide.

Twisting around, Delia could see the outline of *The Dark Dart* at anchor in the bay. The ship's riding lights rose and fell with the swell, making it difficult for her to gauge how far away it was. Slowly, they pulled away from the looming cliffs.

Delia knew how often Madame Esse sat on her balconies with her spy glasses in hand. *She will not be there this late at night*, she thought. *Even if she is, she will not be able to recognise us at this distance, and the way we are dressed.* Nevertheless, she tugged at her hood, making sure yet again, that it covered her face.

While Trojan was rowing, he was musing about their predicament. They had given all their money to Ambry for their passage to Keshia. All being well, they should reach there safely, but then what?

He knew no one in the town, so far away from his own estates. The authorities would have been alerted about runaway slaves and would be on the lookout for them. There would be no hope of returning immediately to Devron. He would face it when they got to Keshia, he finally decided, tired of the circle his mind had been making.

The rowboat ground against the hull of *The Dark Dart*, arousing the sailor who had been dozing on watch.

'Who is there?' he called.

'Dan the cabin boy, with passengers,' came back the answer. 'Drop the rope ladder!'

Getting Delia up the rope ladder from the rocking, pitching rowboat, while enveloped in her cloak, was not an easy task. Trojan pulled from above, while Dan pushed from behind, at the same time, avoiding Delia's lashing boots with dexterity and alarm. Finally they all managed to fall about on the deck. The sailor swarmed down the ladder and returned with their parcels and bundles. The dinghy was then hoisted on board.

Dan gave them a superior glance before saying, 'If you two are ready, follow me.'

They picked up their parcels and dutifully trailed after him down the dark companionways to the low lintel of a cabin. 'You can latch it from the inside,' he instructed. 'No doubt you want a drink and a bite to eat. I'll bring something.'

Delia was amused to find this was the identical cabin where she and Amelia had been incarcerated. However, now the room was neatly set out and the bunks were made up. A small lantern on the table gave a pleasant glow, making the polished wood of the cabin walls gleam.

After latching the door, Trojan flung himself on a bunk and stretched out his arms. 'So far so good, now all we have to do is avoid Ambry.'

Delia arranged their belongings in a neat heap at the side of the cabin, then perched on the single chair in the room. 'If we stay in here, and we are very quiet, perhaps he will forget about us.'

Dan returned with some bread and cheese and two flagons of ale. He indicated a curtain in the corner, saying that was where they could wash and there was a chamber pot there for their convenience. He would see to the necessaries, this was said with a grin. He bid them good night, and Delia snicked the door behind him. She threw off her cloak, snatched the mask off her face, and did a turn in the middle of the cabin.

'Farewell, Madame Esse! I hope I never see you again.' She then sat down on her chair and made a start on the bread and cheese.

Trojan sat up, lifted an ale flagon, and took a great gulp. 'Listen! The sails are going up! We shall be moving soon! Who would have believed we would come back to this ship of our own accord? Hey, save some of that food for me! You have already had those cakes!'

Next morning Dishnigar was far behind them. *The Dark Dart* sailed south, following the coast line. Trojan found being confined to the cabin most irksome. It was only mid morning of the first day, and he was roaming round the cabin like a caged beast.

Delia sat on her bunk and watched the waves splatting on to the coastline. The rugged beauty of the southern shores attracted her. She wondered what lives people lived, in the hamlets they were sweeping past.

'Do come and sit down and watch this scenery,' she cajoled. Trojan, you will make a hole in the carpet!'

'I'm worried,' was the answer. 'Even if we do reach Keshia safely, what are we going to do then?

'We have no friends and no money, and to boot we are escaped slaves.

'I bet Madame's pigeons have been wearing out their feathers dashing back and forth.'

'Don't worry about the money aspect.' Delia reached out a hand and pulled him down beside her. 'Look at these.'

She pulled a knotted handkerchief out of the neck of her shirt. The bundle had been lying hidden beneath her breasts. She undid the knot and displayed the contents on the bunk, beside his knee.

'You didn't steal these jewels?' he asked in horror.

'Don't be silly! Eyas was using her jewels to outfit us, and these were some that were left over. There should be enough silvos here to set us up in Keshia, and then we can decide what to do.'

'I must say that is a huge relief!' Trojan pushed the rings and bracelets around with his forefinger, finally picking up one, a particularly fine, ruby necklace. 'I remember Eyas wearing this,' he said. 'Hasn't she been a great friend? I wish she had come with us.'

'She made her decision,' Delia replied. 'She is safe and secure, with a great future assured for her, which is more than can be said for us brave freebooters.'

'Oh, we will be all right. I'm feeling much more cheerful now. Put these back where you had them hidden, we wouldn't want to lose them.' He watched her tie up the jewels carefully; then she replaced them inside her shirt.

'We must practise our skills,' Trojan continued. 'None of this slacking around on our bunks. Today, we will practise knife throwing.'

He busied himself making a target out of towels, then erected it on the far side of the cabin. By the time Dan arrived with their lunch, Delia was exhausted. Her fingers were stinging and her arm ached. However, she had improved her skill and could hit the target almost as often as Trojan could.

'I want a rest this afternoon,' she pleaded.

'Oh no! We are playing skip this afternoon.'

This consisted of her jumping out of the way, as he tried to tread on her feet. After a little while he changed over, but was too nimble for her to get anywhere near him. Before they were aware of it, the day had gone.

So their days passed. By the time *The Dark Dart* had rounded the Southern Cape they had established a pattern of activities which kept them fit and filled their days.

The meals, apart from the bread and cheese, were not to Delia's taste, so she ate very little. On the other hand, Trojan, knowing he had to eat to maintain his strength, gobbled up both their portions. She became lean and wiry, while he gained muscle. All their exercise kept them healthy.

One morning when Dan arrived with their breakfast his face was agog with excitement.

'We have had to put on more sail because we are being chased! There is a Devron galley after us. It came out of the

223

early morning mist, just past the Cape. It must have been waiting in the lee of the land, waiting for us.

'Captain Ambry is calling all hands to help. You two might have to come on deck if there is a fire.'

'Why would there be a fire?' Delia's face was drawn with worry.

'They might send fire arrows into our sails.' Dan was clearly excited at the prospect of the battle ahead. 'We might have to abandon ship,' he shouted, running up the companionway.

'Bundle everything up together!' Trojan was looking stern and purposeful, sharpening his sword.

'Why are you doing that?' Delia demanded. 'Who are you going to fight?'

'Anyone who attacks us!' Trojan declared.

'Don't be silly. We are passengers on this ship, and the other one is from Devron. We are just going to stay quiet.' Having said this, she sat down on her bunk.

Chapter Fifteen

Troy pulled up the collar of his jacket and hunched forward over his horse's neck, trying to avoid the biting wind, which was gusting over the rain swept plains. He shivered inside the dead rider's leathers. They were too small for him, but did give him a covering against the worst of the wind and weather.

The boots though had been a different matter, but fortunately he had been able to retain his own from the galley, though now much the worse for wear. He had tramped around the slave quarters day and night after he had recovered from his beating, wondering what was to become of him.

His thoughts turned to the day Borin had entered the square. Troy had been standing at the bars across the window, looking out with his hands grasping the cold steel. He had watched the tall, rangy rider with long, dark red hair, stroll over to the Slave Master's office. As he had crossed the square he had looked up, and their eyes had met. Borin had smiled, as one human to another, provoking a grin from Troy, who suddenly had a surge of hope.

Later he was summoned to the office by the slave who brought him his meals.

'You are on your way, boyo,' had been his terse summons.

The Slave Master had unshackled him and had then turned to Borin who was standing to one side waiting. 'What about the collar?'

'Take it off,' Borin had replied. 'There is no place to run to on the plains.'

Troy had straightened up when the collar came off, even though he was naked apart from a breechcloth and his boots.

Once outside the Slave Market, Borin had guided Troy to where he had left Jet and another stallion. Undoing the saddlebag of the other horse, he had produced the leathers Troy was now wearing.

'These will do until we can clothe you properly, when we get home,' he had said gruffly. 'Best to cover the mess someone has made of your back. Can you ride?' Borin looked at his newest acquisition dubiously. He did not look at all prepossessing.

Struggling into the clothes, Troy had nodded assent. He glanced at the horses tethered to the railing. 'Nothing as large as them, though,' he had admitted.

'You'll soon get used to them.' Borin had encouraged, swinging up on to Jet's back. 'Your horse is called Glint. Ben called him that because he thought he had an evil glint in his eye. What is your name?'

'Troy.'

'Well, Troy, mount up, and let us go find the rest of the band. If you treat me fairly, I shall treat you the same. As I said before, there is nowhere to run to on the plains.'

Swinging into the saddle, Troy remembered thinking, 'be careful what you wish for.' He had patted Glint on the neck, and had then urged the dun to follow Borin who was leading the way out of the square.

When they reached *The Endless Tankard* they found the other riders all packed up and waiting for Borin outside the tavern.

Borin had introduced Troy quickly, saying he was the new man to replace Ben, but there was no mention that Troy was a slave he had recently bought. Troy had wondered at that, and then he was grateful, as the other riders treated him as their equal.

They had left the streets of Dishnigar behind, their horses eager to be off, trotting through the cobbled alleys, with the sounds of their hoofs reverberating off the walls. Shaking their harness and flicking their tails, they headed up towards the cliffs. They were pleased when they reached the gravel road, away from the enclosed spaces. It was not until they turned to the right at the top of the cliff that the wind had hit them.

Unused to being outside after his weeks of incarceration, Troy suffered the most from the wicked cold. Now he and Glint had become fast friends, and as the afternoon wore on and the homesteads dropped behind, he began to appreciate being on horseback, despite the cold.

Troy considered the group of people whom fate had thrown his way. They all seemed friendly enough, had included him in their banter, and there seemed no animosity for the new man.

Borin was obviously the leader, yet Jerain also held some stature, and was respected. Merthsandra only had eyes for him, yet she had given Troy a careful summation when he had been introduced to her. He admired her nonchalant attitude, and her horsemanship.

Merthsandra's vibrant personality kept them all alert, and she chivvied them along with her incisive remarks and her witty tongue. Her family resemblance to Borin was strong, though his hair was a dark red and hers was fair. They both rode as if the horse was part of their own body, and their horses seemed to reflect their personalities.

Borin signalled they would stop and make camp. Each rider looked after his or her horse. Troy was glad of this, as he had thought being the only slave; he would be expected to do all the work. However, everyone pitched in to help.

Water was brought, the fire was lit, bedrolls were stretched out, and soon dinner was cooking. Glad of the bedroll he had found attached to his saddle, Troy stretched it out as near to the fire as he could find a place, not already occupied.

Just before he was going to lie down, Jerain appeared at his elbow. 'Here, this might be useful if you haven't ridden for a while.' He held out a small, white pot of ointment.

Troy reached for it eagerly. 'What is it?'

'Oh, some potion my wife had our healer make up. It heals saddle sores and other aches and pains.'

'Is Merthsandra your wife?'

'Good Mut, no! I am married to her sister, Merth. The Horse Lady! The Clan Leader!'

'I'm sorry, I didn't know the clan was led by a woman.'

'You will meet her some day. Good night.'

227

Jerain slipped away into the fire-lit dusk, and then Troy heard Merthsandra's laugh tinkling in the distance. After he had applied the ointment, his pains and aches alleviated, and soon he was drifting off to sleep, more content than he had been since landing on this shore.

The next day the riders were up at dawn. Troy was woken by a rider, who shoved a hot drink at him with a slab of tasty bacon steaming between two pieces of bread. He ate voraciously, suddenly aware of the residual hunger he had suffered in the slave quarters.

Glint was pleased to see him, and soon they were all on their way. Trotting up beside Jerain, he noticed the beautiful animal Jerain was riding. He thought about Juliette, and how he had wished to mate her with one of these great stallions. The likelihood of this happening was receding further and further into the distance with every day that passed.

Troy glanced aside at Jerain who also seemed to ride as if he were part of his horse, in the same way Borin rode. Troy knew he was a good rider, but he was nothing like these Horse Lords, who seemed to be bred to ride.

The next longer stop was at the river where they had stopped on their way to Dishnigar. Taking advantage of the late afternoon sun, Troy went down to the water with the intention of washing his clothes, as they still bore evidence of the death of their previous wearer, and he felt aware of his presence. He would also like losing the stench of the slave pens from his own body, too. To his surprise, Borin had beaten him to the water.

Troy stood on the bank and watched Borin swim to the far side of the river with strong, powerful strokes. When he stood to turn around, Troy was surprised to see a large bear tattooed on Borin's back. Borin swam back lazily, then plucked some soap from among his drying clothes spread out on the bank, and tossed a bar over to Troy.

'You look as if you could do with some of this. My wife, Muria, made it. It brings up a good lather.'

Thanking him, Troy quickly divested himself of his clothes, and then set to scrubbing them as soon as he had immersed them in the water. After, he joined Borin for a swim, his blond hair dark with water now, rather than with dirt.

'That's a great tattoo you have on your back, better than what I have got,' Troy laughed ironically.

'It is a totem,' Borin replied. 'It means I am married to Muria, who is the Horse Lady of the Bear clan. My sister, Merth, is the chief of all the clans. She has some mighty totems and tattoos.'

'I thought Jerain was her husband. If that is the case, what does he wear?'

'He should have a Phoenix, but we left before it could be done. I expect he will call for the Priestesses as soon as he returns home. The tattoos imply status, but they also mean responsibility. They are not to be done lightly'.

'Borin's glance shifted from Troy to where Merthsandra was entertaining Jerain, challenging him to a stick throwing contest.

'It will be a good thing when we all return home,' Borin added. 'You will stay with me when the others go further into the plains, as you are replacing one of my men. How did you learn to ride like you do?'

Troy met his gaze evenly. 'The Princes of Devronia have riding masters,' he stated.

'I see,' was Borin's only comment. He climbed out of the water and went for his clothes.

As the days passed, Troy became more accustomed to the continual riding, and finally his pains and aches subsided. However, he still suffered from the cold, as the wind persisted to sweep over the plain, although the spring sunshine caused the flowers to bloom. The wild blossoms were a constant source of interest to him, as all the plants he had been aware of previously had been carefully cultivated blooms.

Another source of wonder was the night sky. Sleeping in the open on the plain was a different experience from his previous open-air adventures, bivouacking in the forests of Devronia, when out hunting with friends.

Lying on his back, Troy could see the down-turned bowl of the sky, from mountain range to mountain range. The vast expanse made him feel small, and slowly his attitude to life changed. He stopped railing against his fate, and accepted what his present life would be. He thought his fortune could have been worse, being a slave to the Horse Lords was not all bad.

The lifestyle suited him, now he was more hardened, the food was good and the other riders treated him like an equal. It seemed Borin had not bothered to tell that Troy was a slave. The only difference that he could see between himself and the other riders was the fact that he bore no tattoo on the insides of his wrists.

He wondered what had happened to his friends. As they had all been sold before he left the slave quarters, he had no way of telling where they had been taken. He thought Trojan would cope no matter what the situation he was in, but he worried about Delia and Anton.

Delia would cause herself her own trouble, Troy mused, *whilst Anton would be too eager to please.* As for Amelia, he did not know her well. She had always been taken from the middle of the picture by Delia. He remembered her as a quiet, sensible girl, who anticipated what would be required in most situations. He expected a search party was under way for all of them. His mother and father would be very worried, while Lex would consider him a great nuisance.

They were riding at the foot of the mountain, and Troy came out of his day-dream to see Borin and Jerain talking and gesticulating in front of him. Riding closer, he caught the gist of what they were saying. Jerain was wanting to enter a valley, the entrance of which Troy could see as a cleft in the side of the mountain.

'Just because we've killed the first lot of thieves, there is no guarantee that further outlaws haven't banded together there, ready to attack passing travellers,' Borin argued.

In the end, Borin's wise council prevailed, and camp was set up outside the valley mouth. The mules and the packhorses, who apparently were the dead robbers' mounts, were glad to have their burdens eased. Troy picketed Glint, made sure he was happy, and then went to help the muleteers, who were also looking after the packhorses.

Borin and Jerain were sitting besides the newly-lit fire. Jerain was studiously avoiding watching Merthsandra, who was sitting under a tree braiding her golden hair. Looking over the camp, he noticed Troy helping with the pack animals.

'That new man was a good find,' he commented. 'He is a good worker, who gets on well with the animals. The other men seem to find him good company, too. How did you come by him? What was he doing in Dishnigar?' Jerain felt there was a story here he was missing.

Borin did not answer for a moment. He watched Troy brushing an old hack with all the care he would give a prize stallion.

'He is used to dealing with people. He is a prince in his own land.'

Jerain swung around to look at Borin with surprise. 'How did he land up here?'

'I found him in the slave pens. I didn't inquire as to how he got there, no doubt through some unfortunate circumstance. I shall free him, of course, but I expect he will stay at Muria's yurt. No prince would want the world to know he had been a slave, and so badly beaten.'

As the last rays of the evening sun disappeared behind the far mountains on the western shore, dark descended quickly. The riders all gathered around the fire. They were swopping stories of the day, waiting for their evening meal. It was bubbling merrily, hanging from a tripod erected over the embers, while other dishes were keeping warm.

Suddenly, the sound of a pipe could be heard in the far distance. All talk stopped as the riders listened to the eerie sound, which held them motionless beside the fire.

'Where is that coming from?' Borin asked quietly, the hairs on his arms erect with distrust. He was worried about the women in the party if it came to a fight.

'It's coming from the cut in the mountain.' Jesse, a grizzled old rider replied. He spat near Jerain's feet, then continued, 'where he wanted to spend the night.'

'We shall have to find out,' Borin stood up. 'We can't stay sleeping here, not knowing what is in front of us. Before you

231

say anything, Merthsandra, you are staying here.' He then named four riders, including Jerain and Troy, to arm themselves and to follow him in a scouting party.

Troy had a knife and a dagger thrust into his hands by Jesse, as he stood up. 'There you go, boy. You can't go off marauding in the dark, barehanded. Here's an old cloak, too.' He rummaged in his pack, and produced a dark blanket made into a cloak. 'That'll stop the light catching you; keep it over your head.'

As Troy was the only member of the party who had not been in the valley before, he followed at the back. He was stepping on the heels of the man in front of him so as not to get lost in the dark.

Borin led them up a sidetrack he had found previously, and they were soon gathered on the cliff face, looking down on their former campsite.

The sight spread before them quickly eased their fears of armed assassins. The group was formed from a collection of packhorses and caravans. The people were settling for evening and were going about their nightly chores. The piper was sitting on a rock beside their fire; unaware of the furore he had caused.

Three girls were dancing in front of him. They were dark beauties; and their skirts of red, yellow and green, swirled in unison when they spun and stamped, while bells attached to their ankles accented the beat of the music.

Sitting at the doors of the open caravans were some older women, busy preparing vegetables, or doing some mending. The only guard was lying on an outlying rock, with his hat tipped over his eyes.

'Nothing to worry us here,' Borin smiled. He started to stride down the track. When he approached the camp he called out. 'Hullo the camp! Visitors are coming!'

This set up a chorus of barking dogs, who erupted out of the caravans and came to sniff and bark at them. The dogs were followed by a pack of small children, who stood at the edge of the firelight and looked at them with interest.

The piper put down his pipe, and crossed the camp to greet them. Borin stepped forward offering his hand in friendship.

'Good evening. We are from the horse clans, returning home from Dishnigar. The sound of your pipe alerted us to your presence. There are few other travellers on the plains, so we have come to pay our respects. My name is Borin.'

'Who are you?' The piper looked at the other riders, one at a time, with a dour glance. A small wiry man, with brown, crinkly hair, and untrusting eyes, he was not going to be tricked by strangers. He weighed up what Borin had said, and then nodded.

'We are travellers from Keshia, going to Dishnigar. We followed the Grey River, then crossed the plain to Orphur, and have followed the mountains down to here. We are a mixed company, travelling together to keep the wolves at bay. My name is Struan, and these are my daughters.' He gestured to the three girls who had followed him, but were standing with a group of children off to one side.

'If you and your party would like to join us for a yarn and a drink, you would be most welcome.'

Borin glanced at Jerain, who nodded. One of the riders was sent to bring the rest of the party into the valley, then they all trooped over to the fire.

One by one people came from the caravans, curious about the strangers, yet not wanting to put themselves to unnecessary risk, if these armed men suddenly turned on them. However, when Merthsandra and the wives of the riders arrived, the tension eased. Struan, good to his word, called to one of his party to break out a small barrel of ale. As one of his companions did just that, conversation flowed thick and fast.

Troy found himself sitting between an old woman who was draped in shawls and long flowing skirts, with sigils embroidered on the cloth, and a wiry, jumpy little man, who seemed to have difficulty sitting still. The gipsy ancient, was known as Old Maeve, while her greying, unshaven male companion, introduced himself as Timmo.

Timmo came from Dishnigar, and wanted to know what was happening in the town. Troy knew little, apart from the fact the horses had sold well, and that the weather had been very cold.

'It is always cold in Dish,' Timmo agreed. 'I run this trip for old Essa, all the time. I bring her special packets from Keshia. You know what I mean?' He put his thumb to his nose suggestively, his watery eyes blinking at Troy as he leered at him.

'Who is Essa?' Troy asked, not really wanting to know.

'Oh, you would have heard of her as Madame Esse, I suppose.'

'No, I haven't heard of her.'

'You've been to Dish and not heard of the Madam? She's the boss, no one says no to Essa. Would you like a cut of her stash? I have a little extra for personal use. Essa is kind in that way.'

Troy shook his head, and the black cloak slipped down, showing his fair head, while revealing his features in the firelight.

Old Maeve leant forward, and grasped his hand in her skinny one. 'A Horse Lord, you say you are?' She turned his hand over, exposing his wrist to the light. 'Where is your clan mark, my fair boyo?'

'I have joined them recently,' Troy returned. 'I don't have a clan, as yet.'

'Not many belong to the clans who are not born into them. You have the look of a foreigner to me. Where do you come from?'

'I'm originally from Devron.'

Still nodding, and holding his hand, she peered at him closely, then dropped her gaze to the palm of his hand. 'I see,' she said slowly, 'you haven't finished your journey yet, my boyo. There is still a long way to go.'

Troy smiled at her, seeing concern in her old, sunken eyes.

'At least it looks as if I will finish what is intended, if what you say is true.'

She let go of his hand, and patted his shoulder. 'There are not many on the plains like you; take care of the red gold hair.' Timmo gave him a nudge.

'If you are not into hash, perhaps you would like to buy a horse?'

'What kind of a horse?'

Timmo leaned closer and whispered behind his outstretched hand. 'A Horse Lord's mare in foal!'

'Where did you get her?'

'She was loose on the plain in the north. I trapped her in a cut by the mountains.'

Troy thought how he would love to have this mare, a horse of his own. He knew he had the use of Glint, who was a fine animal, but he could be taken away from him when they reached the yurt. Then there was the problem that the mare had been stolen. No Horse Lord would lose a valuable mare. No one would want the chance of a male foal being born away from the plains.

'I would look at this mare.'

'Come with me.' Timmo got up and led the way up the cut towards the end of the valley. Hidden in the thick brush, outlined in moonlight, was a mare the colour of the moonlight herself. She gave a soft snort, when surprised by the sudden appearance of the men.

'What a beauty!' Troy breathed, running a hand over her swollen belly. The mare leant into him, ready to be friends. 'What do you want for her?'

'Two thousand silvos, at least.'

'I'll see what I can do,' Troy countered.

Returning to the fire side, he arranged to see Timmo in the morning, then made his way back to their camp.

The others had just settled for the night, and Troy picked a careful way around sleeping bags, until he reached Borin.

'Lord, I need to have your attention.'

Borin raised himself on an elbow, and listened carefully to Troy's story.

'A mare in foal and stolen? She must be from a yurt to the north, as that is the way they travelled. We must recover her, either by paying or stealing. She must not leave the plains; our people's livelihood depends on it.

'Well done, Troy. I'll talk to you further about this in the morning.'

Borin lay down and considered what he should do. It was against his nature to be underhand in any transaction, but at the same time he was determined not to allow the mare to be sold in Dishnigar.

The trader had asked for 2,000 silvos. Borin decided to offer one and exchange one of the bandits' horses, thrown in for good measure. Having reached a decision he was able to settle down to sleep.

Meanwhile, Troy was still awake. His thoughts centred on the lovely mare and what her off-spring might be like. He knew the foal would never be his, but all the enthusiasm he had for Juliette to have a great foal surged back.

In the morning, Borin called to Troy, and they set off along the path to the valley.

It was still gloomy and wet as the morning sun had not risen over the mountain, and the over hanging trees covered the view of the sky with their canopy of leaves.

As they walked Borin questioned Troy about the mare, and his impressions of Timmo.

'So, you think he's an agent for Madame Esse? He is probably a tricky customer, then. She wouldn't employ a fool.' He shifted his knife, at the same time making sure that it was not hampered by his cloak. 'If he won't bargain it might come to a fight. That mare is not leaving the plains.'

Troy glanced at him and saw Borin meant business, his eyes were fiery and his jaw set in a hard line, with his teeth clenched. This was a side of Borin he had not seen before.

Troy was glad Jesse had loaned him his weapons – who could tell what support Timmo would have amongst the other men in the caravans? As it happened, Troy had had plenty of practice, but had never attacked anyone with the purpose of hurting. Perhaps this was the time he would be blooded, as long as it was not his about to be spilt.

The camp was quiet as they approached, but they disturbed the dogs who came barking.

Timmo came to meet them. When he saw Borin, his expression changed from friendly welcome to unease when he recognised Borin's assured demeanour.

'Good morn to you, Horse Lord. Are you interested in the mare?'

'I would like to see her,' Borin returned. 'I make no bargains without testing the wares.'

'Of course, of course! Come this way, my Lord.' Timmo was all ingratiating smiles, while bending obsequiously.

He waved Troy and Borin ahead of him, up the valley path, all the while babbling about the beauty of the mare.

Pushing through the bushes, Troy saw the mare was just as lovely in the daylight as she had seemed in the glamour shed by moonlight. She whickered to him as if to an old friend, and then allowed him to approach near enough for him to be able to pat her and give her a handful of sweet grass.

Borin examined her from a distance, then looked at Timmo with distaste. 'You stole her, didn't you?'

Before Timmo could protest his lack of guilt, the mare gave a whinny of fear, then swung around on her tether with nostrils dilated and ears quivering. Troy was surprised by her actions as she had not seemed frightened before.

The early morning breeze brought the waft of a rank smell their way, and this was accompanied by the sounds of crashing through the bushes.

In front of them stood a huge, brown bear, with its jaws slavering while it's enormous paws batted at the foliage in front of it. The mare screamed and tried to bolt, pulling at her tether.

Rather than being afraid of the bear, Troy jumped to contain her, fearing she would do herself damage. Timmo and Borin were in the bear's way. As it advanced, Borin stood ready to duck under its guard, but Timmo threw his knife at the bear's snout. It bounced off the hard bone harmlessly, but infuriated the animal further. With a great roar, the bear stood up on its hind legs, then surging forward, grasped Timmo in its paws and lifted him off the ground.

Borin chanced his moment and pushed against Timmo's body to plunge his knife in the bear's open mouth, angling the thrust up into its brain. The bear slumped forward with Timmo lying underneath its enormous frame. Making sure, Borin leaned to one side to put his dagger up through the thick pelt covering the stomach into the heart.

Borin and Troy were shaking and quivering with the aftermath of fear. It took the combined effort of both of them to roll the carcass off Timmo. The bear, in its fury, had crushed and suffocated him. The little man was dead.

Wondering why it had attacked, Borin examined the body of the animal. He found a large swelling in its paw, which he attributed to the spine from a porcupine – the poor beast had been starving and fevered.

'Now we are in a predicament,' Borin observed, as they sat by the mare gaining breath and composure. 'What do we tell the camp about what has happened here, and to whom does the mare belong to?'

He stabbed both knife and dagger into the earth to remove the remains, then wiped them carefully on handfuls of grass. Troy got up and retrieved the knife, which had been thrown so harmlessly by Timmo.

'We'll explain what has happened. How we were attacked by a bear and Timmo was killed, which is true. We will also say the mare belongs to the Horse Lords, which is also true.'

'A royal decision,' Borin countered with a grin.

'A practical one,' Troy answered as he checked the mare.

Their return to the camp created a furore. Timmo's death produced little concern as no one was directly his companion. Old Maeve said a prayer for his soul, and others wished him well on the journey to the Other Lands as he was buried in some soft soil near the brook.

Knives were sharpened, then the men gathered in high expectation to collect bear steaks; some with rejoicing over the expensive pelt, soon to be theirs. Troy and Borin were able to lead the mare away without anyone questioning their legitimacy.

When they emerged from the valley entrance, the other riders were all gathered together, ready to continue their journey back to Muria's yurt. They were very curious about the new mare, and both men were questioned avidly.

Merthsandra ran her hands over the silken coat. 'The mare is in foal. The baby is for me,' she cried.

'No, you don't' Borin replied, over the chatter of conversation. 'The mare is for Muria, as you well know, and Troy gets the foal. He found them, and his bravery saved them both.'

'Nonsense!' Troy was quick to declaim. 'If you hadn't killed the bear it would have had all of us, not just Timmo!'

'It was just that the bear dealt with his namesake,' Jerain decreed. 'I agree, you should have the foal. If you hadn't guarded the mare she might have killed herself in flight.' He gave Troy a slap on the back in friendship.

Merthsandra pushed between them, then turned and pouted at Troy.

'After its mother got such a fright, it will probably be a still birth or a monster, anyway.' She linked arms with Jerain, pulling him away while calling over her shoulder to Borin.

'Come on, let us get moving; night will be on us and we shall still be in this spot. I never want to see this valley again.'

Finding Glint already saddled up and his bed roll on a mule, Troy put a leading rein on the mare and joined the group at the back, just in front of the packhorses. Realising he had missed breakfast and the midday meal was in the far distance, he chewed on a piece of bread left over from the day before, which he found in his saddlebag as he was riding.

Who would have thought that the meeting with Timmo the previous evening would have such an outcome? He could hardly believe it. No matter what sex, the foal was to be his. In a few days he had gained clothes and a horse, and perhaps some day he would gain his freedom.

He thought of the few words he had exchanged with Old Maeve before they had left the encampment. He had told her to look after Timmo's possessions carefully as there was a parcel there for Madame Esse. Old Maeve had laughed and had then replied that Timmo had already left his stash with her.

'I'll see that painted hussy gets her filth,' she had said, 'but she will pay me by letting some young girl escape from Jade to go and live a better life. Perhaps I shall take on an apprentice to look after my caravan.

'Go with Mut young rider! Keep those blue eyes clear and far seeing.'

He had kissed her cheek, then squeezed her hands goodbye.

The rest of the journey to Muria's yurt had passed without incident. Troy's pulses quickened when they saw the outline of the yurt in the far distance one morning. This was the place where he would live in the future.

Muria rode out to greet them with her fair hair flowing down her back. She was wearing a similar outfit, in black, to those Merth usually wore, and her tattoos were bear on her back and lynx on her stomach. As she was only a clan leader, she did not have the royal snakes, but she did have two small bears tattooed on the insides of her wrists.

Borin was overjoyed to see her. All had been well during his absence, and he regaled her with news from Dishnigar. She was delighted with the prices they had got for the horses, and was surprised to hear about the new mare. However, she was dismayed at the thought he had been in danger from the bear. This prompted him to call Troy forward.

'Muria, this is Troy. He will be part of our clan. He has shown bravery and loyalty all the time we have been travelling back. The animals like him and he seems to know what they are thinking.' He thumped Troy on the shoulder, and then said to them both quietly, 'He will be a freed slave.'

Troy flushed with pleasure at the prospect.

'Perhaps we shall be able to arrange the ceremony at the next Horse Fair,' Muria suggested.

Nodding in assent, Borin added 'He is almost as good a rider as a Horse Lord who has been born to the saddle. I think he can keep Glint.'

Muria looked puzzled, so Borin drew her to one side to explain what had happened to Ben. Realising his company was not needed, Troy walked into the yurt as he was curious about his future home on the plain.

Once inside, with his eyes accustomed to the dimmer light, he was astounded at the magnificence of the enclosure. The walls of the tent were decorated with panels of pictures, hunting scenes, galloping horses, mountains, view of the open plain in morning light, and people in different aspects of their daily life. All depicted with vibrant colours and strong, sure strokes.

The floor was strewn with carpets, and every now and then small areas had been enclosed with thick blankets to ensure privacy. In the centre was a long cooking pit, and at the far end of this, away from the main door, was a sheep skin covered bench with piles of cushions surrounding it. All the materials were beautifully embroidered and had gold and silver threads woven into their structure.

He was welcomed by Jesse. He showed Troy where he would sleep. Then sat him on some cushions and asked a passing maid if she would bring some victuals and a drink. Slowly the other riders drifted in, and Troy was surrounded by a laughing, talking group, including him in their number.

As he made his way to bed that night, he was thankful that Borin had found him. It wasn't the life style he had expected, but fate had dealt him a hand he could build on.

Just before he fell asleep, he again had the vision of lovely arms and hands with the pictures of snakes upon them. In the background was the grey wolf guarding them both.

Chapter Sixteen

Swinging up on Sythe, Merth held the baby tied firmly to her chest; she was swathed in a colourful, patchwork shawl. She walked Sythe from the yurt, taking an easy amble over the flatter part of the plain.

This was Alyssandra's first outing. Merthsalla was accompanying them on their afternoon stroll, riding Storm. She was taking her guardianship of her niece very seriously.

At 13, Merthsalla was becoming a beauty, with long fair hair and slanting green eyes.

Listening with half an ear to her chatter about a kitten the trader had given her when he had arrived recently, Merth was marvelling at how easy the birth had been.

It had been fortunate that the priestesses had been staying overnight on a trip back from another yurt.

During the evening her waters had broken. The priestesses had immediately set up their small tent and supervised the birth.

Alyssandra was perfect. Her downy, brown hair curled when damp and her skin was of an olive hue tinged with pink.

When the priestesses had left to continue their journey home, Merthsalla had volunteered to help look after her baby niece. Merth was glad of the child's help, as looking after the yurt was quite enough work as it was.

Andreas had returned to the herd now he could ride again, so that was one responsibility she had lost but only for the time being. In fact, she had lost two tasks she thought with humour, remembering what a burden he had been when he was recuperating from his fall.

She pulled the shawl down a little so she could take a peek at her daughter's face. The baby was sleeping soundly, lulled by the regular, smooth movement of Sythe's canter. *I wonder what Jerain will think of this one*, she mused. *The riders should be back now the late summer had arrived.* She had been expecting them for days, hoping they would arrive before the baby was born.

'So I shall call him Scratch,' Merthsalla finished.

'A good name,' Merth murmured, smiling at her little sister. Her expression altered as her thoughts shifted to Merthsandra. *I wonder what devilry she has been up to?*

She would have been flashing her charms at all the men. Jerain would be bewitched, she was certain. Lifting her head she smelt the evening breeze blowing across the land. The men would be returning from their work with the herds on the plains.

Prince Drun had finally settled. He and Rahadir had become a welcome addition to the riders, unless someone looked at them askance. When that happened their feathers became very ruffled.

'Come,' she called to Merthsalla. 'It is time to go back. The shadows are starting to lengthen.' They turned back towards the yurt.

On their way home they met Redd, Drun, Rahadir, Rolf and Andreas, all looking hot and dusty from their day's work.

Drun seemed to be enjoying his life in the camp. He and Rahadir were being tutored by Andreas, and chivvied by Rolf and Redd, as to how a Horse Lord should behave. They were now even accepted by Boris and Borland, who were frisking around Merth and Merthsalla, barking a welcome.

'Did Ramesh bring any news?' Andreas asked.

'He brought me a kitten!' Merthsalla exclaimed, her eyes shining with pleasure.

'Another animal!' Redd teased her.

'Ramesh did remind me there is a horse fair in the north in six weeks time,' Merth volunteered. 'I have decided to go, and I shall take Prince Drun and Rahadir with me.

'After visiting the fair we shall continue up to the Northern Plain. We will see what progress has been made about the canals. I realise there has not been much time for the completion of such a great project, but it will be gratifying to see it has been started.'

'I'd like to come too,' Redd exclaimed. 'It will be good to visit friends and family at the fair. Perhaps some Horse Lord will fancy me for his daughter!'

'I suppose that means I stay here,' Andreas grumped. 'Someone has to be reliable.'

Drun and Rahadir were having a quick consultation, riding behind the group. Finally, Drun gained sufficient courage to ride up alongside Sythe. Sythe turned his head and gave the other horse a quick nip for his impertinence.

'Horse Lady, what will happen if my father has not had time to start the canals? What if the pigeons did not reach him in time, or not at all?'

'You will come back with us, of course!' She surveyed him calmly, cradling Alyssandra with one arm, while guiding Sythe with the other.

'But surely the word of The Jada will be a sufficient bond?'

'I haven't got the word of The Jada, as yet. I only have the promise of his heir.'

'You insult me, yet again, Horse Lady.' Prince Drun was red faced and angry.

'No,' she replied, 'I only state a fact. Let us wait and see what eventuates. Decisions can be made then.'

With that, Drun and Rahadir had to be content as Merth drew away from them to talk to Andreas about the events of the day.

'I wish I was coming to the horse fair,' Merthsalla said to Redd. 'You get all the luck.'

'Nonsense,' he replied. 'Did I go to Dishnigar? Have I got Lords clamouring for me to join their herds? Tell me about your kitten. I haven't even got one of those!'

Merthsalla kneed Storm closer to her curly-haired brother then launched into a great eulogy of praise for the tiny, black kitten she had left asleep in her bed.

Rahadir was one of the first to dismount when they reached the yurt. He enjoyed the feeling of returning home after a hard day's work. He and Drun had slipped into the life of the Horse Lords and found they appreciated the activity and purpose.

These attributes of life had been absent in their dilettante days of leisure at the court.

Rahadir, in particular, had lost the arrogant attitude of a high courtier. He found he appreciated the friendship offered so wholeheartedly by the people in the yurt. Drun was slightly more standoffish and quick to take a slight, but he was improving too.

Redd took Sythe and Storm under his charge as he led his horse out to picket. All three animals followed him to the click of his fingers, with Boris and Borland leaping about them.

Rahadir was watching Redd, who was wandering away with his nonchalant air, while he had a grimace of envy on his face.

'What's up with you?' Rolf asked, as he passed the group around the entrance to the yurt.

'Oh, nothing really. I just wish I were on such good terms with the animals as you people seem to be. I have learnt to gain their respect, but that is as far as it goes.'

'It took you a while to realise they are individuals,' Roft replied. 'Now you are looking at them with different eyes from when you first arrived. When an animal, like a horse, chooses you, rather than you using it, you will find you understand.'

He patted Rahadir on the arm, then went on his way.

Merth came up behind Rahadir and linked arms with him.

'How is my newest rider?' she asked, smiling at him.

'Much happier, Horse Lady,' he returned. 'I really don't care whether I return to Jaddanna or not. I find the life here suits me.'

'We shall see when we are nearer your city. You may find the pull of the high society stronger than you think. If you do wish to return with us, you will be welcome. Good riders are always needed.'

So saying, Merth preceded Rahadir into the yurt, slinging her jacket on to its peg. In that way, she announced her presence to all who needed her. She then carried on into her own private quarters.

Rahadir joined Drun, who was already seated on their sheepskins, with his hands stretched out to the fire.

'I need new boots,' Drun shifted on his seat impatiently, his eyes taking in all the activities in the yurt.

'Perhaps the trader may have some for sale,' Rahadir suggested, sitting down beside him.

'Fetch him,' Drun commanded.

Rahadir looked at him belligerently. 'Fetch him yourself,' he answered. 'While we are here, we are equal guests of the Horse Lady. I am neither lackey, nor messenger boy for you. If you want boots, find them.'

Drun's hand went straight for his knife hilt, only to find his wrist held in a firm grasp. Andreas had been sitting behind them, and had expected this outcome to the conversation.

'Put it away laddie,' he said kindly. 'I'll have no skirmishing under my nose in the Horse Lady's yurt. Rahadir is right. It is time you did more for yourself. Watch the Horse Lady, does she expect to be waited on? Yet every person in this yurt would die for her, if need be.'

He leant forward and caught a passing rider by the arm. 'Ask Ramesh to trundle over here to share a sip of wine with me, just when you are passing him, would you please?'

'Certainly, Horse Lord,' came the answer.

Ramesh brought a bottle with him.

'Good riding, Horse Lord, and how are you this fine evening, Andreas?'

'I shall be better when we have shared this excellent wine, you have had brought from Keshia. Good of you to come over to spend some time with me.'

'Can I help you in any way, Andreas?' Ramesh sipped the Keshian wine, having savoured its bouquet.

'This young lord needs new boots,' Andreas answered, giving Drun a nudge in his back, with a none too gentle toe.

'Come to my wagon in the morning.' Ramesh pushed his streaked grey, brown locks away from his face with one hand, while pouring more wine with the other. He had taken his cue from Andreas' gesture; his amber eyes glinted with suppressed humour.

'Do you want my trade?' Drun demanded angrily, looking at the wine as he noticed none had been poured for him.

'My boots are not worn out,' Ramesh replied pointing to Drun's feet. 'It is you who needs to try them on. No point in me carrying them all here to find none of them fit you. Good Health!' He raised his glass to Andreas.

Drun pushed Rahadir on the arm. 'Come!' he ordered. 'I find we need to go to our rest.'

Not wanting to annoy him further, Rahadir also rose and they made their way to their sleeping quarters.

'Young colts,' Andreas smiled at Ramesh. 'They all need to feel the rein, no matter where they come from.'

Ramesh agreed, watching the young men walk away with swagger in their steps.

The hush of the yurt was suddenly disturbed by a commotion outside. Rolf, who had just been inside the tent flap, came flying across the yurt to Andreas.

'The riders are back!' he shouted, 'Jesse, Jerain, and the rest.' He was nearly knocked over as Boris and Borland flew past him, barking their annoyance at the unusual sounds outside.

'Let them go,' Andreas said. He rose to go and greet the returned group, anxious for their news and wanting to know how they had fared.

Merth emerged from her quarters, holding Alyssandra up against her shoulder. The baby's hair glistened in a halo upon Merth's dark, green jacket. 'What is all this fuss about?' Merth asked. 'Why are the dogs barking so loudly?'

'The riders are back!' Andreas answered, as he passed her on his way outside.

Standing still, Merth watched the entrance with anticipation. Her heart had given a leap, and now her knees were trembling. She took a deep breath to calm herself, then turned Alyssandra so she faced the front. This was the vision Jerain encountered as he stepped inside.

His handsome face lit up when he saw the scene in front of him. He crossed the room with big strides and clasped them both in his arms.

247

'Sweet Mut! You have our child, and a girl as we expected! What a beauty!' His eyes glistened as he grinned at Merth. 'How well you look! I was worried for you, and I missed you.'

'I have missed you, too. Your daughter is called Alyssandra.'

'That is a pretty name. She is fine?'

'She is perfect,' Merth smiled 'How was your journey?'

'Successful.' He led them to the sheepskin seat. 'We had some wild moments, but we sold the horses for a goodly profit and have some extra to boot.

'We stayed longer at Borin's than I intended. It was good to meet Muria and your brother. If I hadn't tarried we would have been here for the birth.'

Andreas entered with Merthsandra wrapped around his arm. *She looks thinner and somehow tauter*, Merth thought bitterly. *Her actions are even swifter and more predatory*, she murmured to herself. She watched her sister as she enchanted their father, cuddling him, while laughing up at him, her face full of excited conversation.

A few days later, Merth left Alyssandra with Merthsalla for a long afternoon, while she took Sythe for a much needed gallop. It had been a while since she had stretched his legs, and he revelled in the exercise. His hooves drummed across the plain, while his tail streamed behind like a banner.

Life was good, Merth was thinking as they were returning. Jerain was attentive, the autumn stretched before them; the new foals were fit and well, and there was the prospect of the horse fair in front of them.

Slowing Sythe down, she walked him towards the spring where his favourite patch of sweet grass grew. While he was cropping there, she slipped off her boots and paddled in the cool water.

Wandering down the stream, admiring the coloured stones beneath the rippling water, she was about to wade around an overhanging bush, when she heard a woman laugh. Peering through the bushes she was held still in her tracks, as though she had been bound.

Merthsandra was lying naked on the bank, throwing pebbles and twigs at Jerain as he emerged from the water. While Merth watched, horror struck, Jerain lunged for Merthsandra, pinning her down, spread-eagled on the soft earth.

'Now, you demon,' he said gruffly, 'you will get what you have been teasing me for all the time we have been away.'

Merth watched how Merthsandra grabbed him to her, wrapping her long legs around his body. She scraped her nails down his spine, kissing him while laughing deep in her throat. As she arched her back to meet him, her nipples stood from her breasts, lifting to find his stroking fingers.

Turning, Merth tiptoed back through the water, pulled on her boots, and then led Sythe away from the spring. The journey back to the yurt seemed to take an age. She rode grim faced and steely-eyed, her thoughts tumultuous, fitting with the thundering hooves.

When she finally reached her home, Merth rubbed Sythe down, then left him in the charge of a young rider, who was delighted to look after the Horse Lady's stallion.

Entering the yurt she called some retainers to her.

'I want Merthsandra's belongings bundled up in packages suitable to go on a packhorse, if you please.'

'Why, my lady, is she going far?'

'Pack everything, please. No matter the distance.'

'As you will, my lady.'

Spinning round, she found Redd watching her with concern showing on his face.

'What is the matter, Merth?'

'If you would please me,' she replied, 'you will collect my husband's equipage and bring all his possessions outside the yurt.'

With that, she picked up a stool and carried it outside, where she placed it in front of the tent flap. She called to Rolf to bring two packhorses from the herd and then told him to halter them nearby. When that had been completed, she asked him to request food and beverage from the cooks, to be placed in the animal's packs.

She sat waiting outside the tent flap for the rest of that long afternoon. Merthsalla brought Alyssandra to be fed, and then Merth sent the child back inside in Merthsalla's care. Her younger sister looked at her with worry on her face, but did as she was bid, eyes wide over the top of the baby's head.

Merth had an air of steely determination, which showed no change of heart. She was the complete Horse Lord, Head Lady of the clans, at last.

She watched Jerain and Merthsandra approach the yurt. Merthsandra was riding in front. Thunder was prancing, showing off; her silky coat glossy in the rays of the evening sun. Her actions were no doubt inspired by Merthsandra's attentions. Merth considered her, watching her sister's facial expressions. Merthsandra looked as if she had achieved her ultimate desire.

Merth switched her attention to Jerain. As he dismounted he raised a hand in greeting, but he did not look at her directly, shielding his face from her close scrutiny.

When they walked towards her, having given their horses to waiting riders, they became aware of Merth's stillness. Involuntarily they stopped, when they saw their goods heaped beside the packhorses.

'Merth, what is this all about?' Jerain had a note of uncertainty in his voice.

'I think you are well aware of what this is all about,' Merth stated calmly. 'You are both banished from this yurt.

'It is lucky, Jerain, that I put off summoning the priestesses. Now you will not need the totem of the Phoenix on your back, as you will not be the partner of the Horse Lady, nor will you see your baby.

'As for you,' here she glanced at her sister, 'I do not need a scorpion in my basket. You may go whoring wherever you wish.

'No doubt Jerain will take you back to his home land with him, to his people, if they have room for one whose lust outstrips her honour. No, there is nothing more to be said!' This was said with her palm raised, as Merthsandra was about to protest.

'You may go now, the Horse Lady has spoken!' She indicated the bundles and the packhorses. 'Here are your goods. I give you the gift of the horses, and of course, Thunder.' With that she rose, lifted her stool and returned inside the yurt.

Andreas was waiting for her. He held out his arms and she buried her face in his shoulder.

'Best you found out early,' he comforted. 'If a colt strays once, it is hard to keep it in the herd. You will be better off without him. As for your sister, I have known she would bring us unhappiness, her spirit has always been wayward.'

Merth could hardly hear what he was saying, because she was sobbing so hard, burrowing into the leather jerkin he was wearing.

Straightening, she took a deep breath and dried her eyes on the shawl she had tied around her shoulders.

'The dinner needs supervising,' she said, 'and no doubt Alyssandra needs feeding. At least the Phoenix has an heir.' This was said over her shoulder as she gave Andreas a small smile.

During the next few days Merth mourned for her lover, though in her secret heart she had known he was mostly looks and show. *He was still a boy*, she thought, from the height of her 15 years experience. *I was too stern to remain faithful to, when Merthsandra used her wiles.*

Life was busy, what with foals to watch, purchasing from Ramesh, organising the yurt, preparing for their trip to the horse fair, and looking after the baby. She had been alone during most of her pregnancy, and now slipped back into her every day routines without giving Jerain much thought.

At night, she usually went straight to sleep with Alyssandra content in her cradle beside the bed. The odd time she thought of Jerain became less and less, and finally she did not grieve for him any more. The dreams of her blond lover returned. He was often accompanied by the wolf, hovering beside him, with her yellow eyes watchful yet compassionate.

Over the next week she weaned Alyssandra, realising she had to leave the baby behind when she went to the fair. Merthsalla was delighted to be given the responsibility of the baby, though some of the older women in the yurt were really going to take care of such a precious bundle.

Drun and Rahadir were full of anticipation about their journey to the north. They sat around the fire in the evenings with Redd, questioning him about what happened at a gathering. Redd was looking forward to going himself – he regaled them with stories of previous fairs he had attended.

Merth was giving Merthsalla final instructions about the care of Alyssandra. Merth was loath to leave the baby as she was only a few weeks old. However, travelling on horseback with a baby so young was not a sensible option.

As Horse Lady, it behooved Merth to go to the gathering. The council for the tribes would have many meetings. Merth would have to make decisions on points of law, and she would also have to give judgments. It would not be just parties, races, feasting and challenges for her.

The group farewelled Andreas one sunny morning. He and the children were gathered outside the yurt giving messages and parcels for friends and family, who would assemble at the fair.

Ramesh was travelling with them, as a large fair like this one would need all the goods he had to trade. Merth had some riders bringing a string of colts. She also had blankets, which the women had woven, and some fine, leather jackets.

When they set off they numbered a large party. Merth rode at the front, her mind full of Alyssandra and her welfare. She was sure she would be fine, being a strong, healthy baby, but she worried all the same.

She glanced across as Redd thundered up beside her. He was attired in bronze-coloured leathers, which brought out the gold flecks in his brown curls, offset by a bright blue shirt. His face was alight with the delight of the promise of future fun, as well as the hope that he might find a clan leader willing to sponsor him, now he was old enough to be considered to partner a Horse Lord.

I still don't want to lose him, Merth thought, *but if he is chosen I shall have to accept the inevitable.*

'You are looking very gallant,' Merth teased him, her brown eyes flashing wickedly. 'Whose heart do you intend to capture?'

'Give it a rest, Merth,' Redd flushed embarrassedly. 'I have already been given a rollicking by Rolf and the others. You would think I usually go around in rags.'

'No, just usually dirty, grubby, uncared for and smelling of horse,' Merth returned. 'Nice to see you can scrub up so well. That old chestnut of yours is often better cared for than you are.'

Redd patted his horse's neck. 'You are not so old, are you Bow?'

Sythe swung his head to give a nip to Bow, who was coming far too close for his liking. Sythe was feeling edgy with all the energy and activity in the party. Merth was having to calm him with hands, knees and whispers.

Rahadir came up on her other side.

'Having trouble with the stallion, Horse Lady?'

'No more than I can handle, thank you. He doesn't like crowds.'

'Or strangers?' Rahadir teased.

'You are not a stranger now, Rahadir. I think of you as one of the clan.'

'Thank you. That is a compliment.

'After we have looked at the irrigation project on the Northern Plain, perhaps you would like to accompany Prince Drun and myself to see the wonders of Jaddanna and meet The Jada in person?

'We would be honoured to escort you.'

'What a venture that would be!' Merth exclaimed. 'I like the idea, but let us take each day as it comes. Who knows what will happen at the fair, or for that matter, on the Northern Plain? Circumstances might insist I go further as it is. Who knows?'

They camped that night in a gully, which they often used when moving the herds into different grazing grounds. The softly-grassed area had the protection of a circle of thick trees and a small stream of sweet water tinkled through the vale. Fire pits had been dug previously and soon they were arranging sleeping areas and recovering their bedding from the packs.

Merth and the other women found a secluded corner where they placed their sleeping bags, out of sight and out of the wind.

After Sythe had been walked to cool, rubbed-down, fed and watered, he was quite content to stay with Bow and the other horses on the picket line beside the trees. Having seen him settled, Merth wandered over to the fire to join the others for their evening meal. Rolf handed her a tin plate full of food, then leaned across and filled her tankard with beer.

'This brings back memories of our trip to the seeress,' he remarked.

She smiled at him as she accepted the food and drink. 'In more ways than one,' she said, nodding to where Rahadir and Drun were spread out with their backs to a fallen branch. 'I thought we would have had more trouble with them than we have had. They seemed so obnoxious and arrogant when we met them at first.'

'They were spoiled and had little experience of the world, apart from their palace. They didn't know how real people live. Are you going to let them go?'

'Of course. Though it might be interesting to let them take us to Jaddanna. I'd like to meet this Jada of theirs. You must come too. I shall need my trusty escort.'

'I don't know what Andreas will say to us gallivanting across the land.'

'It will all be to our advantage, I am sure. We must make the most of this army digging holes for us.'

'I suppose you are right, as long as we don't fall in them!' Rolf gave her an ironic grin, then applied himself to his food. He was pleased to think she wanted him to accompany her, although he would have done, without Andreas putting her in his care.

A few days later they reached the area where the horse-fair was being held. Already, there were tents set up, and the small valley was full of activity. Children chased each other, or played games around the booths where the traders had set up their wares. Horses were paraded, prodded and inspected.

Chickens, goats, and the occasional wandering pig had free rein, while cows mooed and complained from their grazing area.

People had come from all over Strevia. Each clan raised its banner over the main tent belonging to their Lord. This made a festive, colourful picture spread before them, as they descended into the valley.

Riding down into the area, Rolf held up their Phoenix banner with pride. The huge emblem fluttered and cracked in the wind. There was a murmur of welcome from the gathered crowd as they approached. The Horse Lady comes!

Merth shrugged off her jacket, then spread it over Sythe's rear quarters. She sat up purposefully, then raised her head. No one was going to have the opportunity to ask her searching questions she decided. If she had put her husband aside, it was her business only.

She rode past a group of street musicians, who immediately started to play when they saw her.

Moving steadily on, she pushed through the throng assembled in the square, where tables of food and drink had been set up, then led her party to an open space beyond the temporary village. She was pleased to see this spot had been left vacant for them. Andreas had camped in this small defile many times. It was secluded and near a sheltered stream, away from the main gather.

It was not long before Merth had shed her clothes, kicked off her boots, and was submerged in the cooling stream. The other women joined her, and soon the men could be heard splashing in the water, lower down the rivulet. She was pleased to see Drun and Rahadir had joined the other riders without question.

That evening, dressed in her best amethyst outfit, Merth joined the gather for supper and dancing. When people inquired about her family, she stated that her marriage was over, but the Phoenix had a future Horse Lady. There were smiles and whispers, but Merth overlooked any asides, which came to her ears. She greeted old friends from different clans, and welcomed new pairings that seemed to be more fortunate than her own had been.

She looked for the Bear banner, but as yet, Muria and Borin had not arrived. Knowing they had the furthest distance to ride, she was not unduly worried at their absence. She found she was looking forward to seeing Borin, for all his annoying ways of teasing her.

Rolf took the place of Andreas and escorted her from group to group. He was conscious of her needs and she only had to think of something, a drink, a sweet pastry, or somewhere to sit, and he had produced it.

Redd had joined the musicians, and their steady beat and haunting melodies made the evening more special. It was a beautiful, gentle night, with moonlight streaming down from the full moon, sailing in a cloudless sky. The sky, itself, looked like dark velvet, sprinkled with glittering diamonds.

When she finally collapsed in a heap on a pile of cushions, breathless from dancing, an older man appeared at her side.

Glancing up, she saw he was escorted by a banner bearer, with a crouching leopard as the banner's totem. He inclined his head, then greeted her with a soft, cultured voice.

'Good evening, Horse Lady. I hope your day has been enjoyable?'

Searching her memory, she made the link, man to Totem.

'Horse Lord Leonnus, from the Leopard Clan I believe?'

'The very same,' he replied. He was tall and angular, yet handsome, in a quiet, aesthetic way, with heavy, dark brows and a straight nose. He had an air of quiet confidence, imbued with a touch of humour. 'I was hoping to gain your attention through my old friend Andreas, but I hear he is not attending the gather this year.'

'No,' Merth shook her head. 'He is looking after the herd while I have a holiday. He has not been well this year, and I suspect he is checking up on what I have been doing in his absence. Can I help you?'

'I have come to request the services of young Redd. My daughter, Sara, has had an eye on him, while they have been growing up. Perhaps he would like the Leopard on his back?'

Merth took a big breath. This was another of those moments that took the stuffing out of her legs. She motioned to Leonnus to sit beside her, as she sat down on her cushions rather suddenly.

'I have no desire to stand in Redd's way,' she answered. 'He is a valuable rider and has been my right hand, particularly with Andreas being ill, but if he wants to join with Sara, a Leopard he will be. Your clan works further to the east, does it not?'

'Yes. We are out of the main run of things. This is the first meeting I have been to for a couple of years, though my family has attended, bringing our livestock. That was when Sara saw Redd again. I have not been introduced to him, as yet.'

Merth beckoned to Rolf. 'Would you please go and extricate Redd from the musicians and bring him here? Rolf, tell him there might be something to his advantage.'

Turning to Leonnus, she continued. 'Sara is a lucky girl to be able to choose her own husband.'

'Well, Horse Lady, she usually gets her own way, often by guile and intrigue, I must add. She is our only daughter and our heiress, so her wishes must be considered.'

I wish Andreas had thought of mine, Merth thought bitterly, *then perhaps I would not be Horse Lady, and Merthsandra could have had the lot*!

She continued chatting with Leonnus until Redd arrived. He was delighted with the offer, as he had been secretly enamoured with Sara all through his teens, and this was what he had privately hoped for.

When they had shaken hands on the deal and a date had been set, he went running back to the musicians to give them his good news. Soon, the music started again, filled with gaiety and vigour and the dancers started again. Merth was asked to dance by an admirer, so she was happy.

Chapter Seventeen

Before they left Dishnigar the royal family of Devronia had a conference with their sea captains. It was decided that the second galley and the rescued ship should return to Devron, as there was now only one pirate ship to contend with. Accordingly, the two ships left for home before *The Aurora* left the harbour.

Jack followed the coastline down the south-east coast of Strevia. He continued the policy of visiting each cove and hamlet, searching for signs of pirate settlements.

The land was wild and rocky, with rolling waves coming from the open sea, smashing against the cliffs. The few settlements they did find were dingy huts, clinging to the mean strips of sand strewn along the barren coast.

The people they met were mainly fisher folk, living on the meagre bounty of the ocean. They did have patches of farmed land behind their huts, but certainly there was no excess of food or riches.

Lex clambered aboard after visiting the last of these hamlets before they were going to swing around the Southern Cape.

'A surly lot,' he commented, brushing sand off his trousers. 'As far as news about Ambry and his friends, no luck. The headman there said he hasn't seen any big ships pass by this way for a couple of weeks!'

'Can you trust him?' Joseph asked, putting his pipe in his pocket as he was speaking. He had been leaning on the rail, puffing contentedly, while watching Lex return to the galley.

'Who can say?' Lex returned. 'They might all be in cahoots with a dozen pirate vessels, all waiting for us around the next cliff!'

Jack nodded in agreement, a sardonic laugh accompanying his assent. 'At least the weather is holding fair,' he contributed. 'I would not want to round the Cape in a storm.'

'We might not be finding pirates, but we are going in the right direction for finding Troy, I think,' Lex said. 'A pity we weren't able to rescue Trojan and Delia.'

'We didn't even see Delia!' Joseph exclaimed. 'I wonder how she is holding up serving as a slave?'

'It should improve her character,' Lex grunted, remembering Delia's airs and disgraces.

'Trojan will be responsible,' Jack added. 'He will have planned his escape by now. He will be looking after Delia, making sure she keeps herself out of trouble.' He pictured Trojan's handsome, lean visage with his long, blond hair arranged neatly over impeccable clothes.

Lex and Joseph repaired to the stateroom, while Jack urged the crew to combat the current, as they commenced to round the Southern Cape.

There had been disguised hostility between the King and Lex since leaving Dishnigar. Joseph considered he had been put upon, because Lex was so furious about his heritage and lineage.

The King thought that whatever he did was his business. It was no trouble to him that Lex had always considered the Queen to be his mother. After all, one woman was similar to another – they were about, just to ensure the line continued.

'You are still my heir, Lex.' He stated this firmly, looking directly at his son, as they sat at table for lunch.

'Oh, no!' Lex raised a hand in refusal, his black eyes snapping as he surveyed his father. 'When we find Troy, he will be. If we don't find Troy I'm sure my sister is coping splendidly at home. She will make an ideal, reigning Queen, and she is legitimate. I have other plans in mind.'

'Indeed?' Joseph was taken aback. He had assumed Lex's previous remarks were just irritated sounding off, filibuster in fact. *Who would not want to inherit the kingdom?*

'Yes, I like it here in Strevia. I intend to find suitable employment and seek my fortune here when this trouble is over.'

Joseph gave a snort of disbelief, and then they continued their meal in silence.

Rounding the Cape was a strain on the oarsmen. Fortunately the wind was light, so a sail was raised to aid them. The land jutted out into the ocean with long fingers of rock, which disappeared under the crashing waves.

Jack plotted a course well out to sea, before turning back toward the western coast, well clear of the dangerous protuberances.

Up the rigging, sailors watched for rocks and for the telltale signs of old wrecks, and changing currents. It was a tense time for all, and Jack gave a sigh of relief when they were in smoother waters once more.

The western coast was different from the gloomy cliffs they had experienced in the east. There were sandy beaches and sequestered inlets. Small harbours were the home for local fishing boats – the area seemed peaceful and content. The land appeared fertile and well-cared for, with the farmsteads scattered through the growing crops.

Rounding a headland, a small town came into view. There was a larger bay than they had previously seen leading on to a sandy shoreline.

Jack called out, 'Mister Clark, we will bide here for a while. We will fill our barrels with fresh water, and purchase some supplies. Enter the bay and drop anchor, if you please!'

'Aye, aye Sir!'

Jocelyn was leaning with his back to the rail, watching the activities on the ship. He had really enjoyed the voyage on the galley and was considering joining the navy.

He wondered what Lex's reaction would be if he voiced this desire. He would probably not care what Jocelyn did now, seeing he intended to strike off on his own.

Mind you, Jocelyn's mind wandered on, *Lex was really taken with the lady he met in Dishnigar, and with the horses there. I was quite smitten with Dolly too, and I think she was pleased to meet me, as well. Perhaps both of us will end up there. What a lark! Anyway, things will stay as they are until we find out what has happened to Troy.*

They stayed in the harbour for a couple of days. Jack sent two men up on the headland at the entrance of the harbour to keep watch for *The Black Dart*, or any other pirate ship which might be in the offing.

In the late afternoon of the second day, one of the seamen posted on the headland, came flying down the cliff path without concern for his life or limb.

'Something is up.' Lex watched the man progressing towards the lifeboat moored on the beach. By the time the seaman had rowed the little boat into hailing distance there was quite a crowd gathered on the deck.

'Hullo, the galley!'

'Yes Peters, what is the news?' Jack's tone was crisp.

'The pirate galley has passed the harbour entrance. It looks as if it is on the way to Keshia, Captain. They were making good pace with a following wind.'

'Raise the flag for all hands on board, Mister Clark. We shall set sail in half an hour.'

'Aye, aye, Sir!' came the swift response.

'Do you think he will have Troy on board?' King Joseph's eyes gleamed in the anticipation of finally being united with his younger son. The sea voyage had taxed him, as well as the trouble about Lex's parentage. He felt he was losing his family.

'I doubt it, Your Highness, but we shall stop him in any event, and stop any further schemes he may be plotting.'

The Aurora slid out of the harbour with little fuss. However, when they finally reached open sea there was no sign of *The Dark Dart*. They turned north and set course for Keshia, every minute expecting to see a sail on the horizon. Yet, it was not until early morning of the next day when a faint smudge could be seen.

'There she is, on our port bow!' The lookout bellowed.

'Quicken the drum,' Jack Smart ordered.

The oars were pulled with more vigour, as a promise was made of extra bounty if the pirate ship was captured. This put strength into the backs and muscles of the sailors.

When a wind sprang up from the south later in the morning, a sail was raised, so by the early afternoon the other galley could be easily seen.

The oarsmen rallied with a faint cheer as the sails filled and the galley raced forward across the ocean.

'Are you going to ram her?' Lex asked, as he leaned on the prow, his intent gaze raking the other vessel.

'We shall bid her to have to, first,' Jack replied. 'No need to damage either ship or endanger any lives, if our desires are met with conversation.' He raised a querying brow at Lex, with a questioning look on his tanned face, waiting for Lex's reply.

'As long as they don't attack us first,' Lex answered, grumpily. 'What if they have Troy on board and refuse to hand him over?'

'We will deal with the encounter as it happens, my Lord. There is no point in meeting trouble half way. Furl the mainsail!' he commanded.

The Aurora drifted up behind *The Dark Dart* and a small rowboat was readied.

'Prepare for boarding!' Clark's voice boomed across the water.

With a sailor hoisting a flag of truce, the rowboat crew ferried Lex, Smart and Jocelyn over to *The Dark Dart*.

Ambry was leaning over the side, watching them approach.

'Good day to you, gentlemen. How can I help you?' His voice sounded both amused and quizzical.

'Good day, Captain Ambry,' Lex replied, as he climbed aboard. 'We have reason to believe you have my young brother, the heir to the Devronian throne, on board, perhaps as one of your galley slaves, yet again. We wish to look for him.'

'You can believe all you want,' Ambry answered amiably. 'Your young lad is not aboard, yet you can look amongst my crew to your heart's content. If you so wish, you can purchase any of the rascals that might take your fancy.' Ambry folded his arms across his mighty chest and beamed at them, his grin turning into a chuckle.

'You stay here,' Lex told Jocelyn. 'If there is any sign of the rowboat shifting, come and find me. Lead the way, Captain Ambry.'

'I have no intention of going down amongst the galley slaves. They do their work when needed; that is all the interest I have in them. Mister Clay, take these gentlemen on an excursion around the ship, if you please.'

The enormous master-at-arms shifted away from the shadow of the sail and started making his way towards the companionway. 'This way, Sirs,' Joe Clay grunted.

Lex was appalled by the condition of the poor wretches below deck. Their backs were scarred by perpetual use of the lash, their bodies were covered with seawater sores, particularly around where they were shackled. The men were thin and smelt horrendously. However, he gritted his teeth, then inspected every face, hoping to see the familiar features of his young brother.

Some of the men pleaded to be taken from their shackles, but most bore his scrutiny with grim, mute despair. A few of the livelier ones had ribald remarks to make, giving Lex comments as to his appearance and heredity. He maintained an even composure, though his thoughts considered their remarks to have had some value. Having completed his journey through the bowels of the galley, Lex paused outside a shut cabin door. A young cabin boy loitered near the closed door.

'Don't I know you?' Lex asked. 'I remember! You are Dan, who I met in Dishnigar.'

'You're right, my Lord. Can I help you again?'

'I would like to see who is in the cabin you are guarding so closely, Dan?'

'Paying passengers, incognito, my Lord.'

'Open up, please!'

Dan looked at the master-at-arms for support, but Clay shook his head at him. 'Captain Ambry has given these gentlemen permission to search the ship. Open the door, Dan.'

Shrugging his shoulders, Dan stepped to one side as he thrust the door open.

Lex stepped into the cabin to be confronted by a masked man, who was holding a sword at the ready, to attack. Another masked figure hovered behind the sword wielder.

With an oath, Lex reached for his sword, just as the masked figure dropped his weapon to the deck, causing a clatter.

Lex found himself suddenly enveloped in a sweeping brown cloak which was wrapped around long, powerful arms.

'By all the hells! It's Lex!'

The exuberant voice seemed familiar. Lex pushed away the husky chest in which his face had been suddenly squashed and looked up to see the mask being pulled away.

'Great Mut! Is that really you, Trojan?'

'Yes, it is you big oaf, and look who else is here, I have Delia!'

Delia was struggling to get out of her disguise; she then rushed forward to greet Lex and Clark.

'Ambry didn't say you were on board!'

'He doesn't know,' Delia asserted. 'We came aboard at night and we haven't left this cabin for the whole of the voyage. He only knows he has paying passengers. Have you found Troy?'

'Unfortunately not. We have examined this hulk from bow to stern; you are the only surprises. Well, you had better come away with us, unless you wish to finish your journey here?'

Delia was already gathering together the few items they had brought on board.

'What a turn up!' she chortled. 'We were going spare being cooped up like this, afraid Ambry would turn us into slaves again!' They were soon ready to go up on to the deck.

'Are you going to come with us?' Trojan asked Dan, thinking he could aid the boy to a better life.

'Oh no, sir, thanks all the same. If I stay with the Captain, I know I shall always get back to Dish from time to time.'

Ambry was waiting for them on the deck; idly tapping his velvet clad leg with a large telescope.

'Are you done?' he asked, as Lex stood by his side. 'I told you he was not on board. Now, perhaps, I shall be able to continue on my innocent voyage. You should look in Keshia for your runaway prince.'

He glanced at the couple standing behind Lex, holding their baggage. 'You are relieving me of my passengers, I see. Don't think you will get your coin back because you haven't finished your journey.'

Delia threw back her hood, her face radiant in the sunshine. 'Good day to you, Captain Ambry, we wouldn't dream of asking you to refund our gold. We know how much it means to you.'

'You two!' Ambry stepped towards Trojan who was also flipping back his concealing cloak. 'By the hells, if I had known it was you I was dealing with, no passage would I have given!' Ambry was red in the face with annoyance. 'Where is that cabin boy? Dan!'

'Don't take it out on him,' Trojan laughed. 'He had no idea who we were. As far as he knew we were a couple eloping from an outraged father.'

'Anyway,' Delia butted in, 'we have had suitable accommodation and the food was good. I'll recommend you to all my friends, if they are escaping. Our compliments to your crew, Sir, particularly to the cooks.' She linked arms with Lex. 'Are you ready to go yet?' she asked, smiling up at him.

Without any more discussion, the party moved towards the waiting rowboat. Before he left, Trojan stepped forward and shook Ambry's hand.

'Perhaps we shall meet you in Keshia, if you are still going there. I have no ill feelings about our encounter– we should have evaded you in the first place.'

Ambry put his hand on Trojan's shoulder. 'Fair-minded of you, I must say, my Lord. I am going to Keshia, but only for a short while.

'I fancy taking a run up the Northern Ocean, perhaps to The Bay of Storms, to see what pickings I can find up there. Shall I send word to Madame to inform her where her slaves are?'

'I wouldn't bother,' Trojan returned his grin. 'I intend to visit Madame Esse after we have found Prince Troy. I have unfinished business in Dish.'

With that he sauntered across the deck then dropped down the rope ladder to the waiting boat. He pictured Eyas as he had last seen her, with her long pale hair streaming down her back. The Eagle would welcome him, he was sure.

As the sailors rowed back to *The Aurora* the wind was rising and soon *The Black Dart* had her sails filling in the breeze, before she started to pull away to the north.

Delia's quick eyes immediately picked out individuals in the little group of men clustered forward on the deck of the approaching Devronian galley.

'Good Mut! There is the King! Won't he be surprised to see us!' Her exuberance, when trying to rush up the rope ladder, nearly swamped the small boat. Trojan had to hold the ladder steady in case she slipped and threw them all in the sea.

Before long they were gathered in the main cabin and Trojan had to recount their adventures to the crowd, hanging around to hear the tale of their adventures. When he had concluded, King Joseph sighed and clasped his hands together across his waist, while leaning back in his chair. 'So,' he sighed, 'we are still no further forward in our search for young Troy, he seems to have vanished off the cliffs of the continent.'

'What do you think we should do now, Lex? Shall we follow this Ambry to Keshia?'

'I believe we should,' Lex agreed. 'If we don't look there we shall always wonder if we missed him because of an oversight. Mind you, I believe Keshia is a very large town, and the countryside has estates.

'He could be on an outlying farm, working in a mine, or cooped up in some Lord's boudoir, for all our searching.'

'Usually slaves can be traced,' Trojan interrupted. 'The slavers stick to a pattern of sale and keep records of each transaction.

'I don't like the idea, but we shall have to visit the slave market. We must not forget that Amelia and Anton were also in their hands.'

A wave of nostalgia swept over Delia. She remembered what fun she had had with Amelia, and how the other girl had conceded to her wishes, and yet kept a restraining hand upon her pranks. It was because Amelia had been visiting Devron with Delia that she had been captured in the first instance.

'We must search for them!' she burst out, as a sudden picture of Anton's adoring face sprang into her mind.

'Don't worry, child, that is our purpose,' King Joseph smiled kindly, when seeing her woeful expression.

'Well, if that is the intention, we should get moving,' Jack Smart launched himself out of his chair.

As he left the cabin his voice could be heard.

'Mister Clark, prepare to set sail, if you please.'

Oars dipped in the water instantly, and soon the warship began to make speed. The sails rose, clattering up the masts, snapping in the fair breeze. Once they were secured, the rowers were able to rest, as *The Aurora* flitted like a huge white bird across the ruffles of the waves.

'We shall have to find you somewhere to rest,' Lex said. 'Jocelyn, go and see the purser and ask him what he can devise. The Lady Delia must have some privacy.'

Delia glanced at Trojan, who looked back at her with a prim face but with dancing eyes, as he considered the privacy she had experienced in the cabin they had just vacated. Jocelyn was soon back, saying Delia had a small space, which was being fitted out for her, situated near the main cabin.

The purser had requested a half hour's grace, so he could organise the fitting out of a bunk and other accoutrements. While they were waiting would the gentry wish for lunch?

They all trouped to the dining area, and soon Trojan and Delia were enjoying the best meal they had had since setting sail. Arrangements had been made for Trojan to share Jocelyn's small space.

After lunch, Jocelyn showed Trojan the cabin, then Lex gave them a tour of the ship. Trojan was very impressed with the facilities provided for the oarsmen. He was also astounded at their general physique and virility. What a difference between men doing something because they were employed to do so, and how he had suffered under the whip and the terrible conditions when he was a slave aboard Ambry's galley.

Their voyage to Keshia was uneventful. The water changed colour from clear green to muddy brown as they neared the harbour entrance.

The harbour was a hive of industry. Huge sailing ships, interspersed with dhows and outriggers, were all in constant motion, either entering port or leaving, while those at anchor bobbed in the swell.

Bumboats plied their wares from vessel to vessel, offering everything from fruit to whores, while tattooists, carpenters, barbers and outfitters, raised their voices across the water vouchsafing their abilities. One man had a small boat with trained monkeys on board for sale.

Shags dried their wings on lumps of rock near the coast, their feathers gleaming in the sunlight. The harbour had a pungent aroma of salt and spices, intermingled with the stench of rotting debris and excrement. The sun was powerful, beating through low clouds, and the whole scene shimmered in a heat haze.

Proudly showing the Devronian Royal Standard, albeit drooping in the humid air, *The Aurora* dropped anchor off to the side of the harbour, away from the shipping lanes but still in deep water. There was a small sandy bay close by on the land, with a lane leading off, over the hills towards the main town.

After discussion, it was decided to send Tom Clark to ensure accommodation for the party at a worthwhile hostelry, and then to return with enough horses to enable the royal party to ride into the city.

The crew was given sporadic leave; but was told to ensure they were on deck for roll call in the mornings.

Delia sat on the deck enjoying the late afternoon sun. *The Aurora* had attracted a deal of attention and was now besieged by bumboats. The traders were having rich pickings, as the sailors had not been allowed ashore during the voyage, not even at Dishnigar.

'Look!' she said to Trojan, as he came and stood beside where she was sitting. 'Those men are having pictures drawn on their bodies. What is the purpose?'

'Do you expect them to wash off, Delia? As to the purpose of them, there are many reasons. To draw your attention, to make someone look different, to remind them of someone, to give them a bond to a clan, to feel more handsome; each person has a different reason.'

'Do you think it is terribly painful? I don't like pricking my finger, but I think I would like one.'

Trojan raised an eyebrow at her in surprise. 'I expect it is painful, but as long as the wound doesn't get infected I suppose the pain would be transitory.

'High-born ladies don't have such things, Delia. Where would you want it?'

He was laughing at her. She knew but she was not going to be deterred by him and his opinions.

Extending her right leg, Delia revealed a neat ankle and a well-shaped foot below her workmanlike trousers. 'I would like a rose on the arch of my foot. What do you think?'

'Very fetching, I'm sure. Which of these scoundrels takes your fancy?'

She surveyed the tattooists, and finally chose a small slant-eyed man who seemed to have spotless equipment and was working at speed.

On Delia's insistence, Trojan called the artist over. He arranged for the man to call at her cabin first thing in the morning. Returning to where she was reclining under the awning, Trojan pulled her to her feet.

'Come on! We should go and look at the town while you can still walk. Put on your boots, while I get a boat.'

Soon they were riding along the track heading in to the town. The vegetation was different from what they were used to, the plants more verdant and the flowers prolific. The semi-tropical air suited Delia, and her face was glowing as she turned to look at the ocean, with the shores coming down to the bay.

'This town seems more fun than Dishnigar. What a dour, miserable place it was. I thought we were there for ever.'

'Keshia is much bigger than Dishnigar, and the climate is different. Not only that, the people who live here are different too. Many come from the lands across The Great Sea.

'The people are traders and merchants; they trade from here to other places. Look at those big merchant ships in the harbour and the bay.'

'Perhaps Troy is on one of those.'

'Heaven help him, if he is. A slave on one of those ships would disappear forever. Perhaps Lex will have some better news when we see him.'

They made their way through the fascinating streets, surprised by the activity on the pavements. Delia was impressed with the matching outfits the women wore and liked the idea of the striped awnings everywhere in the centre of the town. She was glad they had left the noisome clutter of the port, with its hidden alleys and roughly visaged populace.

The inn they had been advised to enter was in the middle of the main thoroughfare. It was named *The Yellow Orchid*. The trees surrounding the building had many such; the gorgeous blooms suspending from their leafy branches.

Their perfume was heady in amongst the enclosing trees. As they rode towards the stable, Trojan leaned from his saddle and plucked a bloom for Delia to place in her dark tresses.

'How about a yellow orchid on the other foot?' he teased.

'No thank you,' she replied firmly, 'one will be sufficient.'

Lex was sitting on the verandah of the inn with his booted feet on the guard rail, resting amongst the gaudy heads of canna lilies, which had been planted at the front of the inn. He looked calm and at ease, with a long, cool drink in his hand. He waved to them to join him, when he saw servants coming to take their horses to the stable.

'This seems a fairly decent place,' Trojan commented, shaking Lex by the hand as he rose to greet them.

'The best there is, I think. Our Mister Clark has done a good job. It is certainly a very busy place.' He indicated the foyer of the hotel, which was full of patrons, either leaving or entering, while servants and porters dashed about bearing piles of luggage.

Delia grasped Lex by the arm. 'Have you any news of Troy?' she asked earnestly.

'None, I'm afraid, but I do have other information. Amelia and Anton were brought here in a covered cart from Dishnigar by the slavers.

'No, before you ask, they are not in Keshia. They have been shipped to the Royal Court of Jaddanna, in the north, who knows for what purpose? They were kept away from the other slaves and had special treatment.'

Trojan slapped his fist down on the railing. 'We must have just missed them! From whom did you get this news?'

'I found the slave master in the market, and he had written documentation concerning all transactions. It must be done for legal purposes, he told me. He was a wily character with little pity, but he seemed honest.'

'So where can poor Troy be?' Delia put her hands to her face and sobbed a little.

This was so out of character that both men looked at her in dismay. Finally, Lex guided her to a chair and called for wine.

'Thank you, Lex,' Delia gave him a tremulous smile. 'I'm all right now. It was just the annoyance of missing Amelia and Anton on top of no word about Troy.' She accepted the proffered glass of wine with grateful thanks.

King Joseph had been resting after his sojourn into town, and now joined the party on the verandah. He looked tired and drained. He was finding the humid climate very debilitating. However, he was cheerful enough as he greeted Delia and Trojan.

'Young Jocelyn is arranging dinner for us. Apparently, the inn has an enclosed arbour in the rear, where we can dine, away from the crowds inside in the bars. Will that suit you, my dear?'

Delia assented, and soon they moved to the arranged accommodation, when Jocelyn beckoned them forward.

Jack was already seated at the table in conversation with one of the waiters. Before he rose to bow to King Joseph, he passed a small purse of money to the man while describing Troy's appearance.

'Do you think it will help?' Lex asked, as the man moved out of the arbour with a purposeful air.

'Who knows? We must try every avenue. It is possible that some lord has brought him here in his entourage. If the lord stayed here, Troy could be in the servant's quarters, we can but try!'

Night came quickly and the servants were lighting candles before the party started their supper. It was pleasant eating outside in the candlelit seclusion.

The food was excellent, though rather too spicy for their Devronian palates. Lex did remark he would endeavour to find such recipes in the future, now he had found what delights such spices could inspire.

Delia contented herself with plain rice, fruit and vegetables, not game to try strange flavours in the presence of royalty in case she made a gaffe.

Lex was discussing the news about Amelia and Anton with Jack and Trojan.

'Jaddanna,' Jack mused aloud, 'that is right in the north of the continent. It is very hot there, so I have heard. I have never been so far, but we shall have to go, of course.

'The land is ruled by a man called The Jada. He is a fine ruler, so I have heard, but the country is still run on the lines of outmoded customs. I wonder how we shall be received?'

'Lucky we have King Joseph with us, in that case. Having another despot with us might tip the scales in our favour. I can't bear the thought of Amelia being treated as a lowly concubine.'

'You don't need to worry as much for Amelia as for Anton. As far as I have heard young boys are sought after in a similar vein in that country, quite legally, apparently.'

Trojan put his hand to his forehead in a gesture of distain. 'Let us go quickly, then,' he expostulated. 'The sooner we get there the better. Who knows, we might have news of Troy in the north as well.'

As it was, they could not leave immediately, as some minor repairs were needed to be done to the sails. They left three days later, giving Delia time to wonder whether her foot decoration had been worth the trouble, then she decided it was.

For as the pain lessened, she found she was constantly admiring her pretty rose, and spent her days parading the deck barefooted.

Chapter Eighteen

The lantern gleamed dimly; its fragile beams outlining the forms huddled in a group, in the centre of the hurriedly raised tent. A sudden storm had chilled the air, and constant wind continued to bite across the plain.

As the evening had drawn in, Troy had appealed to Borin for help, as he felt sure the lovely Lustre was about to foal and she needed protection from such extremities of weather.

Borin had called to Jesse to assist him, and soon Troy was able to install Lustre in this hastily erected enclosure. The men had hunkered down around the mare, their presence giving her a feeling of calm and their warmth raising the temperature of the small space, encircled by leather and canvas walls. The ground was covered with plenty of straw.

Lustre strained again. She shifted her hooves uncomfortably, while tossing her head away from the restraining tether, then relaxed with her head lowered, quivering from the prolonged effort. Her soft breath gusted around the waiting men.

'It's taking too long,' Jesse said. 'She's going to need help.'

'Looks like it,' Borin agreed. 'I'll get the rope, you get warm water and soap.'

Troy looked at them in surprise, but they seemed calm and matter of fact as they left to complete their tasks. They returned in moments.

'You hold her head, Troy,' Borin ordered. He was busy stripping off and soon bared his torso. He washed himself thoroughly, then rubbed a lather of soap all the way up his right arm.

Fascinated, Troy watched closely as Borin placed himself at the rear of the mare then gently explored inside her birth canal.

'The foal has its forelegs drawn back under it,' Borin said. 'I can just reach the left leg. I'll pull it forward, you be ready with the rope, Jesse.'

Jesse busied himself making a slipknot at one end of the thick rope.

'Got it!' Borin breathed a sigh of satisfaction, sweat running down his body. 'Pass the rope. Hold on tight Jesse, I don't want this lot to slide in under, again. Now for the other!'

Moments passed. Sweat continued to flow over Borin as he struggled inside the mare; capturing the other foreleg took a deal of effort. At last he was able to call to Jesse to pass the other end of the looped rope.

'Wait until I feel her straining, Jesse, then when I say, pull like mad. I shall have to guide the head so we don't break the foal's neck. Slowly! Now pull! Wait a little!' The tension mounted.

'Now pull again! It's coming!'

Troy found he was holding his breath. With his sheltered upbringing he had never considered what happened when birth commenced. He watched around the belly of the mare, astounded to see thin, delicate hoofs, caught in the loops of the rope.

'Here comes the head!' The men staggered back as a small creature of a silvery colour followed their pull on the rope. They landed in a heap on the straw with the body of the foal spread across their legs. Jesse busied himself drying it off, cutting the cord and clearing its airways. The little animal lifted its head and looked around for its first glimpse of the world. Borin encouraged it on to its feet, then nudged it towards its mother.

'It's a colt!' Jesse cried out in delight. He pulled the rope out of the way, wrapping it up around his arm.

Occupied with gentling the mare, Troy could just see the silvery grey of the foal, topped with switches of black mane and tail. Lustre tossed her head away from him and bent around to greet her new offspring.

'I'll stay for cleaning up, and I'll give her a good warm mash,' Jesse said. 'You two can go and tell Lady Muria her mare is fine, and then you can celebrate the birth of the colt.'

Thanking him, Borin and Troy made their way out into the wind and trekked across to the main yurt. Borin was adjusting his clothing as they went.

He's mine! Troy was thinking, *such a beautiful creature!*

'Do you often have to help?' he asked Borin.

'It depends. If the mare is young and frightened, or if she is old and tired, we have to.

'More often, like this one, when the foetus is lying in the wrong position. They are all so valuable, we can't afford to let anything go amiss, if we can help it.'

They stamped into the yurt letting the leather hanging bang shut behind them.

'Lustre has a great colt!' Borin called out once they were inside.

Muria rose from where she was sitting by the fire, and came to greet them.

'Is Lustre all right? Is the baby perfect?'

'They are both fine. Jesse is looking after them. We should send him a hot drink – he'll be ready for one, I should think. It was hard work.'

'Are you pleased?' Muria turned to Troy with a smile. 'Your first horse, apart from Glint!'

Troy returned the smile and assured her he was delighted. He thought of the army of horses at his disposal in Devron, with a faint chuckle. Poor Juliette would be feeling neglected.

They called for mulled wine, then settled down by the fire.

'We shall have to wait for a few days before we set off to the Horse Fair,' Muria mused. 'Lustre will need to rest and the foal will need to strengthen its legs.'

'Are you going to take her to the fair to sell her?' Dismay made Troy's voice rise to a higher pitch.

'No! No! Nothing like that but I must take her in case someone is still looking for her.'

'Yes, I suppose you must. It was a surprising stroke of luck, the way we found her. That bear did us a favour. I wonder who that devil, Tommo, intended to sell her to?'

'I doubt if we will ever know, now. It was a lucky chance, being able to keep the colt on the plains.'

276

Sipping his wine, luxuriating in the heat from the fire, Troy gazed into the dancing flames. He thought about how he had had such high hopes of purchasing similar animals to the baby he now owned, hoping to strengthen the Devronian strain. Little had he realised how unfounded such a hope had been; yet now he had been given a pure bred colt.

His thoughts turned to the week when all of this had happened.

He had been breakfasting with his father and Lex. Lex had been teasing him about his drinking habits, telling the King how two of the guards had been needed to put Troy to bed the previous night.

The King had explained the reasons for the Kordovan's visit to Devron. He was talking about the importance of trade with the island kingdom. He had requested that Troy escort Delia on a shopping trip.

As Troy had helped himself to breakfast he had caught sight of himself in the mirror above the side board. His reflection had showed fair hair around an angular face, fine-boned with high, prominent cheekbones. He had considered his nose too big and his jaw too firm for classical good looks.

He smiled to himself as he remembered how important his clothes had been to him then. When he had taken Delia and her friend Amelia shopping, he could only think about escaping to his horses.

'What are you going to call him,' Muria inquired, butting into his thoughts.

'He seems too little to have an important name,' Troy returned. 'Let's give him a few days before we name him. He might tell us himself.'

Borin gave a chuckle. 'You must really be becoming one of the Horse Clan, if you are thinking like that. Perhaps you should have your wrist tattooed.'

'I would like that.' Troy's face lit up. He felt he needed to become part of this new life, which seemed to be inexorably spread before him.

He glanced at Borin's wrist, where the bear tattooed there, spread a paw down into his palm. He thought of the huge bear on Borin's back, then smiled at Muria, aware that this gentle lady had them all in the palm of her hand.

'I'll call the tattooist tomorrow,' she promised. 'A tattoo, a small one, like my wrist totem, doesn't take long at all.'

The next day the wind had dropped and Lustre and the new colt were freed into the sunshine.

Troy was astounded at the lines of the colt, and was pleased how sure its movements were, although it was so young. He was unable to spend the day admiring it though; there was work to be done with the herd.

Leaving Lustre and her foal, he whistled to Glint, who came trotting up, eager to begin the day's work.

They had become fast friends and Troy was glad he did not have to forfeit the great companionship he had with the big, rangy animal.

Lustre gave Glint a warning whinny, but Glint had far too much sense to approach her new baby.

On Borin's instructions, the riders took the herd on towards high ground for pasture. While they were moving the animals, Borin was selecting which ones he would take to the Horse Fair, with Muria's approval.

He selected 20 animals of different age and sex. Borin's skill, knowledge and quick eye, made Troy envious of his abilities, though he felt he was learning by example, albeit slowly.

A couple of weeks later they set off for the Horse Fair. Troy had called the foal Streak, as there was a streak of silvery hair in the middle of his black mane. Lustre and Streak seemed glad to be on the move.

Riding Glint, while leading Lustre, Troy kept a close eye on Streak as he trotted at his mother's side.

Muria had a wagon carrying all kinds of goods for the Fair. These ranged from leather jackets to pots of wild honey, potted meats to baskets of sweetmeats. There was a space at the back of the wagon where they could put Streak if he tired.

Troy made a point of travelling with the foal when he did tire, on occasion. He would support the delicate head, stroking the gleaming silver coat, while murmuring words of comfort and reassurance. Lustre and Glint would follow the wagon with steadfast determination in every flick of their tails.

Lustre was concerned with the wellbeing of her colt, while Glint was hurt by Troy's desertion for another. Troy spoke constantly to Glint, making sure his hurt did not change to jealousy. Muria often came to cast an eye over the colt, bringing Lustre a treat, perhaps an apple, or a piece of bread.

Muria had a way with animals and had already endeared herself with her new friend. She had ridden Lustre and they made a fine pair.

The small group was passing the Eastern Mountains, having covered nearly half their journey to the Gather, when Muria called a halt at midday, much to the surprise of Borin and the riders. Borin raised an eyebrow at her in query, concerned over her well being.

'Oh, no my Lord, there is nothing wrong. I would like you to linger here a while, while I visit with the seeress who lives at the foot of the mountain there.' She indicated a narrow track vanishing into the forest of young trees at the base of the mountain.

'I thought that track leads to the Priestesses,' Borin commented.

'So it does, but it forks and leads to the seeress' cave. I shall not stay there long, the animals probably need a rest, anyway.'

'I shall come with you,' Borin frowned against the sun, worry showing in the way he sat his horse.

'No, you are needed here. I shall take Troy with me. I'm sure he will be a fine guardian.' She smiled at Troy, who was delighted to be entrusted with the well being of his Horse Lady.

'At your service, Lady Muria.'

'We shall be back tomorrow.' Muria bent over and gave Borin a loving caress. 'Don't worry, we shall be fine.'

Looking at Troy she continued, 'I have a pack horse made ready, perhaps you would be so kind as to lead it?'

Borin had to content himself with establishing a camp. He realised it would be a good opportunity to examine the horses for wear and tear after the journey, so far, but he still felt disgruntled that Muria had not consulted him, nor had she given her reasons for visiting the seeress.

He watched the three horses trot away from the camp, then disappear into the bushy foliage of the forest.

Sighing, Borin shrugged his shoulders, then called the riders to him, so he did not have to shout his orders for camp preparation.

He was soon involved in examining the horses, and was quite pleased they had stopped, when he found one or two with hooves which needed attention, and another with a cut which had to be stitched.

The day passed quickly and he was tired enough after his work to seek his blankets early.

Muria and Troy soon found the glade where Merth had camped when she visited the seeress. Elated, Troy surveyed the provisions, which had been carefully stored for the next visitors to the spot.

As he built a fire for their evening meal he vowed to himself that in future he would always leave the necessaries for camp making, wherever he stayed. Muria soon had a meal going while he tended the horses.

'Surprising how many horses have been up and down this track,' Muria commented, her eyes following the telltale tracks of hoof prints disappearing into the gloom of the forest.

'Didn't Lord Borin say the priestesses lived this way, as well as the seeress? Perhaps they have many visitors. I should think their services are called on regularly. Do you want to visit them as well?'

Muria glanced at him through strands of long, blonde hair, which she was brushing. Her hair had reddish highlights where it reflected the firelight.

'No, not this time. A lot depends on what the seeress says, as to whether I shall be calling the priestesses in the future.'

Troy nodded, not knowing what to say. He busied himself building up the fire while he turned her remark over in his mind. How could one woman's decision affect the outcome of another's future?

Muria put her brush away, sat up straight and changed the subject.

'Are you looking forward to the Horse Fair, Troy?'

'Indeed, yes! Lord Borin has promised to give me my freedom there. How will this be done?'

'Oh, all the Horse Lords gather together and any announcements like that are declared in public. Lady Merth will give her consent, I'm sure.

'What did you do, before you were captured by the slavers? I'm sure it must have been something to do with horses. Were you a stableboy?'

'I have been quiet about it, Lady Muria.'

'Are you ashamed of your past?' A worried wrinkle appeared on her forehead as she thought she was alone in the forest with a man she knew very little about.

'Of course not! I don't think people will believe me, that is all!'

'Try me.' Muria sipped from her mug, while giving him a constant gaze.

'I am the younger son of the King of Devronia. We were captured while on an official visit to Kordova. I have no doubt they are moving heaven and earth to find me.'

Muria hooked her hair behind her ears so it did not hinder her stare of astonishment.

'You are a prince of the royal blood, in line for the throne?'

'Much good the royal blood did me when the slavers put me to the lash. I bleed as red as the next man, I assure you, and it spills just as quickly.'

'Will you return to Devron once you are freed?'

'I doubt it. My older brother is the heir, so I will not be needed unless something happens to him. I shall send word that I am alive though, because people might be worried and still be looking for me.

'To tell you the truth, I prefer the life here on the plain, working with the horses. My life in Devron was pretty pointless. I was a social nuisance, now I think about it.'

'Borin will be pleased to hear you want to stay. He thinks you are a talented rider, and you are so good with the animals.'

'I'm glad to hear that. At one time, when I was in the slave pens in Dishnigar, I thought my life had ended.'

Muria looked at his handsome profile, outlined against the flickering fire, and gave a quiet chuckle.

'I'm sure you have a great future ahead of you. We will question the seeress about you tomorrow.'

Troy smiled in return. He had little expectation of seeresses. He would do what was needed to please Muria, but to him life was a series of incidents with no pattern to them. Some people had lucky breaks, while others were less fortunate, or were born with poorer prospects. If good fortune befell him, that would be fine, but most days now he had work to do.

With that in mind, he bid Muria good night, then withdrew to his blankets on the other side of the fire.

In the morning they tidied the area where they had spent the night, carefully replenishing the wood stack, and making sure the ashes of the fire were well covered with soil.

The day dawned fair, and the horses made swift progress through the forest to where the track forked.

'It must be this way,' Troy said. 'There are too many signs of passage to the right. I should think most people would visit the priestesses.'

Muria agreed, so they followed the left hand fork. The wood became thicker and the branches grew so closely, little light penetrated between them.

The path was narrow and twisted, covered in foliage, reaching from side to side above them. Soon they had to abandon their horses and continue on foot. When they finally reached the cave of the seeress they were hot and tired, from pushing through the bushes, and traversing the narrow, pebbly path through the canyon. The trees and bushes encroached on the path, giving a feeling of gloom.

'I hope she is here,' Muria rubbed her face with her blue scarf, then flicked her long hair back, tying it up in a bundle with the scarf, so taking the weight off her neck.

'Oh, I am at home,' a husky voice came from behind them. A figure stepped out from between the tree trunks. She was dressed in dark green, with the silky material embroidered with light green, ivy leaves. Her gown hung loosely and billowed around her as she walked. Her dark hair off set her tanned face. She was perfect in this setting.

'Welcome, Lady Muria.' Her glance rested on Troy momentarily, 'and your companion.'

'You may sit here and rest, while I speak to Lady Muria.' She indicated a fallen log near the entrance to the cave.

Troy bowed, then sat where she had shown him. He watched the two women as they entered the cave, one tall and fair, the other slight and brown, but both with an air of purpose and confidence. Muria had come to visit an equal; she would defer to no one.

When her eyes had adjusted to the lamp light in the cave Muria was impressed with the workmanlike lack of clutter.

The seeress had surrounded herself with the tools of her trade and the bare necessities of life. Yet, there were homely touches, such as a bunch of wild flowers, displayed on a side table.

A pot was simmering on the central stove. Lifting a hand in a gesture of welcome, the seeress offered herb tea.

'Well, how can I help the Horse Lady of the Bear Clan?'

'My Lord has returned recently from a visit to Dishnigar. While he was away it came to me we should start a family. On his return, he agreed, but since then my moon blood continues to flow. I wonder whether there is aught amiss?'

The seeress tilted back her head and gazed at Muria, using the rods of her vision. There was no illness to be seen in Muria's aura, she seemed to be in perfect health.

'Let me scry a little.' The seeress moved to the table.

The black liquid in the shallow, silver dish seemed thick and opaque to Muria, yet the seeress was engrossed with the apparitions she could view.

'Your Lord Borin is a strong and healthy man, full of vigour and virility. I see no reason for your lack of flowering seed. Let me drift into the future, just a little.'

Muria sat on the edge of her chair with her hands clasped firmly together. The eager expression on her face was belied by the anxious trembling of her fingers.

She felt her heart thudding unpleasantly.

A faint smile crept around the seeress' lips. She raised her head and turned to stare at Muria.

'Do not be so uneasy, Lady. Your children wait to be conceived. I see twins arriving at the turn of the year. Handsome children they are, a boy and a girl. Perhaps there will be more later, I saw some further shadows, but surely this is enough to begin with?'

Muria laughed in relief. She reached for her drink of cooling tea and had a refreshing drink.

'You have given me much to dwell on,' she confessed. 'I thank you, lady. I have brought a small gift in appreciation of your advice.' She laid a tiny packet on the table.

The seeress glanced at it, but did not open it. 'I will investigate your gift after you have left. Shall I have words with your man?'

'Please do. I feel he has need of purpose in his life. I warn you, he seems to have little trust in your ways.'

'No matter. I shall speak with him. Call him in.'

Muria rose and exited the cave, to find Troy engrossed with the attentions of a small grey cat.

'So! Sasha has found you. You are honoured! Come this way.'

The seeress held back the leather fold so he could enter the cave without it brushing against him.

Troy slid past the small dark woman, surprised at her youth when he was so close to her. He had imagined her to be a mature woman, if not elderly, the way Muria had spoken about her. He felt out of place in the cave, but took the stool she indicated by the fire.

'Lady Muria wishes me to give you council,' the seeress said, sitting down beside him. She put a finger under his chin so she could turn his head, then gazed into his eyes.

Without a word she lifted his hands and inspected them. She gave a small exclamation of surprise as she studied his palms, then gave him a quick, assessing look from under lowered eyelids.

Pulling a handful of polished stones from her pocket, she thrust them into his hands.

'Rub these between your palms, then scatter them for me on this rug.'

She studied the scattered stones carefully, then picked up the two furthest from him and asked him to throw these again. When the stones fell in the same area, she nodded. She spoke softly.

'You have a destiny, which you cannot avoid. No matter what decision you make, you will be a ruler. I see you will be kind and just, and will consider the feelings of others. Animals' trust you, and will always give you comfort.

'I have spoken to your future already. No matter that you are still a slave, your freedom is in front of you. I wish you well in all your undertakings.'

Troy gave a shiver of apprehension as a wave of power permeated the cave. The lights seemed brighter and the fire crackled loudly.

'My thanks, seeress. My Lady Muria awaits me.'

He stumbled out of the cave, to help Muria up from where she was sitting, playing with the cat. They bid the seeress goodbye. She stood at the mouth of the cave watching them as they crunched across the pebbles strewn on the path, while wending their way down the narrow ravine.

Not a word was said on their way back to the horses, as each had much to think on.

Glint was delighted to see Troy, and gave a neigh of welcome as he sensed his approach.

As they made their way through the overhanging trees around the steep hillside track, Troy glanced at Muria's joyful face.

'Did the seeress give you good news, My Lady?'

'She did indeed, Troy. She raised my spirits and assured me I am fecund.' Muria patted her mare, who gave a whinny of appreciation.

'Perhaps we should have offered her some payment for her efforts.' Troy wondered what he could have given her, out of his meagre possessions.

'I did. I left her a small packet of emeralds. They should be sufficient for both of us. Was your visit worthwhile?'

'I hardly know what to think. She did assure me I shall be freed. She also told me some things I have to consider.

'Do you think our fates are always mapped out, and nothing we can do will alter them?'

Muria considered her answer. 'I think there is an over all plan which can veer in any direction, depending on the choices we make in offered situations. Ultimately, our own decisions affect which way our *karma* leads.'

'When I left Devron I did not think anything would alter the pattern of my life. I had a great deal to learn.'

Borin was pleased to see them return. It had taken longer for them than he had expected, and he had been anxious once dusk had started to descend. There were always wolves or marauding bears about in the forests. He could tell how Muria was riding that she bore good news.

'A successful visit, my love?'

'I believe so. Apart from confirming what we wished to know, Troy has been given advice. I'm afraid he did not wish to hear it. Come My Lord, so we can seek privacy. I have much to impart.'

Feeling shut out, Troy guided Glint to where Lustre was grazing in the shade of the wagon, Streak at her side. He slid out of the saddle and stroked the mare's gleaming neck.

'How are you, my lovely? Has this bundle of naughtiness been behaving?' Streak frisked around them, flicking up his heels and giving Glint a nip of welcome.

Troy looked at them in delight. These were his new family, even if Lustre belonged to Muria in name; he would always have a soft spot for her. She nuzzled his pockets, looking for the treats he often carried.

'Not today, my love. Glint has had everything I had.' He led Glint to the stream, collecting the pack horse and Muria's mare on the way. He carefully avoided where Lustre was, as she did not take kindly to other mares in her vicinity, particularly not with Streak running free.

As he tended the animals Troy's mind was in turmoil. How did the seeress know so much? He had a feeling she sensed his past as well as his future. His disbelief in all things mystical had been badly shaken, and now he did not know what to believe.

He had a wave of anticipation as he remembered his recurring dream of the girl with the wolf standing behind her. He pictured the gentle hands stretched out to him, with the snakes curling around her arms. Perhaps his vision would be in his future?

Having tethered the horses he returned to the main camp, where he joined the other riders sitting around the fire, waiting for their supper. Unearthly howls of wolves came from the forest. Looking at the moon drifting overhead, casting a magic glow on every blade of grass, he was glad he and Muria had escaped the denizens of the woods.

Accepting a bowl of soup and a tankard from Jesse, Troy found he was starving. Jesse watched him gobble down his supper then scrape the tin dish with a gobbet of bread to collect all the juices.

'Did the Horse Lady lead you a steady dance?' he inquired, a gleam of amusement in his dark eyes.

'It wasn't the Horse Lady, it was the other one, the seeress. She appeared to know more than was good for me.' He looked at Jesse with an ironic gaze. He did not mean to make little of the experience, but he could not resist raising an eyebrow, while glancing disdainfully down his nose. In this way, he could subdue Jesse's questions without so much as looking at him.

In fact, he was developing a habit not to look at a person directly, but to gaze past over a shoulder into the distance, thus dismissing the person from his presence, alienating himself from the conversation without giving offence. Jesse took the hint and started talking about the next day's ride.

Some days later they were nearing their destination.

The journey had gone smoothly and the horses were in good condition. Troy was pleased to see that Streak was keeping up well now, and did not need to ride in the wagon.

The colt was full of life and energy, though he still kept close to his mother, while Glint kept a watchful eye on him whenever he was in Streak's vicinity.

As they came up to the outskirts of the Gathering, Troy found he was full of excitement with his heart pounding in his chest. Soon he would be free.

He knew that as far as his future was concerned little would change, seeing he had made his decision to stay on the plains. However the thought of being mentally unchained, sent a surge of pleasure through his body. Until now, he had not been so aware of how his bondage had irked him.

The view of the encampment came on them suddenly, as they cantered over a small rise. The colourful tents, topped with the flags and totems of the families, made an impressive sight.

When they reached the open centre, Troy's attention was held by the variety and extent of booths and stalls selling wares from across the land, and possibly from overseas. He was starting to lag behind when Borin called to him.

'There will be plenty of time to investigate here later, we must move on to where the Phoenix has encamped before night falls.'

Laughing, Troy nudged Glint forward to catch up with Borin and Muria.

As they moved through the crowd, people hailed Borin from every tent they passed. Troy had had no idea of the size of the gathering, or how popular Borin would be, nor how many people knew him.

'How is it so many people know who you are?' he queried.

'I told you. I am brother to The Horse Lady of The Phoenix, the chieftain of the plains. Of course people know me, my sister is their leader!'

Jesse, bearing their huge, billowing, Bear banner had led the way since entering the camping ground. Now he veered away towards the far right, so perforce the rest of their group followed him.

'There is the Phoenix!' Muria called gesturing in front of them. Following her indication, Troy saw the magnificent standard flying as totem over a large tent established away to the right, far from the crowd.

'We shall camp beside them,' Muria announced. 'It will be good to meet your sister and make her mine.'

Troy was looking at the entrance to the tent when it suddenly opened and a figure stepped out.

'There is my sister! Merth!' Borin urged his horse forward.

Following him, Troy saw a sturdy, lithe figure, dressed in emerald green trousers and bolero, with her revealed skin covered with swirling tattoos all over her torso. She had long, brown curls, a vivacious face and an air of assurance, coupled with kindness.

As their eyes met over Glint's head, Troy knew he had found his destiny. He looked at the arms with those well-remembered snakes upon them. He raised his eyes to look at the face, previously hidden in his dreams.

The wolf, which had been the guardian of his visions, was pictured on her skin. He raised a hand in homage; aware they were both responding to his thoughts.

Chapter Nineteen

'We should discuss what to do next.' Chun looked tired and strained, his face paler than usual. The effort of burying the bodies of the settlers had taken its toll on both mind and body. He was also anxious about their own predicament.

'As far as I can see, we have three choices,' Anton volunteered.

'We can carry on following the cliff path and hope we reach Jaddanna, we could return to the ship and wait for rescue, or we could wait and try to attract the attention of a passing vessel, while staying here.

All of these options seem full of danger in one way or another. What do you think, Amelia?'

'We must stay here for tonight, as the cliff path would be too precipitous for the horses in the dark. The attackers seem to come from the cliffs, so we should set guards on the top of the cliffs above us, tonight.

I don't believe we should go back, I think we should carry on towards Jaddanna as Chun intended. Do you think we could make our way along the foot of the cliff, instead of being so exposed on the cliff path?'

'If we are on the sand perhaps we could find a boat we could use, or we could still hail a passing ship. I don't think we should stay here waiting to be attacked longer than is necessary.'

'Let's decide in the morning, when we have rested, then maybe we shall be able to see whether we can make our way along the water's edge. We must not abandon the horses either.'

Amelia was thinking of her precious Tam and how attached she had become to the little mare.

Guards were placed and they settled down for the night.

Anton lay on his back looking at the stars, while at the same time listening to the waves slip slap as they crested on the beach.

The air, blowing across the plain, was redolent with wild sage. The scents mixed inextricably with the pungent odour of seaweed and salt.

If it had not been for the threat of the brigands in the offing, or their dubious future in Jaddanna, he would have been perfectly content.

He looked at the still form of Amelia, who was sleeping peacefully, with her hand under her cheek. He considered how much they had experienced together and thought how strong and resourceful she had become, but his heart belonged to Delia.

He wondered if Delia were alive, as he was picturing her bright, lively face, ready to start some scheme or jape. She probably never thought of him; after all he was just a mere squire, while she could have the choice of princes. Nothing could be done about it until they were freed, anyway.

Sighing, he drew the blanket over his head and readied himself for sleep.

Chun was up before dawn the next day. He had been considering Amelia's suggestion of following the beach, so he strode off to investigate the next bay, around the northern headland.

The air was crisp. He walked barefooted on the damp sand, which was cool to his toes, though the sand was hard packed, and ridged by the receding tide. The water was luminescent and soon glistened brightly as the sun topped the heavy cliffs above.

The next bay was a sweep of land, which would take them all day to cross. It looked attractive and had small waterfalls along the cliffs.

The high tide line, strewn with seaweed, did not reach the cliffs, so there seemed no reason for them not to proceed. He turned and returned to camp, eager to commence their journey.

Amelia came to meet him. 'What did you find?' She put a hand on his arm, wanting reassurance.

'A big bay, we will be able to traverse along there. It will probably take us all day, even with the horses, but it seems safer than being so exposed on the cliff.'

'Well then! Let us get started!'

Chun called everyone together and explained what they had decided.

Anton listened carefully while feeling they were probably putting themselves in danger, if they were not able to find a way up the cliff side further up the coast. He consoled himself by thinking they could always return to this spot and start again, if needs must.

The journey was certainly more pleasant, particularly when the tide was out, as they were able to wade the horses in the water, or continue on the hard, dry sand.

When they had to travel nearer the cliffs the horses found it hard going in the soft sand, but generally it had been a sensible decision. They avoided the searing wind at the top of the cliff and were able to find shade in the mornings, before they were completely exposed to the sun.

They found a couple of skiffs, which had been cast up in some storm. With a little ingenuity, the soldiers managed to repair these, so every day there were groups assigned to fishing duties.

Another party was sent foraging on the cliff for birds and rabbits. This was done in the early mornings before the march began. In this manner, they were able to supplement their food stocks and became virtually self-sufficient.

Anton was pleased to find that his worries about ascending the cliffs were unfounded, there seemed to be trails up the cliff sides everywhere they went.

Amelia found she was enjoying herself. Dressed in a pair of cut down trousers and a loose shirt, she waded in the water searching for pretty stones and shells. She looked forward to every day with happy anticipation.

When she had lingered too long and had fallen behind the main party, she urged Tam forward and they galloped to catch up. Gone was the court lady in waiting. She hardened up every day. Her hair was sun streaked, and her skin tanned golden brown.

Splashing alongside Chun one afternoon as they were leading their horses, Amelia glanced at him, then linked arms with him.

'What will you do when we reach Jaddanna, Chun?' she asked, gazing up at him.

He turned towards her with a smile, his usually inscrutable face alive with anticipation. 'It depends on two things,' he replied. 'I will have completed my duties to The Jada, my contract expires this month. Hopefully, I shall have accumulated enough pay to be able to do what I wish.'

'What do you want to do?' Amelia looked at his almond shaped, dark eyes. Her heart skipped a beat, and her legs felt surprisingly wobbly.

'I wish to free you from your slavery to The Jada and marry you, if you will have me. Will you be my wife?'

This new Amelia had lost her shyness. She grasped both his hands in hers, horses' reins and all, leaned forward and reached to kiss him on the lips. 'Of course I will,' she said firmly. 'Where shall we live?'

'My home is in Keshia. I have a small estate with family and friends there. I have a healing practice, which I would like to return to. Would you like that?'

'I did like Keshia, it all sounds wonderful.' He put his arm around her waist and they continued walking through the receding tide.

'Well then, that is settled. We just have to persuade The Jada. Better him than his arrogant son, Drun. I left him with the Horse Lords.'

'Tell me about them.' Amelia had heard about the wild tribes in the centre of the country, but had never met anyone from there. Chun regaled her with the tale of Rahadir and Sythe.

'What a marvellous horse that one must be; not that you are not!' She turned to pat Tam on the nose. 'I know you understand everything I say.'

Anton came galloping back towards them.

'Hurry up you two! We are nearly around the bluff, don't get out of sight!'

'Anton, will you give me away?' Amelia asked, mischief in her eyes.

'So that's the way of it!' He stretched from his saddle to shake Chun's hand. 'You look after my little sister, or you will have me to answer to!'

'Look!' Amelia pointed out to sea. 'There's a ship out there! See that dark mark? I wonder if it is on its way to Jaddanna?'

Anton screwed up his eyes, looking against the sharp light of the dancing waves. He moved away from the others, and climbed a small dune, better to see against the brilliant water. His horse was restless, so he dismounted to steady himself, then shaded his eyes with his hand.

'I do believe it is coming this way,' he called to the others. We shall have to wait for it to approach much closer, before we can tell if it is friend or foe.'

He turned ready to remount his horse and glanced over his saddle at the usually deserted plains, stretching to the horizon behind him. To his surprise there was movement in the middle distance. He stayed where he was, studying the dust cloud, which seemed to be moving rapidly towards them.

A deep griping in his abdomen came with the realisation of what he was seeing. Turning, he yelled down to the others who were still standing in the waves.

'Take cover! We have brigands approaching, coming fast across the plain!'

This announcement scattered everyone to action.

Chun flung himself on his horse and had soon gathered the party together, and was directing them to take shelter by the cliffs. Fortunately, the fallen rocks gave cover, leaving just one small passageway at the side, near the looming cliff face.

Behind the rock fall was the entrance to a small, narrow cave. One by one the horses were led into the cave, and after some insistence from Chun and Anton, Amelia went in to calm them, and to take safety there herself. The rest of the party hunkered down behind the fallen rocks, positioning themselves to resist attack.

Anton placed himself in the narrow passageway leading to the cave. At last his swordsmanship would be put to more than just a test of skill.

'With luck they might not see us,' Anton breathed.

'They know we are here and have been trailing us,' Chun replied. 'We are an easy target and there are only a few of us.' He glanced around at the soldiers grouped behind the rocks; all were ready with knives and swords in their hands.

The men The Jada had sent to guard his son were seasoned fighters, he thought, but so far their skills in battle had not recently been tested. They had had no reason to exercise the skills Anton had taught them on board ship.

'Practise has been kept up and I have a high regard of the men's abilities,' Chun concluded.

The sound of drumming hooves alerted them to the nearness of the raiding party, which had descended the cliffs further around the bay, out of sight.

Without a moment's hesitation, black cloaks fluttering, scimitars raised, while uttering skirling screams, they rode past in groups, circling to attack again.

The view was restricted with swirling sand thrown up by the galloping hooves. The air was filled with the furious screams of attack, the thunder of the horses, and the clash and slash of weapons as the soldiers resisted the attack.

The small party of travellers defended well, knowing their existence was at stake. Raised swords, firmly held in brawny fists blocked the slashing scimitars. Few cuts were received and the fallen rocks stopped and dulled many a ferocious attack.

The leader of the brigands, a dastardly fellow with a patch over one eye, called his group together and they all dismounted. They huddled together, listening to the one eyed leader.

'Stage one over,' Anton gasped, passing around a canteen of water. 'Be ready! They will come for us on foot, now! We must defend the cave at all costs!'

He received nods of assent from all the party, with grim determination showing on every face. Anton helped tie a piece of rag around the forehead of a soldier who had received a slash during the battle. The blood, trickling down his face was filling his eye, reducing his sight.

'Chun will look after you later,' Anton smiled at the soldier, then gave him a thump on his back. *If we do have any later*, he mused to himself, returning to his post by the hole in the rocks.

'Here they come again,' Chun called out.

Anton raised his sword and straightened his back. 'Remember to keep your guards up and hold your positions. They want horses and slaves, but we want dead bodies!'

He took a deep breath while watching the brigands approach. He had always worried if he would lose his nerve in a real fight, or that he would never be able to injure someone with intent, but found he need not have troubled himself.

Anton found self-preservation augmented his skill, as soon as he saw the upraised scimitar descending towards him. With a quick riposte, he slammed aside the broad blade, and then transfixed his opponent through his exposed neck.

As the body slid away, another furious face came around the side of the rock. This one managed a small nick in Anton's left arm, but quickly suffered the fate of his leader.

'We can't last much longer,' Chun panted, wiping the sleeve of his shirt over his eyes, soaking up the sweat. He watched the brigands grouping again, getting ready for another assault.

'We have whittled them down a bit.' Anton pointed to the bodies lying at the foot of the rocks.

'Yes, but there are only a few of us.' Chun glanced down sideways to count their wounded. 'We have lost three to the battle, not dead but badly-wounded.

'One has a blow to the head, one has a badly cut chest and the third has lost three fingers. As well as that, we are tiring.'

'Who is that in the middle?' Anton asked.

'By Mut, it is Amelia!'

'Let her fight,' Anton advised. 'It would be more dangerous trying to stop her.'

Amelia watched her bearded opponent climb up the rock towards her. Her heart was thudding in her chest, but at the same time she thrilled with exhilaration.

She could practise the skills she had gained. The man laughed when he saw her stern face. Chuckling away, he raised his huge sword ready to swing down on her.

As he loomed over her, Amelia lunged forward with her sword, thrusting it up under his upraised arm. With a yell, he dropped his weapon then slid towards her. She leant forward calmly, and cut his throat with a slash from the knife held in her left hand.

Straightening up, brushing her hair out of her eyes with the hand holding the knife, she looked over the rocks purposefully, ready for her next attacker.

Half an hour later there were no more attacks. What was left of the bandits had gathered together in a group at a distance, away on the sand.

'They are preparing for a final attack,' Anton said. He was sticking his sword in and out of the sand to clean it.

'No! They are leaving!' Chun said worriedly. 'They will be going to get others to help them and then they will be back at night fall.' As he said this, the bandits wheeled and trotted off, leading their riderless horses by their reins.

Amelia sank down on the ground. Reaction had set in, and she was trembling with the horror of what she had done. Chun dragged himself around the rocks until he had found her. They threw themselves into each other's arms. Amelia was sobbing, while Chun held her as if she would snap in his arms.

Anton organised the unhurt members of the party to rig up a small area where the wounded could be tended. He then sent off men to find wood for a fire, others to fill water bottles, another group to look after the horses.

Soon, all the jobs, which were necessary to establish order, had been completed, in an attempt to restore normality. Anton remembered to post guards. *If they do come back, we must be ready for them*, he thought.

The bodies of the brigands were hauled together, away from the camp. Chun had ordered for them to be buried in the sand when the men had finished their other tasks.

Everyone had been so busy that the ship, which they had guessed was on the horizon had been forgotten.

When there was a slight respite, one of the soldiers looked out to sea.

'Sir!' he called to Chun, 'look out on the water!'

Chun turned away from the wounded man he was caring for, with an irritated gesture. Astounded by what he saw, he jumped to his feet.

'Quickly!' he called out. 'Get firewood to light a bonfire on the point! That ship is drawing closer. If we can attract their attention, we might escape, even yet!'

'What if it is pirates?' Anton queried, uneasily.

'Pirates or not, the sooner we are out of this situation the better. We have wounded men, little food, and those devils will be returning at sundown! Get moving!'

Before long most of the men were jumping up and down beside the big fire they had built on the headland. Every bit of cloth they could find was being waved.

At last they were noticed, and the great galley changed course, starting to head for the shore. A huge cheer went up from the castaways as they realised they were to be rescued, for good or ill.

'Oh, thank God!' Amelia cried, after she had been peering at the closing vessel. 'That is the royal standard of Devron flying at the mast.'

Aboard the galley, Lex and Trojan were watching the shore approach with interest. They had heard the watch call to the captain, attracting his attention to the bonfire on the hill.

Jack had looked at the stragglers on the beach through his glass and had then decided to alter course to investigate. When they had ventured far enough in the shallow water, the galley was anchored and a long boat lowered. Lex volunteered to go with it.

Delia came on deck and joined the group standing by the rail.

'What is all the commotion about, whatever is happening?' she asked Trojan.

'There are some poor souls marooned on the beach over there. Smart is sending a boat to see if they need rescuing. They have horses there, do you see? Over by the cave mouth. Perhaps they don't need our help, after all.'

When the boat came near the beach, the people around the bonfire came rushing down to greet the sailors.

As Lex waded towards the shore he was astounded to see the familiar figure of Anton running towards him across the sand. Lex threw his arms around Anton, hugging him as tightly as he could.

'You young dog! How did you get here? Are you free? Who is that woman and who are these men? Is Troy with you?'

Anton could hardly speak, he was so overcome with emotion.

'The lady is Amelia, Lady Delia's lady-in-waiting. The soldiers belong to The Jada – they are from the Jaddannese army. This is my friend Chun, he is betrothed to Amelia.'

Chun came staggering up, as the final run across the sand had sapped the rest of his strength. Lex shook his hand, but he was gazing past him at Amelia as she made her way towards him. This was not the Amelia he had remembered at the ball with Delia.

Amelia covered the final strides to reach the group standing at the water's edge. She was wearing her usual cut off trousers and loose shirt, with her sword belted around her waist. Bareheaded and barefooted, she looked like a young boy. Lex surveyed the sun streaked hair surrounding the angular, fine-boned face and was astounded at her composed expression and fluid grace.

'Well met, My Lady.' He bowed over her sun-tanned hand, while meeting her laughing eyes with his own.

'We are all so pleased to see you, Prince Lex,' Amelia returned. 'Have you met Chun, my betrothed?' She turned to Chun and slipped her hand through his bent arm.

'My pleasure,' Lex returned. 'Perhaps we can be of service to you? It looks as if you have been in some bother?' he raised an eyebrow at Anton who was standing near.

'You may well say that.' Anton swung around to survey the cliff tops behind them. 'I think we should get aboard the galley with as much speed as possible, before our friends return in greater numbers. Can we wade the horses out, My Lord?'

'I think we can manage that. It would be a great pity to have to abandon them. I'll ask Jack Smart to lower a gangplank to make a ramp for them.

'You come with me, Amelia. I'm sure we can find a cabin for you. We will leave the men to bring the supplies and the horses.'

'Thank you,' Amelia responded, 'but I must be with my horse when she boards. She will be more comfortable if I am there. I shall bring her one of the first though, Prince Lex.' She smiled at him before turning away.

Lex returned to the long boat delighted with this encounter, yet sad that Troy had not been with the party.

As soon as he stepped foot on the galley, he was bombarded with questions from King Joseph, Trojan and Delia. Lex raised his arms to push past them as he stepped aside.

'Wait! Wait! I shall tell you all in a minute! First I must get Smart to move closer to the shore, if it is possible, and then let down a ramp.'

He left them still demanding news, and hurried to where the Captain was waiting on the bridge. Soon Jack had understood what was needed, and the galley edged towards the shore. Soundings were taken continually, and just before the galley struck the sand, the anchors were lowered, and then a wide gangplank was let down.

Lex returned to the others and gave them the astounding news.

'Somehow or other, Amelia and Anton have got themselves mixed up with some Jaddannese cavalry. They are coming aboard now!'

Delia leant over the side, squinting against the sun, her eyes shaded by her hand.

'Is that Amelia? The one with the long hair, sitting astride that horse? It can't be. She can't ride any better than I can!'

'Things have changed,' Lex laughed. 'Not only is it Amelia, but the man riding beside her is her affianced.'

'There's Anton!' Delia rushed to the top of the gangplank, ready to welcome them all aboard.

'Who did you say the men were?' Trojan asked, watching the horsemanship displayed by the approaching riders.

'Apparently they are soldiers from Jaddanna. They are escorting Amelia and Anton to the city. Our friends are still intended to be slaves for The Jada. However, Amelia's man, Chun, seems to think that if we go there he will be able to get them freed. It is all still a pretty mix up.'

'No sign of Troy?' King Joseph asked, forlornly.

'No, unfortunately.'

The old King looked so woeful, that Lex put a consoling hand on his father's arm.

'Let bygones be bygones,' he said. 'We have four of our five wanderers. Surely we shall find Troy eventually, even if we have to go over the whole continent by foot!'

Trojan helped the sailors bring the horses safely on deck. When Anton appeared, climbing up on the deck, Trojan gripped his arm in both hands.

'Well met! Welcome aboard!' he smiled at his friend.

Anton gave a gasp of pleasure and relief. 'You have no idea how pleased I am to see you too, Trojan. Is Troy aboard the galley?'

Trojan shook his head in despair, his mouth tightly scrunched ironically.

'Who knows what has become of him. We couldn't trace him from Dishnigar. But Delia is here with me.'

Turning, Anton noticed Delia, who was leaning over the side, waving to Amelia. Anton suddenly went bright red and let go of the reins of the horse he was leading.

'Hold on!' Trojan yelled, grabbing the reins, but Anton was off. He dashed across the deck and swung Delia around in a bear hug.

'Who! Oh, Anton!' Delia was delighted to see him. She returned his hug with a kiss. 'I have been so worried about you,' she said, 'and all the time you have been cavorting around with Amelia.'

'Is that what you call it? She will be coming aboard soon. Good news! She is going to marry Chun, so she will be going to live in Keshia. Whatever happened to you?'

'Trojan and I have been playing ladies maids to a family in Dishnigar. We were well-treated and well-looked after, but it was no fun, so we had to escape. What happened to you?'

'By courtesy of The Jada, we were also well-looked after, though what he intends to do with us when we reach Jaddanna, Mut forfend!'

'You needn't go to Jaddanna,' Delia declared, her eyes flaring brightly with emotion as she looked at him. This was not the young, untried boy she had last seen in the slave pens. Now he was an assured young man, with a strong character and a steely look to his eyes.

'Yes we do.' Anton had a firm note in his voice, which sounded as if he had made up his mind about this.

'We must free ourselves from slavery or we will be forever looking over our shoulders expecting to be recaptured.

'Chun seems to think he will have some say in the matter; he thinks The Jada will listen to reason. Who knows?

'If not, I shall have to sell my lands left to me by my father in Devron to ransom us. I must go to the city to complete the bargain.

'There is more to being a slave than wearing a collar.'

Delia looked and saw he still had the iron ring around his neck.

'We were lucky,' she said, 'we were able to lose our collars.'

She stood on tiptoe, leaning against him, to peer over his shoulder at the slight form standing watching the last horse come aboard. She gave Anton a kiss by his ear as she stood up straight again.

'Who is this Chun, Amelia is going to marry? What a peculiar name!'

'He is a healer from Keshia. He was working for The Jada and visited the Horse Lords when in the Prince's retinue.

'When the Prince was detained, Chun brought the rest of the party to Keshia. Come and meet him, I'm sure you will like him.'

Trojan had got rid of Anton's horse and was giving Amelia a hug as she stepped up on the deck.

He surveyed her castaway look, holding her at arms' length, while laughing with a chuckle of delight.

'Well, my dear! Whatever has happened to the demure little lady's companion? I declare, there is a veritable sea wolf before me!'

'Be quiet, Trojan! Stop mocking me. Here, have you met Chun? He and I are going to be wed, so you had better be polite!'

'You are aware I'm known for my politeness.' Trojan greeted Chun. 'I hear congratulations are in order?'

Chun smiled at the lanky figure before him, ignoring the long, blond hair and indolent air, already charmed by Trojan's friendly behaviour.

'I can't accept your good wishes yet, my Lord. We still have to gain her freedom from The Jada, as in a way, so do I.'

Lex suggested that they all repair to the main cabin out of the sun, and surely it must be time for some refreshments?

With alacrity, they all turned and followed his lead, though King Joseph entered the cabin first. He had recovered from his disappointment that Troy was not in their number, and was now eager to hear of everyone's adventures.

The outcome of the discussion was that they really were honour bound to continue to Jaddanna, if only to disembark the soldiers and their horses. Everyone from Devron was curious about the city, anyway.

'A pity we can't send Ambry with them,' Delia said forcefully. 'He has a lot to answer for, and so does his friend Petric.'

Lex and Jack Smart glanced at each other, amusement showing on their faces. Trojan, of course, noticed this by play.

'Tell us what you are thinking, Lex!'

'I'm sorry Delia to be the one to tell you this,' Lex looked rather shamefaced for being caught out, 'but your mother won't be home when you get there.'

'Why not?'

'Well, apparently she was smitten with Petric and has gone off with him to the Southern Isles.'

A stunned silence greeted this news.

Delia broke it by saying, 'Oh, my poor father! It doesn't matter what happens in Kordova as far as I am concerned, now, unless Anton wants to go there. I shall stay wherever he wants.'

Anton took her hand, too overcome to say a word, but with his adoration written all over his face.

'So, it looks as if all our fates are to be decided by The Jada,' Chun remarked. 'Who knows, he might have news of your son.' This was said with an inclination of his head to King Joseph.

Chun, as usual, was feeling concern for all in the company. King Joseph nodded in agreement.

'It looks as if our course is set, then?' Jack Smart queried, raising an eyebrow at Lex.

'Yes, Captain. When you are ready we should set sail to round the Northern Cape on our way to Jaddanna. All agreed?'

The gangplank was drawn up and the oarsmen pulled the galley away from the shore.

Lex was helping find berths for everyone. The girls were quite happy to share a cabin, having much to talk about.

Anton and Trojan were leaning over the side, watching the land recede. As they were watching, a large group of horsemen thundered up on the cliffs above the beach. They streamed down the cliff side, ululating battle cries, while swirling swords and brandishing knives in threatening gestures. With cries of dismay and annoyance when they discovered their victims gone, they swirled around the edge of the sea, with their horses bucking and rearing at the sudden stop.

'Thank Mut we were saved from that lot.' Anton breathed. 'We managed to fight off the first group, but we would have had no hope with that number.'

'Did you fight to the death?' Trojan asked, staring at the bandits on the sand.

'Oh yes!' Anton said grimly, 'even Amelia killed three, and I don't know how many she wounded.'

'The little lady's companion!' Trojan smiled. He leant out over the side and waved at the brigands, who roared more furiously when they saw him.

'Mayhap I shall speak to this Jada about making his shores cleaner,' Trojan mused aloud.

Chapter Twenty

The chieftains had assembled in the morning to give their considered opinions on the legal disputes, which had arisen over the intervening months, since the last gathering of the horse clans.

Merth sat in the centre of the half-circle of men and women, ready to give her final verdict on the cases. Attired as The Riffed One, the cold wind made her feel on edge – she wished to call for her fleeced jacket. She folded her arms to keep the niggly, little chill from sliding up under her bolero.

There were one or two minor cases to begin with. In outlying clans the moral laws of the Horse Lords were not strictly adhered to, particularly if the clans were in touch with other races, such as those who came from near Keshia.

Merth had decided that outlawing thieves and rustlers was the best decision. Her love of life, and respect for other people, ensured she was a magnanimous leader.

In her judgements there were no arbitrary rules, resulting in flogging or branding. She was amazed when one of the supplicants standing in the centre of the half circle, was one of her own riders.

She remembered when she had been newly promoted to her position – she had given judgement against this man about a saddle. She had thought at the time that she had raised an enemy.

He told the assembly about how he had expected to gain the saddle after the death of his father, and how with summary justice it had been given to another.

When Norsa had finished speaking, Merth stood.

'I have given judgement on this matter in the past. I shall withdraw until a consensus of opinion has been delivered about this man's plea.'

She strode away from the judgement circle and went towards the fire, where it had been placed on the other side of the glen.

She looked around the crowd as she was sipping a hot drink, looking to see if Jerain or Merthsandra were amongst the throng. She was glad not to see them.

If they had come to the Gather she would have had to outlaw them from the plains, something she had no wish to do.

She saw Borin on the other side of the fire chatting to Redd. They looked more alike now Redd was getting older.

Merth wondered where the man she had dreamed about so often was at that moment. He was not amongst the crowd, so he was probably working with the horses.

The pulse in her neck started to throb at the thought of him. Her knees had a peculiar, rubbery feel, as she circled the fire to speak to her brothers.

Borin welcomed her with a hug, and Redd grabbed her by the hand.

'What are you doing here? Escaping from giving the judgements?' Redd was laughing at her flushed face.

'Oh, I'm just waiting for something to be settled by the council, as I have already had a part in it. Muria is looking well, Borin.'

Muria was sitting in the council on behalf of the Bear Clan.

'Of course she is! I look after her like you told me to.' Borin gave her a grin.

'Who is that fair-haired man who was with you last night?' Merth ventured, getting more flushed by the minute.

'He is a slave I want you to free. I have two reasons to come before the council and he is one of them. Oh look! They are calling for you.'

Merth returned to her seat with rosy cheeks and a feeling of anticipation. She would see her dream man again!

The council had upheld her first decision concerning the saddle. Norsa had accepted the ruling with ill-grace. He had announced he would change clans, and was now offering himself as a rider for a different totem.

Merth thought this was a trifle foolhardy as she would not have held it against him, because he had sought further justice. If no other clan would take him, he would have to leave the plains to find further work.

The day dragged on. She found she was restless, then realised she was waiting for Borin to be called to take his turn. Finally, Borin approached with the tall, fair-haired stranger walking with him.

Unaccountably, Merth found she was sitting up straight with her tummy tucked in, hands clasped firmly in front of her, while licking her lips to ease a dry mouth. Avidly, she watched the slave come towards the group sitting in judgement.

When Borin had made his plea, saying that Troy had fulfilled all of his duties, had helped in times of trouble, and had been a friend and mentor, the council all agreed he should be a free man.

Merth raised her head and looked straight at the new rider. She met the steely, blue eyes with a smile in her own brown ones.

'Well, Sir! Do you join with the Horse Lords, or do you go back to your own home?'

Troy looked at the regal beauty and serene countenance of the woman with whom he intended to spend the rest of his life. 'I shall stay with the Horse Lords if the Lady Muria will have me,' he returned.

Muria has plenty of riders,' Merth stated. 'I have just lost a good man. Borin can I ask you to release this man to me, so I can employ him as a rider for the Phoenix?'

Borin was taken aback. He enjoyed Troy's company and skills, but he could not refuse Merth, if she really wanted Troy.

'My pleasure.' He bowed.

'Go find the priestesses,' Merth ordered, looking at Troy. 'They will put the Phoenix on your wrists, so you don't need The Bear. Come to my tent this evening and we shall discuss your future employment over a glass of celebratory wine.' When she smiled her face lit up, revealing her sudden inner warmth.

Troy was overcome. What with gaining his freedom, while at the same time being bound in the chains of love, he was tongue-tied.

He looked forward eagerly to the evening, hoping he would finally be alone with Merth. Bowing to her, while extending his right hand in the way the Horse Lords greeted or farewelled each other, Troy retreated, looking to find Jesse; hoping his friend would help him find the priestesses, whoever they were.

Borin had watched while so much had not been said, between Merth and Troy. Then with a little laugh of bemused pleasure, he turned once again to the council.

'Now I have a further dilemma to put before the chieftains,' he declared.

'When we were returning from Dishnigar on our annual horse cull, we came across a vagabond called Tommo.

'Unfortunately a bear killed him, but that is another story. In his possession was a beautiful mare, who was in foal.

'As the mare was obviously from a herd belonging to a Horse Lord, I took charge of her. Since then she gave birth, and I gave the colt to my slave.

'The mare I gave to my wife, for safekeeping. If no one has lost such a mare, my lady Muria, is willing to give her a home. If she is claimed we feel some proof of ownership is called for, and we would need some recompense.'

With this over, he bowed to the assemblage and withdrew to the side. No claim was raised by any of those present.

Muria vouchsafed to keep the mare, now named Lustre, in her possession. If anyone laid claim to her, she would interview that person herself. The judgements continued for the rest of the afternoon.

'I thought you were going to be a Bear,' Jesse growled, as they returned to their encampment after Troy's visit to the priestesses.

The small Phoenix tattoos had only taken a few hours, and Troy was well-pleased with the result. It had given him an instant feeling of belonging, which he had never experienced before, not with the Bears, or even at home in Devron, where his every wish could be satisfied.

'Well, you are right. I had hoped to be a Bear, too,' he returned, throwing his arm around Jesse's shoulders, 'but when the Lady Merth claimed me for the Phoenix, what could I do?'

'I suppose I shall see you now and then,' Jesse grumbled, 'what with The Bear being her brother I guess there will be some toing and froing. Didn't you want to go home?'

'No,' Troy said firmly. 'I am a younger son, who has been a slave, and I bear the marks on my back to prove it. Even if something happened to my brother, I must have lost the respect needed for a prince. I would just be an embarrassing nuisance. Better, I stay here and start a new life with the Phoenix.'

'A prince, did you say?' Jesse was looking at him with wide eyes and an open mouth.

Troy laughed. 'I'm just another rider like you! Let us see if we can find some beer! I would also like to spend some of this coin Borin has given me, on new clothes that fit. I saw some merchants over where those booths were. Come on!'

Soon they were sitting under a large tree, each holding a bun with steak inside, in one hand, with a large tankard of frothing beer in the other.

Troy was much more comfortable now he had trousers and a jacket, which fitted him. He had also found some finely woven, coloured shirts in autumn shades, which offset his fair hair and drew attention to his complexion. As these had caught his fancy, he had bought one of each.

He was now wearing an olive green, linen shirt. His brown leather trousers and jacket were fringed and embossed, but he felt he could put up with their ornamentation for their feel and cut. Now the tailor had his measurements, he had promised a set of more workmanlike leathers.

Troy stuck out his legs and surveyed his boots. They were scuffed and dirty, but they were still comfortable. He remembered worrying about getting them dusty the day he took Delia shopping. He gave a chuckle, thinking about that young boy who was emulating being a dandy. The boots would do for a while yet. As Troy and Jesse sat chatting, finishing their beer, Borin found them under the tree.

Calling for more beer, including one for himself, Borin flung his length down beside them.

'I guessed I would find you here,' he said. 'My you are looking smart!' Borin surveyed Troy and a surprised smile crossed his face.

'I thought it was time I was wearing something that was big enough for me,' Troy replied with a smile. 'You never said your sister was such a beauty!'

'I hadn't realised it myself.' A big grin stretched across Borin's face.

'Having a child has changed her. She has been telling me about my niece, Alyssandra, a fine little demon apparently, left at home in the yurt.

'Oh, by the way, Merth said for you to call on her this evening, after the evening meal is finished.' He glanced at Troy, surprised to see he had changed colour. *The beer must be pretty strong,* Borin thought.

That evening Troy could hardly wait for the last meal of the day to be over. As soon as the dishes had been cleared away, he tidied himself up, using water from a nearby stream, then made his way to where the Phoenix emblem fluttered in the cool, night breeze.

I belong to the Phoenix now, he thought, a feeling of pride surging through him, as he admired the red and yellow totem. He stood outside Merth's small tent, unsure what to do.

The rider on duty, who was lounging by the door, spoke. 'If you have come to see The Riffed One, just step inside. She will call you when she is ready.'

Troy pushed aside the tent flap and came face to face with the back of Merth's jacket. He stood there admiring the embroidery.

'Come inside.' The soft welcoming voice stirred the strings of his soul. Pushing past the jacket, he saw Merth standing by her fire, with her hands resting on the heads of two massive hounds, one on each side of her. He waited just inside the entrance way, wondering how far he dared approach.

Merth smiled, a slight alteration to her face, which suddenly gave spirit and animation to her features. She gave the hounds a push.

Realising this was a kind of test, Troy stood motionless. Boris and Borland padded across and sniffed at him. Boris licked his hand. While Borland planted his paws on Troy's arm, then looked straight in his eyes. After this, both dogs sat down on the ground behind him, near the tent flap.

'Welcome!' Merth whispered. 'My guardians have given you leave to approach.'

Troy strode forward and offered his hand, pointed down towards her.

Merth gripped his hand in both of hers, then turned it over, looking at the small Phoenix on the inner side of his wrist, still slightly inflamed.

She raised her head and looked into his vibrant blue eyes. 'The man of my dreams. I have waited for you for many days.' She ran a finger over the tattoo on his wrist. Troy bent and kissed the back of the hand, still grasping his.

'My Lady, the shadowy figure I have seen in my nightly wanderings, has only shown me these.' He stroked the snakes on the backs of her hands. 'The wondrous face I have only seen today.'

'My seeress told me to watch for you,' Merth replied. 'I was afraid I would never find you.' She pulled his hand and together they moved toward the sheepskin rug spread before the fire.

'Your name is Troy? Borin mentioned something about you being a lost Prince? Is there trouble in this?'

Firmly grasping the proffered hand, Troy assured her there was no trouble. He told her that the only reason he would return home was to set the fears of his relatives at rest. He stated that it was his intention to spend the rest of his days in the shadow of the Phoenix.

'Well then,' Merth breathed, looking at him in delight, 'perhaps you would like to guide the Phoenix in the future? I am in need of a husband to guard my herd.'

'It will be an honour,' Troy croaked, a tremor in his voice.

Merth slid her fingers in his hair, where it was falling over his face. She tightened her hand and pulled him forward into an embrace.

As they kissed, desire took her. This was her man, chosen by fate to be her partner. She was aware of the wolf of her childhood standing by his side.

Troy closed strong arms around her, then kissed her again, soundly. The shadow lady of his dreams was warm and luscious beyond belief.

When Merth stretched out on the sheepskin under him, Troy responded passionately.

Later, exploring and examining, Merth ran her hand across his shoulder.

'What happened to your poor back?' she queried, raising herself on her elbow to gaze into his face.

'I was foolish. I would not accept my fate, so I was whipped into submission.' He gave a little laugh. 'It was worth it all, because it ensured I would come here to find you!'

'I shall have to hurt your back, again.' Merth looked troubled, not wishing to cause him more pain. 'If you are going to be my mate, you will have the Phoenix on your back, like mine.'

She rolled over, dropping the rug, which was covering her. Troy admired the wonderful picture on her back. 'I shall be able to bear the pain for your sake,' he said quietly.

'It might hurt more on your scars, but at least it will cover them. You won't have the big tattoo until we return home, anyway. It would take too long while we are here.

'I intend to visit the Northern Plain after we leave here. I shall be taking Prince Drun and his friend Rahadir on to Jaddanna, to return them to The Jada.

'This will take some time, probably a month there, a week at the palace, then six weeks returning home. I shall instruct the priestesses to have their tents ready for you then.' She rolled over again, settling the rug around her shoulders.

'I'm surprised you are not already married,' Troy said, lifting her hand to kiss each finger.

'I have been,' she said calmly. 'I have a little girl. I put my husband aside, when he betrayed me with my sister. I had to banish them from the clan. I don't know where they've gone.

'Fortunately he had to travel on a mission for our clan, before the Phoenix could grace his back. You must realise it is not a small thing, to be the mate of The Riffed One. There are rules and laws, which must be followed.'

'Did you love him?' Troy was uneasy, waiting for her answer.

'I thought I did. Later, I realised it was only physical attraction, not a soul thing. He did not anticipate my needs, and neither did I, his. I did not choose him, my father arranged the marriage.'

'I still have to face that hurdle. What is your father like?'

'Andreas is big and blustering, and expects to be obeyed. At the same time, he is kind and thoughtful, and has a feeling for the future. He will agree to whatever I decide for my own good. He will like you,' she smiled.

The dogs had been lying by the tent flap all the time they had been together, now they started to bark and whine.

'Someone comes whom they know and like,' Merth stated, pulling on her clothes.

Troy jumped up, searching for socks and boots with one hand, while shrugging into his shirt with the other. The rider outside was talking to someone.

'Who is coming?' Merth demanded. 'Be quiet Borland! Boris, heel.' She walked over to the tent flap.

'Oh, it is you!' she smiled at Borin as he pushed inside.

'You can be the first to congratulate us,' she said to her brother, 'Troy has consented to wed me. You did me a huge favour bringing him here!' She gave Borin a hug.

'It is said that like calls to like!' Borin laughed. 'I always knew he was someone special!

'Redd asked me to come and find you. He is celebrating being asked by Leonnus to join the Leopard. He wants you to meet Sara. You will have your news to tell as well!'

314

Borin stretched past Merth to grasp Troy's hand. 'Muria will be sorry to lose you. She has been counting on you staying with us.

'You will have to leave the colt with Lustre for a while. When he has grown some, you will be able to visit us to claim him.'

Troy nodded. He started to consider what would happen to the horses. 'May I keep Glint?' he asked.

'The Horse Lady's Lord can have anything he wishes.' Borin's dark eyes sparkled with a flash of amusement.

'I think you have let yourself in for more than you have bargained for.' He punched Troy on the shoulder. 'Anyway, come on both of you. Redd is waiting for us and a party is beginning!'

Troy was glad he had purchased some better clothes, as he and Borin escorted Merth to the Gathering Square. Merth introduced him to dignitaries as they were greeted, and every rider who passed, acknowledged Merth with lowered outstretched hands.

The news went around the camp like lightning. The lady Merth had chosen a new Lord to be her chieftain. A stranger from across the water! Rumour had it, he could be royalty!

Troy's background and upbringing stood him in good stead, and soon he was holding his own and making conversation with those around him, giving as good an impression as he could.

Redd came flying up to the group around Merth, brown curls in disarray, but with a big grin for his sister.

'There you are! I have been looking for you everywhere! I want to bring Sara to meet you.' He grasped Merth by the hand as if to pull her away, then noticed Troy standing beside her.

'Redd, you must meet the future Lord of the Phoenix.' Merth's eyes were twinkling as she grabbed her younger brother into an embrace. 'We both have things to be thankful for,' she murmured, 'come and be introduced to your future relation, this is Troy.'

'I'm sure my sister has made an excellent choice, My Lord. She rarely makes an error. Please be welcome as our future Lord of the Phoenix and of the plains.'

Redd reached out to shake Troy's hand, measuring him up and finding he approved.

The rest of that evening was one of the happiest Merth had ever experienced. Good wishes abounded and soon the party was in full swing. The musicians played tunes to dance to, and soon the air rang with shouts and stamping feet.

'Time for your party piece,' Borin laughed at Merth, with the well-remembered gleam in his dark eyes.

'Must I?' Merth relinquished Troy's hand while breathing a sigh. She stood and signalled to the players.

Immediately they stopped their music long enough for people to return to their seats, then started a tune Merth often used for her dancing.

It was a lilting melody with a steady beat, which escalated until she was a whirling picture of violet and silver, with her totems undulating like living pictures.

Before the music had finished, she had grabbed Troy by the hand, and had then made him the focus of her passionate movements.

She finished by leaping off the ground into his arms, then kissed him firmly, while her skirt continued her line of flight and wrapped itself around his legs.

Borin started to pound his heels. 'The Horse Lords!' he yelled, raising his glass. Everyone drank to the toast with heels drumming and glasses raised.

Merth lifted Troy's arm. 'Troy of the Phoenix!' she shouted. 'Toast a welcome to my new Lord.'

'Troy of the Phoenix!' came back the reply.

Troy woke the next day with one of the worst hangovers he had ever experienced.

He found he was lying on the sheepskin in Merth's tent, but she was nowhere to be seen. Opening one eye, he searched the tent, surprised she had left without a word.

He struggled into his clothes and was just about to leave, when the tent flap opened and she returned with Boris and Borland at her heels.

She was bringing breakfast, which included a mug of something dreadful. When he pushed it away she insisted that he finish it.

'I give this to my father regularly,' she maintained, 'it always does the job.'

'What! Finish it off, completely?' Troy was nearly gagging.

'Better out than in, if that is what is necessary,' she said decidedly.

Later on in the morning, when Troy was feeling considerably better, he took Merth to visit Lustre and her colt.

'They are both beautiful,' Merth enthused, waving to Borin and Muria who were also coming to admire.

'Muria, how nice to see you.' Merth gave her sister in law a hug. 'I have a boon to ask. Will you shelter the colt with Lustre, while Troy and I visit the Northern Plains?'

'My pleasure,' Muria agreed. 'You can come to the Bear when you return.' She gave Troy a pat on the arm, then looked at him serenely. 'Your young one will come to no harm,' she promised. 'Jesse will make sure of that!'

Jesse blushed scarlet when everyone turned to look at him. He had been feeding Lustre when the others had arrived. Troy strode over to him, shook him by the hand, then pulled him into a firm grip.

'Thank you for looking after me when I first came to the plains. You helped me and made things easier for me.'

'It was good to have your companionship,' Jesse returned. He bowed to Merth, lowering his stretched hand, 'My Lady!'

The colt scampered over to Troy searching for tidbits in his pockets.

'When are you going north?' Borin asked Merth.

'As soon as I can collect everyone together,' Merth replied. 'Prince Drun and Rahadir are full of impatience now they are on their way home, and I must say, I am curious about what has been happening on the other side of the river.'

'It is a pity we can't come with you,' Muria said. 'We must get home as there are things to be done. One thing we must do is call for the priestesses.'

'Oh, indeed!' Merth grasped her hand, 'blessings be upon you, if that is the case. We will have need of the priestesses too, when we return. Troy will have to fly the Phoenix, but there is no hurry on that.'

Two days later, the party set off. Troy found that Glint was quite capable of giving Sythe his own back, and soon the two horses were companionable, though Sythe did tend to push ahead.

When Troy was introduced to Prince Drun and Rahadir, he was amused when Merth established his credentials.

She had raised her head, looking Drun firmly in the eyes. 'I must present you to the Lord of The Riffed One, Prince Drun. Prince Troy, may I present Prince Drun from Jaddanna?' Her stance dared him to think or say anything unseemly, like making remarks about a former slave.

Drun and Rahadir had made all the correct noises and had both been polite and well mannered to Troy.

Now they trotted behind Merth, Troy and the dogs, who were leading the party.

It took almost a week to reach the Grey River. One afternoon they entered a small forest, and when leaving the trees they heard the sounds of the water. On the other side of the stream deep trenches had been cut, with channels running away from them. These were filled with water, and the whole plain was lush and verdant.

Lifting her gaze, Merth realised the land was empty, no trace could be seen of a moving creature.

'Oh dear,' Merth cried, 'I don't know whether to be pleased or angry. It looks as if your cattle have been returned home, Prince Drun, and the army disbanded.

'They have done a good job, but only on the northern side of the river. I thought we were going to benefit from their labour on the southern side as well.'

Drun stood in his saddle as he studied the vista in front of him.

'Never fear, Horse Lady. There must be some mistake.

'When we speak to my father about the land I will ensure that if we come back to this side of the mountains in the future, that the trenches will be completed on this side of the river also.'

Merth had to be content with this, though there seemed to be too many ifs and buts in the promise.

As they crossed the northern plain, Merth dropped back to converse with Rahadir.

'How are you feeling, now we are approaching your home?' She indicated the far mountains looming majestically in the distance. 'When we cross through that gap you shall be in your own land.'

'I am glad to see Prince Drun will be returned to his father as promised, Horse Lady.'

'You are ducking the question,' Merth laughed. Leaning across she put her hand on his arm. 'Do not worry! I shall not keep you to your promise. If you wish to stay in your family tents I shall understand.'

'We shall see,' he smiled at her in return. 'I do believe the life of a rider with the Horse Lords will prevail. Not only that, in a couple of years our lovely Merthsalla will be looking for a husband.'

'I hadn't realised that was in the wind. She has stolen your heart already? She is just a child.'

'A competent child, My Lady, or you would not have left your daughter in her care. She is your second in command, all but for her age, and so beautiful without any guile.'

'Would you wear the Phoenix on your wrist?'

'I would be honoured to be asked,' he replied.

'So be it, then!' Merth nodded, as she urged Sythe forward again.

The weather remained calm as they traversed the plain, with sunny days and cool nights.

Every night was filled with delight and passion for Merth and Troy. The fair-haired, angular man Merth had dreamed about, turned out to be a considerate, incandescent lover.

As for Troy, he found his Horse Lady to be full of wiles, with hands that found places he was unaware he had.

Every aspect of Merth was erotic. Her perfume drove him wild with desire, and her every movement conveyed controlled sensuality, without contrivance.

Not only their bodies and youthful virility were in accord, but also their minds.

Both bred to rule, brought up with responsibility and respect, it was a delight to be able to relax in one another's company, with a merge of souls.

Every day dawned with the promise of the joys of future passion.

They crossed the rift in the mountains much sooner than they had expected. Prince Drun asked if he could lead the party, now they were travelling in his land.

Merth assented and dropped back, calling Roft to raise the Phoenix banner behind the prince's colours, which Rahadir held fluttering in the breeze.

'I wonder what happened to Chun and my royal guard?' Drun commented to Rahadir. 'Little did I think we would be returning as hostages. Neither did I think I would be so pleased to see my father, when we set out.'

'Let us hope he will be glad to see us,' Rahadir added. 'We are bringing potential trouble with us.' He glanced back to where Merth and Troy were riding behind them.

The land on the other side of the mountain was green again. There was a gentle rain falling, and soon the riders were soaking wet as it penetrated through their garments. Herds of cows could be seen in the distance, all looking well-fed and contented.

'It seems the transference of the herds has benefitted us,' Drun remarked, running an experienced eye over the nearest group of cattle.

The road they were travelling on cut through the verdant countryside in a straight line from the rift in the mountains to the city of Jaddanna. It appeared to be much used and well travelled. The rain ceased as they left the greenery when they moved north. The climate got hotter and drier every day.

'The army must have returned this way,' Rahadir commented one morning.

'Not so long ago, either,' Drun urged his horse forward. 'If we hurry we might catch up with them.'

'Why do you want to?' Rahadir asked. 'You will see them soon enough. Watch for the dust cloud, we are better keeping well behind them.'

Drun could not understand his attitude. For himself, he would take pleasure in having the company of the army officers he trained with. Obviously Rahadir was not so sure.

Chapter Twenty One

The Jada reclined on a sumptuously-padded bench in his turret room, high above the palace. He always enjoyed this time of year, when the winds blew the stagnant heat out of the opened windows of his lofty sanctuary.

He plucked the soft silk of his robe away from his body, then settled himself comfortably on his pillows. From his high vantage he could see the entrance to the bay.

The port of Jaddanna was a busy place, full of shipping of many kinds. There were fishing skiffs, bum boats, floating rafts, pleasure boats flitting about haphazardly, and barges carrying anything from coal to excrement.

By the wharves, houses were built on stilts; they were surrounded by the boats of those who cleaned the city, or those who fished for a living in the harbour.

Raising his gaze from the hubbub around the wharves and piers, The Jada noticed a ship entering the bay. Under full sail was a galley, quickly coming into view.

As he watched, the sails were reefed and the oars came into play. He admired the seamanship, which was evident in the concerted dip of the oars.

Searching amongst the papers upon his table, The Jada found his eyeglass, raising it he examined the flag sailing from the mast of the strange craft.

'The royal pennant of Devronia, I do declare!' he murmured to himself. 'Now what would they want in Jaddanna?' He rang a small silver bell, summoning his vizier.

'Be so kind as to send a message of welcome to the royal highnesses of Devronia who have just arrived in the harbour. They should tie up along side my royal barge. Then send an escort to guide them to the palace. Do you know any reason why they should visit us?'

'No, Your Excellence. I have only now seen the ship. There have been no previous indications from them. I shall send messengers immediately.'

As The Jada watched, a long boat, rowed by sailors of the Jaddannese navy, intercepted the royal galley of Devronia. After lengthy communications, both boats threaded through the traffic to reach the berth next to the royal barge.

Still looking through his glass, The Jada noticed a familiar figure on the deck of the Devronian galley.

'Chun! I'm sure it is! How did he manage to get on that ship, I wonder?

'He has some of Drun's guard with him, by the look of it, though I don't see Drun. A curious business. I wonder where they have come from?

'I doubt if Chun has been to Devronia, I thought he was in the middle of the Horse Plains.' He rang his silver bell again.

The vizier must have been waiting outside the turret door, as he was there immediately, with a look of expectancy on his wrinkled, old face.

'I shall return to the throne room to receive my guests, I will have my repast there. Please arrange for some suites of rooms to be prepared. By the look of it we shall have some important visitors this afternoon.

'No doubt they will need places to rest and refresh themselves. I shall need more appropriate clothes, rather than this robe. Call my body servant to bring something to the throne room, if you will?'

'As you wish, Your Excellence.' The Vizier bowed himself out.

Delia and Amelia were waiting on the deck for the men to get changed. The girls were still attired in the clothes they had used on the journey.

Although Amelia had a few of the garments she had purloined from the pleasure galley, she preferred the freedom of her pants and shirt.

Lex appeared, dressed in clothes suitable for a royal prince of Devronia. He surveyed the two girls with a jaundiced eye.

'You two look like a couple of pretty pirates. Is this how you are going to greet The Jada?'

'He won't care what we look like,' Delia announced, with a flick of her hair. 'Anyway, we don't want him to take a fancy to Amelia, when we want him to free her.

'As for me, it doesn't matter what I look like, as long as Anton wants me.'

Joseph came on deck, puffing with the effort of climbing the companionway.

'Well, are we all ready? Here comes Trojan, all we need now are Chun, Anton, and Jocelyn. Of course, we can't forget him.'

Chun sauntered from the other side of the deck where he had been organising the Jaddannese soldiers and the luggage.

'Do you intend to ride to the palace, Your Highness?'

'Oh, I expect we should take carriages,' Joseph replied.

'If that is your wish, I shall send the horses to a stable I know, close to hand.'

'Take care of my mare,' Amelia insisted.

'Of course I will. Tam will have the best of care.'

Suitable carriages were summoned to the dock. Joseph and Lex, accompanied by Trojan and Jocelyn, were soon ensconced in the first.

Coming behind, in the second carriage with Chun, were Anton, Amelia and Delia. They were pleased with the informality this arrangement gave them.

The route to the palace first passed through the slum area of the city, near the docks. People seemed to live their lives on the streets. Amelia was amused to see a barber plying his trade under an umbrella on the sidewalk.

The shops opened out on to the streets, with their wares decorating the pavements. Hawkers were interspersed among the crowd, while little fires were burning for people who were cooking. Surprisingly, domestic animals roamed at will.

Slowly the activities of the slum quarters gave way, as much wider tree lined roads, with houses set behind walled gardens appeared. The carriages were able to move freely here, without danger of knocking someone over.

The Jada's palace could be seen on the top of a hill. It was gleaming white in the sunshine with its towers and minarets outlined against the blue sky.

Chun drew attention to the topmost turret. 'That is where The Jada spends his free time,' he told them. 'He will have spotted us from the turret with his glass; that is why the sailors came to guide us to our berth in the harbour.

'The Jada always knows what is happening.'

'Is he frightening?' Amelia asked, looking at Chun anxiously.

'No. I couldn't say that.' Chun gave her hand a squeeze. 'I'm sure you and Anton will be all right now. The Jada is a reasonable man.'

The carriages swept over a bridge into the open parkland, surrounding the palace. Delia was enthralled with the various animals, which could be seen from the carriage window.

'Look! There are elephants!'

'Yes,' Chun agreed. 'They are the elephants, which are used in processions. They helped the army clear the rift in the mountains.' He carried on to explain how the earthquake had allowed the cattle to be moved to find pasture.

Soon the carriages had arrived at the palace. The party assembled in a stateroom, which had been set aside for their use.

The vizier appeared in the doorway, bowing low.

'Welcome, Highness!' His eyes sought Joseph's. 'When The Jada is ready to receive you, I shall come for you. For the moment, please refresh yourselves with these delicacies.' He indicated a table set aside with food and drink. Bowing again, he withdrew.

Returning to The Jada, the vizier said, 'your visitors are here, Excellence.'

'Who has come?' The Jada asked, languidly. He was always fatigued when wearing the heavy state robes.

He signalled to the fan bearer to commence waving the fan. The perfumed air hung heavily in the enclosed throne room.

'According to Chun, who accompanies the party, there is the King of Devronia, the Prince of Rhodia, The Duke of Desra, named Trojan D'Auton, two ladies from Kordova, and two squires. Apparently one lady and one squire are being delivered as new slaves to your palace.'

'What a curious mixture of company!' The Jada folded his hands on his lap and seemed to be examining his rings carefully.

The silence extended for some time while he gave thought to the matter. The vizier stood on one foot, and then on the other as he waited.

Suddenly a message bearer entered the throne room, under the escort of two palace guards.

The Jada beckoned him forward and released the slip of paper from his message wand. Having read what was written, he passed it to the vizier.

'A token of great joy!' exclaimed the Vizier. 'Prince Drun returns, and also Rahadir! Who are these other people with them? Do you know, Excellence?'

'A party of Horse Lords, I should think, led by their Horse Lady. My, we are popular today! It will take them some time to get here, as they are coming by foot from the stables. Show in the party from Devronia, if you please.'

When the visitors entered the throne room, The Jada rose and went to greet them. He grasped King Joseph by the hand, then reached across to pull Lex towards him.

'What a pleasure to meet neighbours, face to face.' He spoke with animation, real enthusiasm in his voice. He led them to a seating area, leaving his imposing throne empty.

'King Joseph and Prince Lex, I presume, and who is in your retinue?'

Lex answered. 'May I present my friend Trojan D'Auton, and my brother's squire, Anton, My Lord. Also, may I introduce the Lady Delia and the Lady Amelia from Kordova, and my squire, Jocelyn?' Lex turned to usher Chun forward, but The Jada had already seen him at the end of the line.

'Well, old friend, I see you have landed on your feet again. Which of the company are my two slaves?'

Chun came forward and dropped to his knees. 'Your Excellence, I beg you to free my future wife, and my best friend! They became slaves because of bad luck, not by ill-doing. I would plead for mercy in this case!'

'Your future wife?' he looked at Amelia carefully, as Chun grasped her hand and drew her to his side.

'Well, I suppose I can be magnanimous, and give her to you as a wedding present. No further flirtations with my daughters, though! What of the young man?'

'I can vouch for him!' Lex spoke up. 'He has been my brother's squire for years.'

'Not only that,' Chun added, 'he has taught the cavalry who were with us, how to improve their sword skills.'

'I suppose he is too valuable to be left a slave, if all you say is true. Young man, will you enter my employ to teach my soldiers all these military skills? Shall we call you Master of Arms?'

'My pleasure, Sire. As long as my future wife may stay at my side.' Anton was overwhelmed, while Delia blushed scarlet.

'Another beauty to bless my court!' smiled The Jada. 'Is there any other reason Devronia is in Jaddanna?'

'Indeed there is, sir.' King Joseph was looking his most pompous. 'We are searching for my second son, Troy, Prince of Ardarth. He was also captured and forced into slavery with these friends. Have you had any word of his whereabouts?'

To his disappointment all answers were in the negative. Piecing together all they knew, the trail leading to Troy went cold in Dishnigar.

The Jada clapped his hands for servants.

'Take my guests to their apartments so they can rest from their journey. Tonight, we shall have a feast to celebrate their arrival.'

To Delia's and Amelia's chagrin, a servant arrived at their apartment bearing a selection of beautiful robes from which they were to choose garments, which might be suitable for the court function that evening.

Both girls succumbed to silken sheaths with satin under garments. Delia chose a dark, ruby red, while Amelia had a shimmering grey, shot through with opalescent green. Maids arrived to help them with their toilets, while also bearing soft slippers to match their robes.

'I do find this comfortable,' Amelia murmured to Delia. 'I suppose we shall have to play our parts, while we are here.'

'It is all right for you,' Delia replied, 'you will be going to Keshia, where you will be able to be as you like. I shall have to conform to the whims of the court.'

At the same time, she was admiring her dark beauty in a full length mirror on the wall.

'You will be able to come and visit us,' Amelia replied. 'That red really suits you.'

In due course they were all seated at The Jada's table enjoying courses of exotic food, the like of which, they had never tasted. Lex and King Joseph, aided by the others, regaled The Jada with tales of their sea voyages.

The Jada was particularly interested in Trojan's tale of the brigands on the coast, to the west of Jaddanna.

'I shall clear that nest of vipers out,' he declared. 'A contingent of the army will be dispatched tomorrow.'

The vizier appeared at The Jada's elbow. He leaned forward and whispered in the bended ear.

'After you have ensured there are enough places at the table, send them in.' The Jada had an amused look on his face.

The vizier spoke to the servants standing near, and the other end of the table was quickly supplied with places and chairs. The vizier gave a slight nod.

Suddenly, the double doors were opened by the guards; Prince Drun stood in the doorway.

'Welcome, my son,' The Jada called. 'Bring your companions with you.'

To everyone's amazement, Prince Drun, flanked by Rahadir, who turned to offer his arm to the most exotic creature anyone had ever seen.

Merth took Drun's arm and walked with stately calm into the room. She was wearing her amethyst outfit, with purple and silver ornaments in her hair. Her tattoos caught the light and the wolf on her stomach seemed to leap from her body. As her arms moved, so the snakes writhed, holding all eyes in fascination.

The Jada rose to his feet, ensuring everyone else stood too.

'Welcome Horse Lady to Jaddanna. Thank you for returning my son.'

As he spoke Troy entered the room. He had waited for Merth to be announced, before he had walked forward. As he was standing behind Rahadir, no one noticed him for a moment, as all eyes were on Merth.

Then uproar broke out.

'It's Troy!' Delia shouted.

Lex ran from his place to hug his brother. Anton, just a step behind, checked to make sure it was Troy, as he looked so different. King Joseph, overcome with emotion, sat down suddenly, needing a stimulant. Luckily, close to hand was his wine glass.

Merth stood to one side, amazed at all the commotion. Only when Chun came up to welcome her and explained who everyone in the room was, did her expression lighten.

'Oh, so these are all Troy's relations and friends?' she questioned Chun.

'Indeed, Horse Lady. They have been searching land and sea to find him.'

'Luckily I found him first,' Merth flashed Chun an impish glance. 'They can't whisk him away from me now.'

She turned, and moved over to thank Drun for escorting her to his father's court, then went and slipped her hand into Troy's. Introduce me,' she murmured.

'Your Excellency, My Lord King, Prince Lex, may I introduce my wife, The Totem, The Lady of the Horse Lords.'

Delia gave an audible gasp. She gazed at Merth with astonishment. 'However did you find her, Troy?'

Delia was looking at Merth's riffs with open admiration.

The Jada knocked on the table with his knife. 'Now if we all sit down, perhaps the stories can be told for the delectation of all. Please be seated, ladies and gentlemen.'

Trojan pushed his chair over by his friend. 'Are you fit and well?' he asked. 'I have spent many a night worrying about what became of you.'

'I am fine now, thank you. I did suffer in Dishnigar after you were all taken away. It took an age for me to recover from that brutal lashing.

'I was fortunate to be discovered by The Riffed One's brother. He's been a gentleman and treated me like a brother, for all I was a slave. I was set free by him, under the auspices of my lady. What happened to you?'

'Delia and I played servants for Madame Esse in Dishnigar. We escaped with the help of Madame's adopted daughter, Eyas. Would you believe we sailed again on Ambry's boat?' He continued with his story, much to Troy's amusement and surprise.

Merth was talking to The Jada.

'Thank you for giving me the opportunity to make the acquaintance of your son, Your Excellence.'

'Well, my dear, I believed you should know we intended no harm to your Northern Plain, although we acted in haste and without your permission. I did not want to go to war over some grass.'

'No, we came to an agreement. However, I do hope your army intends to finish the job on the southern banks, next year?'

'I make that a promise,' The Jada nodded. 'We hope we will have sufficient fodder without trespassing again, but the trenches will be dug even if we do not use the land.'

Troy caught Anton's eye across the table. He gestured for Anton to join him.

'I will not be needing a squire in future, Anton. I shall not be returning to Devron.'

'Neither will I, My Lord. I am staying here in Jaddanna. I have been appointed The Jada's Master of Arms.'

'So all my sword training was worth it,' Troy laughed.

'Indeed, it was. I am going to marry Delia. She has no wish to return to Kordova, particularly as her mother is not there now.'

Merth excused herself from The Jada and King Joseph, then moved down to be at Troy's side.

'Have you told your father you are the Lord of the Horse Lady and what it entails?' she queried.

'This minute.' Troy rose from his chair and moved to kneel at his father's chair.

'My Liege,' he began. 'I am the Lord of Horse in Strevia, so I must renounce my slight hold on Devronia's throne. I shall not be returning to Devron.'

King Joseph covered Troy's hand with his own.

'Good luck, my son. I'm sure you will be happy. The Lady Merth has wondrous charm.'

'I must offer my abdication, too, father,' Lex stated from his other side, his dark eyes looking firmly into the King's. 'I have decided to return to Dishnigar, and Jocelyn is coming with me. We have unfinished business in the town.'

King Joseph looked at the others seated at the table.

'Trojan, I must beseech you,' he said. 'Are you returning to Devron with me?'

'I am, My Liege.'

'Perhaps there is a princess there in search of a husband?' The King smiled at last.

'Perhaps I might be honoured,' Trojan nodded, stretching his legs under the table.

'My Lady,' The Jada spoke to Merth. 'It seems to me as if all the strands of fate have sat in your hands. A little tug here, a little slack there, so you have gathered everyone here together. Well done, Lady of the Horse Lords.'

Merth smiled and assented by bowing her head low with her fingers firmly entwined in Troy's.